# THE LAVENDER BRIDE

## ALEXANDRA WESTON

Boldwood

First published in Great Britain in 2025 by Boldwood Books Ltd.

Copyright © Alexandra Weston, 2025

Cover Design by JD Smith Design Ltd

Cover Images: Shutterstock

A CIP catalogue record for this book is available from the British Library.

Paperback ISBN 978-1-83603-995-2

Large Print ISBN 978-1-83603-996-9

Hardback ISBN 978-1-83603-994-5

Ebook ISBN 978-1-83603-997-6

Kindle ISBN 978-1-83603-998-3

Audio CD ISBN 978-1-83603-989-1

MP3 CD ISBN 978-1-83603-990-7

Digital audio download ISBN 978-1-83603-993-8

This book is printed on certified sustainable paper. Boldwood Books is dedicated to putting sustainability at the heart of our business. For more information please visit https://www.boldwoodbooks.com/about-us/sustainability/

Boldwood Books Ltd, 23 Bowerdean Street, London, SW6 3TN

www.boldwoodbooks.com

*For my Dad, Peter Weston.*

# PROLOGUE
## SHEFFIELD, ENGLAND, APRIL 1946

I creep down the stairs, carefully stepping over the third one from the bottom which squeaks. The hall is in darkness but the door to Father's study is ajar and a sliver of light slices across the brown hall carpet. I ease my coat off the rack and slip it on. Into the pocket goes my lipstick. Father doesn't approve of women wearing cosmetics. I'll apply the lipstick outside the newsagents using their shop window as a mirror. I tiptoe to the front door. Very gently, because it sticks on damp nights, I ease it open. The smell of wet earth gusts into the hall. The door creaks and I freeze.

'Is that you, Audrey?' Father calls from his study.

I glance behind as my heart rate accelerates. I could make a dash for it. It's Freddie's last night before he goes back to university in Birmingham. We're going to see *The Harvey Girls* with Judy Garland and I'm *that* excited about it! Not just because Judy Garland is amazing and talented and such a great singer. But because this is my last chance to see Freddie until June which is ages away.

If I make a dash for it, I'll catch such a lecture when I get back. I'll get sent to my room without supper and told to read my Bible until I'm a more dutiful daughter. It's better to face it head on and then at least I'll be saved the diatribe on sneaking out.

'Yes, Father.' My shoulders hunch as I close the door. I feel myself shrinking, becoming more insubstantial with every footstep I hear coming towards me. I turn and Father's silhouetted in the lighted doorway, his tall, spare figure looking even more austere with the light behind him. His hair is dark like mine but thinning, leaving acres of forehead as it inches away. There's a line of puckered scars down the side of his face, a legacy of his time in the trenches in the Great War. He holds the *Daily Mail* in one hand, his pipe in the other.

'Where are you going?' His voice is even but that's not necessarily a good sign. He flicks on the light and the sudden illumination shifts the scene. I'm no longer hiding in the shadows.

My hands twist in front of me and my voice sounds faint as I say, 'Only to the pictures.' I shove my hands in my coat pockets to stop them betraying my emotions. 'I'll be back by nine.'

'Have you finished typing my sermon?' Father's the minister at the Methodist church. Since I started secretarial college in September, he expects me to type his sermon. He's also got me taking the minutes of church meetings as an opportunity to practise my shorthand. As if I don't spend enough of my days trying to decipher the blasted obscure symbols.

'Yes, Father.' This at least I've done right. My head comes up. 'It's on your desk.'

'Very good.' He folds the newspaper and tucks it under his arm as he takes his tobacco tin from his pocket. 'You're not going with Freddie Greenwood, are you? You know I don't like you spending time with that boy.'

My hands tighten into fists in my pockets because this is an argument we've had a dozen times before. I don't understand why

Father's suddenly taken against Freddie. We've been friends for years, but about a year ago, Father suddenly decreed Freddie was no longer welcome in our house as he wasn't 'a suitable companion'. He'd muttered some guff about Freddie filling my head with dreams and nonsense and then refused to speak about it again. The more I shouted, the less he'd say. The powerlessness turned inwards like a dagger. I hated Father but I loathed myself too for not being able to stand up to him, for being too weak to make him see how utterly and completely wrong he was. Since then, it's only the dreams of Hollywood and of the life Freddie and I will have when we get there that keep me going.

My fingers fasten around the lipstick in my pocket that I bought with my own money. My chin comes up. I'm seventeen and in a few months, I'll be in full-time employment. I'm not a child any more. 'I am going with Freddie. He's my best friend...' My voice clogs with emotion because Freddie is the only person who understands. 'And I barely see him now he's at university.'

'Audrey, we've talked about this,' Father says wearily as he takes matches from the pocket of his worn tweed jacket. 'Freddie is not a suitable companion for you.'

'But why not?' My voice rises. I am sick and tired of living by his antiquated rules. 'You keep saying that but you won't tell me why.'

'Freddie is a bad influence.' Father strikes a match and then puffs at his pipe until it lights. In the pause, my hand twitches to reach for the door handle and escape into the night. 'He fills your head with nonsense about film stars and Hollywood.'

'It's not nonsense!' My hands form fists, the nails digging into my palms. How can I be related to this man who doesn't understand me? It makes no sense that we're the same flesh and blood. 'It's the only thing keeping me going. I'm bored to death at college. If you'd let me stay on at school like I wanted—'

'Girls do not need an education. You'll be married soon and then what use will a higher certificate be?'

'I want to do something more with my life than get married!'

As my voice rises, I hear the kitchen door firmly closed. Abruptly, the hall feels smaller and colder. My stomach tightens. However much I hope that this time will be different, Mum never takes my side. Yet I cling forlornly to the hope because without it, the loneliness of living in this house will suffocate me.

'Nonsense! All girls want to get married. It's a woman's purpose in life.' Father takes his pipe from his mouth and gestures with it. 'As the Bible says, "Urge the younger women to love their husbands and children, to be self-controlled and pure, to be busy at home, to be kind, and to be subject to their husbands."'

'I don't want to be subject to a husband!' The words are an affronted shriek. 'I want to take photographs like Lee Miller.'

Photography is my passion. At school, I was encouraged by my art teacher, Miss Stewart, who lent me a camera. Now she's no longer part of my life, I read books from the library and study the photographs in *Vogue* and the movie magazines but it's like learning to swim without ever getting in the water. I'm chock full of theory and ideas with no opportunity to put them into practice. Sometimes, the intensity of the urge to capture a moment on film makes my fingers twitch. The first thing I'm going to do when I start working full-time is buy myself a camera.

Father sighs deeply as if I'm physically causing him pain. 'I should never have let you go to that grammar school. Filling your head with ridiculous ideas about what women can do. Women belong in the home and that's the end—'

'They didn't stay in the home during the war, did they?' My hands knot with anger because he's blinkered and stupid. My neck juts forwards as I fling the words at him. 'They were Land

Girls like Esther and in the forces and working in the steel mills. Even Mum was in the WVS.'

To be fair, Mum mainly served tea but my sister, Esther, who is two years older than me, joined up to be a Land Girl when she was seventeen. She worked on a farm in Lincolnshire and returned home only to get married. She and her husband Bill live in Grantham and I miss her dreadfully.

'You'd do well to forget that, Audrey.' Father takes a step towards me. 'It worked out fine for your sister. She's a good girl but a lot of them were no better than they ought to be. Getting themselves into trouble—'

It's like a light bulb going on. Is this the reason he doesn't like me spending time with Freddie? Because if it is, I can reassure him and we can finally stop arguing about it. 'Is this why you don't want me to see Freddie?' My words tumble over themselves. 'Do you think I'm going to end up expecting? It's not like that between us. We're friends. Like we've always been.'

Although I wish it wasn't *exactly* like it's always been. I really, desperately want Freddie to kiss me. What happens after that which makes a baby, I'm still not sure about and annoyingly, Esther won't tell me, even when I offered to give her all of my chocolate ration.

'This is not a suitable discussion for a seventeen-year-old girl.' Father's knuckles whiten as he grips the stem of his pipe. 'If these are the kind of ideas you're getting from going to the cinema then it's time you stopped.'

'No!' I stand up straighter and shout the word in his face. 'You are not taking the cinema away from me. Or Freddie.'

Life simply wouldn't be worth living without them. The cinema on a Saturday evening is the one spark in my drab, dull weeks at college. Seeing Freddie (even if it only is during his university holidays) is the only time I can really be myself.

Without them, I'd wither and waste away in this house filled only with duty and faith.

'While you still live in my house, you'll obey me.' Father stalks across the hall towards me. He towers over me, making me feel painfully small. I fight the urge to cower away from him. My shoulders tense as my hands go clammy. I should just give in. It'd be easier. Freddie would understand. It's on the tip of my tongue to murmur, *Yes, Father*. Then an image forms of Freddie waiting for me outside the cinema. My friend. The one person who makes me feel good about myself. My spine straightens. I'm not giving in. Father's not going to take my only true friend away from me.

'Why should I when all of your ideas are Victorian?' I force myself not to look away from the intensity of the anger in his eyes. 'You're stuck in the past. You're a fossil.'

I yank the door open. Drizzle falls like a curtain. I have my foot on the threshold when Father grabs my arm.

'You will do as I say, girl! Take your coat off. You're not going out tonight.'

I hate him being this close to me because it always ends with a slap. I cringe back but he's holding my arm too tightly for me to get away. I'll have bruises tomorrow. His face is blotchy with anger, his scars painfully pronounced. His nostrils dilate, making his nose hairs quiver. I hate him. I do. He's the worst thing in my world. I wish he were dead!

My blood pounds in my ears. I have to get out of here before the slap comes. I snatch his pipe from his hand and hurl it across the hallway. There's a crack as it hits the wall. It breaks into two pieces as it falls, tobacco spilling from the bowl onto the carpet.

'You insolent little wretch!' he shouts in my face, spittle hitting my cheeks. 'Now look what you've done!'

I have to get away. I have to see Freddie. Only he can help. I twist in Father's grip, wrenching my arm free. Off balance, I stumble down the step, jarring my ankle.

'You will see the error of your ways.' Father's voice is pitched low to make sure the neighbours don't hear. 'Bible study and no supper when you get back. I'll mark the chapters for you to read on respecting your elders.'

I don't look back. 'I don't care!' I stride up the path, past the vegetable beds filled with beans, onions and carrots to supplement our rations, throw the gate open and slam it behind me.

I turn on my heel and march away from him. I have to get to the cinema, to Freddie. Once I'm with Freddie, I'll be all right. I'm shaky with adrenaline, my hands trembling as I straighten out the sleeve of my coat. There's cooling sweat under my arms. I turn the corner and suddenly, my legs feel weak as a kitten's. I lean against a wall and bend over, pressing my hands against my stomach.

What have I done? Father will be furious for days because of the broken pipe. He loves that blasted pipe far more than he loves me or Mum. He certainly spends far more time with it. There'll be endless pages of the Bible to read when I get home and verses to copy out and I'll have to do it all without supper or a fire. This is how the disrespectful daughter is punished. But why should I respect him when he's such a bully? He takes everything away from me that makes me happy. First photography because it's not suitable for a girl, then school because girls don't need an education. I can't let him take Freddie away too. Because if I didn't have Freddie and our dreams of Hollywood then there'd be nothing worth fighting for. I'd shrink until I was nothing but the dutiful daughter Father wants.

I blow out a long breath as I straighten up. I'll show him! Freddie and I *will* go to Hollywood, we'll get married and we'll be happy.

I start walking again, summoning the daydreams of our house in the Hollywood Hills with the white walls and the red roof. There'll be roses around the veranda. We'll go out for dinner at the Brown Derby and spot the movie stars. There'll be glamorous parties that I'll go to in beautiful frocks. I won't be the Minister's daughter any more. I'll be sophisticated and beautiful and feel like a million dollars.

My heartbeat drops, my breathing steadies. Nothing can hurt me when I'm dreaming about Hollywood. Freddie and I will be safe there. Away from Father and bullies like him. We'll be happy. I just know we will!

I was too young then to know that life doesn't work that way. Those dreams sustained me through the dreary post-war months that followed. I clung to them like a life raft when my world turned upside down. Hollywood was my Shangri-La. Little did I realise that, when I finally got there, Hollywood would sink me.

## PART I

# OCTOBER 1951–FEBRUARY 1952

INTERVIEWER: The early fifties saw the height of McCarthyism which led to the Hollywood Blacklist. What was it like to live through that?

REX TRENT: You have to remember the background. Russia had developed their own atomic bomb. There was a deep fear there'd be another war. This time with nukes. Senator McCarthy was convinced there were Communists in positions of power in the US and that they were giving secrets to the Soviet Union. Then his cronies got it into their heads Reds had infiltrated Hollywood and were using movies to spread pro-Soviet propaganda. That was baloney, as anyone in the industry could have told them, if they'd been willing to listen.

— INTERVIEW WITH REX TRENT –
BROADCAST ON HIS SIXTY-FIFTH BIRTHDAY, 27
FEBRUARY 1989

# 1

## HOLLYWOOD, CALIFORNIA, OCTOBER 1951

Rex Trent is rising high in the firmament of Crown Pictures' stars. The twenty-seven-year-old heartthrob is a welcome addition to the ranks of Hollywood's most eligible bachelors. Rarely seen out with the same girl twice, Rex confesses he's having far too much fun to think about settling down.

— *PHOTOPLAY*, OCTOBER 1951

'Hi, I'm Rex Trent.'

I look up and then tilt my head back further until I finally see his face. He's *that* tall! My jaw drops as awareness zips down my spine. He's proper handsome too! That jaw! Those eyes! I feel slightly lightheaded just looking at him.

Automatically, I run my fingers through my hair. I've dreamed of this moment since I got the job with the Dirk Stone Talent Agency and discovered Rex Trent is its most famous client. I wish I'd known he was coming in today and I'd have worn something better than this plain old blouse and navy dirndl skirt.

His hair is dark brown and a little tousled as if he forgot to brush it this morning. As I look more closely, I see those unforgettable eyes are a soulful brown. His chin is shadowed by stubble but I can still see the dimple in it. The photographs I've seen of him (and I've looked at lots!) didn't prepare me for the size and breadth of him. He's wearing a navy blazer with a white, open-necked shirt with a chartreuse stripe. I can't help but notice that his shoulders fill the blazer out beautifully. There's no wonder the fan magazines call him 'the beefcake'.

His eyebrows raise as he crosses his arms. Oh, boy, how embarrassing! Heat streaks across my face. I hastily lower my gaze to my desk. *Say something, Audrey. He's famous but he's still a client. You've got to speak to him.*

'Hello, I'm Audrey Wade.' I sound primly English, without a trace of my Yorkshire accent, but my voice is high-pitched and strained. 'I'm Dirk's new secretary.' My blush deepens. My first time speaking to a bona fide movie star and I sound like a strangled duck. I take a deep breath and add, 'Is Dirk expecting you?' This time, my voice is level but my accent is back, the vowels as flat as pancakes.

Rex blinks, frowns. 'Yes, he said I had to sign some papers.'

His voice is curt with a hint of frustration. I blink and look down. This is not how I imagined him. I've had a crush on him since I saw him in *Emma*, an adaptation of Jane Austen's novel when he played Frank Churchill, and thought him jaw-droppingly handsome. He was funny and self-deprecating in the role and that trait came through in the interviews I'd read too. I wipe my sweaty palms on my skirt. What was I thinking? Of course he's not going to be like Frank Churchill. That was acting and this is real life. Freddie always said I had trouble distinguishing between the two and here I am, proving him right. There's the familiar lurch of loss at the thought of Freddie. I push it away. This is not the time.

'Of course.' I smile, hoping it looks confident and professional, as I push my chair back and stand. Unfortunately, the fabric of my skirt gets stuck between my chair and the leg of my desk and I have to yank it free. *Yes, very dignified, Audrey!*

Rex doesn't return the smile. Disappointment needles me. He has such a wonderful smile. He's always smiling in the photographs in the film magazines. Can't he spare just one of those heartwarming smiles for me?

The papers are the extension of his contract with Crown Pictures. Dirk's been negotiating it for weeks. As I walk around my desk, he takes a step back but I still pass within inches of his chest. I'm five foot six and he towers over me, making me feel absolutely tiny. His cologne is richly spiced. It smells enticing, elegant and expensive. Glancing up, I see Rex looks a lot more tired than he does in his photographs. There are purple shadows beneath his eyes and lines around his mouth. Could that be why he's not as charming as I expected?

'If you'll take a seat for a jiffy, I'll see if Mr Stone can see you now.' My voice sounds breathy as if I'll pass out at any minute.

*Come on, Audrey. Pull yourself together and don't muck this up. Rex is too important to the agency for you to behave like a dazzled bobbysoxer. Do you want Dirk to fire you? Because that's the fastest way back to the typing pool at the insurance company. And then how will you keep up with the rent?*

I make myself inhale deeply as I gesture to the leather chair underneath the window. There's one hopeful already sitting there waiting. Such a lot of hopefuls come through the agency's doors that I don't bother learning their names until Dirk signs them. This one's perched on the edge of the matching sofa, clutching his headshots.

'You don't expect me to sit on that, do you?' Rex points at the chair. His beautiful mouth is twisted into a sneer. 'Why hasn't

Dirk got a new chair? I'm sure as hell earning him enough to buy a new one.'

He's not wrong about the chair. The springs are shot and have a habit of poking you in places you'd much rather not be poked. I'm mortified that he's mentioned it. Somehow, this feels like my fault, even though the chair was in situ long before I started working for Dirk. Sweat blooms in my armpits. I look around frantically as if another more comfortable chair will materialise.

The young hopeful leaps from the sofa and gestures for Rex to take it. I breathe a sigh of relief as I cross to the filing cabinet. Ginny looks up from her typewriter. She's secretary to Will Tranby, who's the agent to many established theatre performers. She's a couple of years older than me with shrewd, blue eyes and a turned-up nose. She wears her light-brown hair in a ponytail and is always well dressed.

Ginny's eyes roll towards Rex and she mimes fanning herself. I grin quickly at her as I take Rex's contract from his file. As I turn round, I'm astounded to see he's lying on the sofa. His eyes are closed, his hands neatly folded across his chest. Because of his height, his feet stick off the end. The young hopeful looks astonished to see Rex's famous head at that angle.

For a second, my brain takes in only the composition. The light from the wide window above, the tall man lying on the sofa like a wounded hero. Golly, I wish I'd got my camera with me. But Dirk would not be happy if I snuck photos of his clients when they weren't looking.

'Mr Trent,' I say quietly. 'Are you all right?' Is he sick? I can't imagine why anyone would lie down on that sofa if they weren't. Could that be why he's been a tiny bit grumpy with me?

'I'm beat.' His eyes don't open. I'm not even worth the effort of lifting his eyelids. My heart plummets. Instantly, I feel smaller.

For a second, I want to cry. This is the first genuine movie star

I've met and he's being rude. Worse, he's making me feel small. This is not what I dreamed of back in England when fantasies of Hollywood were all that got me through my school days and the dreary post-war years. In my daydreams, the film stars were always charming and made me feel wonderful. They were definitely never rude or unfriendly.

For the whole of the five months I've been working for Dirk, Rex has been in Europe first on holiday and then filming *The Three Musketeers* in France. He plays Aramis, the restless romantic with a mistress in every town. It sounds thrilling! Working for Dirk hasn't cured me of my love of movies. If anything, being on the inside and knowing what's coming up makes me even more enthusiastic. Ginny laughs at me. She's been working for Will for three years and says no one impresses her any more but perhaps Rex will be the exception.

Abruptly, I wish I'd never met him in real life because then I could have kept alive the dream of him as the perfect man. Not that any man is *actually* perfect (except maybe Cary Grant). I'm not *that* naïve.

I tap on Dirk's door and then enter. The room smells of cigarette smoke and peppermint as Dirk's perpetually either smoking or crunching mint balls. He's on the telephone, his feet on his desk, his chair tipped back. He holds up one finger, which means 'wait'. If he points at the door, it's my cue to leave the paperwork on his desk and go back to mine.

On the wall behind my boss's desk are photos of his clients, all with effusive messages of thanks to Dirk for his hand in developing their careers. Rex's head shot is centre of the top row as befits the agency's most famous name. The wall to the left of the desk is covered with signed photos of everyone who's anyone in Hollywood. Closest to me are Humphrey Bogart, Cary Grant, Irene Dunn and Lauren Bacall. I focus on Cary Grant's superbly handsome face. What advice would he give me about dealing with Rex Trent? Cary is English too. He crossed the pond to seek his fortune in Hollywood. Did he ever feel like I do? Baffled by the sheer unreality of it? Unable to work out how a poor boy from Bristol ended up as one of the most lauded stars in Hollywood? Perhaps I should have changed my name too. Left plain old Audrey on English shores and arrived in Hollywood as Adele or Ava.

'She won't do it for less,' Dirk barks into the telephone, pulling me back to the here and now. He's mid-forties, spare and wiry with a restless energy he pours into his work. He's got a weak chest that landed him a desk job in the war. 'Stop wasting my time and get back to me when you can put a decent offer on the table.' The receiver is forcibly returned to its cradle. Then Dirk grins at me as he swings his feet off the desk. 'That was *The Jack Benny Program*. I'm making them sweat.'

Dirk goes the extra mile for his clients. He's both ruthless and relentless on their behalf. In exchange, he expects total loyalty. They take his advice and no one else's. In my four months here, I've seen two young starlets dropped for listening to someone else's words of wisdom about their careers rather than Dirk's.

'Rex Trent is here to see you,' I say as I put the contracts on Dirk's desk.

My boss smooths his moustache with nicotine-stained fingers before picking them up. 'He should sign these in blood after the rigmarole I went through with Harry King to negotiate it.' He reaches for another mint ball and pops it in his mouth. 'Send him in. And bring more coffee.'

Reaching the door, I still. Rex is motionless. His eyes are closed, his face relaxed. He can't be asleep, can he? I approach and a small snore escapes him. I look at the young hopeful. He shrugs as if to say, *He's famous, he can sleep if he likes.*

I should wake him. Dirk's expecting him. I cough and say, 'Mr Trent?'

As if my voice disturbs him, he huffs out a long breath and then turns over. His broad back is towards me, the fabric of the blazer straining across his shoulders.

What do I do? Find him a blanket and let him sleep? Or prod him until he wakes up?

I turn to Ginny and mouth, 'He's asleep.'

Her eyebrows shoot up. She crosses the room to join me.

'Sure is,' she whispers. 'You'll have to wake him.'

I reach out to touch his shoulder but then I snatch it back. I don't want to be the one to do it. What if he's furious with me for waking him? I do not want to deal with Rex's anger. Seeing him irritated has been bad enough.

I glance at Dirk's office door. He'd wake Rex without a second thought. He's got a very important contract to sign. Dirk would say snoozing can wait. Rex's shoulders rise and fall as he breathes. He must be absolutely exhausted to fall asleep on that sofa. He may be one of Hollywood's hottest rising stars but right now, he's as vulnerable as a baby. If the agency really does go the extra mile for its clients, shouldn't we accept the unorthodox and let our client take the nap he clearly needs?

'I can't do it,' I murmur.

Ginny shrugs next to me as if to say, *It's your funeral.* I hope to goodness she's not right and Dirk won't fire me for this.

I turn to the young hopeful. Could Rex's slumber be his lucky break? I tiptoe to the coffee maker, fill a cup and take it in to Dirk. 'Mr Trent is indisposed—'

'What?' Dirk snarls. 'You just told me he was here.'

'There's a young man to see you instead.' I clear a space amongst the sea of papers and yesterday's *Hollywood Reporter* to put his coffee down. 'I think he's got potential.'

A large part of my job is sifting through the hundreds of letters Dirk receives every week. Almost every applicant is good-looking, many are undoubtedly talented but only a handful have the magnetism that makes a movie star.

Dirk sighs. 'He'd better be good, kid. And make me a lunch reservation at Scandia – twelve thirty for two.'

I nod and send the young hopeful in. He smiles gratefully at me, which is almost undoubtedly premature. Dirk's brutal with those who don't make the grade. There's a strong chance he'll be out on his ear in ten minutes.

I settle back at my desk. As my fingers hover over the type-writer keys, I glance over at Rex Trent again. Seeing him like this stirs memories of Freddie. Freddie wasn't as handsome or anywhere near as tall. Yet that vulnerability reminds me of my lost friend. If only I could tell him about this most confusing encounter. But Freddie is gone from my life. He chose a different path and made it entirely clear I had no part in it. My stomach clenches at the memory.

I thought coming to Hollywood, living the dream we'd had growing up would heal me. That I'd never feel small and lost once I arrived in LA. But it turns out I'm still the same Audrey even here. I pretend to be like everyone else but inside, I'm quaking in case they find out I'm worthless, just as Father always said. Freddie used to lift me up. Without him, there are days when I'm fragile as finest crystal. I miss him so much, I'm sometimes surprised people can't see it. That they don't know I'm broken-hearted, not for a lover but for my best friend.

I take a deep breath to push through the wave of sadness and then pick up my telephone to call the restaurant. I keep my voice low as I make the reservation. Still Rex doesn't stir. Even the rattle and ding of my typewriter doesn't wake him. The young hopeful leaves, head down. Another who didn't have the ineffable quality Dirk's looking for.

I keep glancing over at Rex, alert for any sign he's stirring. Will he be embarrassed as people often are when they fall asleep in front of strangers? Or angry with me for letting him sleep? Perhaps he'll feel better after he's had some rest and be more like the man I've seen in the films and read about in the magazines.

At twelve, I go out for lunch with Ginny as usual. I'm curiously unwilling to leave Rex, as if I'm the one protecting his slumbers. I look back over my shoulder as I leave the office. Will he still be there when I come back? It's unlikely. Dirk will have no compunction about waking him.

'Who'd have thought it?' Ginny says as we walk downstairs. 'He really must have been exhausted.'

As we eat, we talk about her boyfriend Nathaniel and their plans for the weekend. She asks me whether I'll risk another date with Dan, a pilot I met through a friend who's an airline hostess. I've been out with him twice and he's spent the entirety of both dates talking about himself. 'Probably,' I tell her. 'Even Dan's better than sitting at home on my own on Saturday night.'

Weekends are the worst. During the week, work keeps me occupied but my weekends can feel very empty. That's when the gloom can set in. I've made a few friends in Los Angeles but many, like Ginny, are busy with their boyfriends. Ginny's the closest I have to a genuine friend and yet I still feel a gulf between us. Her life has been full of sunshine, siblings and sports (Ginny plays golf, tennis and badminton). She's from a large, boisterous and well-to-do family from Pasadena. Her father is a partner in a law firm, her mother attends fundraisers and is a member of the Daughters of the American Revolution. They're the kind of people who'd have been wholly out of my sphere back in England and that makes me uneasy when I accept their hospitality as I always worry they'll realise I don't quite come up to the mark.

'That's the problem with pilots. They're like actors,' Ginny says with a laugh. 'Egos the size of California.'

Is that the case with Rex Trent? It didn't seem that way from all I've read about him and when I've heard him interviewed on the wireless. Yet this morning's grumpiness could be down to ego. Was he angry at having to wait to see Dirk and being forced to deal with a mere secretary? He's not the first bad-tempered actor I've dealt with while I've been with Dirk and previously at Arden & Arden, the theatrical agents I worked for back in London.

I've always put it down to artistic temperament and accepted it as part of my job. I've never been as sharply disappointed as I was with Rex. I *really* did like him such a lot before I met him.

Ginny dashes to the drug store. I pick up a packet of Pall Malls for Dirk as he's like a bear with a sore head if he runs out of cigarettes. I return slightly earlier than usual, running up the stairs in my ballerina flats. Will he still be there? Will he sleepily wake up, blink at me and offer that heart-stopping smile? Might he apologise for being rude earlier and bring me flowers to say sorry? And then I'll be delighted and thrilled and know he's the absolute nicest man in Hollywood.

Heart thumping, I open the door a crack and peer inside. He's gone. The fantasy evaporates. 'Cheerio, Rex,' I murmur. Suddenly, I feel cold and tired and reach for the cardigan I keep on the back of my chair.

My sister, Esther used to say that my dreams wouldn't keep me warm. Those words feel painfully true right now. She'd laugh at me for creating such a bubble of expectation around Rex. But it was such a beautiful, glittering bubble. Letting it go brings me down to earth with a bump. Now I'm just the secretary again.

After plumping the sofa cushions and refilling the coffeepot, I return to my desk. On it are the contracts I gave to Dirk earlier. I turn to the last page and see Rex's signature. The handwriting is neat, almost childlike, each letter perfectly formed.

I sigh out a long breath of frustration. I'd thought working for Dirk, I'd meet famous people, that they'd get to know me and I'd become part of the Hollywood set. But all I get to do is make coffee, type letters and post contracts. There's no reflected glory in being the girl who sends Rex Trent's contract back to Crown Pictures. Even today, when I was within touching distance of a movie star who *actually fell asleep* on the sofa next me, doesn't get me any closer to my dreams.

Ginny's return prompts me to square my shoulders before rolling a clean sheet of headed notepaper onto my typewriter. I don't need Dirk to dictate letters of this kind. I've done this time and again. The stock phrases flow from my brain to my fingers. I paperclip the letter to the contracts and return them to Dirk's desk.

Dirk returns late from lunch. 'Indisposed, was he?' he says to me as he passes my desk. 'You're too soft, kid.'

I cross my arms and meet his gaze. 'He was exhausted. It was only common courtesy to let him sleep.' As Dirk opens his mouth to argue, I add, 'We need to replace that chair. Rex refused to sit on it. He said with the amount he earns the agency, you should be able to buy a comfortable chair.'

'He obviously didn't have a problem with the sofa.' Dirk huffs out a breath that's heavy with peppermint. 'Damnit! Get W&J Sloane on the horn and get them to send something over.'

'Just the chair?' I ask as he turns away. 'Because it'll look odd if they don't match. You don't want your best client to be unhappy.'

'You think I'm made of money?'

I wait. Dirk protests first and thinks second.

A beat later, he adds, 'Fine, get both.' After another beat, he says, 'But that's the end of it. I'm not having you and Rex bleeding me dry.'

There's a thrill in hearing our names paired like that. I smile as I say, 'Thank you, Dirk.'

'Huh!' At his office door, he snarls, 'Where's my coffee?'

Once he's back in his office with the door closed, Ginny flashes me a thumbs up. I pour the coffee and take it through to Dirk. Then I find W&J Sloane's number in the directory and they promise to send me a catalogue in the mail.

The rest of the day passes in the usual way. As I take dictation and type, I'm distracted by thoughts of Rex. Does he fall asleep with strangers all the time? Or did I do something which put him at his ease? I want to believe it's the latter, that he sensed I'd understand. Is that why he reminds me of Freddie, because despite Rex's grumpiness, he seemed at ease with me? Because Freddie and I were always easy together. Until, of course, we weren't.

* * *

When I get home to my tiny apartment on Fairfax Avenue, I'm restless, flitting around the small space, unable to relax. I moved here shortly after I started working for Dirk, the deposit eating up what was left of my inheritance from my Great-Aunt Violet. It has a living area downstairs which includes the kitchenette with cheery yellow cupboards and a fold-out Formica dining table. Stairs lead to the tiny mezzanine which holds my bed. Beneath the stairs is a petite bookshelf which I found in a thrift store and painted white. I share a bathroom down the hall with Miss Miles who works at Central Casting and Mrs Nowak who has a job at City Hall.

The flat may be small but it's light and bright. I've spent every spare dime to make sure it's nothing like the house I grew up in. It came furnished but as nothing matched, I've done my best to hide the furniture. The sofa and chair are covered with orange, white and yellow striped Mexican blankets. The brown carpet is largely hidden by a geometric patterned rug in the same colours. I replaced the lampshades with zingy yellow ones from the Five and Dime store. Upstairs, there's an emerald-green counterpane on my bed which was another Five and Dime store find.

What I don't have, and never will, is an ashtray. I don't want this space to smell of smoke as home did. Father's pipe smoke permeated every room and clung to my hair and clothes when I went out. It felt like I carried a constant reminder of him everywhere I went.

The only reminder of home is a photograph of Esther and Bill with my nephew David and my niece Ruth. It's framed in a cobalt-blue plastic frame that glows when the sun floods through the window. The bright colours remind me that this is my space and I decide who comes into it. It's the first place I've ever lived that feels like a sanctuary, where I know I'm safe when I close the front door behind me. That feeling is worth every cent that goes on rent.

After I've eaten, I settle on the sofa and pull out the bundle of film magazines I've accumulated since I moved to LA. As I flick through then, I spot plenty of mentions of Rex, snippets about upcoming films, interviews, photographs. I spend a lot of time looking at the photos, at his handsome, smiling face. There's not one in which he doesn't look delighted with life. I re-read the interviews. The down-to-earth charm I remembered comes over in every line. He seems enchanted by every experience, thrilled to spend time with the interviewer, captivated by the movie business. There's not a hint of the grouchy man I met this morning.

He must have been feeling off-colour, that's the only explanation. He was exhausted after filming *The Three Musketeers* and the long journey home.

I get ready for bed and once I'm snug beneath the green counterpane, I allow the fancies to form. Rex will come back to the office. I'll be wearing my best blue and white dress, he'll ask me to have coffee with him to say sorry for the other day and we'll go to Schwab's Pharmacy (where Lana Turner was discovered) and he'll be just as charming and gorgeous as he is in the magazine interviews. And we'll get on so well that he'll ask me out again and I'll be taken to The Cocoanut Grove and Earl Carroll's and Ciro's. I've never been to a nightclub but I've seen them in the movies. My imagination provides me with an off-the-shoulder satin dress in emerald green with yards and yards of skirt which makes my waist look tiny. We'll dance the slow foxtrot, his strong arms cradling me. But when I look up, it's not Rex's face I see but Freddie's, bruised and shadowed as it was the last time I saw him.

## 2

Tony Young is teaching Rex Trent to surf and these boys are having a divine time at Venice Beach this week!

— *EYEWITNESS*, NOVEMBER 1951

Rex does not return. Every day when I go into the office, I hope he'll come in. A week later, Dirk tells me Rex is on a publicity tour for *Redwood Canyon*, a Western in which he's got third billing. The newspapers report that at the New York premiere, his bobbysoxer fans are screaming for Rex and ignoring the film's more established stars. His date for the premiere is veteran stage actress Tallulah Bankhead, who must be fifty if she's a day. She's still a striking woman though and they look relaxed and elegant together on the red carpet.

I spend a good fifteen minutes, when I should be working, fantasising about going to a premiere with Rex. He'd look debonair in his dinner jacket, I'd wear an elegant designer gown with a crinoline petticoat beneath, evening gloves and jewels. We'd walk up the red carpet hand in hand and I'd lift my chin as I stand and smile for the cameras, thinking of Father and Freddie, who told me I'd never make it in Hollywood.

The telephone ringing snaps me out of my reverie but the daydream doesn't fade. Over the following days, it becomes the place I retreat to when the world feels too much. When my body is going through the motions of washing up or ironing, my mind is on the red carpet with Rex Trent. Some days, the dream feels more tangible than the dull reality of being a secretary and I come back to the everyday feeling cheated that I've got filing to do and the post to get ready.

Rex may be absent but his name is a constant presence at the agency. Dirk is lining him up for *Sealed with a Kiss*, a romantic comedy with America's sweetheart, Brenda Ball, but Harry King is driving a hard bargain on the fee to lend him to Ransome Pictures for the movie.

I agree to another date with Dan, who takes me to Lindy's and then spends the entire evening telling me why the troops in Korea will show the Communists who's boss and why Truman is a lousy president. During dessert (a rather lovely lemon cheesecake), I drift off into daydreaming about Rex again. It's only when Dan says, 'At least McCarthy is doing something to root out the Commies and the faggots,' that I snap back into the present.

Anger floods through me. 'McCarthy is a bigot and a menace.' My hands start shaking and my spoon drops into my dish with a clatter. 'My father is just the same so I know one when I see one.'

Dan throws his napkin onto the table. 'I don't have dinner with Democrats.' Then he stares at me as if he's never seen me before. 'Or are you a Red?'

'Don't be ridiculous!' I shove my chair back. I feel the eyes of the other diners on me as I snatch up my wrap. Most of the time, I just want to fit in, even if it means putting up with boring idiots like Dan. But there are things I won't stand for and Dan's just hit one of them on the head. 'I'm just someone who's seen other people treated badly because of prejudices like yours. Thank you for dinner, Dan. Don't call me again.'

As I walk away, I keep my head up. I'm shaky and yet elated. My heart feels fluttery and desperate like a caged bird. For once, I spoke out. I didn't let Dan get away with it as Father always did. I was brave for Freddie and everyone like him. Even though Freddie will never know, it was the right thing to do.

Tears prickle behind my eyes. I miss Freddie so much. He always understood. I never felt powerless and voiceless with him. Until that last day when suddenly I did.

I reach the front desk. My voice is wobbly as I ask the maître d' to call a taxi. Back in England, I'd walk home, but no one walks in Los Angeles, especially not in red, patent kitten heels. I self-consciously shift my weight from side to side as I loiter in the entrance of Lindy's waiting for it to arrive. I glance over my shoulder again and again. *Please don't let Dan leave until I'm gone.* When the taxi pulls up, I dart outside and blow out a long breath as I climb inside. In a few short minutes, I'm unlocking the door to my flat.

I slip off my shoes and climb the stairs. Beneath my bed is a shoebox. Careful of my wide, red skirts, I tug it out and lift the lid. Inside is my old life. There's not much: the ribbon from the tartan dress I was given by Great-Aunt Violet on my tenth birthday; my Brownie badge; a note from Miss Stewart, my art teacher, telling me not to give up on photography; a clipping from the *Sheffield Daily Telegraph* of my photograph that won second prize in their VE Day competition; the copy of *The Wizard of Oz* that Freddie read to me from as the bombs fell in 1940. At the bottom of the box, tied with a yellow ribbon, are the few photos I brought with me. Ones of Mum, Esther and Freddie.

It was taken in the summer of 1945 before he went to university. I remember the day perfectly. We'd taken the bus to Bakewell, eaten our sandwiches by the river, throwing the crusts to the ducks. I had the camera I'd borrowed from Miss Stewart and I'd taken the photo of Freddie beside the bridge. He was squinting at the camera, his hair ruffled by the breeze, his hands sunk into the pockets of his blazer.

Emotions surge through me as I look at his face. How can I miss him so much when I'm still angry with him? If only he hadn't lied. Hadn't said those terrible things. Hadn't made me feel as small as Father used to. Then I might have understood.

I run a finger over his face. If only I could tell him about this evening. Let him know I stood up for him. But those days are long gone.

A sour sadness washes through me. I put the photo back in the box, close the lid, push it back beneath my bed. Freddie chose a different life. One without me in it.

* * *

When I wake up on Sunday morning, anxiety is chewing at my guts. As I get myself a bowl of cornflakes and eat it at the fold-down table, I see again Dan's face as I shoved my chair back. What if he tells everyone that I'm a Red? You can't be too careful in Hollywood with the House Un-American Activities Committee hauling people in to ask them if they are or ever were Communists.

I should have been more careful. What if I'm never asked out on another date because I'm known to sympathise with subversives and queers? Women aren't supposed to have thoughts of their own. Especially not young, single ones who want to get married. The magazines make it very clear that it's a woman's role to agree with whatever their man thinks. If that's what marriage is then it's not much different to being a daughter. I hated Father telling me what to think and believe. It's hard to believe I'd take it much better from a husband, no matter how much I loved him.

I thought the world was changing during the war but the freedoms women enjoyed have shrivelled and died since VE Day. It felt viciously unfair that Esther got to join the Women's Land Army at seventeen but those choices weren't available to me because I was too young. I'd longed to join the WAAFs which would have taken me far from Sheffield but the war ended before I was old enough. Since then, women have been relegated to jobs which are considered suitable – teacher, nurse, secretary – and expected to forget they'd been riveters, mechanics and ambulance drivers when their country needed them.

It's baffling how quickly the world has forgotten how strong and resourceful women can be. We've been shoved back in our boxes and it's stifling to have scented that freedom and feel it yanked away again. To be expected to sit quietly while idiots like Dan blither on.

Getting angry again won't help. It's Sunday and I've got laundry to do. I strip my bed and stuff the sheets into the dirty washing bag. With *Photoplay* in my hand, I haul the washing across the street to the launderette. Fortunately, it's still quiet. I push open the door, releasing the smell of washing powder and sweat. A middle-aged lady reading next to the dryer nods to me.

Once the machine is going, I sit on the bench and open up *Photoplay*. There's a photograph of Rex at the Los Angeles premiere of *Redwood Canyon*. This time, he's accompanying Olivia Swift, who had a string of hits in romantic comedies before the war but more recently has taken on serious dramatic roles. She's a stunning strawberry blonde in her late thirties. I covet her midnight-blue evening gown. Rex's smile is as magnetic as always.

I rest my head against the wall, close my eyes and shove away the noise of the washing machines. I replace it with a big band playing as Frank Sinatra sings. The smells of the launderette waft away and the only scent is of roses and lilies. Rex and I are dancing the waltz in a beautiful ballroom filled with flowers. We glide effortlessly across the floor and as the music fades, he smiles at me. My heart flips. I'm alive with sensations, safe in his arms and yet gloriously aware of every gorgeous inch of him.

The fantasies keep me going as the washing machine churns on, as I fill the dryer and watch it turn and then, back in my flat, as I make my bed and iron my clothes ready for Monday.

* * *

Two weeks pass. The new furniture is delivered. The green tweed upholstery brightens up the office. Dirk complains at the cost but as he takes every opportunity to sit on the sofa, I think he's secretly pleased.

The following week, Dirk is preoccupied. Whenever I go into his office, he's on the telephone but nine times out of ten, he stops speaking until I've left the paperwork and closed the door behind me. He asks me to buy *Eyewitness* for him. It's a scandal rag packed with gossip the studios don't want to get out. When I ask why he wants it, he mutters something about 'it being good to know what those sharks are saying'.

While Dirk is out at lunch, I pick up *Eyewitness*. On the front page is a photograph of rising star Marilyn Monroe on a date at Ciro's with Charlie Chaplin Jr. The implication of the article is that Monroe is dating Chaplin (described as the son of Holly-wood royalty) to further her career. I shake my head. I saw Monroe's latest, *Love Nest*, last month and I'd say she's one to watch. *Eyewitness* fails to mention *Love Nest*, instead focusing on her being voted 'Miss Cheesecake of 1951' by the troops in Korea. I huff out a long sigh. That is utterly unfair. She's a talented actress and all men want talk about is her looking good in swimwear!

On page three is an article about Rex and one of the agency's other client's, Tony Young (real name, Terry Stoker), saying they've been seen surfing together at Venice Beach. Tony is brother to Ida Young, dancing sensation, who's got a glittering career ahead of her at MGM. Ida was once a client of the agency but left after a falling-out with Dirk.

The article starts with a shot of Rex and Tony in swimming trunks carrying their surfboards up the beach. I'm distracted by seeing Rex with so few clothes on. His chest is muscular, his arms perfectly shaped, his legs like tree trunks. The outer door opening makes me snap the magazine closed and I hurriedly return it to Dirk's desk.

The problem, whatever it is, must go away because Dirk is more relaxed the following week. On the Wednesday afternoon, he drops two signed letters on my desk and then leans on it. 'Got any plans after work?' he asks.

'I've got camera club at eight,' I tell him as I fold the letters and slide them into envelopes. Camera club is the highlight of my week. For two hours, I get to be a photography buff and not worry whether anyone thinks it inappropriate for a woman to be interested in composition, exposure settings and metering. It was daunting joining as they're all far more experienced than me. The only other woman is Rita, who has rather taken me under her wing. She's a widow in her sixties who takes incredible landscapes and allows me to use the darkroom in her house on Doheny Road.

'That gives us plenty of time. Come to the Cock'n Bull with me for a drink.'

I freeze as dread walks icy fingers down my spine. My

breathing snags as his proximity suddenly takes on a different meaning. Ginny's not at her desk. There's no one to help me if I need it. Dirk's not the first boss who's made unwanted approaches. Back in London, my middle-aged boss pinned me between two filing cabinets and grabbed my breasts. Only the fact that I had a staple remover in my hand and didn't hesitate to apply it where it could do most damage stopped the encounter from being much worse. I'd been immediately sacked. Righteous anger had propelled me out of that office with my head held high. I couldn't let that slimy toad see how much he'd upset me.

As I'd trudged back to my digs through the pouring rain, my umbrella struggling to cope with the deluge, the anger had dissolved. I'd felt cold to the bone, shaken and nauseous. My brain had replayed the incident again and again. Each time, the physical reaction felt worse until I had to stop and vomit in the gutter. Acid still in my mouth, I'd stood by the Thames for a long time, wondering where I'd gone wrong. I was nineteen and entirely alone in the world. I was furious with Freddie for letting me down. He should have been there for me when I was hurt and upset but Freddie didn't want to know me any more.

That afternoon had been the closest I ever came to packing up and getting the train back to Sheffield. Only the knowledge that Father would blame me for what happened with my boss stopped me. In his eyes, it was always the woman's fault. I knew he'd tell me that if I'd dressed more modestly or behaved more demurely, it wouldn't have happened. I couldn't give him the satisfaction of being right. He'd told me I'd never make it on my own, that I was too much of a dreamer to stand on my own two feet whether that was in London or Hollywood. I had to show him he was wrong.

So I'd squared my shoulders, faked a reference and, through some quirk of luck, landed the job at Arden & Arden.

I'd worked there for over a year but I was never more than the secretary. Famous people swanned in and out but no one noticed me. I felt more insubstantial than I had in my previous jobs, as if through proximity to fame, I became out of focus. I told myself it was English snobbery, that I could never fit in where class and accent were so highly prized. I told myself it would be different when I got to Hollywood. But it isn't really.

As Rex Trent proved, I'm still barely visible. Being Dirk's secretary doesn't feel all that different to being 'the Minister's daughter'. I want to be seen for who I actually am. Instead of being labelled by the men in my life.

Back in the here and now, Dirk's waiting for an answer. He's looming over me, taking up too much of my space. My heart rate is erratic. Sweat prickles under my arms.

'Plenty of time for what?' I ask as I open my desk drawer and fumble for the staple remover. My hand closes over it, just in case.

'What kind of question is that?' Frowning, Dirk shifts his weight and takes a step back. I breathe a little easier. 'You've been here six months. You're smart. I think you can do more. If you want to?'

My jaw drops. I blink as my mind scrabbles to catch up. I release my grip on the staple remover. This is what I've hoped for since I started working for Dirk. I'd never have got an opportunity like this if I'd stayed in London. Could this be the start of a life where I'm respected for what I can actually do, not just for my typing speed?

'I do want to.' My chin comes up. 'Definitely.'

Once he's returned to his office, I press my hands against my pounding heart and let my head drop. I jumped to the wrong conclusion. Dirk's a married man who appears devoted to his wife, Lillian. Yet I can't blame my body for its reaction. I'd been unprepared once and I will never allow myself to end up in that situation again.

Could this be my chance to be finally seen? To prove I can do more than type and make the coffee? Could I be the one negotiating on behalf of clients or escorting them to the studios to meet talent scouts? Just the idea makes me feel fizzy with excitement. If I pull this off, then Father and Freddie will *really* have to eat their words!

\* \* \*

The Cock'n Bull is what Hollywood thinks an English pub looks like. Timber beams divide the ceiling, the walls are wood panelled, and the carpet is checked. There's a picture of King George VI on the wall. A suit of armour stands in an alcove. The place smells of cigarette smoke and grilled cheese which is definitely not authentic. (Only two ounces of cheese a week was the hardest part of rationing for me. I used to have dreams about cheese sandwiches!) The clientele is far more illustrious than at most English pubs. Bette Davis and Orson Welles have been known to drink here.

Dirk's seated at one of the tables, but I notice he's not alone. For a second, I hesitate. Dirk doesn't just drink here for the Moscow Mules. If he's chatting to a studio exec then he won't want to be interrupted. Then Dirk sees me. As he raises a hand, the man with him turns. I realise it's Rex Trent and my stomach does a little flip.

I can hardly believe my eyes! I've been longing to see him again but I wish Dirk had warned me. I feel crumpled and sweaty and there's a smudge of ink on the front of my blouse from when I replaced the typewriter ribbon this afternoon. I run my fingers through my hair as I cross the room to join them. If only I'd reapplied my lipstick before I left the office.

Then Rex smiles and, honestly, my heart skips a beat. It's like a thousand-watt bulb has been turned on and happiness radiates from his skin. I cannot believe *that smile*, the one I've seen on the screen and in the magazines, that I've dreamed about every night, has been turned on me. It's as if he's a magnet pulling me towards him across the room and I'm powerless to resist.

'I don't want to interrupt,' I say as I reach their table, speaking to Dirk as my gaze flits to Rex and then away again. Beneath the excitement at seeing Rex, I'm disappointed that my chat with Dirk will have to be postponed. 'We can do this another—'

'Join us!' Dirk gestures to the chair next to Rex. 'You two have met, haven't you?'

*Really?* I frown as I pull out the chair. He must be serious about me doing more at the agency if he's happy for me to sit down with him and his best client.

'I think I owe Audrey an apology,' Rex says as I sit. 'Last time, I fell asleep, which wasn't real polite when you first meet a lady.' He offers me a shy smile which is just as beautiful as the first one. I blink as my mouth goes dry and my heart jumps. He pushes his dark hair back with a strong hand. I watch the muscles in his arm flex before it comes back to rest on the table mere inches from mine. Oh, boy! He really is swoony!

'Please don't worry about it,' I manage to say. 'You were clearly very tired.'

'I sure was.' Rex looks downcast for a second. 'Aramis is a great role but all that fighting and horseback riding sure was tiring.'

'It'll be worth it,' Dirk says. 'I've a good feeling about this one.'

Dirk's feelings are legendary in the business. He has a gift for spotting stars and spent a fortune on Rex before his career took off, sending him for acting, singing, dancing, fencing and horse-riding lessons as well as coming up with his stage name.

'What are you drinking, kid?' Dirk asks me as he gestures towards the bar.

'A Moscow Mule, of course,' I tell him. As the drink was invented here, it would be rude not to try it. I won't deny that there's a thrill in thinking how appalled Father would be if he could see me now. He despises women who go to pubs, has strong views on temperance and thinks Hollywood deserves a similar fate to Sodom and Gomorrah. In his eyes, I am supping with the Devil and he'd caution me to use an extremely long spoon.

Rex asks for another beer and Dirk crosses to the bar, stopping to talk to a tall man in a shabby suit on the way.

'Dirk tells me there's a new sofa and chair at the office and I've got you to thank for it.' Rex turns those remarkable, dark-brown eyes on me. I abruptly feel rather lightheaded, as if all of the air has been sucked from the room.

'I only reminded him that he didn't want to make his best client unhappy.'

'Good for you.' Rex gives me an appraising glance and I blush. 'What's he like as a boss? I hope he doesn't make you stay late on a Friday night?'

I laugh as I press my hands against my heated cheeks. It feels naughty, talking about Dirk behind his back. It makes me feel like a child again, giggling with Freddie after church.

'He's all right. I've had far worse. I just have to make sure his coffee is strong enough and not forget to buy Pall Malls and mint balls.'

Rex hoots with laughter and a flush of pride spreads through me. I made Rex Trent laugh. Well, look at me! Not bad for the girl who left Sheffield with nothing.

'What is it about him and mint balls?' he says. 'I've seen him request them at restaurants and while everyone else is eating, he just sits there crunching away.'

'It's his thing. He told me once that if you want to get noticed in Hollywood, you have to have a thing that everyone remembers you by.'

'I didn't know that.' Rex looks suddenly pensive. He taps his fingers on the table before shooting a sideways look at me. 'So what's your thing, Audrey? Other than being very pretty indeed.'

It's as if someone has snatched my breath away. My fingers cover my parted lips. *Rex Trent thinks I'm pretty! Oh, my giddy aunt!* The urge to pinch myself to make sure I'm not daydreaming is very strong indeed.

'I'm not sure I've got one,' I manage to say. 'Not yet.'

'Maybe it's that you're English,' Rex says. 'Your accent is real cute.'

'Oh!' I look at him with wide eyes. 'You really think so?'

'Sure, I do.' He frowns as he peers at me a little more closely. 'Why do you look like you don't believe me?'

I take a breath, wondering how much of this I want to share. He's different today, exactly as he seemed in the magazine interviews. He's looking at me, one eyebrow raised, and that gives me the courage to explain.

'Well, I don't talk proper like.' The words are pure Yorkshire and I laugh at Rex's puzzled look. 'I mean, I don't talk like the Queen or as they do on the BBC. At the agency I worked at in London, that was very much a problem.'

'Well, that sounds real stuffy.' As Rex smiles, crinkles surround his eyes. It's hard to look away. Not that I want to. Not at all.

Then behind his shoulder, I spot Dirk returning carrying the drinks. My lips press together as I try to hide my disappointment that my time alone with Rex is about to end.

Dirk gives a beer to Rex, keeps a martini for himself and pushes a substantial copper tankard across the table towards me. I blink. This is taking the old-world charm a bit far, isn't it? I peer into it, hoping it's a lot more ginger beer than vodka.

Dirk raises an eyebrow at Rex, who shakes his head very slightly in reply. I glance between them. What's that about?

'I saw a bit of England while I was away.' Rex shifts in his seat, slanting his body towards mine. 'I had a fine time in London. Went to the Tower, saw the changing of the guard at Buckingham Palace, took a ride on a London bus.'

I smile at his obvious enthusiasm. 'I used to take one of those buses to work every morning.'

'How long did you live in London?'

'Three years.' I left home when Father banned me from seeing Freddie. I'd followed him down to London only to be... My stomach clenches as it always does at the memory of that time, leaving me a little breathless. I shake my head. This is not the time to think about that.

'That's not where you're from then?' Rex asks.

'No, I grew up in Sheffield.' I pause to see if there's any recognition of the name in his eyes. His dreamy, dark eyes look blankly back at me so I add, 'It's where stainless steel comes from.'

Rex frowns. 'I thought that was Pittsburgh.'

Dirk laughs. 'Nearly right.' He pushes a bowl of roasted nuts across the table to Rex. I take a sip of my drink and gasp as vodka scours the back of my throat. 'That's got a kick like a mule,' I say.

'You did ask.' Dirk grins as he lights a cigarette. 'Just don't let Senator McCarthy seeing you drinking it or he'll think you're a subversive.'

For a second, I freeze. Then I realise he's ribbing me. Of course he is. No one in America knows about Freddie.

Feeling Dirk's gaze on me, I fake bravado to hide my slip. I raise my tankard as if I'm proposing a toast. 'To Senator McCarthy. And if he can't tell the difference between a drink and a political party, he should get his eyes tested!'

'Christ, Audrey!' Rex gives a startled laugh. 'People have been blacklisted for saying not much more than that.'

'I'm only saying what's obvious. McCarthy is a bully and bigot.' I cross my arms as my chin comes up. 'Anyway, they're not going to bother blacklisting a secretary.'

'Just don't take us all down with you, kid.' Dirk winks at me. Then he adds, 'Moving to safer subjects, why don't you tell Rex why you wanted to come to Hollywood?'

Dirk sounds like an anxious teacher prompting their prize pupil. I glance at him. Have I ruined things by talking about McCarthy? I just see red when it comes to that bully. He's turning Hollywood inside out with his questions and his stupid list.

Dirk nods encouragingly and Rex tilts his head expectantly so, feeling I've got to behave nicely now, I pick my words carefully. I don't want Rex to think I'm a loose cannon. He can't guess that McCarthy reminds me of Father and it's far too soon to share with him the realities of growing up with a dictatorial parent during wartime.

'The cinema was my favourite place when I was growing up.' My smile comes easily as I'm transported back to the Star Picture House on Ecclesall Road. 'I went every week and saw whatever was on. Musicals, weepies, westerns, they all felt like magic to me, a world away from grey old England. Sheffield was bombed very badly in 1940—'

'Gee!' Rex says, leaning a little towards me. 'Were you okay?'

'I was fine.' His obvious concern warms me and makes me

speak more confidently. 'Our house wasn't hit. But a lot of people died and were injured.' I swallow around the lump in my throat. Too many people. Such horrendous ways to die. 'A huge number lost their homes. My father opened the church to provide temporary accommodation.'

Rex darts a look at Dirk, who nods in response. Anxiety creeps back in. What is going on? There's some subtext here that I'm missing.

'Your Father's a minister?' Rex asks.

'Yes, a Methodist minister.'

'Audrey taught Sunday School,' Dirk adds and my eyebrows shoot up. Why has he mentioned that? The last thing I want Rex to know about me is that I was a Sunday School teacher. It makes me sound as dull as ditchwater.

'You did?' Rex gives me a gentle smile. 'Well, ain't that just the nicest thing!'

He beams at me. I blush because his gaze is so intent. I feel like I'm floating on air.

Maybe the Sunday School revelation wasn't the worst thing after all. I'm staggered Dirk remembered, though. I mentioned it months ago, just after I started working for him.

'I'm not sure I was very good at it.' I risk another sip of my drink. It's growing on me, the warmth of the ginger beer complimenting the sharpness of the vodka. 'Father pretty much foisted it on me once I turned fourteen.'

Another look passes between Rex and Dirk. I glance between them to try to divine what this unspoken communication is about. Dirk smiles blandly at me. Rex tosses a nut up in the air and catches it in his mouth. Then he grins at me and all other thoughts go out of my head.

There is something adorably childlike about him. It reminds

me again of Freddie. He's got the same playfulness and ease with the world that Freddie had when we were growing up. I drink again, hoping the vodka will drown the sadness I feel.

'I was in the Navy during the war.' Rex leans in as if imparting a confidence. 'I was an aircraft mechanic on carrier ships repairing fighter planes.'

I didn't know that. It's not been mentioned in any of the articles I've read. An image forms in my head of him in overalls doing something technical to the inner workings of a plane. A hero with a spanner. How dreamy is that? 'In Europe?' I ask.

He shakes his head. 'No, I was in the Philippines.' He tosses another nut in the air but fails to catch this one in his open mouth. It falls on the floor. Rex simply shrugs. 'So when did you come to America?'

'April last year. I...' When I followed Freddie down to London in 1947, I thought we'd make good on our plan and be on the first liner across the Atlantic. But it didn't work out like that. My hands knot in my lap as I remember the bitter words we exchanged the last time I saw him. 'I wanted to come before but I had to save up. Luckily, when I turned twenty-one, I inherited some money from my great-aunt and booked my passage.' The bequest was £500. For someone earning £4 10 shillings a week, it was a life-changing amount of money.

Knowing I had enough to live on even if I struggled to get a job, I set sail. Arriving in New York was like walking into my dreams. I'd seen *On the Town* with Gene Kelly and Frank Sinatra only a week before I left and it felt unbelievable to be actually walking in Central Park and down Broadway. Everything in New York was bigger. The skyscrapers, the cars, the people. They didn't look pinched and deprived as everyone did in England. America was bursting with confidence and you could see that simply in the way people walked down the street and how they dressed.

I couldn't believe the food. There was so much of everything. Yet after ten years of rationing, I'd forgotten how to enjoy it. I swiftly learnt to ask the waiters for the smallest portions as if I was an invalid recovering after a long fast.

It was easier to indulge with clothes. Clothes rationing had ended the year before and I owned one New Look dress but I'd been too broke to buy much back in England. Saks, Bloomingdales and Macy's were a slice of heaven, full of clothes that were feminine, emphasising curves rather than hiding. I splurged on a new wardrobe. There was no way I was going to arrive in Los Angeles looking drab in my wartime Utility garments.

After a glorious, heady week in New York, I took the train to Los Angeles. I'd arranged to stay at the Mary Andrews Clark Memorial Home which is run as a YWCA but looks like a French château. I shouldn't have worried about finding work. My excellent typing and shorthand speeds made it easy to get a job. Secretaries are always in demand which, annoyingly, was the point Father made when he insisted I go to secretarial college.

Initially, I worked at an insurance company, which was not very different to some of my jobs in London. It was frustrating to be in Los Angeles but still have no part in the film business. Then in May this year, Phyllis, who had a room down the corridor at the Mary Andrews Clark Home, asked if I'd be interested in meeting her boss, Dirk Stone. Phyllis was leaving to get married and she knew I'd worked for a theatrical agent back in London.

The interview was at Scandia, Dirk's favourite bar. It's got a distinctly Viking feel to it, being decorated in dark leather with horned helmets, drinking steins and sheepskin rugs. Dirk was constantly being called away to the telephone, leaving me for long minutes on my own when I felt painfully self-conscious.

Apart from the blonde waitress, I appeared to be the only woman there. Dirk would return to say, 'That was New York. They want Ann Roberts on the Ed Sullivan show,' or, 'That was Universal. They want to loan Rex Trent. I'm making them sweat.' I'd blinked at the famous names. In the brief periods Dirk was sitting at the table, he asked me next to nothing about myself. I was convinced I'd blown it. This had been my one shot at getting a job in the movie business and it'd come to nothing. As he got up to leave, I started to thank him for his time, thinking I'd never see this man again. 'You start Monday,' he said. 'Be there at nine o'clock. Phyllis will show you the ropes.' Then he walked out, leaving me staring after him with my mouth open.

I'd come all this way. I'd uprooted my life, not once but twice, and now I was finally going to work in the movie business. I wanted to tell Esther and Mum and Freddie. They'd be over the—

Then the reality hit me. Only my sister would want to know. Mum and Freddie were lost to me. The missing, which I carried every day, was suddenly as sharp as a blade through the heart. I'd done it. I'd showed them but I couldn't even tell them.

'And you like it here?' Rex asks, interrupting my thoughts. 'You don't miss England?'

'I love it here.' I beam at him. 'There are things I miss about home but Los Angeles is an amazing place to live.' The list of things I miss doesn't include the rain, the cold winters or Father.

'Telephone for Dirk Stone,' the barman calls. Dirk stands and strides to the kiosk built into the panelled wall, which leaves Rex and me at the table alone again.

Rex gives me another of those shy smiles. I smile back at him. He's so different this evening to when we first met. It must have been the exhaustion that made him grumpy that day. There's no other explanation because he's completely charming today.

Into the pregnant pause, he says, 'How would you feel about having dinner with me on Friday?'

I stare at him as my eyes widen. Dinner with Rex Trent? I blink at him as the shock fades and excitement zings through my body.

'Of course, if you've got plans...' Rex adds, turning away and taking a gulp of his beer. He's misread my hesitation. Thought it was rejection, rather than overwhelming, earth-shattering surprise. Because moments like this do not happen to secretaries from Sheffield. And yet it just has and I have to make him see that I'm completely and totally delighted.

'No. No plans.' My hand reaches out and touches his sleeve. 'I just didn't expect... That is, I didn't think—' I break off because I cannot finish that sentence. I can hardly tell him he didn't seem interested in me.

He shifts back to face me. 'Then you'll come?' He looks eager, as if I'm going to make his day by saying 'yes'.

'I'd love to.' I smile widely as excitement bubbles through me. It's actually happening! I'm going on a date with Rex Trent! This is the best moment of my entire life. The dreams which gave me solace during my school days and the grim post-war years in London are coming true. The only thing that's wrong is that Freddie isn't here to see it. Will I ever get used to living without him? Will the hole above my heart where our friendship used to reside ever heal?

'Swell!' A big grin sweeps across Rex's face. He looks like a child on Christmas morning. There's something so appealing about that and it sweeps me back into this incredible moment. 'Would Villa Nova be all right?'

Villa Nova is a romantic little Italian not far from the office. It's also a known hangout of some very famous names – Bing Crosby and John Wayne are regulars. This is so thrilling! It's going to be absolutely incredible to go there with Rex Trent. I must be the luckiest girl in Hollywood right now!

'Wonderful,' I say, my voice vibrating with excitement.

'Write down your address,' Rex adds, 'and I'll pick you up at seven.'

I do as he asks and hand it to him. As he reads it, I take a quick gulp of my Moscow Mule. Do they put fairy dust in these tankards? Because that seems like the only explanation of how this has happened.

Back when it was a game to us, Freddie and I talked about who we'd meet in Hollywood. I always teased him that I'd go out with movie stars and, oh boy, did I want that! But in my heart, I always believed I'd marry Freddie.

I grip my skirt with shaking hands as I push the memories away. I made such a mess of things back then. But I couldn't allow Freddie Greenwood to derail my plans. I'm here in Hollywood and I'm about to go on a date with a movie star. You can stick that in your pipe and smoke it, Freddie and Father and everyone else who told me I was a fool to move here!

'I can't wait!' I say to Rex.

He smiles at me again but this time, it doesn't have the movie-star wattage behind it. I'm wondering what to say next when Dirk emerges from the telephone kiosk. As he strolls back to join us, he raises an eyebrow and Rex nods. Did Dirk leave us alone together on purpose? Did he know Rex wanted to ask me out and that's why he invited me for a drink this evening?

I look at my boss with new eyes as he retakes his seat. Maybe he's more of a romantic than I thought. Perhaps that's what his long-suffering wife sees in him. I wonder if Rex will tell Dirk of our plans but the conversation moves on to Rex's next movie role. He talks excitedly about meeting Brenda Ball and the team at Ransome Pictures.

I drift off as they talk. Images of Friday float through my brain. Rex is wearing a navy suit with a pale-blue shirt and a dusky grey tie. I'm... Then the image dissipates as reality once again intrudes on my dreams. I look down at my navy skirt and plain white blouse with the ink smudge on it.

I've got absolutely nothing to wear!

## 3

Rex Trent tells us about his favourite things: cars, surfing and dating the coolest girls in town.

— *MODERN SCREEN*, NOVEMBER 1951

I tell Ginny as soon as she gets through the door on Thursday morning. She hesitates and then says, 'Just be careful. Remember what we said about actors. Egos the size of California.'

'Rex isn't like that.' I cross my arms, disappointed that she's not living this moment with me. 'He was adorable last night.'

'Did Dirk talk to you about doing more at the agency?' Ginny hangs her jacket on the coat rack before crossing to her desk.

'No.' I've almost forgotten about that in the excitement of being asked out by Rex. If Dirk did indeed engineer Rex and me meeting again then I feel a bit of an idiot for believing he wanted me to do more at the agency. I'm not sure I'm ready for Ginny to see that, though. I make a show of straightening the papers on my desk as I say, 'I'm sure we'll talk about it another time.'

But perhaps we won't need to. If it goes well with Rex then

maybe I'll be leaving to get married in a few months and I can hang up my secretarial hat forever. Wouldn't that be something!

I always knew I didn't want to be rushed into matrimony as Father intended. Paired off with the suitable son of one of the influential members of his flock, going from schoolgirl to wife with barely a moment in between to find out who I am and what I want. But I'm twenty-three in January and plenty would say that's getting a little long in the tooth. I don't want to end up an old maid like Great-Aunt Violet.

And marrying Rex wouldn't be like marrying someone back home. He wouldn't expect me to turn into a boring old house-wife. It'd be fun and parties, premieres and film shoots.

I float through Thursday in a perpetual daydream. But on Friday, nerves have kicked in. What will we talk about? Will I feel out of place in a swanky joint like Villa Nova? What if I don't know which cutlery to use? I ask Ginny and she tells me, 'Start on the outside and work your way in.' Then I start worrying again about what to wear. How will I afford anything fancy enough?

I've precious little saved as the apartment eats up all of my salary. I bought a lot of clothes when I was in New York last year including a couple of evening dresses but, when I tried them on last night, neither the red that I last wore to Lindy's with Dan or the blue floral one felt right for this evening.

He's taking me to the joint where Vincent Minelli proposed to Judy Garland. I can't go in any old dress. It needs to be absolutely perfect!

In my lunchbreak, I go to Saks. It's far more expensive than where I usually shop. The whole atmosphere feels rarified as if it's a temple to clothes and glamour. With the help of a very atten-tive shop assistant, I spend most of next week's wages on a sapphire-blue dress with a portrait collar. Looking at myself in the mirror, I look older and feel almost glamorous enough to be stepping out with a film star.

Back in the office, I struggle to concentrate. What will Rex wear? I hope it's a suit or a sports jacket. He looks really dandy in smart clothes. What will we eat? I like Italian food but it can be difficult to eat with dignity. Maybe I'll avoid the pasta and have a salad. Salad is always good. After I realise I've typed 'salad' instead of 'salary', I give up and do the filing. I can't seem to stop myself from glancing at the clock but every time I look up, the hands have barely moved.

My telephone ringing is a welcome distraction. I snatch it up. 'Dirk Stone Agency. Audrey speaking. How may I help you?'

'Gee, I'm real sorry, Audrey.' I recognise Rex's deep voice immediately. 'But I can't make it tonight. The studio has scheduled an interview with one of the fan magazines and I can't get out of it. Can I call you next week?'

The bubble of excitement pops. My shoulders droop as disappointment sinks through me. I'm not going on a date with a movie star. I've been stood up by a movie star. Of course I have! Why would he want to go out with a girl like me? I'm nothing special. I've been a ruddy idiot getting my hopes up and now I've got to tell Ginny. She pretty much warned me this could happen.

'That'll be fine.' My voice sounds choked. I clear my throat before I speak again. I don't want him to hear how upset I am. 'I know you're a busy man.'

'You wouldn't believe,' he says with a soft laugh. 'You're the best, Audrey.' Then he's gone and I'm listening to the dialling tone.

As I put the handset back on the receiver, I feel weighed down by loss. Not just of this evening's date but of the dreams which have kept me company since I first met him. It's as if there's lead in my stomach now. All of the fairy dust has fled and I'm back to being plain old Audrey Wade, minister's daughter.

'Was that Rex?' Ginny asks.

I nod as tears threaten. I feel utterly flat. Did Rex ever really mean to go through with the date? Or was it a joke to ask the English secretary out and see how desperate she was? Was that what those glances shared with Dirk were all about? Did they have some kind of bet to see if Rex could get me to say 'yes' to dinner? Oh, God, if they're laughing about me behind my back then I'll have to find another job. I can't stay here to be ridiculed. I press my fingertips against the corner of each eye to stop the tears falling. Thank goodness Dirk's out. He'd have a fit if he saw me crying in the office.

'Oh, honey.' Ginny gets up and crosses the room. 'Did he say why?'

I repeat what Rex told me as I fumble for my handkerchief.

'On a Friday night?' Ginny says. 'I didn't think journalists were that dedicated.'

I twist the handkerchief around my finger. 'Or movie stars.'

Ginny gives me a hug. 'Forget about him. Put that fabulous new dress on and come dancing with Nate and me.'

Nate's a junior architect at a firm Downtown who dotes on Ginny. I don't want to put a dampener on their evening and I also don't fancy playing gooseberry all night. 'Thanks, but maybe next week.' I rest my head against her shoulder. 'I'd be no fun tonight and one of us should go out and have a good time.'

'Seems a waste of a great dress but okay.' Ginny pats my shoulder. The warmth of her sympathy makes me blurt out what's really hurting.

'I feel like such a fool for believing he'd go out with someone like me. I'm nothing special. I'm definitely not pretty or glamorous enough to date a movie star.' My hands flutter with agitation. 'I should have known—'

Ginny pulls back and grips my shoulders. 'Did he say that? Because if he did—'

I shake my head. I don't want her to think worse of him than he deserves. 'He just said he couldn't make it. Because of the magazine interview.'

Ginny tilts her head. 'Right, then maybe I'll hold off threatening him with my seven iron!' I manage a weak smile at the image of Ginny menacing Rex with her golf club. 'Honestly, honey, if he's going to treat you like this, he's not worth your tears. Come out tonight and we'll find you a nice guy. He might not be a movie star but he'll treat you right.'

I know she wants to cheer me up but it's too soon. The dreams of Rex are still too vivid. I need time on my own to lay them to rest.

'Ask me again next Friday.' I'm touched by her support. This is what friends are supposed to do for friends. Not stab them with words like icepicks and shatter their dreams into a million pieces. I force a smile as I add, 'I'm lucky to have a friend like you.'

She tilts her head as she lets me go. 'Right back at you, honey. Now promise me you're not going to sit at home on your own tonight?'

The idea of going home, hanging up my beautiful new frock and cooking myself a simple supper on the two-ring burner in my flat makes my stomach sink. Usually, I'd go to the cinema but, although the darkness always soothes, I don't need movie stars this evening. The other place I retreat to is the darkroom, which is always a balm in times of trouble.

'I'll ring Rita,' I tell Ginny as I take my address book from my handbag. 'See if she's in tonight and if I can use her darkroom.'

I've got a roll of film I took on Santa Monica pier last weekend that's ready to be processed.

'It wouldn't be my choice for a Friday night but if makes you happy...' Ginny, like many others, thinks my obsession with photography a little odd. Father told me it'd make me 'unmarriageable'. Informing him that my heroine, Lee Miller, had been married twice didn't help. He spat that he'd rather see me dead than a divorcee before sending me to my room without any dinner.

Rita answers on the third ring and is happy to let me use the darkroom. I promise to be with her at about six and she adds that she'll cook for us both if I've no other plans. There's a lump in my throat as I assure her that I've 'no plans'.

The rest of the afternoon drags painfully but once it's finished, I drive home to collect my roll of film. I can't bring myself to hang the beautiful frock up. I shove the Saks bag to the back of my wardrobe. As I'm closing the door, I catch sight of my reflection in the mirror.

I look sad and pale, my complexion dull. There's a world of hurt in my blue eyes and my dark-brown hair has lost its curl and lies flat against my head. Yesterday, I felt attractive and assured, brimming with confidence. Rex liking me was an elixir that transformed me from plain old Audrey to the glamorous and special someone I always hoped to be. This evening I've shrunk again. All of the old doubts have returned.

The urge to take off my girdle, put on my housecoat and eat cheese sandwiches with my feet up on the sofa is very strong. But I've promised Rita and, unlike Rex, I'm too well brought up to break an arrangement.

I put the roll of film in my handbag, pick up the car keys and force myself out of the door.

* * *

There's a lot of time to think in a darkroom. It's a process which requires time and patience. As I watch the image solidify in the bath of developer solution, it's as if my feelings are going through a similar process. The swirl of emotions settle into a pattern I understand. Like the darkness of the cinema soothes and restores, the darkroom brings me to a better understanding of myself.

The date with Rex felt like a ticket into the world I've dreamed of since I was twelve. That's ten years of daydreams and fantasies about this town.

For six of those years, the dream was shared with Freddie. We were going to come to Hollywood when the war ended. We'd buy lovely clothes and eat all of the foods that had been rationed for so long. We'd go to glamorous parties and dance with film stars. Freddie wanted to design sets. 'I'll be on the credits,' he used to say as his hands sketched out a cinema screen. '*Set design by Fredrick Greenwood.*'

Always at the end, I'd say, 'And we'll get married, Freddie.' I'd imagined our house: a white-painted bungalow with a red roof and a rose-covered veranda.

'Yes, we'll get married,' he'd reply.

'And we'll have four children,' I always said next. I wanted two boys and two girls. I'd named them after my favourite film stars: Cary and James for the boys, Ingrid and Dinah for the girls.

'At least four,' he'd say.

I loved that daydream. When Father was in a rage, when he yelled at me so loudly that spittle sprayed my face, that's where I took myself in my head. When I was sent to my room yet again, denied food or a fire until I mended my ways, I comforted myself with knowing that one day, I'd live with Freddie in Hollywood, we'd have a family and I'd be happy.

Then Freddie shattered the dream into a million pieces. It was only the words I'd uttered in anger and desperation that spurred me to make the dream a reality. 'You wait, Freddie Greenwood! I am going to go to Hollywood and I'm going to be a success and I will marry a film star. And you'll be stuck here in boring old England!'

That's what had driven me to risk everything once Great-Aunt Violet's legacy turned up. I'd show them! Father and Freddie would have to eat their words.

I peg the prints up to dry, cross my arms and sigh. But the reality of living in Hollywood isn't glamorous. I have rent and bills to pay, a flat to keep clean and clothes that need hauling to the launderette. In that way, it's not much different from life back home in England except it's sunnier here. It makes me happy to be able to sit in a park on a March day or go to the beach at Santa Monica in the summer after I've finished work. But those are pleasures which have nothing to do with the dreams that brought me here.

What I didn't realise until I got here is that Hollywood doesn't welcome anyone with open arms. Those who have stardom or power hang on to it and those who want it have to work, hustle and pray for a bit of luck to get them inside the hallowed ground of the film studios. I learned that pretty quickly after I arrived. You see them everywhere in Los Angeles: waiting tables, tending bars, cleaning cars as they wait and hope for their lucky break.

I'd thought dinner with Rex was my lucky break. Now I'm just a secretary again. Waiting and hoping for something exciting to happen.

Once the prints are dry, I take them down and open the door. The smell of sizzling beef makes my stomach rumble. I walk through to the kitchen. Rita wipes her hand on her apron as she turns to me. On the outside, with her razor-sharp, grey bob, twinset and glasses on a chain around her neck, she looks like a comfortably off grandmother. Inside, I've learned, beats the heart of an artist which only since her children have left home has she been able to set free.

'Let's see them then.' I hand the prints over and she slips her glasses onto the tip of her nose. The photographs are candid shots from an afternoon on the pier at Santa Monica, snapping women as they talked to their friends, ate an ice cream, walked their dog.

She flips through them and then stops. She studies the print for a long moment. My stomach does an uncomfortable little flip. Rita's got a great eye and I value her opinion.

'This one,' she says, holding it up to me. It's a girl about my age with her boyfriend. He's got his back to the camera and is slightly out of focus. I took it because I liked her dress: the swirl of her skirt as she moved, the way she'd accessorised it with a matching necklace, gloves and sunglasses.

'Look at her face,' Rita says. I peer at it, trying to see what she's seen. The lens has zoomed in on the look of desire and hope written on her features. That's how I felt this morning, lit up by anticipation and aspiration. On top of the world because Rex Trent liked me and wanted to take me out. I hope this girl didn't have it ripped away as cruelly as I did.

'There's a whole story in that shot,' Rita continues. Then she nods. 'This one goes in the exhibition.'

I blush with pleasure and relief. The exhibition is in early February at the Biltmore Art Salon which sounds very grand indeed. I've been really worried I wouldn't have anything good enough, that I'd be the only member of the club whose work didn't make the grade.

Rita smiles at me as she hands it back. 'Now,' she says, 'are you going to tell me why a pretty girl like you isn't out on a date on a Friday night?'

My face crumples. I dig my fingers into my palms to try to stem the tears. Rita won't want to hear this. My parents were always appalled if I cried. It always resulted in a lecture followed by being required to read the Bible alone in my room until I'd got my emotions back under control.

'I'm so sorry,' I say as scrub at the tears on my cheeks.

'Hey now!' Rita pats my back, slightly awkwardly. 'Whoever he is isn't worth it if he makes you cry like this.'

My voice is lost in the torrent of emotion spilling out of me. The patting is calming. She's not angry with me for crying. That's a surprise. 'He's Rex Trent,' I manage to say. 'I was supposed to be going out tonight with Rex Trent.'

'Gee! That hunk of beefcake?' Rita guides me into one of her kitchen chairs. A cocktail glass is pushed in front of me. 'I was making gimlets to drink before dinner. Start from the beginning and tell me everything.'

I take a sip of the cocktail. The lime cordial is sour on my tongue and then the gin kicks in. It's unsettling to be treated as if I've a right to have these emotions, that it's all right to cry when I'm upset.

Rita nods encouragingly. Slowly at first and then as the gimlet eases the lump in my throat, the words fall over each other as I tell her about Rex's invitation and this afternoon's cancellation.

'Here's what you're going to do,' Rita says when I've finished. 'He might be a movie star but it sounds to me as though he doesn't know when he's got a good thing going. You've got to make him see that. Men think with one part of their anatomy and I ain't talking about their stomach!'

I've had so little experience of men. I've dated but nothing has ever been serious. After Freddie let me down, I've found it hard to trust.

'Do you really think he's interested? That he'll ask me out again?'

Rita tilts her head and looks at me as if I'm a photograph she's assessing. 'You're a good-looking girl, with a nice figure and you've got more about you than most of the airheads in LA.' The praise is unexpected and to hear it from Rita means a lot. She's a straight-talking woman and wouldn't flannel me. 'Sometimes, men need a little push in the right direction,' she continues. 'And that's what we're going to give him.' As she lists her advice, my heart lifts because if Rita thinks there's still hope then I'm not giving up. I've left everyone and everything I knew behind to get here and create a life for myself. My dreams cannot die because of one cancelled date.

**4**

_____

Rex Trent's darkly brooding role in _Redwood Canyon_ shows how far he's developed as an actor.

— _LOS ANGELES EXAMINER_, 12 NOVEMBER 1951

I spend the weekend assessing my clothes and putting together outfits that meet Rita's requirements and show off my bust and small waist. While I'm waiting at the launderette and then doing the ironing, I daydream about what Rex will say when he calls me next week. He'll reschedule and next Friday will see me at Villa Nova just as I hoped. There's an undercurrent of anxiety in the fantasies now. I can't seem to shake the fear that he'll cancel again and sometimes, my imaginings see me sitting alone in Villa Nova waiting for him to arrive.

On Monday morning, I follow Rita's advice to the letter and arrive at the office dressed to the nines. Ginny tells me how nice I look. Dirk smiles cryptically when he sees me but doesn't offer any comment. I keep up the regime for the entire week. Wearing outfits that show off my figure, ensuring my make-up is flawless, reapplying my lipstick after every meal. But it's all wasted as Rex doesn't come in.

* * *

I go to see *Redwood Canyon* as soon as it's released. It's on at The Orpheum, a beautiful movie theatre in Downtown. There's such a thrill seeing Rex's name on the brightly lit marquee outside the theatre. I know him! How exciting is that!

Before the main feature is the Movietone newsreel. *Latest Atomic Test in Nevada* shouts the title. I flinch as my stomach flips. The mushroom cloud blooms on the screen, billowing up as it delivers unutterable destruction and I feel sick. I turn my head away but I can't block out the deep voice of the narrator as he praises American ingenuity and reassures us that the atomic bomb will keep us safe.

I find that impossible to believe. I've lived through a bombing raid and still have nightmares about it. Knowing I could be vapourised should the Russians decide to drop an A-bomb does not help me sleep easily in my bed. It feels like the entire world is living on a precipice and one wrong move – which could quite possibly happen during the war in Korea – will lead to anni-hilation.

It's a relief when the feature starts. Rex struts onto the screen looking broodingly handsome and I finally start to relax. I've met this man! It's wonderful to see his face again, even if it is on cellu-loid. I settle back in my seat and let the story take me.

Rex plays the young gunslinger with a dark past. I'm jealous of his co-star, Eliza Yorke. I want him to touch *my* face so tenderly, to look at *me* with eyes full of adoration.

Afterwards, coming out into a LA evening full of cars, brightly lit shop windows and neon signs is a shock. I feel dislocated from the modern world, still inhabiting the ruggedly beautiful landscapes of the movie.

* * *

Ginny asks me to go to a dance with her and Nate on Saturday night and I put off saying yes as I'm still hoping against hope that Rex will get in touch.

He finally rings on Friday lunchtime. 'Audrey,' he says. 'How have you been?'

It is dreamy to hear his voice. 'I'm fine, thank you.' My voice betrays my agitation, sounding high-pitched and a little shrill. 'How are you?'

'Real good.' There's a hesitation and I hold my breath, hoping that what comes next is the invitation I've dreamed of. 'Look, I'm heading up to Malibu with a friend to do some surfing. I'll call you when I get back.'

It's like a bucket of cold water has been thrown at me. All of my beautiful hopes and dreams are drowning.

'Righto,' I manage to say even though my lips feel numb. 'Have a good trip.'

'Oh, and can you put me onto Dirk?' he adds. 'I need to speak to him about this new director Crown have brought in.'

'Hold on a jiffy.' I transfer the call then cross my arms and curl over them as if that will hold in the dreadful pangs of disappointment.

He still doesn't want to take me out. He couldn't even be bothered to ring me earlier in the week to tell me he was going away. He's left it until he needed to speak to Dirk and I'm just an add-on to a business call. Is that how he sees me? The girl who's only good enough for a date if he's got absolutely nothing else to do that evening? That makes me feel even smaller and more foolish.

I should have done as Ginny said and gone out with her and Nate. I should have given up on Rex because he's clearly given up on me.

Who's this friend he's going to Malibu with? I picture a beautiful starlet with red hair like Rita Hayworth who looks stunning in a bathing suit. I instantly hate her!

Ginny's at lunch so there's no one to see me as I leave the office and go to the ladies' toilet. I stare at myself in the mirror. I look older, more polished, attractive. I've seen the appreciative glances of men I've passed in the street this week, the smiles that have been thrown my way. But it doesn't matter because Rex hasn't been into the office and now he's going to Malibu and it could be ages before he gets back. Will he ring when he returns? I want to believe it but it's getting harder and harder.

I don't want to wait and hope and dream for another week only for it to end in another frustrating letdown. But how sad would that be? To give up on all I've dreamed, to accept that my life in Hollywood will only ever be typing, filing and making coffee. I could have stayed in London to do that.

I was going to show everyone who thought I was a fool for coming to America. I could have used Great-Aunt Violet's money to rent a little flat in London, buy nice clothes and go on dates with respectable young men with jobs in a bank or the civil service. Men who were on the lookout for a pretty, amenable wife.

But I wanted more. I always have. I was *that* close to getting it but it blew through my fingers like thistledown and now it's worse than if I'd never met Rex.

Ginny will tell me to forget him and look for a nice, ordinary guy at the dance tomorrow night. But what nice, ordinary guy can compete with Rex? Ginny doesn't understand what I'd be giving up if I settled for an ordinary guy. I've come so close! I know the elation of being asked out by a movie star. The confidence of believing he's chosen my company over everyone else's. The thrill of expecting to walk into a glitzy restaurant on his arm.

For a few short hours, I felt like a million dollars. I want that feeling back.

* * *

Rex's trip to Malibu must be a long one as the weeks keep passing and I don't hear from him. Sometimes, I still allow myself to dream about him but it's bittersweet now. I know it's only a fantasy.

On Thanksgiving Eve, I work through my lunchbreak so I can leave early. Ginny's got tickets for the grandstand on Hollywood Boulevard for us to watch the Santa Claus Lane Parade. I went last year with some of the girls from the YWCA, peering through the crowds at the procession of floats, marching bands and, of course, Father Christmas on his sleigh.

Ginny's had the day off to help her mum prepare for Thanksgiving and I've arranged to meet her and Nate outside Grauman's Chinese Theatre before we take our seats. I'm a little early so I spend time looking at the handprints of stars that cover the forecourt. Famous names abound including Humphrey Bogart, James Stewart, Ginger Rogers and Judy Garland. Rex's name isn't here yet. It's an honour that will no doubt be on its way if he keeps on having hits like *Redwood Canyon*.

At five thirty, I move to the entrance to the forecourt and lean against the wall. It's already dark and although it's not cold by British standards, for LA, it's a little nippy. I button my navy topcoat and arrange my navy polka dot rayon scarf to fill the gap at my throat.

Beneath the brightly lit Christmas trees attached to each lamp post, there are crowds of people flocking along Hollywood Boulevard towards the parade. There are groups of lads and girls, couples hand in hand and many families; the children alight with excitement, bouncing as they walk hand in hand with their parents.

I've brought my camera with me, even though using it with the flash is a skill I'm still trying to perfect. I'm hoping this evening will provide interesting subjects for photos. The final cut on the exhibition will be made immediately after Christmas and I've still got only one photograph that shines enough to have any hope of being included. Rita's got half a dozen at least and, although I know she's far more experienced than I am, that spurs me on to give it one last try.

An elderly couple walk hand in hand across the entrance to the forecourt. They're slow and stately amidst the bustle. It's their clothes that snag my attention. She's dressed in fashions from before the war: a fitted jacket with a built-in cape, a felt hat sporting a jaunty feather. He's natty in a three-piece suit with a fedora and a brass-topped walking cane. If I can just frame it right then this might be a decent photograph.

I get the camera out and check the light, one eye still on the couple as they proceed across the square. Once I've got the setting right, I take a few quick steps until I'm slightly ahead of them. I've got one shot at this. That's the challenge of candid photography. As soon as the subject notices me, the moment is lost. I wait, one breath then another, until the man's cane arcs out and then I press the shutter. The flash lights up the night. The couple look in my direction. I turn away, camera hidden in the folds of my coat. I take a step back and bang straight into someone.

The collision jars me and automatically, I reach out to steady myself. My hand connects with an arm. My grip tightens on the camera.

'Whoa!' a man exclaims.

There's a confusion of impressions. Bone and muscle, rough fabric, the smell of coffee. A clatter as something hits the pavement.

'I'm so sorry,' I say.

The man is in his late twenties. He blinks at me from pale-blue eyes. Or are they grey? It's hard to tell in this light. Whatever colour they are, they've got remarkable thick, dark lashes. He's a few inches taller than me, with a lithe, athletic build, untidy, dark hair that falls across his forehead and a six o'clock shadow across his chin. He's dressed in dark trousers, a cream jumper and a baggy navy jacket.

'Can you see them?' he asks.

'Sorry?' I hastily fasten the case around the camera. 'See what?'

'My glasses.' He gestures at his face. 'Blind as a bat without them.'

I snatch them up from the pavement. They have heavy, black frames and are luckily unscathed. I hand them to him with another apology. My hand brushes his and electricity zips through me and I glance at him to see if he's felt it too. He pushes the spectacles into place, blinks at me through the thick lenses and a flash of surprise passes across his features.

'I can see you now,' he says. 'You were just a blur before.'

'I'm really sorry.' Without thinking, I reach out towards his arm again. My fingers hover an inch above his sleeve before I pull them back. What am I thinking? Haven't I been impolite enough by barging into him? 'I should have been more careful.'

He waves his hand as if to dismiss the apology. 'No harm done.' He nods at my camera. 'Did you get your shot?'

He must have seen the camera before his glasses fell off. 'I hope so, although I'll not be sure until I develop it.'

He tilts his head as if reassessing. 'You do that yourself?' There's surprise in his voice.

I raise my chin; I hate being considered a clueless amateur just because I'm a girl. 'Yes, a friend has a darkroom she lets me use. I'm hoping this photo will be good enough for the exhibition my camera club is putting on in February.'

His eyes widen as I mention the exhibition.

'An exhibition, heh? You must be good.'

What did I say that for? Now it sounds like I was bragging. Heat streaks up my cheeks. 'Well, the rest of the group are good,' I mutter. 'I'm still finding my way.'

He blinks those amazing lashes as he studies me through his glasses. 'You take candid shots?'

'Mainly.' I pull my shoulders back. 'There's a raw beauty in candid shots. I aim to capture people as they really are. That's when you get to the truth.'

He looks at me for a long moment as if considering. 'Stripping away the artifices we all hide behind, you mean?'

'Exactly!' I grin, delighted to have met someone who understands. My hands sweep out as they always do when I'm excited. 'It's in the moments when we believe ourselves to be unobserved that happens. That's what candid photography captures.'

'How long have you been interested in photography?' he asks. A small boy of about eight wearing a cap and a woolly scarf darts past us, his feet barely inches from mine. Instinctively, we both take a step back and, as we do, the man's arm extends as if to shield me from further intrusion.

'Since I was at school. I had a wonderful art teacher, Miss Stewart, who encouraged me.' As I speak, I peer at his face to see if he's genuinely interested. His gaze meets mine and he nods slightly and that encourages me to add, 'I've always been interested in light and colour and composition. It's when you make them all work together that you get something really special.'

A frown passes over his face and then he says, 'You're English. From the north. I was trying to place your accent. It's clearer when you're passionate.'

I blush at the word 'passionate'. Yet it doesn't sound like a bad thing when he says it. 'I'm from Sheffield in Yorkshire.' He's the first person I've met in Los Angeles who's identified my accent so precisely. 'Do you know it?'

'I changed trains there once.' He fiddles with his glasses, before adding, 'I was in Norwich with the Eighth Air Force.'

The US Air Force brought a huge number of bombers and airmen over to Britain during the war. They flew incredibly dangerous bombing raids deep into German-held territory. We didn't know it at the time but thousands of airmen died and equally large numbers were captured.

He adds hastily, 'Don't go thinking I was some glory boy pilot. I was only a humble radio operator.'

I raise an eyebrow as I say, 'You were still up in the sky to get shot at.'

He smiles a little ruefully. 'Yeah, that did happen.' He reaches into one of the wide pockets in his jacket and pulls out a handkerchief. Then he takes his glasses off and gives them a thorough polish. 'I'm from Oregon so the flat lands of Norfolk were an alien world to me. When I got a few days' leave, me and a buddy hopped on a train and ended up in the Peak District. They weren't mountains like at home but, they were sure as hell better than Norfolk.'

Hearing him talk about it conjures up images of the rugged hills of the Peaks, only a short bus or train ride from Sheffield.

There's a sharp twinge in my chest as I take a step closer to him. 'Where did you stay?'

'Matlock. You know it?'

'Of course! I went on a Sunday School outing to Matlock.' It was only once, in the summer of 1939. Father was in holiday mood, his sternness masked as he joked with his congregation. Freddie and I took a pedal boat out on the boating lake and giggled the whole time as we struggled to get it to go in a straight line.

I tense, ready for the cold thrust of pain that always comes when I think of Freddie, but it's muted. Is it the festive air of this evening that's made it more bearable or something else?

'You sound like you miss it.'

It's on the tip of my tongue to deny it but then I hesitate because the truth is more complicated than that. 'I shouldn't,' I say softly. 'I couldn't wait to leave but it's,' I press my hand against my heart, 'still in here.'

The man nods as if he understands. He opens his mouth to speak and then his gaze shifts beyond my shoulder. 'Are you waiting for someone?'

I hear running feet and turn to see Ginny dashing across the forecourt, one hand holding onto her burgundy hat. I'm relieved to see her and yet disappointed because he'll say something polite and leave. I don't want that. It's so rare to meet someone who's interested in photography and talks to me about home.

'Yes. My friend, Ginny,' I say. 'We've got tickets for the grandstand.'

The man nods. 'Enjoy the parade.' As he starts to walk away, he adds, 'Nice meeting you.'

'And you,' I call after him. He smiles at me over his shoulder before disappearing into the crowd.

'Sorry!' Ginny puffs as she joins me. 'The traffic was terrible.

Nate's parking the car. He told us to go ahead and get our seats. He'll meet us there.'

'Don't worry. We've still got time,' I tell her. I glance at where the man joined the crowd but there's no sign of him.

'Who was that?' she asks.

'I don't know. I bumped into him while I was taking a photo.'

Ginny shakes her head. 'You could have got a name. He's a good-looking guy under all that hair.'

'He's not my type.' I cross my arms as my chin comes up. He's not tall or broad and he looked like he'd been pulled through a proverbial hedge. His eyes were beautiful though and I felt that zip of electricity as we touched.

Ginny rolls her eyes as she takes my arm. 'Because your type is hunky movie stars?'

'Yes, it is.' I nod decisively. Or at least, I want it to be. If only Rex would do as he promised and call!

I press my lips together. I'm not going to think about that now. It's the start of Thanksgiving. The whole country is celebrating. This year has already given me such a lot to be thankful for: my (almost) dream job, my friendship with Ginny and meeting a movie star.

Yet as we walk up Hollywood Boulevard, it's not Rex I'm thinking about but the man I bumped into with the beautiful eyes.

5
_____

Rex Trent and Tony Young spent Thanksgiving weekend in Malibu. The pair stayed at the exclusive Malibu Beach Colony, hideout of many a movie star seeking privacy and seclusion.

— *EYEWITNESS*, DECEMBER 1951

I enjoy the parade and return home with a roll of film to develop. As I cook scrambled eggs on the hotplate, my mind wanders to the man I met earlier. Who was he? In retrospect, I agree with Ginny; it was a mistake not to find out his name. I run through the few things I know about him but they don't add up. Some people, like Dan, fit perfectly into a mould. This man was a bundle of contradictions and doesn't fit at all. He was unconventionally dressed even for California. He clearly knew something about photography but didn't talk about his own work. He'd been part of a bomber crew and yet didn't want me to think him brave.

That evening, when I'm curled up in bed ready for sleep, it's not Rex's face I see but the mystery man from the Chinese Theatre. It was so nice to talk to him. He spent time in England, he understands photography. For the brief minutes that we chatted, I felt I didn't have to pretend. With him, it was all right to be a camera obsessive even though I am a woman, to admit that I do sometimes get homesick. I wonder what he would have said if Ginny hadn't arrived when she did. I felt he understood. He, too, has been far from home.

As I fall asleep, I picture him in his American Air Force uniform. His hair is shorter, his cap angled over one eye. Maybe he went to dances and jived with Land Girls like Esther. Maybe he fell in love with one, married her and brought her over as a GI bride.

With that, I punch my pillow, turn over and conjure up Rex's smiling face.

* * *

I spend Thanksgiving day at Ginny's parents in Pasadena. It's wonderful to be part of such a warm, funny family who all seem devoted to each other. I'm sad to leave and return to the silence of my little apartment. That weekend, I see *An American in Paris* with Gene Kelly and Leslie Caron and absolutely love it.

The newsreel before the picture shows the latest hearings of the HUAC. A succession of witnesses: actors and actresses, screenwriters, directors, producers are called before the Committee and asked the same question: 'Are you or have you ever been a member of the Communist Party?' Witnesses who refuse to answer may end up in prison like the Hollywood Ten (a group of ten screenwriters and directors who refused to cooperate with the Committee and ended up imprisoned for contempt of Congress). Admitting you were once a member puts you instantly on the blacklist and out of work. Worse for some than unemployment is that they'll be asked to name the names of subversives. Failure to do that can again lead to the blacklist. It's a witch hunt, pure and simple, and it makes me even more furious with Senator McCarthy who's still waving his list of Commies around Washington DC.

Dirk and I never do discuss my role at the agency. It makes me a trifle resentful that he held out that hope and then whisked it away. I keep on typing letters and making his coffee just as he likes it but with a heavier heart. Dirk regularly asks me to buy *Eyewitness* and I always flip through it before I put it on his desk. One week, there are photos of Rex strolling down the street in Malibu with Tony Young. I'm relieved that he was away with a friend and not a glamorous starlet like I'd feared.

\* \* \*

On the first Saturday in December, I visit the Alpha Beta grocery store in my neighbourhood. As well as my own groceries, I select tins to send to Esther. I send a food parcel every couple of months and always select things we couldn't get in England during the war (like tinned pineapple) or that are still on the ration (Bill has a taste for corned beef). This one will go with their Christmas presents and provide a few treats for the Christmas period.

With two bags full of groceries, I turn in to the Five and Dime store. This is my first Christmas in my own place and I want to make it as splendid as my tight finances will allow. I'm still counting the cents after splurging on the evening dress. Rita has invited me to join her family for Christmas Day, which I'm looking forward to. It'll be amazing to experience an authentic Californian family Christmas.

I pick out a handful of decorations which sparkle with glitter but won't break the bank. Next weekend, I'll get a tree even if it's tiny.

I'm making my way through the other shoppers when a deep male voice says, 'Audrey?'

My heart leaps. I'd know that voice anywhere. I turn and see only a shirt front, but when I look up, I see Rex smiling down at me. 'I thought that was you,' he says. 'What are you buying?'

'Just a few decorations,' I manage to say. My heart is galloping. It's so unexpected to see him here. He looks utterly out of place among the mops, washing lines and plastic cups. But it's also lousy because I look a fright. I have no make-up on, my hair (recently cut à la Leslie Caron) needs a wash and I'm wearing a shapeless old cardigan that came from England with me. I've broken every one of Rita's rules because I never dreamed I'd see Rex Trent in the Five and Dime store.

'You know Tony?' Rex gestures to the man standing beside him. Tony Young is a good-looking guy with tousled, blond hair and razor-sharp cheekbones but Rex outshines him like the sun next to the moon.

'Nice to see you.' As I turn to him, I remember that he was booked to see a talent scout at Universal this week. 'How did you get on at your screen test?'

He frowns. 'He told me it's a shame I don't dance like Ida and I should take more acting lessons.'

'That's good news,' I say, repeating the words I've heard Dirk say a hundred times. 'They only say that if they think you've got potential.'

'Thank you, Audrey. That's what I've been telling him, but he won't listen to me.' Rex nudges his friend, who shoots him a look I can't interpret. They're clearly thick as thieves and that makes a flare of jealousy shoot through me.

Rex turns back to me and gifts me with one of his heavenly smiles. 'I'm glad I bumped into you. I owe you dinner and dancing.'

My heart does a little bounce of excitement. *So he's not forgotten!* My grin splits my face until I remember Rita's rules about not looking too keen and rein it in a little.

'I think it was only dinner but I'd love to go dancing too.'

'Swell!' Rex beams as if I've bestowed a wonderful gift on him. 'I'll ring you on Monday.'

I see Tony's eyes narrow as I say goodbye to them both. I don't know why it bothers him that Rex has just asked me out but it dims my delighted grin a little.

I contain my excitement until I've paid for my decorations and left the store. When I'm on the pavement, I spin round, tilting my head up to the overcast sky as my bags of shopping spin out.

He's going to take me dancing! He's glad he bumped into me! He's going to call! I hear footsteps approaching and hastily come to an ungainly stop, the shopping colliding painfully with my legs.

As I walk home, I'm planning what he'll say and what I'll reply and, by the time I reach my front door, I'm imagining us dancing. I'm humming 'Some Enchanted Evening' as I turn the key in the lock.

After I've put my groceries away, I open the wardrobe door and yank the Saks bag out. Beneath the yards of snowy tissue paper, the dress is a little creased but otherwise just as beautiful. I hang it on a padded hanger and line my dress shoes up beneath it.

When Rex rings, I'll be ready.

\* \* \*

He doesn't call on Monday. Or Tuesday. My heart leaps every time the telephone rings and I endure the piercing disappointment each time the caller turns out to be somebody else. By Wednesday, I've given up hope.

It hurts to be lifted each time I see him and then sink into despair when he doesn't call. My life feels like the rollercoaster ride on Santa Monica pier. Ginny's witnessed my ups and downs and keeps telling me to forget about Rex but that would feel like giving up in so many different ways.

Especially as Rex seemed genuinely pleased to see me on Saturday. What's changed between then and now? Is he too busy? Is that why he finds it difficult to remember to call when he said he would?

The telephone rings just as I'm getting ready to go out for lunch. I snatch it up and am stunned when his deep voice says, 'Hey, Audrey! How do you feel about dinner and dancing tomorrow night?'

My heart soars. He didn't forget! He *was* pleased to see me on Saturday, and he actually wants to take me out. However, Rita's warned me not to sound too eager. I've got to make him believe I've other men queueing up to take me out. 'I'm busy tomorrow but I'm free on Friday.'

I hold my breath, feeling a little sick. If he's busy on Friday, I'll kick myself. *Please, please...*

'Sure, Friday's fine. Is Romanoff's okay?'

My breath catches. Romanoff's is the fanciest place in town. 'Absolutely,' I manage to say.

'I'll book a table,' Rex says, clearly unaware that I'm too stunned to speak. 'I'll pick you up at seven. I've got your address.' With that, he's gone and I'm left staring at the handset.

'What is it?' Ginny asks. 'Not bad news?'

I shake my head. 'It was Rex,' I say, my voice breathy with astonishment. 'He's asked me to go dancing on Friday evening at Romanoff's.'

'Golly! I take it all back. He must really like you if he's taking you to Romanoff's. Now you finally get to wear that beautiful blue gown.'

I look at her with wide eyes. What if I'm not suitably dressed? What if everyone else is in taffeta and furs? 'Is it all right for Romanoff's?' I do the mental maths to see if I can run to a new frock but it's impossible. I simply can't afford anything else.

'It'll be perfect.' Ginny leans forward, her bust resting on her typewriter. 'But if you're worried, I'll lend you my velvet stole. It'll go nicely with that blue.'

I thank her and try to get back to work but I'm hopelessly distracted. The only thing I can think of is Rex. What he'll say, what he'll wear, what we'll eat.

When Dirk emerges from his office, he says, 'You look a lot happier than you did an hour ago.'

'Rex called.' I grin up at him. 'We're going to Romanoff's on Friday night.'

'Hallelujah!' he says, which seems like an odd response. I didn't realise he cared so much about my love life.

\* \* \*

Thursday and Friday pass in a paroxysm of anxiety. Every time the phone rings, I expect it to be Rex calling to cancel. But he doesn't and on the dot of seven on Friday evening, there's a knock on my door.

I'm ready. I'm wearing the beautiful dress with a crinoline petticoat beneath to make the skirts stand out. My legs are encased in the sheerest nylons I've ever worn. Ginny's white, velvet evening stole is around my shoulders. My hair is styled like Leslie Caron and my make-up is impeccable.

I wish Freddie could see me all dressed up ready to go on a date with a movie star. Exactly as I said I would!

I hop from foot to foot for ten seconds so I don't seem too eager. Inside, I'm a mass of nerves. What if I muck it up? What if I can't think of anything to say or say the wrong thing? What if I let him down by not knowing how to behave at a fancy joint like Romanoff's?

I open the door. Rex fills the doorway in his dark-blue suit paired with a pale-blue tie. He smiles at me shyly. 'You sure look pretty.'

'Thank you. You look very nice too.' Then I don't know what else to say. In my daydreams, the conversation has always flowed effortlessly but faced with him, I feel awkward and gauche. What do I, Audrey Wade, from Sheffield have to say to a film star?

'Shall we?' he says as he offers me his arm. Oh, my giddy aunt, I actually get to touch him! I'm painfully self-conscious, aware of every inch of him as I slip my hand into place. There's pure muscle beneath the fabric of his suit.

'I'm sorry this has taken so long,' he says as we walk down the stairs. 'It's been a whirlwind since I got back from France.'

There's a sky-blue Buick convertible parked at the kerb. Is that Rex's? My eyes widen as he opens the off-side door for me. It is and I'm going to ride in it to the restaurant! This may be the most exciting moment of my entire life. If Freddie could see me now, going to Romanoff's with a movie star in a swanky convertible that gleams with chrome.

For a second, it feels hollow without him. The friends I have here don't understand me as Freddie did. They didn't endure six long years of wartime privations in Britain. For Ginny and Rita, the movies are simply entertainment. For Freddie and me, they were a lifeline. A promise that a different world existed and that we could escape our narrow-minded parents and the suffocating world we lived in.

'Have you been to Romanoff's?' Rex asks as we drive down Wilshire Blvd.

I nearly smile. What kind of salary does he think Dirk pays me? 'No, never. This is a proper—' I kick myself for the slip into Yorkshire '—real treat for me.'

He takes his eyes off the road to glance briefly at me. He makes driving look effortless. One hand on the wheel, his other resting along the door frame. 'They say the guy who owns it is a Russian prince.'

My eyes widen. I read about the Romanovs at school and it really didn't end well for the Russian royal family. 'I thought they all died during the Russian Revolution.'

Rex huffs out a breath. 'Who told you that?'

I open my mouth to say, *Miss Cook, my history teacher*, but then I close it again. He sounds offended that I've doubted him. Father always said men didn't want women who were burdened with brains. 'I can't remember,' I murmur. 'I might have got it wrong.'

'I hope he's there tonight. He's a real crazy guy. He lets his dogs eat at the table with him with napkins and everything.'

'Gracious!' I bite my bottom lip to keep from saying anything more. Romanoff's feels rather less glamorous now I know the fellow diners include dogs.

We turn onto South Rodeo Drive. It's easy to spot the restaurant as it has a pink wall with a large sign with the distinctive double R logo. There are a few couples waiting to go in and I hastily scan the women's clothes to see if I'm suitably dressed. My frock seems to fit the bill. I'm grateful for Ginny's stole as they're all wearing furs or evening capes.

A parking valet takes the keys. Rex takes my arm again. In my daydreams, there's always been a shiver as we touched but I don't feel anything. Maybe it's because I'm a bag of nerves.

We walk up the wide steps and past the couples waiting to get in. I glance at them to see if they're offended by us jumping the queue. 'Golly, is that Rex Trent?' I hear a lady whisper to her husband. I glance behind me; she's staring at me with no attempt to conceal her interest. I feel elated, and a wave of mischief washes over me. I wink at her as if to say, *Yes, I'm the one with the movie star, lady.* She turns away, hiding her face behind her clutch bag.

The maître d' welcomes Rex like an old friend and I press my clammy hand against the fabric of my frock. My petticoat rustles as we cross the floor and the carpet is so plush, my heels sink into it. We're shown to a single booth in the dining room. The table-cloth is snowy linen with an arrangement of pink roses and white carnations in the centre of it. The waiter is as perfectly attired as Jeeves and he hands me a velvet-covered menu with the same double 'R' logo embossed on it.

I am relieved that the menu is principally in English, although there's the odd French word thrown in there. It includes frogs' legs which I've no intention of trying. 'What do you recommend?' I ask Rex.

He looks pleased that I've asked. 'The Waldorf salad for starter. Then I always have the fillet mignon which is a fancy way of saying steak. The chocolate soufflé is legendary. You've got to have that.'

Having lived on miniscule amounts of meat back in England, fillet steak always seems overly extravagant to me. How can one person eat all of that at one time? It would have fed a family back home.

I take Rex's advice on the Waldorf salad and the soufflé but settle on the salmon for my main course. Rex orders for me and once the waiter has departed, I look at him expectantly. He stares blankly at his hands. I smooth my linen napkin over my skirt and wait, thinking he'll speak but he doesn't. On the stage across the dancefloor, the band is playing 'The Way You Look Tonight', yet the silence between us stretches until it is uncomfortable. I have to say something but what?

The moment of mischief I felt as we entered has gone. I feel completely out of my depth in this world of privilege and elegance. Will everyone know I'm only a secretary? That I have no right to be here?

I glance around the other booths. I'm not the youngest diner but the girls younger than me are with their parents, laughing and talking as though they have been born to this life. I feel like an interloper. I stare at the array of perfectly polished cutlery in front of me and remember Ginny's advice: 'Work from the outside in.'

If only Rex would say something. I fidget with my watch, turning it round and round on my wrist. My doubts multiply. I bet the starlets he usually dates don't struggle to find things to say. They're not gauche and embarrassed as I am.

The waiter brings the wine and offers it to Rex to taste. He gives it a perfunctory sip and then nods. Glasses are poured for both of us. I take a sip to ease my dry throat. As the waiter walks away, Rex leans closer to me and says, 'I never know what to say when they offer me the wine. I don't know a good one from a bad one.'

So he feels awkward here too! It's such a relief to know I'm not alone. 'I've never been anywhere this ritzy,' I confess. 'I had to get Ginny to tell me which cutlery to use.'

'Oh, I know that one.' His large hands fan over the silverware. 'Dirk taught me.'

That makes me blink. It's hard to imagine my boss taking the time to instil manners in his clients.

'Have you been with the agency for a long time?' I knot my hands in my lap to stop myself from fiddling with the smallest fork.

'I came to Los Angeles after I left the Navy.' He knocks back half of his glass of wine in one gulp. 'I did all the stuff everyone does who wants to get into the movies. I took acting lessons, put together a resume, got headshots done and sent them to every studio and agency in town. Dirk took me on when no one else would give me the time of day. I owe him a lot.'

'How did you get your break?' I've read about it in the magazines but I've been in Hollywood long enough to know those stories are often cooked up by the studios' publicity departments.

'The first screen test I did was for Crown and I froze. I was sure I'd blown it.' Rex takes a second gulp of wine as if to drown the memory and then tops up his glass. 'Then the camera guy said he'd forgot to put the film in the camera. I was so relieved, I felt lightheaded. The talent scout said, "Go again," and this time, I could do it. It was as if the relief had kicked out the nerves. I nailed the lines, hit my mark and remembered to look at the camera for the close-up. Crown signed me a week later.'

'You must have been really great,' I say. 'Dirks says Harry King only wants the brightest and the best.'

'Crown's been good to me.' Rex drinks more wine. He seems more relaxed now. Whatever was bothering him earlier seems to have disappeared. 'They've worked real hard to build my career.'

'And it's paying off.' I lean forward. 'You've got top billing in *Sealed with a Kiss*.'

'Equal billing.' Rex shakes his head ruefully. 'Brenda's agent wouldn't agree to anything else.'

Again, I feel like I've put my foot in it. 'Are you looking

forward to getting started?' I know from all the letters I've typed that principal photography begins in January.

'Sure. It's a swell script by Marie Calvez. She's one of the best scriptwriters in the business. The Agnes Carlyle series was a big hit for Ransome and she wrote for Aidan Neil and Dinah Doyle in the thirties.'

'Oh! I loved those films.' I clap my hands together. 'I used to go to the matinee every Saturday with my friend Freddie and the Neil and Doyle musicals were our favourites.'

Saying Freddie's name in these surroundings feels strange. In my dreams, our younger daughter was called Dinah. I shake my head to try to shift the wash of sadness. I can't think of that now. This is my new life. The one he chose not to be a part of.

'You'd like Marie,' Rex adds, nudging me gently. 'She's got no time for McCarthy either. She was part of the Committee for the First Amendment and went to Washington DC with them in '47.'

The Committee for the First Amendment were a group of high-profile actors, screenwriters and directors who objected to the investigation by the House Un-American Activity Committee into Communist propaganda and influences in Hollywood and supported the Hollywood Ten. Although Senator McCarthy is not a member of the House Un-American Activity Committee, he's the one who lit the blue touch paper by going around saying he'd got a list of Communists living in America.

'Good for her.' It's great to hear about someone who was brave enough to stand up against McCarthy. 'But I heard lots of the Committee were penalised and ended up on the blacklist anyway.'

Suspicion in Hollywood circles has reached such a fevered state that even being part of the Committee for the First Amendment has ended some careers. Others, like Humphrey Bogart, have had to make very public statements that they're not a Communist.

'Other studios might have fired her for it but Leo Ransome's too smart to lose one of his best writers.' Rex stares into his wine glass before his gaze rises to meet mine. 'I admire her for speaking out and damning the consequences. I wish I was that brave.'

I stare at him, taking in the breadth of his shoulders, the strength in his arms. He's physically a hundred times stronger than me but is he trying to tell me that inside, he's a coward? That he'd testify against his colleagues as others have done in order to save their own careers? Something stirs in the pit of my stomach, an uncomfortable emotion that I can't define.

I know all too well the dangers of not standing up to a bully like McCarthy. You end up trapped and voiceless. I can't believe Rex wants that. He must simply not understand what's at stake. 'I think you'd do the right thing.' My chin comes up as my voice rises. 'No one wants to be pushed into a corner but, if that happened, I think you'd come out fighting.'

'Thank you, Audrey.' He smiles that million-dollar smile and my heart gives a little flip. 'I like that you have faith in me.'

Our Waldorf salads arrive and as I carefully pick up the smallest knife and fork, Rex winks at me. As we eat, he talks about his time in France filming *The Three Musketeers*. He makes me laugh with an anecdote about getting lost driving around the Loire Valley and ending up at a vineyard where he drank so much wine, the owner had to drive him back to his hotel. Before our desserts arrive, I'm surprised to see him order another bottle of wine. I'm only on my second glass. He tops his glass up but I shake my head when he offers to do mine. I rarely drink wine and I'm already feeling pleasantly relaxed.

As we eat the chocolate souffles (which are just as incredible as he promised) I ask him about his travels in Europe and he tells me how much he enjoyed Italy.

'The Italians understand how to live,' he says. 'I wish I could live there.'

It took me so long to get to Hollywood, it seems impossible anyone would want to leave. 'Aren't you happy here?' I ask.

Rex looks down at his empty dish for a long moment. I bite my lip. Have I been rude? Is that a question I shouldn't have asked?

'I'm living the life I dreamed of when I was growing up,' he says slowly, still not looking at me. 'I'm a movie star. I live in a swell house. I get to take pretty girls out to Romanoff's.'

He doesn't sound happy about it, though. Is he like me and finds reality doesn't quite match up to his dreams? Can even movie stars be disappointed?

Then he scoots to the end of the booth and stands. He towers over me as he holds out his hand. With the light behind him, for a brief second, his handsome features look anguished. Then he smiles and says, 'I did promise you dancing as well.'

I put my hand in his. Touching him feels comfortable and easy. Disappointingly, there's still no pulse of awareness.

Rex leads me through the other dancers. I feel eyes on us as we cross the floor. I wonder how many of the women are wondering who this unknown girl is with Rex Trent. I square my shoulders and keep my head up. No one knows I'm just a secretary from Sheffield. This magnificent man has chosen me as his date and that gives me confidence to face the stares.

The band starts playing 'A String of Pearls'. I've dreamed of this moment, how my heart will flutter as his arms come round me, how he'll smile down at me and I'll see in his eyes how much he cares. But he doesn't look at me and my heartbeat doesn't react at all. Is it because I'm nervous? Is that why I'm not feeling the things I'm supposed to feel?

He's so much taller than me that it's difficult to maintain ball-room hold. My left hand doesn't reach his shoulder but has settled in the middle of his extremely toned upper arm. It's disconcerting to look up and only see his square-cut jaw. His lead is assured and it's easy to follow him. I try to relax but I'm worried about doing it wrong. I don't want to stand on his perfectly polished toes in front of all of these people. That would be humiliating.

We dance a waltz and another foxtrot. He chats a little between songs, telling me about his mum teaching him to dance when he was a boy. I relax a little but not enough to really enjoy it. As the band switches to a quickstep, Rex leads me back to our table. I'm smoothing my skirts out when he says, 'Shall we go?'

I stare at him with wide eyes. Already? It's barely ten o'clock. No one leaves a date this early unless it's been a disaster. Have I done something wrong? Should I have talked less or laughed louder at his jokes?

'I've got to be up early in the morning,' he adds.

'Of course,' I murmur politely because that's what the woman must do. She's been invited by the man. If he wishes to leave early, she has no choice but to agree. I gather up Ginny's wrap and my evening bag.

He summons a waiter and requests the bill which he pays with an obscenely large pile of notes. Rex doesn't speak as we walk back through the restaurant. My heart sinks. Somehow, I've messed this up. My one chance at dating a movie star and it's ending in a silence I don't understand.

Heads swivel in our direction as we pass. Are they wondering why we're leaving early? Will the gossip tomorrow be that our date wasn't a success?

As we wait for the valet to bring round the car, I glance up at him. His face is closed off, his eyes downcast, his magnificent shoulders slumped. Freddie's moods could switch like this. One moment, he'd be buzzing with energy and ideas, then darkness would sweep over him and he'd retreat from me. It puzzled and frustrated me as we were growing up. I used to ask myself time and again what I'd done to upset him. It was only much later that I worked out what caused it.

But that can't possibly be the case with Rex. I've read the magazines, I've seen the photographs of him with starlets. He must just be tired, that's all. He's got an early start in the morning. That prompts me to ask, 'What are you doing tomorrow?'

'Tony and I are going back to Malibu.' He grins. 'We'd originally planned to go tonight but I put it on hold for our date.'

I stare at his face. He looks happier than he's done all evening. And that's at the thought of spending time with Tony. An evening out with me at this beautiful restaurant with music and dancing hasn't lit him up like that. Is there something between him and Tony?

Then I shake my head. No, I'm being an idiot. It's because I was thinking of Freddie that I've put two and two together and made one hundred and nineteen. Rex has dated plenty of women. I know because I've seen the photographs and been speared with jealousy. I'm imagining things because this evening has not been the success I hoped for.

I rub my hand across my chest. I had one shot at a date with a movie star and I've blown it. Freddie was right; my dreams are childish. I'm not glamorous or pretty enough to date a film star. One evening out doesn't count. He has to ask you out multiple times to be dating and Rex isn't going to do that with me.

I'll never get another chance like this. I've come all this way, left everything I know behind for the dream of a life in Hollywood and I've failed. Tears prickle behind my eyes. I'll have to do what Ginny keeps telling me and meet a nice, normal guy. But how do I settle for normal after experiencing a night as exquisite as this?

When the car pulls up outside my apartment, I wait until Rex comes round and opens my door.

'Thank you for an enchanting evening,' he says as he takes my hand.

I blink at him in confusion. He's barely spoken for the last twenty minutes. How does that qualify as enchanting?

'Goodnight, Audrey.' His lips brush my cheek. A feather-light touch and then he's heading down the stairs. 'I'll call you,' he says over his shoulder.

I stand and watch him go, my fingers pressed against the skin he's just kissed. Rex Trent has kissed me! Okay, not on the lips so it's not exactly as I dreamed. But it's a start. He must have enjoyed the evening or he wouldn't have kissed me. Would he?

I take my key from my bag and open the door. And he'll call and we'll go out again and next time, it will be absolutely perfect.

## 6

Rex Trent was seen out with an unknown lady at Romanoff's on Friday night. The pretty brunette seemed to be having the time of her life as she danced with the Hollywood heart-throb.

— LOUELLA PARSONS, *LOS ANGELES EXAMINER*, 12 DECEMBER 1951

The week that follows is a whirlwind. Rex sends me a dozen red roses on Saturday, with a card that reads:

*To beautiful Audrey, I'm counting the minutes until I see you again, Rex x.*

I press it against my chest and waltz around my tiny living room. He thinks I'm beautiful! He can't wait to see me again!

I write to Esther telling her all about the date and what a marvellous time I had. Esther and Bill go for tea with our parents every other Sunday and I imagine Father's face turning puce with rage when Esther shares my latest news.

On Monday morning, Ginny shows me the snippet from Louella Parsons's gossip column about our date. It seems utterly unbelievable that I've been referred to as 'the pretty brunette' by the most notorious gossip columnist in Hollywood. I snip the article out of the newspaper to keep.

On Tuesday, Rex telephones and asks me if I'd like to have dinner with him at Villa Nova on Thursday. I feel like I'm floating on cloud nine as I say, 'Yes.'

When I see Rita, I tell her all that's happened and she smiles proudly and says, 'Attagirl!' I count the hours until our date on Thursday evening. Ginny's a little taller than me but the same dress size and she lends me a dark-green evening frock for the occasion. When Rex turns up at my door on Thursday, I feel like my heart will burst.

There's a photographer waiting outside the restaurant. Did he know we were coming or, as it's a popular spot for movie stars, does he wait outside hoping someone famous will show up? Rex is all smiles. We pose underneath the awning. Rex puts his arm around me and I take the opportunity to lean into him, smelling the woody scent of his cologne. The flash is blinding, leaving me blinking as we go inside.

We're shown to one of the dimly lit, red, leather booths. Villa Nova is delightful and nowhere near as intimidating as Romanoff's. I drink Cinzano, eat chicken Milanese and feel as glamorous as Ava Gardner. Rex is utterly charming. While I'm with him, all my doubts and anxieties fade. I feel special. I love hearing him talk about the realities of filming. It's a glimpse behind the magic curtain and although he tells me it's a lot of hard work with early calls and late finishes, it still sounds like the best job in the world. I ask how he relaxes at the end of a long day at the studio and he says he likes to fix cars (he's got three including the Buick he picks me up in) or surf. 'I feel most alive on my surfboard,' he says with a great beaming smile. 'It's the only time I feel really free.'

I'm reminded of what he said about Italy at Romanoff's. I'm more relaxed this evening and feel confident enough to probe a little. 'Why don't you feel free the rest of the time?'

His face closes down. 'Too many people have an opinion on who I should be. It's exhausting.'

I'm itching to ask more but it's obvious he doesn't want to talk about it. I let the conversation drift to our plans for Christmas. He's going back to Illinois for the holidays and I explain that Rita's invited me to spend the day with her family. We talk about Christmases growing up and he's surprised when I explain that during the war, presents were either second-hand or homemade. The affection is clear in his voice when he talks about his parents and his younger sister, Edie.

The only dampener on an otherwise perfect evening is when we're leaving. A middle-aged man with thinning, grey hair stands up from one of the barstools, barring our way. 'Rex Trent,' he says in a loud, southern drawl. 'My daughter loves your movies.'

Rex doesn't reply. I glance up at him. His face is closed down, his jaw tense.

'Can I have an autograph?' The man picks up a paper napkin and pats his suit pockets looking for a pen. 'It'd mean the world to her.'

'No.' Rex pushes past the man. I smile apologetically at the man as I follow.

Out on the pavement, Rex hunches his shoulders. 'I hate autograph hunters.'

'I'm sure he didn't mean any harm,' I say mildly.

'That's easy for you to say. You don't get this everywhere you go!' Rex turns to me. His head juts, his hand sweeps out, gesturing to the restaurant. *'Can you sign this? Can I have my picture taken with you?'* He draws out the vowel sounds, mimicking the man inside. 'Can't I go anywhere without being harassed by idiots like that?'

Unbidden, the memory of my first meeting with Rex slides into my mind. I put his rudeness then down to tiredness, but was I wrong? Was it because he deals every day with intrusions like this? That as a movie star, whose face is known to millions, he can never go unnoticed? Yet as a fan, I know how the slightest brush with stardom can make you feel special.

'It only happens because people love you,' I say. His hands twitch as if to push my words away but I keep talking, 'It must be very annoying and goodness knows, you should be allowed a night off, but I know how much it would have meant to that man's daughter. She'd have felt like a million dollars to have your autograph.'

Rex's lips press together. I tense. Is he about to turn that anger on me? Instinctively, I take a step back. Then he ducks his head and rubs the back of his head.

'Aww, shucks, Audrey. You've made me feel like a real heel.' He reaches into the pocket of his blazer and pulls out the bill he's just paid. 'You got a pen?'

I fish the ballpoint I always carry out of my handbag and hand it to him. He rests the paper on one hand, scrawls his signature and then hands it to me. 'Will you take it to the guy in there? I'll bring the car round and pick you up.'

With that, he strides away into the car park. His slumped shoulders make me wonder if I've done the right thing. Should I have agreed with him? Have I ruined our evening by trying to make him see things differently?

I guess only time will tell. If he never invites me out again then I'll know I blew it. I hurry back inside, tap the man on the shoulder and hand him the autograph. He looks momentarily stunned.

'How did you get him to change his mind?' he asks.

I shrug, a little embarrassed by the question. 'I explained how much it'd mean to your daughter.'

'It sure will,' the man says. 'Darlene will be thrilled.'

As I dash back outside, I picture Darlene as a slightly chubby bobbysoxer. She's a lucky girl to have a father who cares so much. I envy her that.

Rex doesn't speak on the drive back to my flat. Is this my fault? If I'd not spoken out, could the evening have ended differently? I gnaw on my bottom lip as my hands twist in my lap.

Rex is still silent as he escorts me up the stairs to my apartment.

'Thank you for a lovely evening,' I say and then, unable to bear the awkwardness any longer, I add, 'I'm sorry if I spoke out of—'

'No, you were right.' Rex's smile is the full thousand watts. It makes my heart thud against my chest. 'It's pretty neat to give happiness to someone just by signing a piece of paper. You made me realise I've got that power.'

Power is a strange way to express it but I'm relieved he's not angry at what I said. Maybe Rex is one of those rare men who can accept a woman having an opinion.

Rex continues, 'I see why Dirk thinks you're a smart cookie.'

'It'd be nice if he said that to me,' I say tartly. It still smarts that he's not revisited the conversation about me doing more at the agency.

Rex laughs softly. 'You know him better than that!' There's a tiny hesitation before he adds, 'Will you be home Saturday afternoon?'

'Yes. Why?'

'I'd like to drop by if that's okay.'

'Of course.' I gaze up at him. Will this be the moment when he kisses me? He leans in and I hold my breath. *Please let him kiss me! Please!* I close my eyes as my heart beats erratically. His lips brush my cheek. The touch is fleeting, there and then gone. I take a deep breath to avoid sighing with disappointment.

He gives me a shy smile from the top of the stairs. 'Goodnight, Audrey.'

I close the door behind me and shake my head. Is it me? Have I got something stuck in my teeth? Does my breath smell? I cup my hand over my mouth. I smell the coffee we've just drunk but nothing worse. The mirror reveals that my teeth are fine. Ginny's dress is snug, hugging my breasts and my waist, but most men wouldn't complain about that. What is it that's making Rex hold back?

\* \* \*

Louella Parsons's Saturday column includes the photograph taken outside Villa Nova. She names me as Rex's date but her claws are out as she wonders why a heart-throb like him is dating his agent's secretary. The implication that I'm not good enough plucks at my weakest spot. I *always* feel I'm not good enough. I most definitely do not need Louella ruddy Parsons telling the whole of LA that.

'How dare she?' I say to Ginny, acid burning in my stomach.

'Honey, if you're going to date Rex, you've got to get used to it. The whole world is going to have an opinion on your relationship.'

I brandish the newspaper at Dirk when he arrives at the office. 'Have you seen this?'

'Didn't need to. I'm the one she rang to find out who you are. You can thank me she spelt your name right.'

My mouth drops open. Louella Parsons telephoned him! I had no idea he was on those kind of terms with Hollywood's Queen of Gossip.

'You could have got her to write something nicer,' I shoot back.

'Forget it, kid.' Dirk takes his hat off and hangs it on the coat stand. 'The newspaper'll be in the trash tomorrow.'

I'm not sure that helps. Do people forget that easily? Dirk clearly believes they do but I'm not so sure. My stomach quivers. I battle every day with feelings of worthlessness. I'd thought going out with Rex and finally living the life I'd dreamed of would banish them but the doubts and insecurities are still there. Being seen out with Rex gives my confidence a heady and wonderful boost. That's what made me wink at the lady at Romanoff's but then it faded in the silences and awkwardness of that evening. I felt it again at Villa Nova as we had our photographs taken and this time it stuck around, only disappearing when Rex once again didn't kiss me.

Is Louella right and I'm fooling myself to think Rex likes me? We've only been out twice. Yet he's sent me roses and asked to see me tomorrow. That counts for something, doesn't it?

I'm unsettled and distracted all morning. Dirk is more understanding than usual when he finds a rash of typos in an urgent letter to Barney Balaban at Paramount. He tells me to take a long lunch and redo it when I get back.

On Wilshire Blvd, everything is decked out for the festivities. There's an enormous Christmas tree complete with fairy lights and a star on top. The shop windows are filled with elaborate displays in red and green, silver and gold. The Salvation Army band, their uniforms bright in the winter sunshine, plays carols.

It's pretty perfect, especially compared to scrimp and save wartime Christmases when I longed for some of the cheer I saw on the silver screen. Yet it doesn't warm me. I feel like I did as a child with my nose pressed to the glass of Cole Brothers dreaming of owning one of the beautifully dressed dolls and yet knowing I never would.

In Saks, I search for the perfect Christmas gift for Rex. We've not talked about exchanging gifts. Is it too soon in our relationship to be considering it? Ginny seems to think so. But Rex has asked to see me tomorrow before he heads home for Christmas. If he arrives with a present and I haven't got him anything, I'll be mortified.

But what do you buy a movie star who can afford anything and everything he wants? That question is particularly tricky seeing as my finances are anything but rosy.

For twenty minutes, I wander from one room of the shop to the next. I run my hand over a display of lambswool sweaters and realise I don't know what size he wears. I pick up a glass vase that I think is beautiful but as I've not been to his home, I have no idea what he likes.

I stand completely still in the middle of the store. What do I really know about this man? He's talked about work and a little about his family. I know he likes to surf and fix cars but I can't buy him a surfboard or a spanner.

'Can I help you?' a shop assistant asks. She's mid-twenties but with a kind smile. That gives me the courage to confess.

'I'm trying to find something for the man I'm dating but we've not been seeing each other very long and I don't really know what he likes.'

'Maybe a scarf or gloves.' She guides me into a room which is filled with scarves, gloves, belts and ties in all of the colours of the rainbow. 'Thoughtful but not too personal.'

We settle on a cashmere scarf which is as soft as thistledown and a pair of sky-blue, leather driving gloves to match his Buick. I manage not to wince at the price. I'll be living on toast for the rest of the month and all the way through January but it'll be worth it to see Rex happy.

\* \* \*

On Saturday, I'm in a frenzy of anxiety. What on earth possessed me to invite a movie star to my apartment? In all honesty, he invited himself and I said yes but that doesn't change the fact that he lives in a mansion in the exclusive Bird Streets and I have a flat that even the real estate agent called 'petite'. I clean and tidy, shove all of my fan magazines under the bed and hide anything else I don't want him to see in the wardrobe.

Rex's presents are wrapped and ready. I popped to the grocery store this morning and bought ground coffee because I know he likes it and the fragrance pervades the small space.

I stand by the window and look out into the branches of the tea tree that grows beside the road. Usually, the motion of the leaves in the breeze calms me but it's not having that effect today.

There's a knock on the door and I dash to open it. A Christmas tree fills the entirety of the doorway, smelling of resin and forests. I pull back. I can't afford a tree this big. 'I think you've got the wrong apartment,' I say. 'I didn't order—'

'Hey, Audrey, it's me!' My eyebrows shoot up as I recognise Rex's voice. He shifts the tree to one side and his face appears between the branches. He looks delighted, that childlike glee in evidence again. 'You said you'd not bought a tree yet.'

'I haven't but this is—' I can't believe he's done this. It's incredibly thoughtful but I have no idea how he's going to get it into my tiny flat.

He gestures to a bag by his feet. 'I got decorations too.'

I open the door wide and he manoeuvres the enormous tree inside. It's taller than he is, the top of it brushing the ceiling. I pick up the bag of decorations and put them on the sofa. Together, we shift the furniture aside so the tree can stand in front of the window.

'Thank you,' I say. 'It's beautiful.'

'I wanted you to have something nice for Christmas.' He ducks his head and then darts an uncertain look at me. 'I wish I could spend it with you.'

I stare at him, suddenly feeling a little breathless. 'I wish you were too.' I take a step towards him.

Something flickers across his face that I can't read. He steps back and snatches up the bag of decorations. 'I hope you like them. I picked the prettiest ones.'

I blink. Why does he say one thing and then do something completely different? It's like a game of snakes and ladders. One minute, I'm up, feeling high as a kite because he likes me. The next, I'm tumbling down a snake as he backs off again.

'I'm sure I will.' I want to go to him and look at the decorations but he's holding the bag like a shield in front of his body. Maybe he needs time to relax. 'Would you like some coffee?'

After I've poured us both a cup, I switch the radio on and find a station that's playing festive songs. Rex hums along with Bing Crosby as we decorate the tree together. We don't say a lot. I exclaim over the decorations which definitely didn't come from the Five and Dime store. The ones I'd got look a little tawdry next to them. For the top of the tree, he's brought a star.

'Just a jiffy.' I dash upstairs and snatch up my camera. 'Righto, now I'm ready.' I kneel on the rug, ready to capture the moment. The shutter clicks and the flash goes off at the exact second he puts the star on the top of the tree.

'Did you get it?'

'I think so.' I'll have to develop the film to find out but I've a good feeling about it.

I hold onto the camera, hoping he'll want to take a photograph of me in front of the tree, but he slumps down on my sofa. 'It looks real pretty. You got any more of that coffee, Audrey?'

I fill his cup but don't pour another one for me. I'm feeling a little jittery but whether that's from too much coffee or having Rex here, I can't tell.

Rex's arms are stretched along the back of the sofa. Is that an invitation for me to sit beside him? Will his arm come round me? Will this be the moment when we finally kiss?

I perch on the edge of the sofa and glance at him. He takes another sip of coffee. There's still nearly a foot between us. I shuffle my bottom backwards. His hand is just behind my left shoulder and I lean back against the sofa cushions. My head brushes his hand and he pulls back as if I've scalded him. He leaps to his feet. 'I've got something in the car for you.' He hands me his half-drunk coffee and then he's gone.

I stare at the cup, my throat feeling dry. What on earth just happened? We'd been having such a lovely time. What am I doing wrong? The guys I've been on dates with have been all too keen to canoodle in the cinema or try their luck once they'd driven me home. I'm used to pushing them off at the end of the night. Why isn't Rex the same?

I shiver and wrap my arms around myself. This isn't like Freddie. It just can't be.

The door opens and Rex ambles back into the room. He's holding a perfectly wrapped box with a tartan bow around it.

'This is for you. It's fragile.' He hands the box over, our fingers briefly brushing as I take it. He looks down, frowning uncertainly. 'I hope it's okay. I had to ask the guy in the shop. He said this was the best and you deserve the best.' He looks so unsure, my heart aches. How incredibly sweet of him.

'Thank you,' I say. 'I'm sure I'll love it.'

'I wanted to get you something real nice. It sounded like you didn't get many gifts when you were growing up.'

My face flames. Oh, no! Did he think my tales of wartime Christmases were a plea for nice presents? That was the last thing I intended.

'I didn't but that doesn't mean... That is, you didn't have to—' I break off, my confusion about our relationship stifling me. This feels like dating and yet nothing has been said or done to confirm that. If only I knew how he feels about me. I turn away to put the box on the coffee table and when I straighten, his gaze meets mine. I could look into his beautiful, brown eyes forever.

'I wanted to.' He takes my hand, his voice suddenly serious. 'I like you, Audrey. I want to see more of you after the holidays. Can we do that?'

My mouth goes dry. He is the most confusing man I've ever met. Even more than Freddie and that's saying something! He blows hot and cold and I never know where I am with him but I absolutely know I want to see him again.

'Yes!' I throw my arms around him and give him a hug. His body is as solid as a tree trunk. For a long moment he's entirely stiff and then slowly, as if he's unsure, his arms come round me to hug me back. It feels wonderful to be held by him. He smells of woody cologne and pine needles.

He pulls away again quickly and we're left standing in the middle of my brightly patterned rug. He stares over my head at the tree. I look at my feet as my throat constricts. Could I make it any more obvious that I want to be kissed? No other man I've ever spent time with would have turned down that invitation.

Except Freddie.

Memories crowd my mind, but I shake my head to try to shift them. This is Rex. It's not the same. I've read a hundred articles about him dating. He must, despite being a film star, be shy.

I cross to the bookcase and pick up his presents. 'These are for you.' I hand them to him. 'They're not much. I wasn't sure what to get you.'

'Aww, that's real kind of you, Audrey. Thank you.' He smiles shyly at me and then he seems lost for words. He stares at the rug for a long moment. 'Enjoy the tree and have a wonderful Christmas.' He kisses me on the cheek before grabbing his coat from the arm of the sofa. 'I'll ring you as soon as I'm back.'

The door slams behind him. I shake my head in confusion and gaze up at the brightly coloured baubles and the silver star on top of the tree. Would he go to all of this trouble if he didn't like me? No, of course he wouldn't.

I just need to be patient. Maybe Rex needs more time to get to know me, that must be it. When he gets back after Christmas, we'll go out again and we'll kiss and everything will be absolutely fine.

I sink down on the sofa. But what if it doesn't? What if it's like Freddie all over again? The memories crowd around me and I can almost smell the smog of that October evening in Sheffield...

## 7

SHEFFIELD, OCTOBER 1946

The tension in the cinema is palpable as we watch Cary Grant sprint up the stairs in the evil Nazi spy's mansion. *Notorious* is the most exciting film ever. Please let Cary Grant get to Ingrid Bergman in time! I reach across the arm dividing our seats and grip Freddie's hand. He shoots a quick glance at me then he twists his hand so our fingers interlock.

On the screen, Cary opens the bedroom door and sees Ingrid Bergman, limp and helpless in the bed. I hold my breath and then he says, 'I love you.' There's a collective sigh from across the auditorium. He's been beastly to her all the way through the film but finally, he's admitted how he feels!

He carries Ingrid down the stairs and out to the waiting car. He's saved her! They can be together. I press my free hand against my heart as the credits roll. I'd thought Cary Grant debonair and handsome but after seeing him in this film, tortured, brooding and utterly gorgeous, he is now my absolute favourite.

As the house lights come up, I turn to Freddie. 'That was the absolute best! Cary Grant was incredible!'

'I thought you'd say that.' Freddie grins as he releases my

hand to shrug on his overcoat. 'Has he deposed Gene Kelly in your affections?'

I've had a crush on Gene Kelly since I saw him in *Cover Girl* with Rita Hayworth. 'Definitely!' I put my beret on, adjusting it so it angles over my left eye. 'It's Cary all the way for me now.'

'You're so fickle!' Freddie laughs as we exit the auditorium. 'You'll be daydreaming about someone else next week.'

'No, I won't!' I cross my arms and glare at him. 'I'm in love with Cary Grant and it's going to stay that way.'

'I know you, Audrey.' Freddie tugs his cap onto his head. 'I give it a month before you're head over heels about someone else.'

I purse my lips, not wanting to admit he's right but I'm not finished with the film yet. 'Hitchcock's use of lighting was amazing. Did you see the way he used it to create mood and tension?'

Freddie raises an eyebrow. 'More photograph books from the library?'

I raise my chin. 'I bought one. It's champion. It's got sections on composition and lighting and using foreground and—' I blush as I see Freddie's face. He's the only person who accepts my passion for photography but even he doesn't want that much detail.

'Only you, Audrey Wade!' I hear the affection in Freddie's voice and smile.

As we reach the stairs, he slings his arm around my shoulders. It's something he's done for years but tonight, I'm fiercely aware of his proximity. Every nerve ending seems to be alive to his slightest movement. The heat of his hand on my shoulder, the lithe movement of his legs as we descend the stairs in unison. Is he doing this because he likes me as I like him? I don't know because he's Freddie and we've always been this easy together.

I want this to mean something because what Freddie doesn't

know is that I spend as much time daydreaming about him as I do about movie stars. With his arm around me, it feels like we're properly a couple, leaving the cinema on a Saturday evening. Not caught in this strange hinterland between longstanding friendship and, for me, longing.

As we reach the pavement, his arm slides away. Instantly, I feel smaller. I button my coat against the chill evening air. The smog has settled while we've been in the picture house. The air is damp and heavy with smoke. The lights from the cinema glow a dim yellow and barely penetrate more than a few yards. A tram looms out of the mist, rattles past us and disappears.

I glance at Freddie. We've just watched a film about a man who can't admit his feelings for a woman he loves. I don't want to have to get poisoned by Nazis before he admits he loves me. I follow Freddie's gaze; he's looking with peculiar intensity at a tall young man with ginger hair who nods at Freddie as if they know each other. Abruptly, I feel as if I have been poisoned. My stomach burns.

'Who's that?' I ask sharply.

'Dunno.' Freddie's eyes continue to follow the man as he walks away.

Then why is he so interested in him? This is my time with Freddie. I don't need any ginger-haired lad bursting in on our last evening together. It's enough that I've had to hear all summer about his friend Michael. I cross my arms. 'You looked like you knew him.'

'I've seen him around.' Freddie shrugs. 'You'd hardly miss him with that hair!'

The words sound forced and uneasiness stirs. What is going on with him this evening? We were having a great time watching the movie but now it's as if he's a long way away.

We start walking up Ecclesall Road and I say, 'Will I see you before you go back to Birmingham?'

Freddie's going into his second year at Birmingham University studying architecture. I'm jealous and frustrated that he gets to follow his dreams whereas I was sent to secretarial college and spend my days typing letters about the sale of steel.

'Well, you'll see me at church tomorrow.' Freddie's parents are dedicated members of Father's congregation. To keep the peace with his family rather than because of any deep-seated faith, Freddie comes to church on Sundays during his university holidays. I know perfectly well he doesn't step foot in a church otherwise but I'm pretty certain I'm the only person in Sheffield who's aware of that. 'Other than that, probably not. You'll be at work during the day and I'm busy in the evenings.'

Annoyance spikes. Why can't he fit me in? Is it so much to ask that we have another evening together? 'Every evening?' My voice rises. 'Doing what?'

'Things I can't tell a nice girl like you about!'

'Freddie!' I biff him on the arm, possibly a little harder than he deserves, and he laughs.

Is he avoiding me? Jealousy and confusion squirm in my stomach. I've seen so little of him over the summer. I'd been looking forward to him coming back so much, counting the days until I'd see him again. But it's not been like the old days; there's a distance between us now. He talks pretty constantly about Michael, who seems a paragon of every virtue. Every second sentence has been, 'Michael's family live in Putney...' or, 'When Michael and I saw *King Lear*...' They seem to have done everything together during Freddie's summer term.

Freddie's face lights up when he talks about him and I hate it. Freddie's my friend. I don't want to share him with this Michael who I don't know but am absolutely certain I wouldn't like. It's only when we go to the cinema that it feels like it did before he went away. Audrey and Freddie against the world.

Cars pass, creeping slowly through the smog, their headlights blazing. A lad on a pushbike emerges from the murk. He tips his cap and winks at me as he passes. I duck my head and blush.

Jim, one of the apprentices at work, asked me out for a drink last Friday. He's the same age as me, pimply, slender and obsessed with Sheffield Wednesday. Goodness knows why he thought I'd want to go. I'm absolutely certain I've not done anything to encourage him and I said no. When I told Freddie, he said I should have gone. 'Give the poor lad a chance. You never know, he might surprise you.' I'd crossed my arms in a huff as anger and disbelief surged through me. Freddie knows me better than that. Or at least he used to before he went away and started spending all of his time with ruddy Michael.

And what about our plan to go to Hollywood? I couldn't do that if I was with Jim. For the first time, I'd wondered if Freddie had grown out of our dream to move to Hollywood.

The thought chills me because I need that dream. It's a light at the end of the very dull tunnel of my working days. It sustains me during the bus ride across town, the endless hours at my type-writer followed by tiptoeing around at home to avoid sending Father into one of his rages. One day, when I've saved enough money and the government finally allows foreign travel again, I will escape my parents and this city and sail across the sea to Hollywood. There'll be sunshine and parties and glorious food and Father will no longer be able to tell me what to do.

'I wish your degree wasn't so long,' I say abruptly into the silence. 'That means we can't go to Hollywood until 1950.'

'But think of the money you'll have saved by then. If you don't spend it all on photography books!'

'I bought one!' I shoot him a look of amused irritation. 'I'm saving up for the camera in the pawnbroker's window. It's a good one but after that, every penny goes in the Hollywood fund.'

'Think of the sunshine. Won't it be incredible to live some-where sunny!' Freddie says as he takes my arm. 'And the clothes. I shouldn't care because it's bourgeois but damn, I really want new clothes.'

I don't know what bourgeois means and it annoys me that he uses words like that these days. The important thing is he still wants to go. *This* we still share and it's got nothing to do with poxy Michael. I snuggle closer to him as we walk.

'And we'll go to the Brown Derby and eat wonderful meals with meat and butter and cheese.' My stomach growls at the thought. They've been long years of privation during the war and I'd give a lot for a lamb chop or Welsh rarebit.

'Oh, cheese! Stop it!' Freddie groans. 'I'll get a job at a movie studio designing sets.'

'We'll go dancing at The Cocoanut Grove and meet movie stars.'

'And you'll be the toast of Hollywood.' Freddie spins me round and I squeal in excitement.

As I stop, I bump into him. His face is close to mine and his eyes widen. This has got to be the moment, hasn't it? I've dreamed of this for so long. I lean in and kiss him. His lips are soft but there's a rasp of stubble which is not unpleasant. I close my eyes as my senses flood with scent and sensation. Then Freddie jerks away.

'What are you doing?' His eyes darken with anger.

Uncertainty and confusion are a damp blanket thrown in my face, but I can't let him see that. 'I'd have thought that was pretty obvious.' I cross my arms and look him straight in the eye.

'Don't ever do that again.' His voice is icy. I've never heard him so cross. He turns on his heel and walks swiftly away from me. In a few short yards, he's swallowed by the smog.

Is this my fault? Did I do it wrong? I've never been kissed before and I've waited for this for so long and I wanted it to be heart-stoppingly perfect but he's ruined it.

I blow out a long breath. If he wants to be like that then I should leave him to it. There are other boys who like me. I'll go dancing with Jim and we'll see how Freddie likes that. My head droops. Only I don't want to go out with Jim. I want to be with Freddie.

I take off at a sprint down the road. Pedestrians and obstacles materialise out of the fog and are swiftly absorbed by it again. I pass a couple walking arm in arm, an old man in a flat cap and a young woman pushing a pram with a muslin draped over the hood to keep the smog from the baby. The fabric of my skirt bunches around my knees, slowing me down. My beret lifts and I clamp a hand on my head to steady it.

I catch up with Freddie by the newsagents. He's not waited for me which stings. Why should it be up to me to dash after him when he gets upset? Then I spot his hands shoved in his pockets, his eyes downcast. I blow out a long breath and stifle my irritation at him. I know these signs. I have to tread carefully.

'Wait!' I call as I catch up to him. I don't risk touching him. Not when he's like this. 'I'm sorry, Freddie.'

He doesn't look at me. I fall into step beside him. I can't let us part on bad terms. To not see him again until Christmas knowing that we'd not made up would be agony. But what to say? Jokes usually work when he's in moods like this. I rack my brain to come up with something. I test it out in my head then keeping my voice light, I say, 'I must have mistaken you for Cary Grant.'

'Because we look so much alike?' Is that a hint of amusement beneath the grumpiness? I glance at him but his gaze is still fixed on the pavement.

'Well, you're both tall and dark. Admittedly, you're slimmer but, you know, on a dark night—'

'To a blind woman.' He gives me a wry smile. 'You do talk rot, Audrey.'

I shrug to hide my relief that he's speaking to me again. 'It's a talent.'

Silence stretches between us as we walk. It's not far until I'm home. Then I'll have time to try to work out what's happened between us. I must be bad at kissing. The problem is there's no way to find out if you're any good until you do it. Maybe I should try kissing Jim just to make sure I'm doing it right. But then he'd definitely think I like him and I'd have to go out with him and— I sigh as tears prickle behind my eyes. Why is it all so complicated? Why can't Freddie like me as I like him? We've been the best of friends for eight years. We always said we'd get married. So why doesn't he want to kiss me?

The post box outside our house emerges from the fog. The net curtain in Father's study twitches. I spin on my heel and yank my handkerchief out of my pocket. I scrub at my lipstick. If Father sees me wearing it, I'll catch such a telling off.

'Hey!' Freddie catches my hand and there's a tingle where we touch. 'Leave some skin on.'

His hand drops away as I stare at the ruby stain on the handkerchief as if I've transferred the sensation of Freddie's lips against mine to the fabric. Maybe the handkerchief knows where I went wrong because I sure as anything don't have a clue.

'One day, you'll be far from here.' Freddie's gaze meets mine and there's an intensity to it. 'He can't hold you back forever.'

I gaze up at him as I blink back tears. His dark-blond curls are damp and his skin looks pale in the gauzy light. Why can't it always be this perfect between us? I bite my lip. He wouldn't say things like that if he didn't care, would he? But if he cares, why doesn't he want to kiss me?

'Hollywood,' he says, extending his hand palm up. This is our ritual. The way we've always sealed the promise.

'Hollywood.' My hand clasps his, my skin slightly warmer than his. Our fingers grip for a second before we pull apart.

I stare at him. If this was a movie then he'd kiss me now and it'd be utterly perfect. But this is Sheffield and real life doesn't work that way.

Out of the corner of my eye, I see the net curtains twitch again. 'I have to go.' I take a step back, my eyes not leaving his. 'I'll see you at church.'

'What's the sermon?'

'Romans 6:23,' I recite. I typed it yesterday evening, feeling like my fingers might bleed as I hammered out every barbed and bitter word from Father's pen. '*For the wages of sin is death.*'

Freddie grimaces. 'Did you tell him I'd be there?'

'No.' The hair lifts on the back of my neck. 'Why on earth would you think that?'

'No reason.' He waves as he turns away. 'I'll bring a book.'

Freddie's been bringing a book to church since he was fifteen. I, however, as the Minister's daughter, have to sit on the front row and can't get away with tricks like that.

As I walk up the garden path, my shoulders hunch. I stuff the stained handkerchief deeper in my coat pocket. When I open the front door, the hall smells of damp clothes and stewed tea.

'Audrey!' Father calls from his study.

My heart sinks. If he's seen me with Freddie then I'm in for it! 'Coming, Father.' I slip off my coat and shoes.

'Was that Freddie Greenwood?' he says as I step through the door of his study. He's sitting beside the fire reading the *Daily*

*Mail.* His pipe smokes in his hand. 'You're spending too much time with that boy.'

Should I argue? I've tried it before and it's never got me anywhere. Right now, I'm too churned up to defend Freddie to Father. He'll sense any uncertainty on my part. 'You don't need to worry. He's going back to university next week.'

'Best place for him.' Father nods and returns his attention to the newspaper. I'm dismissed. Relief makes me feel a little light-headed. I hurry through to the sitting room where Mum and Esther are huddled around the wireless. Esther's staying with us for the weekend as her husband, Bill is on nights.

'You want some toast?' Mum asks. When I nod, she adds, 'I've saved you a bit of cheese and there's some treacle pudding for afters.'

I slip into the chair she's vacated. It's warm from her body and I pull the crocheted rug over me and snuggle into it.

'Good time with Freddie?' Esther looks up from her knitting with a smile. She knows exactly how I feel about Freddie.

'Sort of.' I bite my lip. Esther went out with plenty of boys when she was a Land Girl. Maybe she can help me understand why Freddie's so confusing. 'I kissed him and he didn't like it. He told me not to do it again.'

'Oh, Audrey!' Esther laughs as she runs a hand over her rounded belly. She's expecting her first baby which is due in January. 'You're supposed to wait for them to kiss you. Boys don't like it when you're too forward.'

I lean forward and clutch the arm of Esther's chair. 'You think that's all it is?'

'I'm sure that's all it is.' Esther takes my hand and gives it a squeeze. 'You need to start playing hard to get.'

'It's Freddie!' I pull back and spread my hands. 'I've known him since I was nine.'

'That's why it's even more important to let him make the running. You don't want him thinking you're fast.'

'Fast?' I lean back with a snort. 'As if I'll ever have a chance to be fast with Father around!'

Esther gives me a long look as she picks up her knitting again. 'What?' I say.

'You won't want to hear it.' She reaches the end of the row and switches the needles over. She's making a bootee from fine white wool. Its tininess pulls at a yearning deep in my belly.

'Esther!' I say as I cross my arms. She might be about to be a mother but she's still infuriating.

She lays the needles down on her lap. 'It's going to be a long time until Freddie's out of university and got a job.' She holds up a hand as I open my mouth to object. 'Just listen. The fastest way out of this house is with a ring on your finger.' She holds her hand up and wiggles the finger with her gold wedding band on. 'Do you really want to spend another four years here waiting for Freddie? There are plenty of decent blokes out there who'd give you a nice home and be a blooming lot easier to live with than Father.'

I stare at her as the implication of what she's saying sinks in. 'But you love Bill, don't you? You didn't marry him just to get out of here?'

Her hand goes to her belly again and she smiles. 'Of course I love Bill. But it's not all romance and big gestures like you see in the films. It's more about the little things, like kindness and building a life together.'

It sounds dull as anything. I open my mouth to object, to tell her I want more, but Esther smiles again. If only she didn't look so blinking happy.

'I know you have all these dreams but dreams won't protect

you when he's,' my sister tilts her head towards Father's study, 'in one of his rages. A husband will.'

Something inside me curdles. I cannot allow my life to become that small. I don't deny it's worked for Esther; I've seen the change in her since she left home and married. She used to be perpetually nervous but that's fallen from her since she left this house. But I want more from my life. I want adventure and romance and to take photographs and I want Freddie by my side as I do it.

'Just think about it,' Esther adds. 'I hate leaving you here, knowing what he's like.'

My throat clogs with emotion. I *really* miss her. We'd been allies against Father's wrath and without her, it's like being stuck in no man's land on my own, never knowing when the next volley of anger will strike.

Mum bustles back in with a tray of tea and toast. As she tends the fire, I bite into the toast and let my thoughts float away. Is Esther right? Am I holding out for an impossible dream? It's not that I really believe I'll marry Cary Grant. I'm not *that* much of a dreamer!

But if Freddie will one day kiss me like Cary Grant kissed Ingrid Bergman then it's worth sticking it out at home. Because together, we'll escape not only Sheffield but the small life that Esther's content with. We're going to Hollywood and, once we get there, everything will be absolutely perfect.

# 8

## LOS ANGELES, CALIFORNIA, DECEMBER 1951

A little bird tells me that Rex Trent is heading home to Illinois for the holidays. Will the budding romance with his agent's secretary survive the separation or will the English Rose be looking for other company to keep her warm over the festive season?

— LOUELLA PARSONS, *LOS ANGELES EXAMINER*, 24 DECEMBER 1951

The whole flat smells of pine resin. It's like sleeping in a forest. The beautifully wrapped box sits beneath the Christmas tree. The gift tag reads, *To Audrey, Happy Christmas, Rex* in the same careful handwriting with which he signed his contract with Crown. I'm disappointed he's not said 'love Rex' or added even a single kiss after his name. There was both on the gift tags I attached to his presents. Was that too forward? Are we not on those terms yet? Or will we never be because he, like Freddie, will never feel like that about me?

Then my gaze returns to the Christmas tree. Would he give me a huge tree plus decorations if we weren't going out?

I can't resist the temptation to feel the weight of the box and try to work out what might be inside. As Christmas approaches, the box becomes endowed with significance because if it's the kind of typical gift you give a woman then that's an indication of how he feels about me. I need to prepare myself to be only one in a long line of pretty girls who've come and gone in Rex's life. But if it's something he's chosen because it matters to me then there's hope that this relationship is as significant to him as it is to me.

I place the parcel from Esther next to the box, the brown paper drab next to the bright wrappings of Rex's present. There's no word from my parents. They have my address but they've never used it.

Christmas Eve sees Louella Parsons digging her claws in again. Any pleasure I feel at her referring to my budding romance with Rex is immediately cancelled out by her implying I'm a tart who'll be looking for someone else as soon as he leaves town. I'm bristling with anger when Dirk arrives. He takes one look at me and says, 'Cool it, kid. She's not worth it.'

I wave the newspaper at him as my voice rises. 'Has Rex seen this? What if he thinks there's some truth in it? That Louella knows something he doesn't?'

Dirk hangs up his hat before he turns to me. 'Rex isn't going to start thinking you're a floozy because Louella Parsons drops the hint in her column. He knows 90 per cent of what she writes are lies.'

'That's easy for you to say,' I tell him as I sink back into my chair. 'You're not the one she's implied is a cheap hussy.'

Dirk pops a mint ball into his mouth before he answers. 'Kid, I'm going to give you the same advice I gave Rex a long time ago. Don't read Louella or Hedda Hopper or the scandal sheets. While you're dating Rex, people will have opinions about you. Doesn't mean there's any truth in them. Most of the time, they're only saying what they think will sell more newspapers.'

'I hate that she gets to say these things.' My hands splay with frustration. 'She's stealing my story and turning it into something else.'

Dirk gives me a long look. 'That's the price of fame. If you don't want it, then don't date movie stars.'

'But,' I sink back into my chair, 'that's so unfair.'

'Welcome to Hollywood, kid.' His smile is so wry, you could hang a hat on it. 'Now where's my coffee?'

Dirk lets me finish at 3.30 p.m. and as I go into his office to say cheerio, he takes a box of chocolates from the bottom drawer of his desk.

'Happy Christmas, kid,' he says as he hands them over. The box is gold with a gold bow. 'You've more than earned these.'

The praise is as unexpected as the gift. Since our aborted chat about my position at the agency, he's not said anything at all about my ability to do my job. I thank him, wish him a Merry Christmas and leave. As I put the box in my handbag, I can't help wondering if his wife Lillian bought the chocolates for me. There'd be a certain irony in that seeing as I bought and wrapped the presents for Dirk to give to her.

* * *

On Christmas morning, I'm awake just after seven. It feels strange to wake up in my own flat with no one else around. There's a strange ache in my chest this morning that feels a lot like home-sickness. I'm not due at Rita's until eleven so there's nearly four hours to fill. I tread softly down the stairs from the mezzanine in my pyjamas and switch the radio on. Perry Como is singing

'Winter Wonderland', which reminds me of the Christmas of 1938 when it was actually snowy. I was nine, eager, excited and a decent aim with a snowball. Christmas Day was a gift of snowball fights with Freddie and making a lopsided snowman with Esther.

I open the curtains to see the sun rising over Downtown and for once, it makes me sigh. I love Los Angeles but Christmas in sunshine will always feel strange.

I make myself a pot of tea and switch on the Christmas tree lights but even they fail to make me feel festive. I wrap my arms around my chest to keep in the longing. Quite what I'm longing for I'm not sure. Home wasn't like they sing about in the songs and I don't want to be back in Sheffield with my family, tiptoeing around to try to avoid upsetting Father. I do want to belong somewhere with someone, though, to have a true home where I can be absolutely myself. Could I have that with Rex? Logically, I know it's far too soon to be wondering and yet he's already shown more kindness than I'm used to. The Christmas tree, in all of its glittery glory, is a more tangible statement of festive cheer than ever happened at home.

It takes huge self-control but I open the parcel from Esther first. Inside is a yellow cotton cardigan which she's knitted herself. It's got a wide welt that nips in at the waist and pretty pearl buttons. I'm touched that, with two small children, she's found the time to make this. I rest my hands on it as though Esther's touch will come through the yarn she's knitted. There's an envelope with a drawing of a Christmas tree that four-year-old David has coloured in for me, wrapped around a photo of my niece and nephew. David, standing proudly beside his two-year-old sister, Ruth, who's still at the adorably chubby stage. A tear streaks down my cheek, followed by another one. They're growing up so fast and I'm not there to see it.

I pour myself more tea to steady myself before I pick up the present from Rex. I peel away the beautiful wrapping paper and reveal a box with the word 'Leica' on it. I gasp. There must be some mistake. Leica makes excellent cameras but they come with a very hefty price tag. He couldn't have, could he? With a fluttery feeling in my stomach, I lift the lid and, beneath layers of tissue paper, is a beautiful camera. I lift it out, marvelling at the efficient grace of it. It's the camera of my dreams if I'd ever dared to dream that big.

Next to it is the instruction manual which I'm definitely going to need, a leather case and two rolls of film. I put it in its case and then carefully place it on the coffee table, lining up the film next to it. I'm both shocked and thrilled that he's given this to me. I'd not thought he'd taken much notice when I'd mentioned camera club but he must have squirrelled the information away. Thinking of him going to the shop and asking for a camera brings a warm glow to my chest. This *must* mean he takes us seriously. This is a present from the heart, an unbelievably thoughtful and generous gift.

But there's a tightness in my chest that I can't explain. The presents I gave him are pretty paltry compared to this. I hope he's not disappointed this Christmas morning when he finds he's only got a cashmere scarf and a pair of gloves from me.

I stare again at the camera. It's beautiful but it's too much. We've only been out a couple of times and he barely knows me. This is the kind of gift you'd give after years together, when you know that person inside out. I'm still barely certain that we're dating and it's unsettling to be the recipient of such generosity.

I stand up and walk to the window, brushing against the lower branches of the tree as I pass. The needles prickle through the fabric of my pyjamas. The sensation shocks me out of this daze of surprise. I need to speak to him. I have to thank him for this incredibly generous gift but I have no way of contacting him until he's back in Los Angeles. I sigh out a long breath. This is why he's so confusing! He's given me this extravagant yet perfect present but not left me his parents' address or telephone number. If we were truly dating, wouldn't I have a way to contact him to say thank you?

\* \* \*

Christmas at Rita's is like being enveloped in a warm hug for the entire day. This is family life like I've never experienced it. There are jokes and banter between the four siblings, grandchildren running about and more food than I've ever seen on one table. I wear the cardigan from Esther which Rita compliments me on. I take the camera to show her and her eyebrows shoot up before she gives a long whistle of appreciation. 'Your beefcake did good!'

I grin as pride engulfs me. She thinks he's mine! If Rita, who's the wisest lady I know, believes that, then isn't it time I stopped worrying? I need to let the past go and start enjoying the here and now with Rex.

## 9

A NEW ROMANCE? Rex Trent's latest date is former Sunday School teacher, Audrey Wade. Audrey's his agent's secretary. Did their eyes meet over her typewriter?

— *PHOTOPLAY*, JANUARY 1952

The days between Christmas and New Year drag painfully. I feel more homesick than I've done since I arrived in America. I also miss Rex and the anticipation of our dates. I keep busy by learning to use my new camera and going to the cinema to see the new Ida Young movie, *Snowtime*, which is an MGM musical spectacular. Ida shines as the aspiring actress hungry for her big break. Not for the first time, I wonder what happened between her and Dirk and why the agency no longer represents her.

Too much time alone allows the old demons to haunt me. I worry Rex will meet someone prettier and more interesting while he's in Illinois or simply realise he can do better than me. He's a movie star with untold wealth. I'm just the girl from Sheffield who types Dirk's letters.

It's a relief when the festivities are over and I've got work to focus on again. Dirk takes Lillian to Palm Springs for the first week of January, leaving me with a long list of things to do in his absence, one of which is taking Sally Berry, one of the agency's newest signings, to Crown Pictures for a screen test.

Determined to look as professional as possible, I wear my navy dress with a matching jacket that nips in at my waist. A red shell cap, belt and gloves makes it a little less severe. Even though I've not heard from Rex yet, I know he's on set on the Ransome lot so there's no hope of bumping into him while I'm at Crown. There's still a huge thrill when I drive beneath the huge, golden crown that decorates the white, arched gateway. If Freddie and Father could see me now!

We're directed to one of the large buildings decorated in the art deco style. A receptionist shows us into a waiting area. Sally's breathing is a little ragged; her foot taps incessantly. Hoping to quell the nerves or at least distract her, I ask her about her family and hometown in Kentucky. By the time the talent scout calls her in, she's calmer and smiles gratefully at me.

Seeing me sitting alone, the receptionist says, 'She'll be at least half an hour. Why don't you go to the commissary and get yourself a cup of coffee?'

I follow the directions she's given me, trying not to look wide-eyed and starstruck as I pass the sound stages. Sadly, all of the doors are closed but I hear jazz emanating from one of them and long to know what's being filmed inside. A woman wheels a rack of dresses past me, their crinoline petticoats fluttering in the breeze. A movie camera is wheeled past on a complicated-looking trolley. I'm almost too distracted to spot the single-storey building that's the commissary. It's only when I register the smell of frying bacon I realise I'm right next to it.

It's mid-morning and the place is pretty empty. The walls are white painted with beautifully lit photographs of the studio's stars on the walls. A woman dressed as if she's just got off a wagon train across the Prairies reads a script at one of the wooden tables, two men in paint-splattered white overalls chat to the middle-aged blonde behind the counter. I wonder who else has eaten in this place. No doubt Rex knows it well but there'll be other big names who dined here like Dinah Doyle, Aidan Neil and dancing sensation Ann Roberts, who's one of Dirk's most successful clients.

I order a coffee and, as I'm paying, I feel a prickling on the back of my neck. Instinctively, I turn my head to see the man I met at the Chinese Theatre. He's standing by the door and looks about as stunned as I feel. He's wearing a pale-blue shirt with a periwinkle tie and a grey flannel waistcoat with matching trousers and carrying a buff-coloured folder. What on earth is he doing here?

I automatically take my change and by the time I've put it in my purse, he's joined me at the counter. 'Well, this is an unexpected surprise,' he says. He smiles at me and my heart does a strange little flip.

'What are you doing here?' I ask, feeling slightly flustered by my reaction.

He grins, his eyes lighting up behind his glasses. 'I work here.'

I blink at him in surprise. He works at the same studio as Rex? Of all the strange coincidences! Does he know I'm going out with Rex? Our picture's only been in the paper once. If he doesn't read Louella Parsons's column, he'll likely not have a clue who I am or who I'm (supposedly) dating. He certainly doesn't look as if he's anything but pleased to see me.

He raises a hand to the blonde behind the counter. 'Usual, please, Thelma.'

'Right you are, Jack.' She gives him an indulgent smile as she pours coffee and slides a tube of M&Ms across the counter to him.

Jack suits him. It's a strong name but with a hint of mischief.

As he pays, I try to work out what to do. It's thrown me how pleased I am to see him. Should I say politely, 'Nice to see you again,' and take my drink to another table? Is that what Rex's girl-friend should do? *But you've not heard from him since the weekend before Christmas*, a little voice says in my head. Not a call or a note in over two weeks. Is that any way to treat the girl you're dating?

With that, my chin comes up and I follow Jack to an empty table by the window.

As I take a seat, he says, 'So what brings you to Crown?'

'I work for the Dirk Stone Talent Agency.' I take my jacket off and hang it over the back of the chair. 'I brought a client for a screen test.'

Jack's eyebrows rise. In the bright light flooding through the window, I can see his eyes are grey. 'Are you an agent?'

I laugh a little hollowly as I stir sugar into my coffee. 'No, I'm Dirk's secretary. But he's on holi— Sorry, vacation and he asked me to bring Sally here today.'

Jack pushes his glasses up his nose. 'I know what a holiday is. I learnt a lot of English slang when I was over there.'

I look at him with some scepticism over the edge of my coffee cup. 'Really?'

'Now you've put me on the spot.' He laughs and runs his hand through his hair. 'All right, I'd better be *jolly* good at this or you'll think I know *bugger all* and I don't want to *cheese you off*.'

'Nicely done,' I laugh. 'You almost sound like a native.'

'Only almost?' Jack winks. Then he offers me his hand across the table. 'I'd better introduce myself seeing as we keep bumping into each other like this. I'm Jack Sorenson.'

'Audrey Wade.'

As I take his hand, a pulse of awareness zips up my arm. *Really?* I want to say to my body. *Why don't you do this with Rex?* Why does the zing happen with Jack, who, although attractive, isn't my type at all?

I glance at Jack to see if he's felt it too. He's smiling at me. It's not like Rex's thousand-watt smile. This is gentler, a smile that warms rather than blinds.

'What is it you do at Crown?' I ask hurriedly as I take my hand back.

'I'm in the props department. I make props and help to ensure they're in the right place on the set at the right time.'

My eyes widen as I listen. 'That sounds fascinating. What films have you worked on?'

Jack reels off a list of titles including *The Three Musketeers*. I blink. Knowing he's worked on one of Rex's pictures makes me feel strangely uneasy. It'd be all right if I could convince myself I'm not interested in Jack but my body keeps giving me these moments where I'm absolutely aware of how attractive he is.

'Were you in France for *The Three Musketeers*?' I ask, my tone perhaps a little sharper than it should be.

Jack opens his tube of M&Ms before saying, 'Rick, one of my colleagues, was on the location shoot. My job was making rapiers, muskets and everything else you'd find in seventeenth-century France.'

This is my moment to say, *I know Rex and he told me how much he enjoyed that shoot* or something like that. Yet I don't do it. I don't want to talk about Rex right now. I don't want to face the confusions and uncertainties of our relationship. I certainly don't want to have to explain to Jack what Rex may or may not be to me.

'I've been here eighteen months,' Jack adds, offering the M&Ms to me. 'Before that, I was at the Pasadena Playhouse.'

The moment to talk about Rex is gone. I take a red M&M and, before I pop it in my mouth, ask, 'What brought you to Crown?'

'You can do things in the movies that just aren't possible in theatre. It's exciting and we get much bigger budgets to play with.' He fishes a brown M&M out of the tube before saying, 'What made you become a secretary?'

'My father.' The chocolate suddenly tastes sour on my tongue. 'He had strong views on women's education.'

Jack quirks an eyebrow. 'You mean he thought you didn't need one? I thought guys like that went out with the Victorians.'

'Maybe over here. Sadly, they're alive and well back in Yorkshire.' Instinctively, I cross my arms, putting a barrier between me and Jack's questions. 'I wanted to stay on at school but Father sent me to secretarial college.'

Jack considers for a moment. 'Well, I guess the joke's on him seeing as you now work for a Hollywood agent.'

It's tempting to mutter, *I don't think he'd see it that way*, but I have a sense Jack doesn't miss much and that would likely lead to a conversation I don't want to get into.

Jack holds the M&Ms out to me again. 'Did your photograph come out?'

Grateful for the change of subject and thrilled he's remembered, I take another M&M and say, 'Afraid not. It was overexposed; it's always a risk with the flash. But I got a couple during the parade that I'm happy with. The final decision on what goes in the exhibition happens this weekend so I'm keeping everything crossed.'

'When is it?'

'The opening's on 1 February at the Biltmore Art Salon.'

'The Biltmore?' Jack's eyebrows shoot up. 'How did you get in there?'

The Biltmore Hotel is a Hollywood institution. It hosted the

Oscars ceremony many times before the war and pretty much every Hollywood luminary has stepped between the ornate pillars that guard its front door.

Heat creeps up my cheeks. I hope he didn't think I'm bragging. 'Mitch, who leads the camera club, knows the manager. They had a gap in their programme and they let us take it.'

'Well, I hope it goes well. I might—' Jack glances at his watch and instantly, his face changes. 'Darn it, I've got to run. I have to get these drawings to my boss. He's got a meeting with the producer at eleven.' He pushes his chair back and stands. 'Good to see you again, Audrey.' He offers me his hand. Again, I feel that jolt of electricity as we touch.

'And you, Jack.' I like saying his name.

He smiles and then he's out of the door. I watch him walk away. He's not tall and powerful like Rex but there's a compact energy about him which is very appealing. He turns and glances over his shoulder as he reaches the path and I blush at having been caught staring. I give him an awkward little wave. He raises the buff-coloured folder in acknowledgement.

I hastily drain my coffee cup and check my watch. It's time I returned to collect Sally. I feel bad for not giving her a thought. I should have been hoping and wishing the screen test goes well but she went entirely out of my head when I saw Jack.

Fancy him working at Crown! It's one of those strange coincidences I'd have thought impossible until I started working for Dirk and realised that Hollywood is actually a pretty small town.

As I walk back, I button my jacket. At least I'm looking good today. Not that it should matter. I'm with Rex, after all. I really should have said but the trouble with dating a movie star is that it sounds like bragging. Also Jack's not given any hint he's interested in me. Admittedly, he looked pretty pleased to see me but he might have a girlfriend or even a wife for all I know.

I cross my arms. If I see him again, I'll mention Rex. Then I blow out a long breath. If he ever blinking well calls, that is!

* * *

Back at the office, eating my lunch at my desk, I open *Photoplay* and start reading. In Cal York's Hollywood gossip column is the photograph of Rex and me taken outside Villa Nova. Although I look sophisticated in Ginny's dress, the caption refers to me as *former Sunday School teacher.*

I can't decide if I'm delighted or peeved. I've read *Photoplay* and fan magazines like it for years. Now I'm actually within its covers but they've made me sound as dull as ditchwater.

Ginny comes over and takes the magazine from me. 'Nice to see my dress in *Photoplay*. It'll be making all my other clothes jealous because it's famous.'

I roll my eyes at her. 'They've made me sound like my maiden aunt. Who told them I taught Sunday School?'

Ginny nods at Dirk's office door. Even though my boss is in Palm Springs, I can feel his hand in this. I wish he'd asked me before he told *Photoplay* about my past. I've come all the way to Hollywood and now everyone knows me as the former Sunday School teacher.

'Why would he want everyone to know that?' I demand.

She shrugs. 'You know Dirk. He'll have his reasons.'

That doesn't reassure me. I feel unsettled for the rest of the day. It feels wrong that Rex's and my relationship is being proclaimed to the world when I'm feeling so uncertain about it. If he'd only called when he got back to LA then it'd be all right. It's his silence that's causing all of these doubts. Of course he's busy with the new film but doesn't he have five minutes to pick up the telephone? Not for the first time since I started seeing Rex, I wish

I had a telephone at home. But that's far beyond the likes of me. I have to save my dimes to use the public telephone in the entrance hall to the block of flats.

When I get home, I stare at the photograph, trying to remember the way I felt on that night out at Villa Nova. I was excited, thrilled to be asked out again. We had a lovely evening until the man asked for the autograph.

Then my thoughts slide to Jack. I see him grin at me, remember the way he made me laugh, feel again that rush of sensation as we touched. I like him. He's interesting and interested in me which is pretty rare in the men I've dated. I wonder what he was going to say before he realised the time. Could it have been *I might come along*?

I shake my head. Of course not. Why would he be interested in an exhibition of amateur photographers even if we are holding it at the Biltmore? He was just being polite. That's all. I'll probably never see him again.

After I've eaten, I write to Esther, telling her about Rex. I clip the photograph from *Photoplay* and include it with my letter. Putting the words on the paper steadies me. Rex will call soon and we'll go out dancing again.

Yet the daydreams are harder to summon when I go to bed. There's something itching at me that's getting in the way of my fantasies. I wrap my arms across my chest and tell myself it's an itch I don't want to scratch. I want Rex. Everything will be fine when he calls.

Telling yourself everything will be fine is easy. If you repeat it enough times, it starts to feel true.

Until, of course, it isn't.

## 10

'You're lying.' I throw out the words as if that will stop the flood of accusations coming from Father's mouth. Cold dread settles in my stomach. I wrap my arms across my middle, protecting myself against Father's words.

'I assure you I'm not.' Father gestures for me to take the chair on the other side of his desk.

We're in his study. On his desk books are neatly aligned, the *Methodist Recorder* is open in the centre of it; his pipe sits next to his tobacco tin. Above his head, flypaper is suspended. Mum changes them every morning and already there's a cluster of shiny bluebottles stuck to it. Outside the window, the sun beats down. Between the rows of peas and beans, the marigolds and hollyhocks are withering from lack of rain. After the terrible winter and the floods that followed it, August has brought day after day of blazing sunshine.

'Freddie was arrested on Wednesday night,' Father says. 'I persuaded the police to issue a warning seeing as he's never been in trouble before.'

There's a buzzing in my head. I can't take in what he's telling me. Freddie arrested? I see him in a police cell, the cold clang of the door as it closes, Freddie terrified and alone. I shake my head. It's not possible. And today is Saturday. Why am I only hearing about this now?

'What did he do?' My throat is dry and the words come out as a barely comprehensible croak.

'Something reprehensible.' Father's lips tighten. 'That's all you need to know. His parents are distraught.'

I squeeze my eyes shut as if that will push all of this away. Behind my lids, a picture forms of Freddie's mother sobbing. She's a small, plump lady who adores her only son. I imagine Freddie's father, a tall, spare man always dressed in a three-piece suit, standing beside her, patting her shoulder as she cries.

'As good Christians, Freddie's parents have barred their door to him—'

The mental image abruptly shatters. 'What?' My voice rises. 'How could they? What can he possibly have done that's that bad?'

'Calm yourself, Audrey.' Father sounds as if he's talking to a two-year-old and that fuels my anger. 'I appreciate this is a shock.'

'Of course it's a shock!' My hands fly out to punctuate my words. 'Freddie's my best friend and you won't tell me what he's done that's so bad.'

Father sighs heavily. 'Do not take that tone with me, Audrey. You must allow me to be the judge on this matter.'

'No!' My voice is high and shrill. 'I want to know what Freddie's done. I'm not a child any more.'

'Yet you persist in behaving like one.' Father leans back in his chair, steepling his fingers in front of him. 'I was in the trenches fighting for my country when I was your age.'

I throw my hands up. He always brings this up when I disappoint him. I'd have done my bit if I'd been allowed to during the last war but I was too young. But I do hold down a job, help around the house, type his dratted sermons and pay for my board. Yet he persists in treating me like a child.

I stand and pace away from him. My chest is tight. He's making me feel small again. But I'm not having it this time. I put my hands on my hips and take a deep breath before I turn back to him. 'I'm going to ask once more, Father. What did Freddie do?'

'I've told you all I'm going to tell you.' Father stands too. His voice is taut, his patience stretched wafer thin.

Usually, I heed the warning and back down but not today. This isn't only about me. He's lying to break up our friendship. Father's tried many tactics before but I didn't think he'd descend to baseless lies about my best friend.

'Fine! I'll go find Freddie and ask him.'

'You will not.' Swift as a predator, Father's hand shoots out and grips my arm. 'I told you for a long time that I didn't think your friendship suitable but you persisted. Circumstances have proved me right and I am going to spell it out in words of one syllable seeing as you appear to need that. You will not see Freddie Greenwood again.'

The cold in my stomach floods my entire body. I want to scream at the sheer unfairness of it, but I clamp my jaw shut. How can he do this to me? Does he not care about my happiness at all? I almost laugh at that because the answer is brutally obvious now. He cares only that I follow his rules and am seen to be the good daughter.

Well, that stops here! I have had enough of doing what he wants. I'm old enough to make my own decisions.

'Sit down, Audrey.' Father's hand tightens around my upper arm, forcing me back into the chair. His fingers are digging into my flesh, hurting me. 'I know you're upset but as a good Christian girl, you will respect my views.'

He's stronger than me; I can't pull away without really hurting myself. Slowly, I lower myself back into my chair. My heart is pounding, my hands shaking. I drop my head to hide the tears of anger and impotence. Father releases my arm and I wrap it across my torso, folding the other arm protectively over it.

I take a long moment to steady my breathing, then I look him straight in the eye. 'You're asking me to give up my best friend because of something he's done that you say is reprehensible. I need more than that. I'm an adult and it's about time you started treating me like one.'

Father sighs heavily. Somehow, the sound implies that I'm the one being utterly unreasonable and it's a trial to have to deal with me. 'You're a young woman.' He annunciates the words slowly as if the argument has addled my senses. 'It is my job as your father to protect you from certain ugliness in the world.'

My brain races trying to make sense of what he's saying. What ugliness? Is this something to do with sex? Only that would make Father talk in riddles. What's so terrible that Father won't talk about it?

'Was he with a prostitute?' My voice comes out as barely more than a whisper. 'Is that why you won't tell me?' I may have led a sheltered life but I do know that they exist. The thought makes my stomach curdle. How could he? After I've been waiting for him, how could he go off and do *it* with someone else?

'Audrey! There are things which we do not discuss in this house and that is one of them.' He raises his hand, palm out, stopping further discussion. 'My decision is made. As long as you live in my house, you will obey my rules. You will not see Freddie Greenwood.'

The cold stone in my stomach leaches into my veins and runs

all the way to my fingers and toes. It's come to this, has it? I have to choose between Freddie or my parents. Freddie, who I'm angry with if he *has* been with a prostitute but who I love with my whole heart. Or this man who's threatened, controlled and bullied me my entire life. I will not regret leaving Father but if I lose him, I lose Mum too.

That causes a deep crater of loss to open up in my chest. Not to see Mum every day will be dreadful. But she always takes Father's side, always silently backs him up.

I look across the desk at Father, at his steel-grey hair, his ruler-straight nose, the puckered line of scars, his cold, blue eyes. A clarity comes over me, armouring me against the consequences of the words I'm about to speak. Because this will change everything.

'Then I won't live in your house any longer.' I stand swiftly this time, not giving him chance to grab me. 'And when I'm far away living my life, I want you to remember that you made me choose.'

Father goes entirely still for a long moment. Then he strides from behind his desk to tower over me. 'You ungrateful little wretch! I'm trying to protect you.'

'No, you're not.' I tilt my head back to meet his gaze. 'You're trying to make sure I do what you say, like you always do. But I've had enough. You don't get to make decisions for me any more!'

His hand is a blur. It strikes my cheek, knocking me sideways. I stagger to keep my balance as pain radiates across my face. My vision blurs. I blink away tears, wipe my nose on my sleeve and press my hand against my face. The pain has a heartbeat, a pulse and it's focused on my cheekbone. It's hard to find my voice. He's not hit me in over a year. I'd forgotten the brutal shock of it, the unforgivable indignity. The way it makes me want to crawl away and curl in a ball.

'Go to your room,' he says.

I force myself to stand tall, to look him straight in the eye. He will not cow me this time. 'I'm going to my room, Father, but only to pack my bags.' I'm proud of the steadiness of my voice, that I don't let him see how much I hate him in this moment. 'I'm not staying another night under the same roof as you.'

'And where are you going to go? There's no point running to Freddie. He's gone to London.'

I grab the back of the chair to steady myself. London? Why didn't Freddie tell me? Tears threaten. I'm fighting for him and he's gone and left without telling me? That's not fair. That's not the way we treat each other. I bet ruddy Michael's at the bottom of this.

The name kicks the gears in my brain into action. I've got Michael's address because I wrote to Freddie when he stayed there at Easter. I'll write to Michael. If Freddie's not with him, he'll know where he is.

I can't let Father see my hurt. He knows too well how to turn my doubts against me. I fold my arms across my chest like a barrier and raise my gaze to stare Father straight in the eye. 'Then I'll go to London too.'

'I cannot believe you're running after that degenerate.' Father spits the words out, spittle falling on my face.

'He's not a degenerate. He's my friend.' How dare Father speak of Freddie like that. 'We've got plans. We're going to Hollywood together and—'

'Grow up, Audrey. Girls like you don't go to Hollywood. They get married, settle down and have babies and the sooner you accept that, the better.'

The words are painful barbs, digging beneath my skin, burying themselves in my heart. If I stay, that is my future. Marriage to a man approved by Father and babies as soon as I can pop them out. I feel lightheaded and sick. It's as if all of the air has been sucked from the room. I will suffocate if I stay and all my hopes and dreams will wither and die.

'Maybe I am a dreamer.' My chin comes up. 'But I'm brave enough to stand up to you because you're a bully who browbeats his family into agreeing with him and however long I live, I never want to be like you.'

Instinctively, I flinch, ready for the next blow, but he walks back behind his desk, making it a barricade between us. 'Get out of my sight,' he says.

\* \* \*

A strange numbness comes over me as I pack my cardboard suitcase. I feel oddly far away, as if I'm watching myself fold my clothes, stuff my stockings in my felt hat to make sure it keeps its shape and wrap my camera in a cardigan to keep it safe. Once it's done, I stand by the door and take a long last look at my room. The anaglypta wallpaper is obscured by a collage of photos that I've cut out of my film magazines and *Vogue*. Cary Grant, James Stewart and Gene Kelly have kept me company over the years. Lee Miller's photographs have provided inspiration.

Will I be back? Will I ever again sleep in the bed, put my clothes in the wardrobe, brush my hair in the mirror? A weight lodges in my windpipe. I press my palm there as if that will help me breathe past it, but the weight is keeping the tumult of emotions contained and if I dislodge it, I will break. I have to go or I'll never be brave enough. I close the door behind me.

As I walk downstairs, I see my parents standing in the hall. Tears streak Mum's face. I utter a wordless cry, dropping the case as my hands automatically raise to hug her.

Father's arm snaps out to stop me. 'You've made your bed, Audrey. Don't come crying to us when it all goes wrong.'

My chin wobbles. He won't even let me hug Mum? What kind of tyrant is he?

'I'll give you one last chance to reconsider because once you leave this house, you are no longer my daughter.'

My knees wobble as the finality of what he's said stuns me. I thought it'd be my choice whether I returned or not. I never thought he'd cast me off. I stare mutely at Mum. Hoping against hope that she'll speak. But she stares at the carpet, wiping tears from her eyes. I love her so much. How can I walk out and never see her again?

But how can I not? Father has made it entirely clear that I have no place in this house if I don't do exactly what he says. If I stay, I will suffocate.

At least I'm not going through this alone. Freddie's been cast out too. If he can face it then so can I. Whatever Father thinks, I will create a life for myself. One that's full of love and excitement and adventure. A life that is nothing like the stultifying one I've endured living in the same house as him.

'If that's supposed to make me change my mind then it's not going to work.' My chin comes up even as I struggle to speak around the enormous lump in my throat. I look past him to Mum. 'I'm sorry, Mum.'

'It's all right, love.' She looks at me for the first time. Her eyes are glassy with tears. How can she do this? How can she let Father dictate everything in their lives including whether their daughter stays or not? 'Let me know you're safe,' she adds softly.

Father tuts as if that's the last thing he cares about. He takes something from her and reaches across the three feet of carpet that divides us to hand it to me. It's my ration book. I stare at its buff-coloured front page with my name and address written on it.

Mum's always taken care of the rations, making sure we're all fed. Now I'll have to do that. The enormity of what I'm doing starts to sink in. I truly will be on my own.

I feel sick as I take my summer coat from the rack. It's too hot to wear it. I fold it over my arm, put my straw hat on and pick up the case again. This is really it; I'm leaving home. I look around the hall with its shabby carpet and faded wallpaper. I stare at the glass bowl on the side table that's stood in the same place on the same crocheted doily for as long as I can remember. My gaze shifts to the framed picture of two kittens above it, to the row of neatly paired shoes beneath the table, to the matching tasselled lampshades that cover the wall lights. None of this will change. It will all stay exactly the same as it always has. And if I stay, I'll be like that bowl, forever static because that's the way Father likes things.

I take a deep breath to push the sick feeling down and reach for the door handle. 'Goodbye, Father.' His face is austere and remote. His eyes flick towards me and then away. He doesn't speak.

I look behind him to where Mum stands. 'Bye, Mum.' My voice catches, tears finally start to fall. I stare mutely at her, hoping she'll do something, say something to make this ghastly moment better.

'Cheerio, love,' she whispers.

The 'love' is a punch to my gut. There's a pain inside me so deep, I can't name it. I want to sit on the bottom steps and howl, it hurts so much. But if I do, Father will think he's won and I can't let that be.

I straighten my shoulders, open the door and step out into the relentless sunshine. Tears stream down my face. I taste salt as they reach my lips. At the end of the path, I look back but the door is already closed.

\* \* \*

I ring Esther from the station. I'm barely able to speak for crying. She tells me to get on the first train to Newark and she'll meet me at the station. I write to Michael while I'm waiting for the train. The letter is awkward, full of crossings out as I struggle to find the words to send to this man I've never met but have heard so much about. On the train, I stare unseeingly out of the window and try not to cry.

At Newark, I climb out and Esther's waiting on the platform with David in his pram. She takes one look at my face and pulls me into a hug.

I cry all afternoon. Esther makes me tea and toast, holds me as I sob. David sits on my lap, his tiny hands fastened around my fingers. His gurgles stir the bone-deep love I have for him and my tears stop although the ache in my chest doesn't shift. If Bill's surprised to arrive home and find his suddenly homeless sister-in-law sitting at the kitchen table, he doesn't show it. He pats me on the shoulder and tells me I can stay as long as I need.

For four days, I sleep on Esther and Bill's sofa, spend my time playing with David and trying to block out Esther's well-meaning advice to let Bill help me find a job with the railway.

On Wednesday morning, a letter arrives from Freddie. He's with Michael, he's fine, he's got digs in Camden and gives me the address. He says it's all been a misunderstanding but he won't be returning to university and is looking for a job in London. But I've known him a long time and I can read between the lines. He's not fine at all.

I write a letter to work telling them I'm leaving and catch the lunchtime train to London King's Cross. Esther and David come to the station with me. As Esther hugs me, she slips a ten-bob note into my hand and whispers, 'You're always welcome with us.'

I try to give her the money back but she won't take it. David is asleep in his pram. I press my fingers to my lips and transfer the kiss to his downy cheek. He doesn't stir. I hope he knows how much his auntie loves him when I'm far away. Esther and I are both crying as I climb into the third-class compartment. The whistle blows and the train jerks into movement. I wave to Esther and then settle back in my seat.

I'm two-thirds excitement and one-third trepidation. I've never been to the capital. As the locomotive steams southwards, I tell myself it'll be all right when I see Freddie. That his face will light up when he sees me and he'll swing me round and finally he'll kiss me because he'll know that I've chosen him. I've put him before my family, my sister and my nephew. That's what you do for the people you love. As the train passes Peterborough and Stevenage, I daydream about the life we're going to have together.

The dream sustains me as I battle through the crowds at King's Cross and plunge into the confusion of the Underground. It keeps me going as, on the hottest day of the summer so far, I carry my suitcase through the streets of Camden, past bombed-out buildings, until I reach the address Freddie's given me.

Trepidation kicks in when I see it's three storeys tall, white paint flaking from its once elegant façade, weeds growing in the small front garden. I climb the steps and after wiping sweat from my palm, reach for the brass knocker. A strip of peeling black paint falls off as I knock.

I hear footsteps inside. The door swings open and a young man about Freddie's age stands in the doorway. He wears a blazer and crumpled trousers. He ushers me inside, apologising for the untidiness. The hall is crammed with bicycles, bundles of leaflets are stacked against the wall and a poster of Joseph Stalin frowns down at me from the wall.

I gasp as my eyes widen. A chill skitters down my spine as I automatically follow the young man into a sitting room. There's a waft of something sour underneath the stench of cigarette smoke and damp. He asks me to take a seat and says he'll get Freddie.

Dirty net curtains cover the elegant window, shrouding the room in gloom despite the bright sunshine outside. Three armchairs huddle around the soot-blackened fireplace. Tacked to the wall is the red flag of the Soviet Union with the gold hammer and sickle in the corner and a star above it. On the coffee table is the *Daily Worker*, its bold headline reads:

US Warns Britain Off Soviet Trade

Beside it sits a dirty teacup, *Animal Farm* and a three-quarters-empty bottle of milk. I take a seat in the chair which sags least.

I stare at the door, waiting for Freddie to appear. This has all got to be some terrible mistake. He can't be living here. These people appear to be Communists. I hear Father's voice say, 'something reprehensible'. Is this what he meant? I blow out a long breath. No, that doesn't make sense. Father would have been only too happy to tell me about Freddie's political views. And you don't get arrested for being a Communist.

At that moment, the door creaks open.

## 11

Does Ann Roberts know about her date, screenwriter Irving Bridges', past? We can't believe he's not told her he was once in the Communist Party. But if she knows, why's she still seeing him?

— *THE LOS ANGELES TIMES*, 10 JANUARY 1952

Rex finally calls me on the day Dirk returns from Palm Springs. He apologises for not calling sooner, saying he's been very busy with filming. I thank him for the beautiful camera, my words tumbling over themselves in my enthusiasm.

'I'm real glad you like it,' Rex says and then adds, 'A little bird told me it's your birthday on Friday. How about I take you to Villa Nova to celebrate?'

It's pretty obvious the little bird is Dirk but although I've been miffed by his silence, I'm thrilled to be asked. Whatever it is that's going on or not going on in our relationship, I'm not going to turn down another evening at Villa Nova with Rex.

He's utterly charming all evening. He orders a bottle of champagne to celebrate. I'm entranced by the performance of it, the heavy bottle topped in gold foil, the silver bucket of ice, the waiter who opens it with careless precision, the white cloud that blossoms from the bottle as the cork pops, the bubbles that fill my coupe glass. The taste is headily delightful.

It's a moment to savour, all right. Drinking champagne in a swanky restaurant with my movie-star boyfriend is a very long way from Ecclesall Road.

Over dessert, Rex gives me my present. It comes in a square box which is a hefty hint that it's jewellery. Under the tissue paper is a double-strand pearl bracelet. The clasp is hidden behind a circle of gold dotted with diamonds and sapphires. I stare at it, open-mouthed. It's the prettiest (and very likely most expensive) thing anyone has ever given me. As with the camera at Christmas, it's a little overwhelming for a girl who grew up with not much at all.

'Thank you,' I say breathlessly. 'It's beautiful.'

'Put it on.' Rex points at my wrist. 'I want to see you wearing it.'

As I struggle one-handed with the clasp, Rex leans over and takes over. I smell the deep spiciness of his cologne. The urge to touch him is overwhelming. I catch his strong, square hand as he leans back.

'I love it,' I say, staring deep into his brown eyes. 'Thank you.'

'You're special to me, Audrey.' He gives my hand a little squeeze. 'I wanted you to know that.'

I blink at him as my heart fills with warmth. Is this how falling in love feels? I don't know. The only man I've ever loved was Freddie, but thinking of him makes the champagne curdle in my stomach. I look down. The moment has gone and yet Rex is staring at me expectantly. I summon a smile as I say, 'You're special to me too, Rex.'

He smiles a little shyly. 'Aww, shucks, Audrey. That means the world to me.'

Once Rex drops me home, again kissing me on the cheek as he says goodnight, I sit on the sofa with a cup of cocoa and think about the evening. Why don't I feel more? We have a nice time together but where's the passion? Other men have struggled to keep their hands off me but not Rex. Is it me? Or is it the two of us together that doesn't work?

Unbidden, Jack walks into my thoughts. I remember that thrill of awareness as we shook hands, the little spark that ran through me as our eyes locked. I want that with Rex but it's not there. Do you need it for a relationship to work?

I remember Esther telling me that love isn't about romance and big gestures like in the films but kindness and building a life together. That sounded really dull back then and it still does. I'm dating a film star but do I need to accept that, even with him, life isn't like the movies?

\* \* \*

At work, Dirk is caught up with a crisis. Gossip queen Hedda Hopper uses her column to claim that Ann Roberts, one of the agency's most successful clients, is dating a Communist. The man in question is Irving Bridges, a respected screenwriter.

I feel really sorry for her. What a situation to find yourself in! I bet she had no idea. In the fevered paranoia that's engulfed Hollywood since the HUAC started investigating again, being in a relationship with a Communist could be enough to end her career.

Dirk asks me to ring Ann to arrange for her to come in to see him. 'Listen for any clicks on the line, kid,' he says, standing over me as I pick up the receiver. 'I need to know if the Feds are tapping her phone.'

My eyes widen. 'They do that?'

'Sure. But try to sound natural, okay? I don't want them to know we're onto them.'

Feeling absurdly self-conscious, I dial the number. As it connects, I press the receiver tight against my ear. As Ann picks up, there's a couple of sharp clicks. If I wasn't listening for them, I'd have just thought it was a bad line. Dirk is watching me intently. I nod. He turns away from me and lets out a stream of swear words.

'Hello?' Ann says.

'Miss Roberts. This is Audrey from the Dirk Stone Talent Agency.' I sound tentative even to my own ears. I hate the thought of a Federal agent listening to this. How is that fair? America's supposed to be a free country and, as it's not illegal to be a Communist, how can it be wrong to date one? 'Dirk would like you to come in for a meeting tomorrow. There's a matter he needs to discuss with you in person.'

We arrange the time and then just before she rings off, I add, 'This is a very bad line. I wouldn't use it if I were you.'

'I don't think that's any of—' she exclaims sharply and then her voice abruptly softens. 'I see. Thank you, Audrey.'

'Cheerio, Miss Roberts. We'll see you tomorrow.'

As she ends the call, the clicks come again.

'I told you to keep it natural!' Dirk snaps as I put the receiver down. 'You practically told them we know they're listening.'

'I couldn't bear her not knowing. It's so unfair.' My hands bunch into fists. It's McCarthy and his bully boys ruining everything again. 'What if she'd kept using the phone and said something they can use against her?'

Dirk paces away from me, rubbing the back of his head. 'Yeah, okay. Maybe you did the right thing.'

'What do the FBI expect to find? She's only dating this Irving fellow.'

'Anything the HUAC can use.' Dirk cracks his knuckles. 'Hopefully against Irving Bridges, not Ann herself, but there are that many pink slips flying about it's impossible to know who's next.'

A pink slip is a subpoena to appear before the HUAC. They've been the death knell to far too many careers over the past few years. The blacklist keeps on growing and Dirk won't want to see any of his clients' names on it but especially not Ann's.

The following day, Ann arrives in the office looking like she's going to a funeral, in a black suit with a pillbox hat. The half-veil hides her red-rimmed eyes. I usher her straight into Dirk's office. He pours her a whisky from the bottle he keeps in the bottom drawer of his desk even though it's only ten in the morning. I close Dirk's office door and return to my desk.

'Just shows you can't be too careful who you date.' Ginny's got her arms folded and a look on her face that I've never seen before.

'It's hardly her fault the chap turned out to be a Communist.' I'm appalled that Ginny can be so judgemental. 'I bet she didn't have a clue.'

'How can you not know you're dating a Red?'

'They don't spend their whole time quoting Karl Marx and whistling "The Internationale",' I say sharply. If they did then I'd have known what to expect when I got to that house in Camden.

'Golly, Audrey!' Ginny leans back and looks at me as if I've grown two heads. 'You sound as if you know one!'

I shake my head as I unjam two typewriter keys that have got stuck together. *Not any more*, I want to say. *Not for four long years. And I've missed him every one of those days.*

After Ann leaves, Dirks calls me into his office. 'Looks like it's her dresser who's the rat. Christ!' He opens his cigarette case and takes out a Pall Mall. 'You can't trust anyone in this town any more.' The click of his lighter punctuates the sentence. 'I thought it was bad in '47 but this is like watching Rome burn. How's anyone supposed to make a decent movie when everyone's looking over their shoulder wondering if they'll be the next to end up on the blacklist because they once spoke to someone who was a Communist for ten minutes in 1938?'

I've not heard Dirk get angry about the blacklist before. It makes me like him a little bit more. There is a heart under that cynical exterior after all.

'What will happen to Ann?' I ask. 'Will she be blacklisted?'

Dirk blows out a plume of smoke. 'Not if I can help it, kid.'

\* \* \*

The following day, I arrive home to find a buff envelope with the words 'U.S. Immigration and Naturalization Service' in bold letters across the top of it. I feel a lift of excitement. I applied to renew my visa before Christmas and this should be confirmation that they're going to grant it.

But it isn't. My heart plummets as I read. The INS are in receipt of my application but will carry out checks to ensure my continuing eligibility before they extend my visa. I am required to attend a meeting at an address Downtown on Tuesday, 12 February. There is a list of documents I must bring with me which includes my passport and proof that I'm in employment.

I sit down abruptly on the sofa as my knees feel a little weak. What does it mean? Why might I not be eligible? I've done everything that I was told to when I got the first visa at the US Embassy in Grosvenor Square. I'm working, which is the key thing, and I've applied to renew my visa in good time. What's changed in the past two years to require further checks and an interview?

I twist my watch around my wrist as my mind churns through a host of possibilities, all more dire than the one before. What happens if I'm not eligible? Do I get kicked out of the country? Could I be sent home in disgrace? I see myself being escorted to the docks and put on the first boat back to England. To have come this far and fail would be unbearable.

I can't go home. I can't let Father and Freddie be proved right, because they'll both be convinced it's my fault. That I was too much of a dreamer, too naïve to read the application form correctly or send some important document.

If I get sent home, I'll never see Rex again. I'll be alone in digs in grey old London, boring everyone I meet with tales of dating Rex Trent when I lived in Hollywood. They'll look at me askance, not quite sure if I'm a lunatic who's made it all up.

I cannot bear that. To have come this close and then find it all ripped away would tear me apart.

\* \* \*

I'm bleary eyed and grumpy when I get to the office. I make myself a coffee and slump behind my typewriter. Ginny arrives a few minutes later and I manage to let her take her coat off before I pour out my worries. I show her the letter and she frowns as she reads it.

'It's probably nothing,' she says as she hands it back to me. 'Everyone's worked up about immigration at the moment because of the Red Scare. You'll be all right once they meet you.

They're looking out for Soviet spies and people with subversive sympathies.'

I go entirely still. 'What?' I manage to murmur between stiff lips. Because although I'm no Communist, I knew a man who is. What if I'm going to be like Ann Roberts and pilloried for the company I once kept?

'Don't look so worried.' Ginny laughs. 'Just don't tell the INS what you think of McCarthy. I don't want you to end up on the first boat back to England!'

She's ribbing me but it doesn't feel like a joke. I feel myself fall back through time. I remember the dim sitting room, the sour smell of milk that'd gone off, the red flag on the wall. Can the INS possibly know that I once visited the home of Communists? And about my friendship with Freddie? In the summer of '48, while the Olympics brought a brief jamboree spirit to London, I saw a poster with his name on it. He was speaking at an event in Mile End with Phil Piratin, who was a Communist Party MP at that time. Obviously, I didn't go. Freddie had made it perfectly clear he wanted nothing more to do with me, but he must have been important to be asked to speak at the same event as the MP. What if Freddie's now some bigwig in the British Communist Party and everyone who knew him is suspect?

An image forms of Freddie, a little older, his hair cropped shorter. He's making a speech about workers' rights and the abolition of private property. He raises a clenched fist as he finishes speaking and the audience roar their approval.

I shake my head and the image shatters. *Oh, please, don't let that be true!* Let that be only my imagination running away with me. I suck in a deep breath. I have no idea what Freddie's doing now. He may have given up being a Communist ages ago. But what if I end up being deported because the INS think I'm a subversive? Someone in the government threatened to kick

Charlie Chaplin out of America for his political views. If they'd do that to Hollywood royalty, what chance does a mere secretary have?

My heart is pumping like mad. I can't leave Hollywood. Not when I'm with Rex and we're getting on so well. Not before he's even properly kissed me!

*If he ever does*, a little voice whispers at the back of my mind. I push that voice away. It will happen. He's just tired at the moment from filming.

Dirk throws the door open and stomps past my desk. I know those signs. I shove my fears to the back of my mind and head to the coffee maker to get him his first cup of the morning.

As I take it into his office, I say, 'Any news about Ann Roberts?' My voice wobbles slightly.

Dirk blows smoke up at the ceiling before he replies. 'She's dumped Irving. The studio is wavering. They don't want to blacklist her when she's getting such good receipts. We need to play on that. I've lined up a meeting for us tomorrow morning with Harry King for her to apologise to him in person for bringing Crown Pictures into disrepute.'

Will that be what I'm forced to do? No matter the things we said to each other on that last day, Freddie was my friend. If I have to disown him in order to stay in America then it will break my heart all over again.

'Then I've got Louella Parsons to do a puff piece,' Dirk continues. 'She'll paint Ann as a poor dupe who didn't realise the guy was a Red. It'll hurt Ann's pride but it's better than the blacklist.'

I frown. 'Louella will do that?' After my own brushes with the gossip columnist, I'm surprised she's prepared to be so helpful.

'Louella will do anything to make Hedda Hopper look bad.' Dirk stubs his cigarette out and pops a mint ball into his mouth. 'You look glum this morning too, kid. What's up?'

As I explain about the letter, my voice wobbles as anxiety clogs my throat. I finish by saying I'll need a letter from him confirming I work here.

'It's all part of McCarthy's Communist paranoia,' he says, crunching his mint ball. 'You'll be fine once they meet you. Just don't tell them what you think of McCarthy.'

'That's what Ginny said,' I say. Unease stalks down my spine. Apart from sharing my views on McCarthy, I've not done anything that could be thought subversive while I've been here. Would they really go to the trouble of looking at what happened nearly five years ago back in London?

'Write the letter they've asked for, tell them I can't run this place without you and I'll sign it,' Dirk adds. 'Then cheer me up, kid, and tell me when you're next seeing Rex?'

Dirk's fascination with my love life still perplexes me. He never showed any interest in who I was dating before Rex.

'He's invited me to lunch at his house on Saturday.' The thought lifts some of the worry. They can hardly deport me when I'm dating one of America's hottest movie stars, can they?

Dirk grins widely. 'That place could use a woman's touch.'

I fold my arms. 'I think you're getting a bit ahead of yourself.'

He winks. 'We'll see!'

**12**

My worries about the INS lurk at the back of my mind, putting a dampener on my excitement for Saturday's date. I can't stop myself rehearsing what I'll say at the interview. I'll wear black to look serious and responsible. I'll assure them that I have no sympathies with Communism and love the American way of life. If they know about Freddie, I'll tearfully assure them that I had no idea he was a Communist and he's no longer part of my life. I don't have to say that was his choice, not mine.

On Saturday morning, I put on my favourite red and white polka dot dress with my red shell cap. As I drive into the hills above West Hollywood, I'm excited to see Rex again. His words on my birthday are a refrain running around my head. 'You're special to me, Audrey.' They've been like armour all week, shielding me from the doubts and insecurities which are usually my constant companions.

This area of Hollywood is utterly different to the corner I call home. Rex lives in the Bird Streets, renowned for luxury homes and celebrity residents. So called because all of the streets are named after different types of birds. Each house stands behind a gated entrance and I catch glimpses of turquoise pools, stunning gardens and outstanding views.

On Nightingale Drive, I pull up beside two huge wooden gates and press the bell. There's a high brick wall surrounding the house. I can see the tops of trees but there's no glimpse of the house. A moment later, the gates swing open. The drive winds through lawns watered by sprinklers while holm oaks and cedar trees stand like sentries around the boundary wall. I gasp as I catch sight of the house. It's vast. Far bigger than I'd anticipated.

Then I wince as I remember Rex coming to my flat. Pretty much all of it would fit in one of his flowerbeds. What must he have thought of my tiny space when he's used to a place like this?

I stop in the turning circle outside the front door. There's a fountain in the centre of it which creates a gentle tinkle of tumbling water. As I get out of the car, I look up. It's built of dark stone with steps up to the front door. There's a feeling of entering a castle with its curved walls and turret at one end.

The huge front door opens and Rex bounds down the stairs. He's dressed in blue trousers and a pale-yellow, short-sleeved shirt.

'You found it okay?' he asks.

'Just fine.'

He kisses my cheek. There's a sudden rush of sensation, the proximity of his body, his strong arm on my back, his lips on my skin but not the zing I felt when Jack touched my hand.

Rex ushers me up the wide steps and through the door. From my handbag, I pull a box of Hershey chocolates and hand them to him.

'Shucks, you didn't have to, Audrey, but that's real kind. You've brought my favourites too!'

I smile. That's the advantage of having read pretty much

everything that's ever been written about him. I know this kind of information without us having to talk about it.

'My pleasure.' I gesture at the huge hall with the cream marble floor. An elegant spiral staircase twirls upwards. 'Thank you for inviting me to your beautiful home.'

He shrugs. 'It needs a bit of love and care. Let me show you round.'

There's a dining room with the tallest windows I've ever seen. The curtains alone must cost a fortune! Opposite is the kitchen which is bigger than the whole of my apartment. I nod to the uniformed maid who's chopping onions at one of the counter-tops. She's a tall woman in her mid-forties with greying hair pulled into a bun and an impassive face.

'That's Trudie,' Rex says as we move on. 'She's a swell cook. She's doing fried chicken for lunch.'

Downstairs, there's a sitting room sparsely furnished in cream and black and a den with squashy sofas, a record player and wire-less. On the wall is a white and red framed American football shirt. 'Chicago Bears,' Rex says. 'My dad's a fan too. We used to go to games together as a treat.'

The first floor has six bedrooms, each with its own half-bath and a master suite which Rex tells me is so untidy, he can't let me see it. There's marble everywhere and it makes the place feel a little chilly. Every tiny sound is magnified; even in my espadrilles, my footsteps echo.

I can see why Dirk said the house needs a woman's touch. Rugs, pictures on the walls, vases of flowers, maybe a sculpture or two would all help to make it feel less cavernous.

'Have you thought of getting a decorator in?' I ask Rex as we climb the spiral stairs to the second floor.

'I thought about it but I don't want it to be someone else's taste. I want it to feel like mine but I don't know where to start.'

He opens the door at the top of the stairs. 'This is my favourite part of the house. This is why I bought it.'

I step into an enormous space and the hairs on the back of my neck lift. It's a vast, empty space with a distinctly masculine smell of beer, cigarette smoke and sweaty bodies. There's a circular stone bar with a wooden counter close to the door. The bar must be ten feet across and stools perch next to it. Beyond the bar stretches acres of wooden floor. There's a pool table, a dartboard on one wall and a chrome-plated jukebox. Slouchy brown sofas rest in the areas closest to the windows. Enamel signs for beer decorate the walls. I stare around, unable to take in what I'm seeing.

'This is where I have parties,' Rex says as if having a hundred-foot bar in your house is an everyday occurrence. Perhaps it is in the circles he mixes in.

'It's enormous,' I say because I can't think of anything else.

'Sure is!' He beams but his smile doesn't warm me as it usually does. Something inside me has frozen at the sight of this room. It feels utterly preposterous and, when many people have so little, rather obscene. But it's also that Rex thinks it's completely normal that unsettles me.

'I don't get to go out to bars any more as too many people recognise me so I wanted one at home.' Rex crosses the room and switches on the jukebox. 'Come on.' He tilts his head, beckoning me over. 'I've got all the hits.'

My footsteps echo as I cross the wooden floor. I stand beside him, twisting my watch round and round my wrist. I don't know what I expected of Rex's house but it definitely wasn't this. This is a statement of wealth that's oddly lacking in class. I wince because that makes me sound terribly British and snobby to boot, which I'm not.

'You pick,' he says. 'I've got Perry Como, Frank Sinatra, Bing Crosby, Rosemary Clooney.'

'Frank, please.' Maybe a song I know will make me feel less out of my depth.

Rex presses a button and the jukebox whirs and clicks. There's a sultry trumpet and then Frank's wonderful voice fills the space singing, 'Almost Like Being in Love'. That feels a little too apt. Did Rex choose this on purpose? Is he trying to tell me that he too feels this 'nearly but not quite' quality in our relationship? Then I peer at the labels on the jukebox and realise this is the only Sinatra he's got.

I raise a rueful eyebrow even though no one can see. I'm jumping at shadows today. This house has unsettled me, made me painfully aware of the differences between us.

'Come see the view,' he says as he reaches a floor-length window that opens onto a balcony with two wicker chairs and a table. We're higher than the treetops and the view is sensational; I can see across the whole of Los Angeles to the ocean. Rex points. 'Look, there's the sign.' He grins.

The Hollywood sign stands proudly against the hill. Each white letter in stark contrast to the ochre land around it. I wish I'd brought my camera as I dearly want to capture this moment. Rex and me on this balcony with the iconic sign behind us. If anything symbolises how far I've come from dreary old Sheffield, this is it!

'Always gives me a thrill,' I say softly.

'Me too!' Rex puts his arm around my shoulders. Could this be the moment when he kisses me? This would be as perfect as anything I've dreamed of! I stare up at his square jaw as if I can will him to pull me against his chest and kiss me. But he gives my shoulders a quick squeeze and lets me go.

'Ready for lunch?' he asks. 'Trudie makes a mean potato salad.'

* * *

We have lunch in the dining room. The fried chicken is succulent, there's an impressive choice of salads and the bread rolls are still warm from the oven. The only thing that isn't perfect is how angry he gets at Trudie for forgetting to make any coleslaw. I feel so sorry for her as she apologises profusely, her hands twisting in her apron.

After she's left the room, Rex huffs, 'I wanted everything to be perfect for you.'

'I can live without coleslaw,' I say but he doesn't smile.

There's a painful silence which I break by telling him about the letter from the INS but struggle to find the words to articulate how worried I am.

He shakes his head as he listens and then says, 'It'll be fine. Just tell them you're dating me. Then they'll have to let you stay.'

I laugh because it's expected of me but it's not the reassurance I'd hoped for. I actually feel more alone with the problem than I did before.

After lunch, he shows me the garden. I spot the spiky yellow flowers of bird of paradise and there's a profusion of pink, rose-like blooms on the camellias. The terrace opens onto a beautiful turquoise pool surrounded by eucalyptus trees and there's a tennis court which he tells me he's never used.

Next we move onto the garage. He pushes the folding door open to reveal an enormous space. There are racks of tools on the walls, a pair of white overalls hanging on a hook, a radio and a distinct smell of oil. Beside his Buick convertible are two other cars. One has an enormous bonnet, striped paintwork and is propped up on blocks; the other is perfect, a sleek burgundy vehicle that looks every inch a movie star's car.

'This where I have my fun.' Rex gestures proudly around him. 'I got the garage extended when I moved in. Got to have space to play.'

I gaze around me with wide eyes. I remember him telling me he enjoyed fixing cars but I'd not imagined he was actually good at it! It's rather appealing, thinking of him in his overalls doing something technical with a spanner.

'You fixed these yourself?' I ask.

'Sure did.' He runs a proud hand over the burgundy one. 'This is a 1938 Cadillac Sixty-Special. V-8 engine. 135 horsepower. She's a beauty to drive. I'll take you out in her one day.'

Now there's a wonderful thought! Rex and me heading down the coast in this amazing car, getting admiring glances from everyone that we pass.

Rex moves on to the one on blocks. 'I've only had this a few weeks. It's going to need a lot of work but she'll be real cool when she's finished. She's a 1934 Packard Sport Phaeton.' Rex gives the car a proprietorial pat. 'They only built 960 of them so she's a real rarity.'

The cars bring something out in him that I've not seen before: a boyish enthusiasm which is rather swoony.

'Where did you learn to fix cars?' I ask as I can't make any sensible comment about the vehicles themselves. I've no idea what a V-8 engine is or how much horsepower is worth having.

'My dad's a mechanic. He taught me a lot and you know I was an engineer during the war?' When I nod, he continues, 'It's satisfying. I like fixing them up. If I hadn't got into movies, I'd have been a mechanic like my dad.'

'You wouldn't live in a house like this if you were a mechanic.' I laugh but I've still got a point to make. Because sometimes, he does seem to have forgotten the realities of work and money that the rest of us live with.

'No, that's true.' Rex looks disconcerted that I've mentioned it. 'But it's good to have a back-up plan. Just in case my name ends up on that blacklist one day.'

I glance up at him, my eyes wide and my smile tight. 'Is there any reason why it should?'

I won't be ambushed this time. If he's got political affiliations that will cause problems then I want to know before this goes any further. Especially with my INS interview coming up.

'No.' Rex shrugs. 'I'm not much interested in politics. That doesn't mean I don't care about the state of the world. I worry about Russia and the atom bomb and Korea same as most folks. I just don't see that there's much difference whether it's Republicans or Democrats making the decisions in Washington.'

I reach out and rest a hand on his arm. 'Well, I can promise you I'm not a Communist.' There's a slight tremor in my voice on the last word. Fortunately, he doesn't spot it.

'Aww, shucks, Audrey. I never thought you were. You're far too nice a girl for that.'

Is that how he sees me? I'm oddly disappointed. I was brought up to be nice, of course, but I'd like Rex to see more than that in me.

'It's your photography exhibition next Friday,' Rex says as we walk back to the terrace where Trudie's left a jug of iced tea. He pours me a glass. 'Do you want to go out for dinner afterwards?'

I'm thrilled that he's remembered. I want him to come yet I'm worried he'll be disappointed. I've only got two photographs in the exhibition: the one of the girl on Santa Monica pier and one I took at the Santa Claus Lane Parade of a drum majorette.

That makes me think of Jack. I wish Rex took the same kind of interest in my photography that Jack does. But Rex wants to come to the exhibition. Maybe when he's seen my work, he'll understand why photography is important to me.

With that in mind, I beam up at him. 'That'd be wonderful. The opening is from seven until eight-thirty so we could go out for dinner after that.'

'Sure thing. I'll book somewhere nearby.' He chinks his glass against mine. 'And maybe I'll buy your photographs to fill my empty walls.'

'You don't have to do that.' I frown because although I know it's well-meant, it feels a little patronising. 'There are some excellent photographs in the exhibition, though. Perhaps one of those will catch your eye.'

'I know exactly what will catch my eye,' he says with a theatrical wink. I laugh and give him a playful shove. Perhaps I did need to see him on his home turf. He's a different person here. Especially in the garage. That's where he really comes alive.

I smile up at him. Rex Trent, my boyfriend. He's so damned handsome and he makes me laugh. He's kind and considerate and he wants to take me out after the exhibition. How lucky am I?

Then my jaw tightens and I glance away, staring out at the incredible view. Why can't I relax and enjoy this moment? Is it my anxiety about my visa that's tarnishing it or is there something else? Am I scared of trusting again and believing that Rex and I can have a future? Is it because of Freddie that I always hold back, waiting for the sky to fall?

I am living my childhood dreams. So why do I constantly feel it's all going to dissolve into a puff of smoke?

## 13

On Thursday evening, when I get back from work, I check my mailbox. There's a single letter with a British stamp. For a second, I'm excited. Is this the reply from Esther? Then I realise it's not her handwriting, it's Father's. Cold fingers of dread run up my spine as everything snaps into too sharp focus.

I grasp the banister and sprint up the stairs. It's got to be bad news. I've not heard from him in nearly five years. He's only going to be writing now if something terrible has happened. It's got to be Mum. Is she sick? Dying? My thoughts hit a dead end there. I will not even think the absolute worst.

I fumble with the door key, my fingers shaking too much to get it in the lock. Once it's open, I stumble inside. *Please let Mum be all right!* Whatever god is up there, don't let anything have happened to Mum. I dump my handbag on the floor and tear the envelope open.

I hastily scan the letter. There's no mention of Mum. I blink and shake my head and read again. Slowly and carefully this time.

*Audrey,*

*It pains me to have to write to you. I'd thought I'd made myself entirely clear when you left home that you are no longer my daughter. However, it appears that for as long as you bear my name, I share some responsibility for your actions.*

*Members of my congregation have brought it to my attention that you are going out with a certain Rex Trent who is, I am told, a film star. There have been stories in the newspaper about you going on dates with this man. This must stop immediately.*

*The fact that you've chosen to live in Hollywood is bad enough. You know my thoughts on that den of iniquity. I only hope God smites it as he did Sodom and Gomorrah. I have kept your whereabouts from my congregation, simply saying you were working in America. Once these shameful articles started appearing, there have been questions about your behaviour which is making my position impossible. I cannot preach about the dangers of sinfulness when my own daughter is embroiled in such shameful goings on. You are making me a laughing stock within my own congregation.*

*It is clear to me that this Trent is merely out for what he can get and once he's got what he wants, he'll move on to the next silly girl.*

*Your judgement was always weak and easily swayed. Living in Hollywood has clearly destroyed what little common sense you had. I urge you to leave that place before it corrupts you further and return to England.*

*Your dutiful*
*Father*

My knees wobble and I sit down heavily on the sofa. The

letter rustles and I smell pipe smoke. I sniff the paper. It's very faint but unmistakable.

My stomach roils and I feel sick. I dig my nails into my palms. The pain snaps me out of the past. I screw the letter up and stuff it in the waste bin. But the smell remains. I cross to the window and throw it as far open as it will go. Exhaust fumes and the aroma of fried chicken from the flat downstairs float in to me.

I take a breath and then another. It's as if Father's reached across the Atlantic and is yanking me back into his orbit. I shake my head to try to clear it. I'm not a child any more. I'm twenty-three. I live in Hollywood. I have a job. I have a boyfriend. Father can't rule me any more.

I wash my hands, scrubbing at the skin, rubbing around the cuticles. I dry my hands and sniff them. They smell strongly of carbolic. Nothing else.

I glance around my little flat. Father's letter has polluted it. This has been my haven and now it's as if he's been here with his jibes and his lies. *Weak. Easily swayed. Silly.* I can hear his voice saying them. I've run all of this way but it's not far enough. It will never be far enough to get away.

He only wants to control me and if I'm not doing exactly what he wants then I'm worthless to him. After nearly five years of silence, he's written because I'm embarrassing him! Not to find out if I'm all right or if I'm happy but because of my supposedly 'shameful' behaviour.

I stand and pace to the window. I'm too jangled and jittery to sit down or cook myself a meal. There's only one place that helps when I feel this way. I reach for my door key and head out again.

\* \* \*

Cocooned in the darkness, I watch *The African Queen.* I munch my way through a box of popcorn as Katherine Hepburn and Humphrey Bogart bicker and fall in love. The darkness of the cinema eases some of the ache around my heart.

Father can send a letter. He can bluster and storm but he can't reach me across the Atlantic to haul me back. Maybe it's a sign of how much of a success I am in Hollywood that he's felt compelled to write now. He's ignored me for nearly five years. Not a single word in all that time. Yet now I'm living the life he told me I'd never achieve, he wants to stop me.

Well, I won't let him. I'm not giving up Rex and I'm not leaving Hollywood. I'm going to keep on going out with Rex and every time my photograph is taken, I'll imagine it winging its way across the Atlantic back to Sheffield and the disgusted look on Father's face when he sees it.

That way, I win. Not him. I will never let him win again.

## 14

---

'Ready?' Rita asks as she turns from applying lipstick in the mirror. We're in the ladies' cloakroom at the Biltmore Hotel. The exhibition opening starts in ten minutes.

'As I'll ever be.' I turn to Rita and she runs her eyes over me from head to toe.

'Pretty as a picture,' Rita says as she twitches the collar of my green circle dress into alignment. 'You'll do your beefcake proud.'

I've got butterflies doing cartwheels in my stomach but there's also a thrill of pride. My work was good enough to be included amongst some of the best amateur photographers in Hollywood. For a girl from Sheffield who bought her first camera from the pawnbrokers, that's almost as big an achievement as dating a movie star! Any other day, I'd think, *If Father could see me now* but I don't want another poisonous missive through the post.

I've been churned up all day, finding it difficult to concentrate at work, feeling unusually snappy with Ginny. I wish I could talk to her about the letter from Father but with her perfect family, how can she possibly understand? When she asks why I seem a bit blue, I tell her I'm worried about my interview with the INS, which is true but not the whole truth.

If the INS send me home then Father will think I've done as he asked and that will be unbearable. Leaving Hollywood would end my relationship with Rex and again, Father would think he'd won. So much rests on convincing the INS to renew my visa. When Rex gets here this evening, I have to talk to him about the INS. This time, I'll be honest about how worried I am.

Rita's the only person I've told that Rex is coming. I didn't want the others to think I was bragging by announcing he'd be one of the guests. Since I visited his house on Saturday, that armour of confidence has felt stronger. I've spent a lot of time daydreaming about what it would be like to live with Rex in his beautiful home: to eat dinner together on the terrace, to swim in the pool. My imagination fails to find any use for his crazy bar but I decide to gloss over that. Perhaps Rex needs that space as Father needed his study and it's simply something I'll accept.

Only sometimes, it's not Rex's face that I see beside me but Jack's and that jolts me out of the fantasy and lands me back in reality with a bump. He's got no right to turn up in my daydreams. Yes, he was easy to talk to and not bad looking but I'm never going to see him again so it doesn't matter.

Rita and I leave the ladies' bathroom and cross the wide corridor to the art salon. The hotel is almost overwhelmingly plush and opulent. The walls are wood panelled like a gentleman's club, the ceiling is intricately carved and the carpet is so thick, my feet sink into it. I've never been anywhere so luxurious.

The rest of the camera club are standing in a nervous huddle by the drinks table. There's a pall of cigarette smoke above them. The space is overheated and a couple of people are fanning themselves with the exhibition programme. Instead of joining them, I stroll around the space, taking a last look before the public arrives. All of the photographs are framed in plain, black frames to give a sense of unity to the exhibition. There's a wide variety of subjects from snakes to skyscrapers and babies to buffalo. To me, Rita's four stunning landscapes are the stars of the show, capturing the sparse beauty of California.

Mitch, the chair of the group, greets me as I return. He's in his late forties with a thatch of grey hair and permanent smile lines on his face.

The clock on the wall ticks up to 7 p.m. and Mitch opens the tall, black doors. There's a small group of people waiting, including Ginny and Nate.

'Golly, you didn't tell me you were part of such a talented bunch,' Ginny says as she looks around the room. 'Show us which ones are yours.'

As I lead them to the two photographs of mine, the butterflies in my stomach get even more frisky. I care what they think. I know Ginny well enough to recognise if she's simply being nice, but her face lights up when she sees the photo of the drum majorette at the Santa Claus Lane Parade. The girl looks to be about sixteen, wearing a short, sequined dress with a ruffled underskirt. Her baton is still a foot above her head, her hand outstretched waiting for it to fall. Her face full of zest and focus.

'I was standing right beside you and I didn't see this!' Her eyes are wide as she spins to face me. She genuinely thinks it's good and that releases some of the tension I'm holding.

'Why are you typing letters for Dirk if you can take photos that are this good?' Nate asks.

I laugh, pride warming my belly. 'Because I don't get it this right very often.'

I show them the one of the girl at Santa Monica pier, bask in their compliments for a moment and then leave them to enjoy the rest of the exhibition. I chat to Rita's daughter who has come to support her but I can't stop my eyes darting to the door.

When will Rex arrive? My hand closes over the pearl bracelet he gave me for my birthday. I've imagined it so many times over the past few days. Our eyes will meet no matter how crowded the room is. As the whispers of, 'It's Rex Trent' spread and grow, he'll come up to me and kiss my cheek and my heart will almost burst with pride because I'm the one he's come to see.

The minutes tick by. Ginny and Nate are full of praise for the exhibition but then depart as they're going to catch a movie. I keep smiling and chatting but my nerves are trampling on my enjoyment of the evening. My armour of confidence is cracking. My throat feels tight. I touch my bracelet again and again as if that can magically summon him.

What if he's forgotten? He knows the exhibition is important to me. If he can't make it then what does that say about how he feels about me?

The heat is making my dress stick to my back. I get myself a paper cup of punch. It's overly sweet but it eases my throat a little. I glance over my shoulder at the door again. Still not here!

I'm sighing out a long breath when a voice says a little tentatively, 'Audrey?'

It's not the voice I'm hoping for but it's one I know. I turn to see Jack smiling at me. He's wearing a cream sweater over a pale-blue shirt which makes his eyes look bluer. Much bluer. Goodness knows why I'm noticing that.

'What are you doing here?' I ask.

'You seem to ask me that a lot!' Jack grins. 'I remembered what you said about your exhibition and thought I'd come down and have a look.'

'That's very nice of you.' I take another sip of the punch while I work out what to say next. I'm pleased to see him but Rex is due any moment and as soon as he arrives, all of my attention will be on him. 'I hope you won't be disappointed.'

Behind his glasses, his eyes shine with warmth. 'Oh, I don't think I'll be disappointed. I get to see you again, after all.'

I blink as the words sink in. So he does like me like that. For a long moment, I stare at him, trying to figure out what to say. He's interesting and easy to talk to and I can't deny the zip of attraction. But I'm with Rex. I wrap my fingers around my bracelet.

'I'm seeing someone.' I gesture awkwardly towards the door with my paper cup. 'I'm expecting him any minute,' I add because I desperately want that to be true. Yet even as I say the words, something shifts inside me. Rex hasn't come and, because of that, a crack is appearing in my beautiful dreams.

Disappointment washes over Jack's face. It's as if a light goes out and he's been cast into shadow. He looks down, staring at his shoes for a long moment. Then he glances at the door, which is still closed. 'I have a talent for bad timing,' he says. 'He's a lucky guy.'

Heat rushes my cheeks. Not just from the words but from the yearning in them. It stirs emotions I've buried deep. Ones I've not felt since Freddie broke my heart.

'I'm sorry. I shouldn't have said that,' Jack adds. 'I promise I won't keep you when he arrives but I'd like to see your photographs.'

I glance again at the door even though other people's reactions would have alerted me if Rex had arrived.

It feels as if my ribs are tightening, squeezing the breath out of my body. Rex is still not here. The opening finishes in fifteen minutes and even if he's planning to arrive at the last minute and sweep me off for dinner, he's leaving it a bit late. Am I'm about to be stood up by my movie-star boyfriend?

There's heat behind my eyes which means tears are close. I

bite down on my bottom lip. I have a strong urge to dash from the room and hide in the ladies' until everyone, including Jack, who's looking at me far too intently, has gone.

It's that intent gaze that straightens my shoulders and brings my chin up. I do not want to cry in front of Jack. Not when I've just told him my boyfriend is due any minute. Tears now would make it entirely clear he's let me down.

'They're over here.' I gesture for Jack to follow me.

Rita raises an eyebrow as I pass and I shrug because what else can I do? Thank goodness I didn't tell the rest of the group Rex was coming because then I'd be utterly mortified.

'These two are mine,' I say, stopping in front of the majorette. I look sideways at him. I care what he thinks. For reasons I don't understand, I don't want to let him down.

Jack tilts his head and stares at the photograph for a long moment. 'You've got a good eye,' he says. 'What made you take this?'

I mirror his pose, looking at the photograph instead of at him. 'She makes it look effortless and that takes real skill. I wanted to capture who she is behind the sparkle of her costume.'

'You've done that.' He gestures and we move in unison to the photograph of the girl on Santa Monica pier. Again, he tilts his head. I find myself holding my breath.

'What was it you said about there being truth in the moments we believe ourselves to be unobserved?' Jack nods at the photograph. 'You've captured that here.'

I stare at him, my eyes widening. 'You remembered!'

I can't believe he recalls exactly what I said outside the Chinese Theatre. I don't know what to do with that, because so few people have ever taken that kind of care with me. *Even Rex or he'd be here now.* I shove that thought away.

Jack must hear the surprise in my voice because he turns to

me. 'When a beautiful girl crashes into me, I tend to pay attention!' His eyes crinkle. There's a glimmer of amusement in them but as he holds my gaze, I know he's not ribbing me; he thinks me beautiful.

Those eyes! Why do they pull me in? Why do I want to stare into them and not stop? Why do they make me feel a deep yearning? To be held, to be kissed, to be loved.

I tug at my collar. It really is ridiculously hot in here. My hands land on my hips as my chin comes up. 'Why are you so nice to me?'

Jack looks stunned. 'Because I like you. I like you a lot.' He studies my face for an uncomfortably long moment. 'Why is that hard to understand?' He speaks softly as if I'm a wild animal that might startle at any moment.

I look away as heat builds again behind my eyes. I take a breath and it's ragged and uneven. The barbs in Father's letter dart into my mind. *Weak. Easily swayed. Silly.* That's how my own father sees me.

I swallow hard, shoving the tears and the emotions away. I didn't leave home, scrimp and save through the years in London and then sail away from everyone I know to find myself in tears in front of a man I barely know. I did it for the dream of a life in Hollywood. I did it to be with Rex. And I won't allow Father or the INS or Jack to take it away from me.

Suddenly, all of the anxiety, confusion and hurt fuse into anger. 'You have no right to ask me that.' My hand folds over my pearl bracelet to give me strength. 'You hardly know me.'

As I say the last words, my heart knows I lie and it hates me for it. Because I'm denying something essential and true. There's a pulse between us. It's in that jolt of attraction but also because he's interesting and makes me laugh and has eyes that I could fall into. He recognises it too. I can see it in his steady gaze. It's why he came this evening. But what he's offering is impossible.

I may be a dreamer but this is a dream I don't want. I can't want. I'm with Rex. I'm wearing the beautiful bracelet he gave me. I can't have moments of intense connection with someone else. That would make me a tart, just as Louella Parsons thinks I am. But I'm not that person. I do not betray people. Unlike Freddie, I am loyal.

Sadness, frustration and loss flicker across Jack's face so quickly that if I blinked, I'd have missed them.

'Okay, Audrey. You win.' He bows his head and the resignation in the movement makes me want to cry.

Just as he's about to turn away, Rita comes to join us. 'Where's Rex?' she asks.

Her question forces me to face the truth. He's stood me up. Disappointment kneads at my stomach. I tug again at the collar of my dress. 'I don't know.'

'I expected better of him,' Rita says, crossing her arms. 'Even movie stars should be punctual.'

Out of the corner of my eye, I see Jack's eyebrows shoot up. 'Rex is your boyfriend?' he says, taking a step closer to me. 'Rex who?'

I open my mouth but no words come out. I feel hot and nauseous and weighed down with disappointment.

'Rex Trent,' Rita answers for me. 'He's supposed to be taking her out to dinner after the opening.'

My gaze darts to Jack. He's staring at me as if he's never seen me before.

All of the colour drains from Jack's face. 'You can't be!' Shock thrums through his voice.

I tug again at my collar. The heat in this room is unbearable. I need to get out of here before I do something unforgiveable like passing out or throwing up on Rita's patent pumps.

'Excuse me,' I say. 'I need the bathroom.'

I'm at the door when Jack catches up with me. He holds it open for me and I barge through. It's marginally cooler in the corridor.

'Is it true, Audrey?' he calls after me. 'Are you really dating Rex Trent?'

I spin on my heels. Even though he's not here, I'm going to stand up for him because it's the right thing to do. 'Why is it so hard to believe?' I fling the words at him. 'Am I not good enough for Rex?'

Jack shakes his head, looking pained. 'Not at all. You're far too good for him. I can't believe—'

'He promised he'd come.' The fact Jack clearly thinks badly of Rex forces me to defend him. 'He's not usually late.'

Jack raises a single eyebrow. 'Oh, Audrey!' There's enormous sadness in his words and there's a subtext as well. I go cold all over as the doubts I've stowed carefully away suddenly become impossible to ignore. Freddie said exactly those words. But I cannot think of Freddie now.

'Why—' I grab my dress and tug it away from the burning skin of my chest. 'Why do you say that?'

He takes a long breath as if debating what to say next. Then the door flies open and Rita rushes towards me. 'Audrey, are you okay? I was coming after you but Mitch stopped me.'

I grab onto her as the most solid thing in my life. Rita will push all of the doubts away.

'I felt faint. It was too hot in there.'

Rita's arm comes round me, guiding me away from Jack and towards the door to the ladies'. I sink into the comfort of her no-

nonsense fussing. I splash cold water on my face, drink the glass of water she fetches me and try very hard not to think.

\* \* \*

Eventually, I go home because there's nowhere else to go. The silence of my flat unnerves me. I put the radio on. It's playing 'Beautiful Brown Eyes' by Rosemary Clooney which, of course, makes me think of Rex.

There are a dozen conflicting thoughts swirling through my brain. At the top of the maelstrom is the question I've pushed away for weeks and that Jack's words have made it impossible to ignore. Why was Jack shocked that I'm dating Rex? What made him say 'Oh, Audrey!' with such inexpressible sadness?

I clutch my bracelet as if that can bring my belief back. But the magic has gone. If I'm being naïve again, I have to face it. I will not be ambushed again.

A shudder shakes my entire body. I can't hold back the memory. As the smell of sour milk fills my nostrils, I'm falling back through time to that house in Camden with the Soviet Union flag on the wall.

## 15

LONDON, AUGUST 1947

Freddie stands in the doorway. I gasp, my hand automatically covering my mouth. His face is bruised, a greenish hue spreads across his cheekbone and along his jaw. Around his left eye, there's a black and purple shadow. A scabbed-over cut slashes across his forehead, a second, smaller one crosses his cheek. He's dressed in a collarless shirt. His trousers are too big for him and are held up with braces.

'What happened?' I walk towards him, holding my hands out to comfort him. He crosses his arms and doesn't meet my eyes. He detours around me to take the chair next to mine. Disappointment swims up my throat, bitter as bile. I take a step back.

'Oh, this.' His hand brushes across his face as if to dismiss his injuries. 'It's not the first time. Stuff like this happens to people like me.'

I gape at him. He's been beaten up before and not told me? Ten minutes ago, I'd have said that was unthinkable. But since I stepped through the door of this house, that certainty has vanished. I don't know what's going on. And that frightens me.

Not knowing what else to do, I sit down again. His bruises

look worse close up. The skin puffy and tight. 'Who did this to you?'

'There were two blokes. Big ones.' He gestures with his hands, sketching out the breadth of them and, for a moment, I catch a glimpse of the Freddie I know. 'I was with Michael. They didn't like seeing us together.'

My first thought is, why didn't he tell me Michael was coming to Sheffield? The second is whether these blokes know Michael and find him as blooming irritating as I do. Not that I'd stoop to beating him up. No one deserves that.

'Why?' I bite my lip. 'They got something against university students?'

Freddie looks at me flatly, his eyes narrowed. 'Are you really that clueless?'

I stare at him blankly. I've come down here to help him, to be together like we always promised we would. Why isn't he pleased to see me and why is he taking that tone?

'About what? Father wouldn't tell me what happened.'

'Of course he wouldn't.' Freddie briefly glances at me. There's a look in his eyes I've not seen before. A guardedness that makes anxiety seethe in my stomach. 'Reverend Wade got me off with a warning. Though I don't fool myself that was for me. He was trying to protect Mum and Dad and to avoid my name getting in the papers.'

'For what?' I throw up my hands. 'The only thing Father was clear about is that I'm not to see you again.'

'He said that to me too.' Freddie looks away, his jaw tense. 'Told me he wouldn't allow me to pollute his daughter any longer.'

There's a huge lump in my throat and a pulse beating in my temple that makes me feel a little sick. But whatever's happened, we'll sort it out together. Freddie and Audrey against the world as it's always been. With a huge effort, I keep my voice even as I say, 'Tell me from the beginning what happened.'

'I can't.' He stands and moves to the window, peering out through the dirty net curtain. Above his head is a flypaper encrusted with shiny, black bodies.

I daren't go to him. Not while he's like this. I have to wait and let him come to me. 'Why not? We're friends.' My voice is soft and gentle. 'We've always told each other everything.'

'No.' He shakes his head, sadly and wearily as he turns back to me. 'There are some things I didn't tell anyone until I met Michael.'

I cross my arms as my throat constricts. We're back to ruddy Michael again, are we? Why is it always about him these days? My mouth twists as I say, 'Where is Michael? Does he look as bad as you?'

'No, I got the worst of it.' Freddie scratches the scar on his cheek. 'Michael's with his family in Putney. They're not narrow-minded like mine.'

I fight back the urge to scream, *Narrow-minded about what?* He's talking in riddles, just like Father. It makes me furious that they're both keeping secrets from me, treating me like a little girl. I cross my arms and when I speak, my voice comes out louder than I intended. 'I'm not a child. Whatever it is, I don't care. I just want to know.'

He blows out a long breath as he takes a packet of Camel cigarettes from his trouser pocket. 'Fine, but once I've told you, you'll wish you didn't know.'

I give him a long sideways look. 'Let me be the judge of that.'

He takes his time to light a cigarette. I smell the sulphur as he strikes the match. 'Michael and I were in a pub on Wednesday night. We'd had a couple of drinks and that made us careless.' He blows smoke upwards. 'We went outside to the alley behind the pub. While we were together—' He coughs and blushes and it's as if a lead weight has settled on my chest because it takes a lot to make Freddie blush. I hold my breath as he continues, 'These two big blokes came out and beat us up. I told Michael to run and he did although he didn't know where he was going. He was wandering the backstreets for hours.'

There's such affection in Freddie's voice. I may have missed it before but it's unmistakable now. A shudder shakes my entire body.

'Then what?' I say through numb lips.

'The blokes that were punching me had me down on the ground. The police arrested all of us.'

I stare at him, my ears turning red, as suddenly, I know what no one will tell me directly. My body turns entirely cold as the shock sinks in. I have no idea what men do with men but I know it happens.

I desperately don't want Freddie to be *one of those* as Father euphemistically calls it. He's mine and we're going to get married. He wouldn't have said that if he didn't mean it. So he can't be, can he? But why was he arrested if not?

'For what?' I manage to croak past the cold lump in my throat. 'What did they charge you with?'

Freddie's chin comes up and he stares straight at me. What I see in his blue eyes is embarrassment but not shame. 'Gross indecency.' His hands form fists. 'The two louts who beat me up told the cops they'd seen me and Michael kissing.'

Icy cold floods through me. 'You like other men?' My voice is barely a croak.

'Yes.'

My lips pinch together so hard, my teeth grate. I shake my head. I won't believe it. I can't.

'But we were going to get married.'

'Oh, Audrey,' he says, crossing his arms as his body turns away from me. 'You didn't still believe that, did you?'

I flinch. For a long, ghastly moment, I stare at him open-mouthed. Then the pieces start to fall into place and my heart shrivels. The night I tried to kiss him and he pushed me away, his growing closeness to Michael, the men I've seen him staring at, the terrible black moods that come over him.

'Are you all right?' Freddie asks. His voice is flat, devoid of concern.

'Of course I'm not all right!' There's a pain in my chest and a throbbing in my temple. Hot tears press behind my eyes. I bite the inside of my cheek to stop myself crying.

'I'll get you a glass of water.' He leaves the room so fast, it's an insult. He can't wait to get away from me. *Oh, Freddie, why are you being like this? Where's my old friend gone?*

I curl over, holding my head in my hands. I can't believe it. I just can't. I love Freddie. I always have. All of our beautiful dreams and now none of that is going to happen because he's *one of those*. He doesn't love me like that. Right now, it feels like he doesn't even *like* me. I've given up everything for him and he doesn't care at all.

Freddie's footsteps return and I force myself upright, ignoring the dizziness. He hands me an enamel mug filled with water. 'I couldn't find a glass.'

Our fingers brush together as I take it from him and he hastily snatches his hand back as if my touch has scalded him. It's such a small gesture but it makes tears flood my eyes. Because I ached for him to touch me and now I understand he'll never want that.

I sip the tepid water. It eases my dry throat, but does nothing for the muffled throbbing that's building in my head.

'It's not wrong,' Freddie blurts out as he returns to his chair. His gaze meets mine and now there's a fierce challenge in his eyes. 'Michael helped me see it's nothing to be ashamed of. It's just the way I am. A part of me like having blue eyes and curly hair.'

That goes against everything I've been brought up to believe. To Father, it is sodomy, a dreadful sin. Freddie's parents believe that too.

My fingers twist as I say, 'It's illegal. Do you want to be in trouble with the police all your life?'

'The law's wrong. It's not fair to make only one way to love legal and outlaw everyone who doesn't fit.' Freddie's jaw juts. 'It's why I joined the Communist Party. Once the revolution comes, people like me will be free to live as we want.'

I stare at him blankly. He's a Communist too? My mind races as I think back. Have there been clues I've missed about this as well? An occasional rant about workers' rights. Freddie getting drunk when Labour won the election two years ago.

'And that's something else you didn't tell me,' I say flatly.

'You wouldn't have understood.' He folds his arms as he sinks deeper into his chair.

I fold mine against the chill of his words. 'You didn't give me a ruddy chance.'

He laughs hollowly. 'You're not exactly a deep thinker, Audrey. All you care about is photography and Hollywood.'

There's a painful heat behind my eyes. I look down at my polished brogues and try to remember how to breathe. I feel myself shrinking, curling in on myself. I really am worthless if Freddie thinks so. Everything Father has ever said must be true. I press my hand against my middle as if that will sooth the hurt.

'I thought you cared about Hollywood too.' My voice is barely a whisper. There are layers upon layers of betrayal. 'Was all of that a lie too? Did you never mean to go to with me?'

'Maybe at the beginning.' Freddie's voice drops so low, I have to lean forward to catch his words. 'I thought if I got out of Sheffield and away from my parents, I wouldn't feel so wrong. Then I met Michael. I realised it wasn't me that was wrong but the way the world sees people like me.' He sounds enormously weary as if this is a battle he's been fighting for years. He gestures hopelessly, his gaze darting past my shoulder. 'Hollywood was only ever a childish dream.'

I am so tired of being called childish! I leap to my feet. Why is it wrong to hope for a better life? To dream about living in a place that's sunny and beautiful, instead of dreary old England?

'Not to me it isn't!' I pace to the fireplace and turn and stare down at him, anger knotting my stomach, my hands like fists. 'To me, it means everything. I love you, Freddie. I always have. I thought we had a future together.'

He curls over his knees, his elbows tight against his body. Into the long silence, I hear a car pass outside, footsteps cross the floor in the room above our heads, a bluebottle buzzes at the window.

When Freddie finally raises his head, his face is stone hard. 'And you wonder why I didn't tell you?'

The pounding in my ears doesn't block out his terrible words. I move to stand behind the other chair, letting it form a barrier between us. 'You let me believe we were going to get married and have children!'

'Oh, grow up, Audrey!' The harshness in his voice is like a slap. 'If you believed that then you're more of a fool than I thought.'

Every muscle in my body suddenly goes rigid. With one part of my brain, I know that later, I'll be devasted by what he's just said. Right now, I'm simply and plainly furious. Because whatever faults I have, I've been a good, loyal friend and this is not the way you treat a friend.

'I can't believe you just said that.' My voice vibrates with anger. 'What have these Communists done to you? They've turned your head and you're not the person I thought you were.'

Colour rises in Freddie's cheeks as he says, 'I knew you'd reject me when you found out who I really am.'

He's turning everything against me. He's making it all about me when it's him that's in the wrong. He's the one who kept secrets and made promises he had no intention of keeping. All I've done is care about him and try to help and he's throwing all of that back in my face.

'You never gave me a chance.' The words tumble out of me. 'You lied to me. You let me believe you cared!' My voice hitches. 'I believed you and because of that, I've been kicked out by my parents, who never want to see me again,' the hot tingle of tears returns and I have to take a breath to steady myself, 'and I came down to London because I thought you'd want to be with me—'

'I didn't ask you to come.' He gestures at my carboard suitcase. 'What did you think was going to happen? We'd get married and run off to Hollywood together?'

There's such scorn in his words. I've been a blind fool. I put my trust in him and he's stamped on it. The shame of it is more than I can bear. No wonder Father thinks I'm a worthless hussy. I've chased a boy down to London and now he doesn't even want me.

I bite down on my bottom lip but it's too late. Hot, painful tears scorch my cheeks. 'I thought you were in trouble and needed a friend.' I grab my hat and with shaking fingers put it back on. 'Clearly, I was wrong.'

'I have friends.' He puts his hands in his pockets as his chin comes up. 'Michael and the chaps here understand me.'

I close my eyes as if that will stop the words from piercing. He doesn't say, *and you don't* but he doesn't need to. I've known him for that long, he doesn't have to speak the actual words.

I have to get out of here. I scrub tears from my cheeks with my fingers, grab my case and my handbag and head towards the door. My case bangs against the leg of the coffee table, the milk bottle wobbles and then falls.

For a second, I watch as a white pool slowly expands over the marked surface. Spilt milk. I hear Mum's voice in my head saying, 'Don't cry over spilt milk.' But I want to sob and scream and pound the floor with my fists until the hurting stops.

'Go home, Audrey,' Freddie says from behind my shoulder. His voice is inordinately weary. 'London's no place for a girl as naïve as you.'

He's doing it again. Putting me in the wrong when he's the one who's broken everything. I spin to face him. 'If I'm naïve, it's because no one tells me anything. You're just as bad as Father.'

Freddie's lips curl in a cruel smile. I've never seen him look like that before.

'You need to take your head out of the clouds, Audrey. You're eighteen. It's time you stopped dreaming about going to Hollywood and marrying a film star.'

Has everything in our friendship been a lie? All the times he told me to be strong because Father couldn't hold me back forever. Did he never mean a word of it? Well, *I did* and I am going to show him and Father and everyone who's ever doubted me.

My hands clench into fists as I spit the words at him. 'You wait, Freddie Greenwood! I *am* going to go to Hollywood and I *will* be a success and I *will* marry a film star. And you'll be stuck in boring old England. I hope Michael,' I can't hold back a sneer when I say his name, 'and your Communist pals are half as good friends as I've been to you.'

I don't wait for him to respond. I pull the door open and barge through it. Seconds later, I'm standing on the pavement, shaking from head to foot. I march around the corner and then I drop my case on the ground and bend over. My hands cradle my middle, the enormous, gaping hole where my love for Freddie used to be.

I press my hand against my temple where the throbbing is getting more intense. I feel wretched. I need to lie down before I fall. The only other place I know in this city is the YWCA that Esther made me book. I have to get there. Then I can fall apart.

* * *

The bus takes me to Great George Street. I find the YWCA, taking in nothing about it except it's blessedly cool. I manage to say the right thing to the lady at reception, who shows me to my room. It's small, sparsely furnished with a single bed, a bedside cabinet and a chest of drawers. As soon as the door shuts behind her, I fall onto the bed, my feet sticking off the end so as not to dirty the bedclothes.

My head aches as if all of the tumult of emotion is pounding on my skull. I feel hot and sick and unbelievably tired. The whirlwind that swept me up on Saturday morning has deposited me here. Spent, exhausted, heartbroken. I've lost everything.

Shame consumes me. I'm alone in a strange city and the only person I know has made it perfectly clear he's no time for me any more. *Childish, naïve, head in the clouds.* Freddie's words ring in my head. They're sharper than Father's insults; they pierce deeper. Because Freddie *really* knows me. I've told him everything, trusted him entirely and he's thrown it all back at me.

What am I going to do? Who's going to help me now? I don't know how to exist in this world without Freddie.

But all the time, Freddie was building a life without me. A life he doesn't want me to be part of. He's cast me off like a shirt he's grown out of. *Fool, naïve, head in the clouds.* How could he be so beastly? When did our friendship stop mattering to him?

A ghastly thought hits me. Was I simply useful to him back home? Was it handy to have a girl around to help keep his secret? Was he using me for all those years?

I roll onto my back and stare up at the ceiling. I press my hand against my temple as if that will ease the throbbing pain. Freddie Greenwood has played me for a fool and the terrible truth is I've let him. I built a future on daydreams and I shouldn't be surprised that they've turned out to be as insubstantial as clouds.

I sigh deeply. It would help if people talked to girls about homosexuality. How am I supposed to know about these things if everyone conspires to keep me in the dark?

I lie in the narrow bed for hours. The pain in my head is terrible but it doesn't eclipse the pain in my heart.

## 16

### HOLLYWOOD, FEBRUARY 1952

Once I take the blinkers off, it's obvious. Rex has never kissed me because Rex doesn't like me that way. Like Freddie, he's let me believe there's something between us. And like with Freddie, I've blown that up into imagining a beautiful, perfect life that's never going to happen.

In truth, I've been silly and easily swayed, just as Father said. I hate that he's right. That even across the Atlantic Ocean, he sees my faults before I do.

I drop my head into my hands and then curl up on the sofa, hugging my legs into my chest. I'm suddenly cold. I tug the blanket that covers the sofa until it's loose and then wrap it around me. I need its comfort, its warmth.

Rex will never love me. I've been waiting for something to happen that never will. I've created all of these wonderful dreams of the life we'll live together and they're gone now. Broken and shattered. He won't ask me to marry him. Because he's not the marrying kind.

I'd planned it all. I'd seen the dress I'd wear at our wedding, the meals I'd cook when he came home from the studio, the friends we'd invite round for brunch. Those dreams were as real to me as the time Rex and I spent together. I'd lived through every minute of our dates in my head many times before Rex picked me up. How we'd talk endlessly and effortlessly. How the time would fly by. How I'd feel safe and loved in his presence.

How am I going to tell people that we're not seeing each other any more? For the first time in my entire life, I'm the girl everyone envies. To give that up will hurt. Especially as I can't tell anyone the truth and because of that, they'll believe Rex got fed up with me. I'll become just another girl in the string he's dated. I can imagine Louella sharpening her pencil, ready for some spiky comment about how the English secretary was never going to hold Rex's attention for long. I'll be yesterday's news.

And Father will believe I gave Rex up because he told me to. I drop my head in my hands. I can't bear him thinking he still has sway over my life and my decisions even though I'm 5,000 miles away. Well, I'm not leaving Hollywood. Not unless the INS forces me to go.

I unclip my pearl bracelet and lay it on the arm of the sofa. It's part of the lie too.

If only Rex had told me the truth. I know it's an absolutely enormous secret that could destroy his career. But he should have trusted me. I've been lied to again and I hate it!

Why did Rex imagine I'd judge him if I knew the truth? I wasn't as understanding with Freddie as I should have been but I wouldn't have made the same mistake twice. Rex has heard me ranting about McCarthy and his bigotry. Wasn't that enough of a clue that I'd have understood if he'd told me the truth? He didn't have to keep pretending. If he needed a girl on his arm, I'd have happily gone on dates with him and posed for photographs to keep the studio and the newspapers happy. It would have been fun to know we were pulling the wool over the eyes of Louella and her ilk.

Didn't Rex give any thought to how I'd feel when he asked me out? Obviously, the answer to that is no. I've been useful to him, just as I was useful to Freddie back in Sheffield. My hands spike in frustration. When is a man going to like me for who I am? Is it too much to hope that I can be loved as Audrey?

I cross to the kitchenette, pull out the bottle of gin Ginny gave me as a flat-warming present. I don't normally drink on my own. 'The road to ruin', Father would call it. I pour a slug into a glass and add a dash of lime cordial and a spoonful of sugar to make a gimlet. I give it a quick stir and then take a great gulp.

The tartness of the lime hits the back of my throat. I want it to erase the last few hours. To take me back to the anticipation before the exhibition opening when my dreams were still keeping me aloft. Before everything crashed and my beautiful fancies were smashed into the dust.

I sit down heavily on the sofa again. My drink splatters onto my skirt. Oh, for heaven's sake! But it's too much effort to get up and clean it off. I flop against the back rest and stare up at the ceiling.

How could I be such a fool? I must have the worst instincts of anyone in the entire world.

How did I miss the signs? Not just the fact he's never kissed me. From the beginning, he was only going through the motions. And I didn't see it because I was so caught up in the fantasy I'd created of dating a movie star. I was in love with the idea of being with him and completely failed to see that the reality didn't match.

What is wrong with me? I'm not a child any more. I know men like men. And of course Rex can't be honest about that. It's ridiculous to expect it. Not when Senator McCarthy is telling everyone the worst thing you can be is a Communist or a homosexual. My fists tighten at the thought of McCarthy. He is bringing out the absolute worst in people, making them as intolerant as Father.

I blow out a long breath. It's not Rex's fault. He's forced to hide if he wants to keep his career. In the movies, he plays tough guys who love hard and that's what people want to believe he's like in real life. I wanted to believe that was the truth. I couldn't tell the difference between the man on the screen and the man in real life. And I treated my beloved film magazines as gospel when the articles about him dating various starlets were actually camouflage.

Oh, my goodness! All of the breath goes out of me in a whoosh. It was right in front of me. I saw it when Rex was with Tony Young. That ease they had together. I was jealous of it. Exactly as I was jealous of Freddie and Michael and yet again, I failed to put two and two together to make four.

I should have realised when I saw the photographs in *Eyewitness*. But I was so busy admiring Rex in his swimming trunks that I didn't see the hints and innuendos in the article. Are Rex and Tony together? Is he the one he really loves?

I squeeze my eyes tight shut. Does everyone else know? Jack does. What about the rest at Crown? Were they all laughing at the naïve little idiot that Rex was dating? And Dirk? He knows everything about Rex. Is this why he's been so interested in our dates?

Suddenly, the pieces slide into place. Dirk set the whole thing up. I think back to that first drink in the Cock'n Bull. It wasn't coincidence that Rex was there; Dirk arranged it. I remember the sense I had at the time that there was some subtext between them. It's obvious what that was now. Dirk was lining clueless Audrey up to be Rex's latest date.

Why me? Had they run out of starlets? Had the word got round at the studios that Rex wasn't interested in girls so it was a waste of time? I recall Dirk prompting me to talk about myself, telling Rex that I taught Sunday School.

I tilt my head back and stare up at the ceiling. They needed someone clean cut. Who better than the daughter of a Methodist minister? It was all to create a picture of me as pure as the driven snow.

The betrayal chokes me. I trusted Dirk. How could he use me like that?

I rest my head back against the sofa cushions and stare up at the ceiling. It's time to be honest with myself. I wanted the relationship with Rex to work so badly, I've not asked myself how I feel. When you strip away the thrill of dating a movie star, going to glitzy restaurants and having my photograph in the paper, what's left?

Am I heartbroken that this relationship will never go anywhere? Or am I actually a little bit relieved to know it's not me that's wrong? I've not failed. The passion isn't there. It could never be there between Rex and me. He doesn't like me in that way and never will. It's not that I've failed to entice him, that I've not pretty enough to make him fall at my feet.

Somewhere inside, I've known we weren't working. That's why I was so confused over the holidays, why I asked myself why there wasn't any fire between us. I enjoy spending time with Rex. He can be entertaining and funny but he doesn't make my heart beat faster.

Unlike Jack. Which is mortifying because he knew. I never want to hear him say, 'Oh, Audrey' like that again. Damn him with his grey eyes that see too much. I don't want to be seen. I want to hide away from everyone and everything because clearly I am too much of a dreamer to be safe out in the world on my own. Father was right. And Freddie. Because I have been naïve. Painfully, idiotically naïve.

I will never trust anyone ever again. Not Rex, not any man. And most definitely not Jack.

I hear Jack say, 'Why is that so difficult to understand?' and it breaks my heart because I can never tell him. Never, ever, ever. He cannot know that my parents threw me out and I ran away to London after a man who cared nothing for me. He cannot know about the terrors of my childhood and the fear of Father's rages. No one in Hollywood knows about that. No one ever will.

I can't see Rex again. I can tell people I ended it because he didn't show up for the exhibition. Only Jack, with his sad, grey eyes, will know the truth. But I never have to see Jack again. I can hide the enormity of my mistake from everyone but him.

And then there's Dirk. I am going to give him a piece of my mind on Monday morning! I'm half tempted to walk out and then he can...

Except I can't. Blast! I've got my interview with the INS coming up. I have to have a job. If I'm not working, I'm not meeting the terms of my visa and they can send me home. However much I want to throw in the towel with Dirk, I can't. Not yet.

It's a terrible, unholy mess and it's almost entirely of my making. If I hadn't been such a dreamer. If I'd listened to my instincts instead of ignoring them then I wouldn't have needed Jack to tell me.

My head sinks into my hands. Why did he have to be caught up with all of this?

I like Jack. But I can never see him again. I couldn't bear the pity in his eyes.

\* \* \*

I get up late, feeling dazed and lightheaded. The sheer weight of everything that hit me yesterday sits like a rock on my chest. I can't face anyone today. I need to be on my own until I've figured out what I'm going to do.

I open the curtains to find it's raining. Puddles dot the pavement. The leaves of the tea tree are tossed by the wind and the sky is murky grey.

Because in the overcast light of morning, doing nothing doesn't seem like an unreasonable plan. No one needs to know I've worked out Rex's secret. I could let things continue as they are for now. Obviously, Rex will grow tired of me in the end... Perhaps he already has and that's why he didn't come last night? If that's the case, then all I have to do is look heartbroken, which won't be difficult, and wait until I've seen the INS and got my visa renewed before telling Dirk I don't appreciate him keeping secrets from me and he can find another secretary to make his blasted coffee.

If the INS do renew it. I still live in fear that they'll know about Freddie and I'll be kicked out as a Communist sympathiser.

Only a few short days ago, I thought life was on the up and up. How did it all go wrong so fast?

There's only one place to go when I feel this bad. The Four Star Movie Theatre on Wilshire Boulevard is my nearest cinema. The late-morning showing is *Broadway Nights*, one of the Dinah Doyle and Aidan Neil musicals. I settle into the seat, breathe deeply of the scent of popcorn and block out the swarm of bobbysoxers chattering in the seats behind me. When the house lights go down, the darkness is like a gentle hug.

The film is a delightful concoction. Dinah Doyle tap dances so fast, you wonder why her feet aren't on fire. Aidan Neil sings with his wonderful baritone voice and together, they're a joy. Two people having the best time up on the screen for us all to enjoy.

It's exactly what I need. My troubles haven't tap danced out of the door but my head feels clearer as I step out into the grey and rainy afternoon. My stomach rumbles. I've not eaten since yesterday lunchtime and maybe food will make the world feel like a better place.

There's a diner further down the block. As I step through the door, the place smells of frying onions and vinegar. The jukebox is playing 'Come On-a My House' by Rosemary Clooney which is far too perky for my state of mind.

I take a seat in a red leather booth and order a strawberry milkshake and club sandwich. Out of my handbag, I pull this month's *Screenland*. As I wait for my order, I flip through it list-lessly, wondering which stories, if any, are true.

* * *

When I get back to my flat, there's a note pinned to the door in Dirk's handwriting. It reads:

> *Audrey,*
>     *Ring me when you get this. It's urgent.*
>     *Dirk.*

I stare at it for a long moment after I've unpinned it. What on earth could be so bad Dirk drove across town to leave me a note? I do not need this today. Not when I'm furious with him for lying to me.

But is it about Rex? Has something happened to him? My breath hitches as ghastly pictures form in my head. Did he have an accident yesterday as he drove across town to the Biltmore? Is he now in hospital? My mind supplies a picture of Rex in bandages with a broken leg in plaster.

Heart pounding, I dash downstairs to the telephone in the entrance hall. I dial Dirk's home number and get Lillian. 'He said you might call,' she tells me. 'He's at Rex's. Ring him there.'

'Is Rex all right?' I ask, my voice high-pitched with anxiety.

'Far as I know. Sorry, Audrey. Dirk didn't tell me anything else.'

The image of Rex in a hospital bed evaporates but panic is still like rocket fuel in my veins. I blow out a long breath. I'm not ready to speak to Rex. Yet I have to find out what's going on.

A female voice answers. Trudie, his maid. 'May I speak to Mr Stone?' I ask.

'Of course, ma'am.' As I hear her footsteps walk away, I picture her in the enormous hall of Rex's house. Seconds later, rapid footsteps approach.

'Audrey?' Dirk says. 'About time. We need you here.'

'What? Why?' My voice rises as dread floods through me. 'Is Rex all right?'

'Something's happened.' Dirk lowers his voice. 'Rex is fine. But I need you to get over here,' Dirk adds, his tone insistent. 'I can't talk about it on the horn.'

My hand tightens on the receiver. What on earth has happened? Is he worried the Feds are tapping Rex's line? Is that what's got him in a lather? Or has someone found out Rex's secret and that's what he can't discuss on the telephone?

Then another thought hits me and my head drops. Is it Dirk who wants me there as his secretary or has Rex requested that I come? Before I drive across town, I need to know.

'Has Rex asked for me?' If the answer to that is yes then maybe I mean something to him, even if it's only friendship.

'Yes, he needs you.' Dirk blows out a long breath. 'Look, kid, he's distraught. I'll explain it all when you get here.'

My spine straightens as Dirk says, 'needs you'. Whatever the unruly confusion of my emotions, I won't let Rex down. I've carried the regret of failing Freddie. I won't make the same mistake with Rex.

'All right,' I say. 'I'll be there as soon as I can.'

## 17

The enormous gates open and I put the car into gear and head up the drive at far greater speed than last time I visited. The tyres screech as I come to a halt. I run up the wide steps and rap on the front door.

I'm anxious about Rex but I'm still angry at him and Dirk. I smooth out my blue shirtwaister and tug my yellow cardigan into alignment. Whatever is going on, I'll face it looking my best.

'Good afternoon, miss,' Trudie says after opening the door. 'They're in the sitting room.' She crosses the hall, taps on the closed double doors and then opens them. 'Miss Wade is here. I'll bring some more refreshments.'

'Audrey.' Rex leaps up from the sofa as I enter. He looks terrible; his skin is pallid, his eyes bloodshot and there are purple shadows beneath them. 'Thank you for coming.'

'What's going on?' Seeing him, my anger fades. I move towards him, arms outstretched, wanting to comfort him. 'Dirk wouldn't tell me on the telephone.'

'Because phones have ears, kid.' Dirk doesn't look much

better. Deep lines score his forehead, his moustache droops, his chin is unshaven. Neither of them look like they've slept.

'I'm sorry about last night,' Rex says as he gestures for me to sit beside him on the cream sofa. The room smells of cigarette smoke mixed with the scent of the pink roses in a vase on a side table. In front of the sofa stands a circular coffee table and twin black upholstered armchairs, one holding Dirk. 'I know I let you down,' Rex says as I take a seat next to him. 'But I ran into some trouble and I didn't want to lead it to your door.'

My mind is racing. Now I've seen the two of them, it's clear whatever is going on is very bad indeed. Scenarios run through my head, each worse than the one before. Subpoena, blacklist, fired by Crown. Or has someone done the same as me and worked out Rex's secret?

Trudie arrives with pots of coffee and tea. 'I'll pour,' I say to her. Anything to hasten the moment when it's just the three of us and Rex can talk freely.

'I'm sorry to drag you out on a Saturday,' Dirk says. 'I wouldn't have done it if we didn't need you.'

'You still haven't told me what's happened.' My voice rises as my gaze darts between them.

'Rex's career is hanging by a thread.' Dirk leans forward, his arms resting on his knees, his hands clasped. 'But with your help, I can save him.'

I stare at my boss. My anger at Rex has dissipated but I trusted Dirk and he's let me down. Maybe it's time to make him realise I'm not a little girl who can be spun any old story. If they want my help then they've got to treat me like a grown-up.

My chin comes up as I say, 'Is this about Rex being homosexual?'

They gasp and there is a fleeting moment of satisfaction that I've shocked them.

'How did you know?' Rex asks at the time Dirk says, 'Who told you?'

'No one told me.' Although Jack as good as did, I'm not going to mention his name. 'I worked it out.' Now I've got their attention, I'm going to make them wait. With only a slight tremor in my hands, I pour them both coffee, adding cream to Rex's as he likes it and leaving Dirk's black. 'I had a friend who was like Rex back in England. Once I started looking, it was pretty obvious.'

Rex's eyes widen so far, I see the white surrounding his irises. 'Obvious?' His voice is high-pitched. 'How? I've been so careful.'

There's a flicker of remorse for scaring him. 'Only because I know you,' I say, handing his coffee cup to him. 'We've been dating for over a month and you've never once tried to kiss me. You light up when you talk about Tony.' Rex's gaze darts nervously to Dirk's face and that prompts me to ask the next question, 'He's the one you want to be with, isn't he?'

'Yes,' Rex blurts the word out. 'But I'll give him up. I'll do whatever it takes if you'll—'

'We're jumping ahead of ourselves,' Dirk interrupts. 'Out of interest, kid, how long have you known?'

'Only since last night. You two created a very convincing smokescreen with all those stories of Rex dating the latest starlets. It took me a while to work out why the reality didn't feel like I thought it would.' I fold my arms and look Rex in the eye. 'But last night, I was angry you stood me up and I had time to do a lot of thinking.'

'Well, that told you.' Dirk barks out a laugh. 'Don't stand the lady up, Rex, or she'll work out the secret you've been hiding.'

'You must hate me.' Rex drops his head in his hands. 'I'm sorry I can't be the man you deserve, Audrey. I—'

He's apologising? To me? Freddie threw blame and insults

like poisoned darts. Yet Rex, who I've only known a couple of months, cares enough to tell me he's sorry.

I swallow hard over the ache in my throat. I have to make him realise I'm only angry he didn't tell me. I failed Freddie because I didn't understand. I won't make the same mistake again.

'No.' I shuffle along the sofa until I'm sitting next to him and gently put my hand on his shoulder. 'I've read the *Kinsey Report*. I know it's not a choice.'

He looks up, his eyes wide with surprise. 'You really believe that?'

I'm surprised that he's surprised. How much prejudice must he have faced if a bit of sympathy makes him look astounded?

'I do. It's part of who you are. Like having brown eyes and being six foot four.'

I hear the echo of Freddie's words and it makes my heart ache for both of them. What a terrible thing it must be to hide your true self from the world.

'Thank you, Audrey,' he says softly. 'I never thought you'd be so understanding.'

That brings my chin up. 'You didn't give me the chance.' I spear them both with a long look. 'You should have told me. Both of you. I don't like being lied to.'

'It was too much of a risk, kid. How did we know you wouldn't sell the story to *Eyewitness*?'

'Because I've worked for you for the past nine months,' I say as indignation flares in my belly. 'You trust me with clients' secrets all the time.'

Dirk reaches in his pocket for his cigarette case. 'Not ones as big as this, kid.' Then his gaze switches to Rex. 'Why don't you tell her what happened last night?'

I pour myself a cup of tea and as I add a spoonful of sugar, I hear Mum's voice say, 'Sweet tea. Best remedy for shock.' I should have been drinking it last night, rather than that that too-sweet punch.

'I finished early at the studio last night.' Rex turns to me and then hesitates as if weighing the words that come next. 'I picked Tony up and we went down to Will Rogers Beach in Santa Monica. People like us hang out there. I planned to stay for an hour or so, drop Tony off and then come to your exhibition.'

So he did intend to come but only after seeing the man he loves. How often has that been the case? There's no wonder I've been confused about our relationship. Not only could Rex never love me as I wanted him to; he clearly cares deeply about someone else.

'When we left, we were followed. A car was on my tail and I couldn't shake him off. I didn't know if it was the cops or a journalist but I couldn't let them follow me back to Tony's or to meet you at the Biltmore. I didn't know what to do. If they followed me home, then they'd know for certain who I was. We drove around town for hours until I finally lost them. We came home and I rang Dirk.'

There are so many emotions warring inside of me that I feel a little sick. I put my teacup down and take a deep, steadying breath. What surfaces from the maelstrom is anger that he's been put in this position. I grasp that as a drowning woman would cling to a lifebelt. Anger I can deal with. All of those other emotions are too hard to feel.

'Then what happened?'

Rex stands and paces to the window. 'I was waiting for the knock on the door from the cops. It didn't come but Roy Johnson from *Eyewitness* called Dirk at nine this morning. He says they've got photos of me and Tony at the beach and they're going to print them in next week's issue.' Rex sits down heavily in one of the black chairs and drops his head into his hands. 'I'll lose everything!'

I don't doubt *Eyewitness* will publish. It's written by a group of poisonous, bitter individuals who failed to make it in the movie business and want nothing more than to bring down those who have. They've broken plenty of scandals already. Rex would be the biggest scalp they've taken.

Would Crown stand by him? I doubt it. From what I've heard, Harry King expects total loyalty *to* the studio but instantly drops stars if they're embroiled in a scandal.

What will I do if it comes out? Louella Parsons and her ilk will have a field day. I'd be painted across town as the clueless floozy who didn't know her man was a queer. No one will go out with me after that. I'll be a laughing stock.

And once the news hits the British papers, Father will believe he was right to warn me about Rex. There'll be another letter, this time asking why I'm still spending time with degenerates and why didn't I learn my lesson with Freddie.

My chin comes up. Father can eat his poisonous words. Rex needs me. I'm not going to let him down as I let Freddie down. This time, I'll be loyal, whatever it costs.

'To be honest, kid, we're in a tight spot.' Dirk stubs his cigarette out in his saucer. 'I might be able to persuade *Eyewitness* to drop the story in exchange for one that I've been keeping in my back pocket that's just as hot.'

'Only if there's no other way!' Rex says sharply. 'You promised we'd speak to Audrey first.'

My gaze darts between them. Rex bites his lip. He looks even more worried than he did when I arrived. If this scheme of Dirk's will save his career, why is Rex reluctant?

'And we will.' Dirk's tone is reassuring. 'Which brings me to the other part of the plan. We need to get it in the public's minds that Rex is straight. If we do that, even if we can't get *Eyewitness* to pull the story, the public will be convinced they're printing lies. The best way to do that is for Rex to get married.'

Now it's my turn to gasp. I press my hand against the sudden tightness in my chest. To me? Is that why they needed me here?

'I know it's a lot to ask,' Rex says quickly, taking my hand and holding it gently between his. 'You deserve far more than I can ever give you. It'd be marriage in name only but I promise I'd take care of you.' He stares at me and there's pleading in the dark depths of his eyes. 'You'll be saving me and I won't forget that.'

I blink, trying to put it all together but my head is spinning. I take a sip of tea in the hope it'll steady me. They're seriously suggesting that Rex and I get married even though he'll never love me? That we can never be as man and wife should be to each other?

It's dizzying. But Rex is in trouble and I do not want to let him down. But first, there's a question I need to ask. 'Why me?'

'Because you're already dating Rex and you've had some press. It'll look like a whirlwind romance and the public will love that. The secretary who marries a movie star. The public go crazy for that kind of thing.'

I stare at him wide-eyed as my stomach forms an uncomfortable knot. 'Just how long have you been planning this?'

Dirk shrugs. 'You know me, kid. Always one step ahead.' Then he leans towards me and a blast of peppermint hits me as he says, 'You're not thinking about what's in this for you. We can get the INS off your back. As soon as you're married, you'll get a Green Card.'

I shake my head because I can't risk trusting the swell of relief that brings with it if he's not 100 per cent sure. 'It can't be that easy.'

'We'll send Rex's lawyer with you to the meeting.' Dirk tilts his head and smiles at me. 'Think about it. They're not going to send the fiancée of one of Hollywood's hottest stars back to England. You'll be a shoo-in.'

I slump back against the sofa cushions. My visa worries would go away. The INS wouldn't ask questions about Freddie and I wouldn't be branded a subversive just for knowing him. I'd be able to stay in America forever. Father would hate that.

That makes me sit up straight again. Father told me to give up Rex. If I don't agree to the arrangement they've proposed then I'll never see Rex again. His career will be ruined and goodness knows what would happen to mine. Would Dirk keep me on? Somehow, I doubt it. I'm not useful to him any more and know too much; I'll likely be out on my ear and back to typing boring letters about insurance.

When I could be living in this house with this man. All right, it wouldn't be love but we like each other. Are friendship and respect solid enough foundation for marriage? Esther always told me that marriage wasn't like in the movies; that it's about kindness and building a life together. Could I have that with Rex?

'What you're proposing is a lavender marriage,' it's a term Ginny explained to me when I first started working for Dirk, 'which will clean up Rex's image and get me a Green Card?'

'Spot on, kid.'

But there's another factor to consider. One neither of them have mentioned.

'What about Tony?' I say, folding my arms. 'Have you talked to him about what you're planning? Because if he goes to the papers, it all goes to pot.'

Dirk's lips tighten. 'Don't worry about Tony. We'll take care of him.'

'And if you'll do it,' Rex leans forward, his hands pressed together as if he's pleading with me, 'I promise I'll give up Tony.

And there won't be anyone else. I'll be true to you. As true as I would be if this marriage was for real.'

I look away from the intensity of Rex's gaze. I hadn't really considered that but of course that's important. If we're going to maintain a façade of married life, there can't be anyone else. And that applies to me too.

Jack pops into my mind. Jack grinning at me, Jack listening intently, Jack making me laugh. Then his face as he said, 'Oh, Audrey!' last night. I stare at the rug and shake my head. There can never be anything between Jack and me now. I'm too proud to bear his pity.

Dirk and Rex are both staring at me. There's open curiosity in Dirk's eyes as if he's trying to work out why I haven't said yes yet. I rub my hands over my face and then square my shoulders.

'I need time to think about it,' I say.

'How long?' Dirk says. 'Because if I don't get back to Roy Johnson by tomorrow night, he's going to press on Monday morning.'

I glance at my watch. It's nearly half past four. 'Can you give me twenty-four hours?'

'Yes, of course.' Rex jumps in before Dirk can respond. 'And remember what I said about taking care of you. You'd never have to worry about money. You'd have the best of everything: clothes, jewellery, cosmetics. We'd eat out all the time and go to parties. I'd buy you a new car as you couldn't keep driving round in that old jalopy.'

'Hey!' I say. 'I worked hard to buy that car.'

They both laugh. Rex's is deep and rich. Would he laugh like that if we were married? Would we spend evenings together listening to the radio and laughing? Or sneaking into the cinema to watch a movie together?

I stand and Rex ushers me towards the door. 'Ring me tomorrow,' he says. 'I'm the one you'll be marrying. I should hear it first.'

I smile at that. It's the first time it's felt like something more than a business proposition. 'I will.'

'I'm sorry if all of this has been a shock for you,' Rex says softly to me as he opens the door. 'You're right; I should have told you. It was no way to treat a friend. I promise if you say yes, there'll be no more secrets.'

My heart warms as he says 'friend'. He's treating me as if he values our friendship. Not like Freddie, who didn't want me once he'd got Michael.

'Cheerio, Rex,' I say as I step out into the enormous hall.

Trudie materialises from nowhere to let me out of the front door. As I walk down the steps, I fold my arms around my middle.

I feel hollowed out by the past twenty-four hours. The dreams and fancies which have been my companions for so long have gone. I feel cold and lonely without them. But Rex is offering friendship, a home, security.

It's the life I dreamed of but with one enormous omission. He'll never love me. Can I ever accept that?

## 18

In the end, it's the promise of a Green Card that decides me. Although I won't lie, the thought of Father's reaction when he finds out I'm married to Rex is a pretty strong inducement too.

I sleep on it because I've been brought up to think all decisions look clearer in the morning and, when I feel the same after my first cup of coffee, I go downstairs to the entrance hall and call Rex's number.

'It's Audrey,' I say when he comes on the phone. 'I'll do it.'

'You will?' He sounds stunned and incredibly relieved. 'Oh, I didn't dare hope. You're the best! I cannot tell you how grateful I am.'

A warm glow forms in my stomach. I let Freddie down but I'm making it right with Rex. This time, friendship will stand true and we'll make a future together.

'Come over later on,' Rex says. 'I'll get Dirk over and we'll celebrate.'

I'm pleased and slightly relieved that he feels it's a cause for celebration. I'm well aware that the cost of saving his career is giving up Tony and that can't be easy.

\* \* \*

When I stand by Rex's door later that afternoon and look up at the house, it's hard to believe it will soon be my home. I'm a whirl of contradictory emotions: excited yet nervous at the huge change that'll soon happen in my life, anxious about playing my part convincingly and worried about what people will say when they find out I'm marrying my movie-star boyfriend. I know Ginny and Rita will be thrilled when I tell them we're engaged but I wish I could tell them it's a marriage in name only. Lying to them will be very hard indeed.

Rex opens the door himself and sweeps me up in a huge bear hug which takes my feet off the floor.

'Audrey, my saviour!' As he puts me down, he adds, 'I'm so glad you're here. Dirk wouldn't let me open the champagne until you arrived.'

Being called Rex's saviour brings back that warm glow in my stomach. This is the right thing to do. Together, we'll beat *Eyewitness* and all those other people who want to destroy him. That's got to be a good thing.

As I follow him across the hall to the sitting room, he adds, 'We'll get you a ring tomorrow morning. I'll get the jeweller to send some over to the studio for you to try on. Any idea what you want?' He glances back at me, notes my red, polka-dot dress. 'You look good in red, maybe a ruby.'

'Something elegant,' I say firmly, thinking of Elizabeth Taylor's engagement ring from Conrad Hilton, a beautiful diamond in a platinum setting. 'Classy.'

'Diamond then.' Rex grins at me. 'I knew you'd know.'

'Congratulations, kid!' As I enter the sitting room, Dirk comes over and kisses me on the cheek. 'I'll miss you. You're the best secretary I've ever had but I don't mind losing you,' he slaps Rex on the back, 'to this guy.'

I stare at him. I'll have to give up work? Dirk must see the shock on my face as he laughs. 'You didn't think you'd keep working, did you? You can't do that. People would think Rex couldn't afford to keep you.'

'Erm, of course,' I murmur. I'm getting married and with that comes a Green Card. That's the important thing. There's no point getting upset about giving up work. I'll be busy doing whatever movie stars' wives do. It'll be all right. I just need time to get used to the idea. That's all.

'I'll get the champagne!' Rex says.

After Rex leaves, Dirk takes my arm. 'Come in late tomorrow.' Dirk smooths his moustache. 'I'm letting Tony go and in case he cuts up rough, I'd rather you weren't around.'

I stare at him. He's dropping Tony? To lose Rex and his agent in one weekend. He'll be devastated!

'Do you have to?' I ask. 'The poor guy!'

'He's never going to make it. Honestly, I'm doing him a favour getting him out of the business.'

I've worked for Dirk for long enough to know the word 'honestly' invariably prefixes a lie. My eyes narrow. What is he up to?

Dirk pats my arm as if I've agreed. 'Eleven o'clock okay for you?'

'All right,' I say slowly.

'Good girl.'

Rex returns with champagne in an ice bucket and three coupe glasses. He opens the bottle with a muted pop and hands me a glass. 'To my beautiful bride,' he says, clinking his glass against mine.

'You don't have to say things like that when it's only the three of us,' I say, a little tartly.

Honestly, if he'd been this fulsome with compliments when we were dating then I might have genuinely fallen for him and now where would I be? Heartbroken and sobbing as I was after I found out about Freddie and Michael. I never want to be hurt like that again. I know where I stand with this lavender marriage and if that keeps my heart safe then I'm fine with that.

Rex looks miffed which makes me feel bad. Wishing I'd been more tactful, I give him a placating smile.

'Give him a break, kid.' Dirk nudges me. 'He's never got fake married before.'

'Nor have I.' I fold my free arm across my chest. 'I just meant save it for when we need it, all right?'

Rex nods and then raises his glass. 'To pulling the wool over the eyes of Louella, Hedda and *Eyewitness*.'

'I'll drink to that.' Dirk clinks his glass against Rex and mine. 'So when are you two going to tie the knot?'

'There's no rush, is there?' I say at the exact same moment that Rex says, 'Soon.'

We look at each other and laugh. It feels more right than any other moment in our relationship. The constraint between us has gone. We both know where we stand now and from this moment forward, we're in it together.

Dirk looks between us and says, 'How would the fourteenth suit you?'

My eyebrows shoot up. 'Of February? But that's less than two weeks!'

'The papers would love a Valentine's Day wedding.' Dirk knocks back half of his champagne. 'And really, what's the point of waiting?'

'I don't want a church wedding,' I say abruptly. I've thought about this on the drive over and there is no way I can marry Rex in church. I walked away from everything Father holds dear but I was brought up as the Minister's daughter and I can't stand in church and say words I don't believe.

'The courthouse it is then,' Dirk says. 'I'm sure we can get you in there on the fourteenth.'

I press my hand against my fluttering heart. Giving myself more time to think isn't going to help. I've committed to this path with this man. I glance at Rex and he beams at me, that thousand-watt smile that has melted a million hearts.

'All right,' I hear myself saying, 'Valentine's Day it is.'

## 19

Twelve days is a very short time to plan a wedding. My friends rally round me. I ask Rita to give me away as she's the closest thing I have to a parent and her eyes get slightly glassy as she agrees. Ginny will be my maid of honour. She becomes a whirlwind of planning efficiency. I don't think she does any actual work in the days before the wedding; she's always on the telephone to the Beverly Wilshire or the photographer or florist.

I'm barely in the office and when I am, I struggle to concentrate. There's a weight in my middle I can't shift. I tell myself it's the build-up to the wedding, that all brides feel anxious.

Dirk is surprisingly understanding about my dress fittings and meetings with the florist. I buy the latest issue of *Eyewitness* for him as I return from having the blood tests that Californian law requires before you get married. Even though Dirk's assured me nothing bad about Rex will be in there, I'll not believe it until I see it myself. The headline screams:

What Ida Young Did to Become Famous

There's a sour tang at the back of my throat as I read. Is this the story Dirk had in his back pocket? There's a photograph of Ida in a skimpy bathing suit. Inside, there's another photograph: this time, Ida's got her arms around a besuited older man whose face is turned away from the camera. The article claims Ida slept with studio bosses on her way to the top and had a long affair with a married producer at MGM who put her in every movie he made.

> 'Ida wasn't choosy,' a colleague told us. 'She bedded anyone who'd help her get ahead. Man or woman. Married or not.'

I smack the magazine closed. This can't be what Dirk was referring to. It just can't. Because this will ruin Ida's career. She'll never work in Hollywood again. I know they'd had a falling-out but I cannot believe he'd do this to her!

I want to screw up the magazine and drop it in the nearest rubbish bin where it belongs. It's nothing but cheap lies and innuendo.

Instead, I stuff it in my handbag. Dirk will want to see it. If he's offended that it's creased, he can hardly fire me.

As I start to walk back to the office, my mind recalls Dirk saying he thought he could exchange a hot story for the one about Rex and Rex's obvious reluctance. Was that because the story in question would destroy Tony's sister? Is that why Tony had to go? I shake my head. Surely even Dirk wouldn't sink *this* low. But if he didn't, why isn't the headline about Rex? Unless he's inside somewhere. I yank the magazine out again and hastily flip through the rest of it. There's not a single word about Rex.

I rub my eyes to shift the heat that's building up behind them. It's a coincidence that Ida's the lead story. It's nothing to do with Dirk. Yet he dropped Tony Young. I sent the letter terminating his contract with the agency. Was that an attempt to sever all ties between Tony and Rex or has Dirk been more Machiavellian than I suspected?

Back to the office, I go straight to the bathroom and I wash my hands as if that will remove all taint of the lies printed in *Eyewitness*. I study myself in the mirror. My eyes are huge, my face pale and drawn. I look nothing like a blushing bride is supposed to.

Am I somehow complicit in whatever Dirk's done to Ida? I shake my head. I didn't know what he was going to do. I certainly couldn't have stopped it.

Everything is moving too quickly. I feel like I've not taken a breath since Jack followed me out to the hall at the Biltmore. Each day, the painful weight in my stomach seems to grow heavier.

Once we're married, it'll settle down. I'll be a movie star's wife. I'll be living the life I dreamed of. I just need to get through the next few days.

I push open the office door and Ginny says, 'Swell, you're back. The Beverly Wilshire have sent over these place cards for the reception.' She comes towards me holding four printed cards.

I have a ridiculous urge to cry. This is what I should be thinking about. Whether the place cards look pretty and the flowers are just right. Instead, I'm wondering whether Dirk's ruined poor Ida's career and how far he'll really go to protect his best client.

'I like the pink-edged one,' Ginny adds. 'But it's up to you.'

'Pink's fine.' I sit down behind my typewriter.

'Are you all right?' Ginny frowns at me. 'You look a bit pale.'

'Pre-wedding jitters.' I force a smile. 'That's all.' But the knot in my stomach doesn't lift. It goes with me to the interview with the INS. Rex's lawyer is by my side and with his assurances and the sight of my diamond solitaire engagement ring, the grey-suited men promise my Green Card will be issued as soon as they've seen our marriage certificate.

I expect I'll feel better after the threat of being sent home is lifted but I barely have time to think at all.

On Thursday afternoon, I walk into the courthouse. I'm smiling but inside, my stomach is churning.

I stare at the dark-suited man waiting for me. For a brief second, it's not Rex's broad shoulders I see, but Freddie's much slighter ones. My steps falter. I feel Rita's gaze on my face. She squeezes my arm in silent reassurance. Then the man turns and smiles that beautiful, beaming smile. It's Rex. I'm marrying Rex.

*This is my dream*, I tell myself as I repeat my vows. *This is why you came to Hollywood*, I think as Rex slips the plain, gold band on my finger. As the judge declares us man and wife, I repeat over and over, *I'm doing the right thing* and if my smile falters a little, no one seems to notice.

## PART II

# FEBRUARY 1952–FEBRUARY 1953

INTERVIEWER: You've been criticised recently for not taking a stand against McCarthyism. What do you say to people who suggest that?

REX TRENT: You weren't there. Unless you lived through it, you have no idea how scared everyone was. I had my own reasons for keeping my head down. It wasn't only Reds that McCarthy hated. He'd got it in for gays too. I was doing my best to make sure no one knew about my sexuality.

INTERVIEWER: Which is why you married Audrey Wade?

REX TRENT: Exactly.

— INTERVIEW WITH REX TRENT –
BROADCAST ON HIS SIXTY-FIFTH BIRTHDAY, 27
FEBRUARY 1989

## 20

Tonight is the glitzy premiere of *The Three Musketeers*. Attending will be Audrey Trent making her first appearance on the red carpet since her whirlwind wedding to heart-throb, Rex Trent. How will the former secretary acquit herself amongst some of the starriest company in the land?

— *LOS ANGELES EXAMINER*, 29 MAY 1952

I was already nervous about tonight's premiere and I definitely didn't need Louella Parsons making me feel everyone will be watching to see if I put a foot wrong. I've had lessons from Crown's deportment teacher on how to walk, stand and turn on the red carpet. Apparently, I march along in far too much of a businesslike manner and have to learn to glide instead. I tried telling her that there wasn't much call for gliding back in Sheffield but she simply raised a chilly eyebrow and told me to go again.

My gown is a beautiful burgundy satin. An exclusive jeweller has lent me a diamond choker and matching earrings. My hair has been styled by the top hairdresser in Beverly Hills and my make-up done by one of the girls from Crown.

As I look in the full-length mirror in my bedroom, I barely recognise myself. In the amazing dress and fur wrap, I look like a movie star's wife. Wealthy, glamorous, assured. No one will know that inside, I'm terrified of falling over or spilling my drink or saying the wrong thing to someone important.

I turn to the pair of eyes that watch from the bed. They're not Rex's. He's in his own room, putting on his tuxedo and, if I'm not very much mistaken, having a glass or two of bourbon on the sly. It's Muffin who's looking at me with her head tilted. She's a West Highland White Terrier and was my wedding present from Rex. She's my constant companion and I adore her.

'Will I do?' I ask the little dog as I pick up my evening bag and gloves.

She whines as if she understands me and then jumps down, following me downstairs.

Rex waits in the sitting room. His black tuxedo is perfectly tailored to accentuate his height and broad shoulders but his bow tie is undone. He struggles to tie them himself. He's got a glass of bourbon in his hand and I can tell from his flushed skin that it's not his first.

The amount Rex drinks has been the biggest shock of our marriage. I'd seen him drink on our dates and, once or twice, thought he was putting it away rather quickly. That was nothing compared to the amount I've discovered he regularly drinks. Every evening, he's knocking back glass after glass of bourbon and weekends are worse. He can go through bottles at a time.

I've tried talking to him about it but all he says is, 'You don't know how hard it is for me,' which I'm sure is true. Sometimes, I can feel how much he misses Tony and the life he used to live.

'You look stunning, Audrey,' he says as I enter. 'Do a twirl!'

I've learnt Rex gets pleasure from seeing me in pretty clothes. I obligingly twirl around, using the skills the deportment teacher drummed into me.

He lifts his glass as I return to facing him. 'You'll be the prettiest girl there.'

'You look rather dapper yourself,' I tell him. 'Or you will when I've tied that bow tie.'

He perches on the edge of the chair arm and as I walk towards him to knot the tie, Muffin jumps up against his leg.

'Get off!' he yells at her. 'You'll get hairs on my trousers.'

He jerks his leg, or it is a kick? It happens so fast, I can't tell, but her small, furry body is propelled backwards. Her claws skitter for purchase on the marble floor then, with a yelp, she crashes against the coffee table.

'Oh, my goodness!' I'm instantly on hands and knees beside her. 'Are you all right?'

Obviously, Muffin doesn't answer me but she looks at me with reproachful, dark eyes as I run my hands over her back and legs. She gives herself a little shake which reassures me there's no serious harm done but that's no thanks to Rex.

I stand up, fold my arms and face him. 'What the hell do you think you are doing? You could have hurt her!'

Rex knocks his bourbon back in one swift gulp. 'You care more about that damned dog than you do about me. I wish I'd never bought her for you.'

I'm appalled he'd say that. Does he have no idea what Muffin means to me? She's the brightest thing in most of my days. Because the sad truth is I'm both bored and lonely since I married Rex. I don't seem cut out for a life of leisure. I miss working. Perhaps it wouldn't have been as hard to adjust if I had a house to run but Trudie does all of that. In truth, my only purpose seems to be to shop, go to the beauty parlour and out for lunch. I enjoyed it for the first fortnight but after three months, I'm desperate for some purpose to my days.

'I love Muffin. She keeps me company.' I cross my arms over my chest. 'Do you have any idea how lonely it is for me in this house all day on my own? I'd go crazy without her.'

'You live the life of Riley.' Rex flings out the hand holding his now empty glass. 'I'm the one slogging my guts out at the studio and then all you do when I get home is nag at me about drinking too much.'

We're back on the drinking again. Every disagreement we've had comes back to this. I take a long breath, feel my ribs press against the boning in my dress.

'Let's not do this,' I say, forcing myself to sound calmer than I feel. I glance at my tiny, gold cocktail watch which was a surprisingly generous leaving gift from Dirk. 'The car is coming for us in five minutes.'

'Fine!' Rex mutters. He sits again, petulant as a little boy. I move to him to tie his bow tie. His breath stinks of alcohol. Everyone will know he's been drinking as soon as they speak to him. My fingers are shaking as I tie the fabric. I fumble it once and Rex sighs pointedly, sending another blast of bourbon fumes into my face.

The car picks us up. We sit in painful silence. Rex pointedly picks a few dog hairs from his trousers. I smooth my evening gloves on and stare out of the opposite window. I was looking forward to this so much. I've dreamed of going to a Hollywood premiere since I was twelve years old. Now I'm finally going to one and Rex is behaving like a spoilt child. It's infuriating.

I feel like I should apologise but I'm not the one who did anything wrong. *He* should be apologising. But I've already lived with him long enough to know that won't happen.

\* \* \*

Searchlights arc across the sky as we drive down Hollywood Boulevard. I tense as cold fingers of fear walk down my spine. Lights like that were used during the war to spot German aircraft. I remember them lighting up the night sky as we dashed to the Andersen shelter before the Sheffield Blitz.

My breath catches; my chest feels too tight. I put a hand on my breastbone and take a deep, steadying breath. This is Hollywood. No bombs here.

Moments later, we're pulling up outside the cinema. The marquee has Rex's name on it. There are throngs of people waiting, shouting and screaming for the stars walking the red carpet. Closer to the cinema doors will be photographers, reporters and radio people as the whole thing is being broadcast live on KHJ.

I've been told that I have to wait for Rex to walk around the car and open the door for me. He gets out without a word. I sit there, clutching my wrap as my heart pounds in my chest. The door opens and the noise hits me in a deafening roar. Rex offers me his hand and I clasp it tightly as I get out of the car, knees together as the deportment teacher drilled into me. Suddenly, I'm standing on the red carpet and everyone is staring at me. A thousand pairs of eyes are turned my way. My stomach roils. Flash bulbs go off again and again. I blink.

Rex grips my waist. 'You have to fucking smile,' he whispers against my ear.

I paint on my brightest smile. 'Keep it up,' he murmurs as we walk towards the entrance. I'm trying to glide as I've been told to. My petticoats rustle around me.

Part of my brain is stunned that it's my feet on the red carpet, that I'm finally at a movie premiere. Another other part of me is overwhelmed by the noise, the attention, the lights.

People call Rex's name. He drops my arm and goes over to a bobbysoxer, pressed up against the railings that keep the crowds back. She looks as if she's about to faint at the sight of him. I stand, stranded for a moment, and then join him. He puts his arm out to shepherd me forward. Rex is utterly charming to everyone he speaks to. He sounds exactly like he did in all those interviews I read before we met. No one would dream he didn't say a word on the way here.

As we reach the photographers, my hands are clammy beneath my gloves. Rex poses with a casual elegance I envy. I feel stiff, trying to remember to keep my bust out and my bottom in as I've been told. Even as my photograph is taken again and again, I feel invisible. It's Audrey Trent, movie star's wife, that they're snapping. No one sees the real me who's quaking behind her lipstick smile.

'Will the newlyweds give us a kiss?' one of the photographers shouts. I stare wide-eyed at Rex. We faked a kiss for the cameras on our wedding day but that was only one photographer. It feels much more exposing with cameras surrounding us from every angle. I close my eyes and raise my face. His lips brush mine and I feel nothing except the glare of a dozen flash bulbs going off.

* * *

After that, there's a lot of waiting about as Rex is interviewed by the various journalists in attendance. My feet ache in my kitten heels as I make desultory conversation with the wives of other stars in attendance. Do they know that our marriage is fake? Is that why they seem distant with me? Or would they treat anyone like this until they've found their place in the set?

Finally, Rex returns but only to say he's going backstage and will join me on the front row after Harry King has introduced him. As I walk down the aisle of the auditorium, I can't stop myself from scanning the crowd for Jack. I want to see him and yet I don't know how I'll face him. He knows the truth about Rex and he's got to have been surprised by our marriage. But he's not there. I'm both relieved and disappointed by that.

Harry King is first on the stage to introduce the film. Each of the stars makes a brief speech. Rex talks about how much he loved being in France for filming and what a joy it is to work with such a talented crew.

When he walks down the steps from the stage and takes his seat next to me, there is a thrill of pride. I'm sitting on the front row for a movie premiere. If only Father and Freddie could see me now!

The film is magnificent. It's beautifully shot with the French landscape making a wonderful backdrop. Rex finds a vulnerability in Aramis's swagger which I'm sure will win him many more female fans. None of them will know in reality, he's thoughtless and selfish and drinks far too much.

When the house lights come up, Rex is instantly surrounded by people, all wanting to congratulate him on his performance.

Evelyn King, Harry's wife, takes my arm and says, 'Come, my dear. If I know actors, he'll be a while yet. You might as well take a few moments to freshen up.'

After I've used the ladies' room, we wait in the foyer. Jack comes down the steps from the mezzanine. He looks very debonaire in his dinner jacket with his hair slicked back. A little shiver goes through me. He's having an intense conversation with a stunning redhead in a cream sheath dress. My heart squeezes when I see him. He doesn't look round, doesn't see me. Why would he when he's talking to a girl as beautiful as that?

I have no right to be jealous. I'm married to someone else but the red-hot coals in my stomach tell a different story. I watch them leave together and I already know that whoever she is, I do not like her.

'Does everyone from the cast and crew go to the party?' I ask Evelyn.

'The invitation is open to everyone who worked on the film. The stars are always last to arrive, though. They always get a round of applause as they come in.'

Rex will absolutely love that! My husband thrives on adoration. It's as necessary to him as oxygen. Tonight is manna for him. Yet the reality of a premiere is a lot less dreamy than I thought it'd be.

\* \* \*

The Cocoanut Grove is a legendary Hollywood nightspot with Moorish arches, papier-mâché palm trees and a ceiling painted to resemble the night sky. The band is playing 'Nice Work If You Can Get It' but it's almost drowned out by the thunder of applause as Rex walks in beside me. Everyone is on their feet. He beams that thousand-watt smile. Next to him, I feel invisible. No one is here to see me.

Abruptly, it feels like being a child again. I was expected to behave impeccably as the Minister's daughter. My smile falters as I feel the pull of the past. Father glaring at me from the pulpit if I dared to yawn or fidget during his sermon. Rex doesn't notice. He's caught up in the moment. I don't begrudge him it but I'd like to sit down somewhere quiet and just have a moment to myself.

Then I feel eyes on me. I look round and find Jack. He's at a table one row back. His gaze locks with mine. He doesn't smile and neither do I but I feel the intensity of his stare all the way from the crown of my head to my toes.

\* \* \*

There's a three-course meal but I barely manage a mouthful. I'm far too wound up. I listen to Rex and laugh at his jokes. I make polite conversation with Evelyn King, who's sitting on my left, but my mind is across the other side of the club. Is Jack sitting with the stunning redhead? Are they flirting over the lemon cheesecake? I want to know and yet I'm terrified to find out if my suspicions are true. He's every right to find someone else. Yet I hate the idea of it.

I dance with Rex and on the way back to the table, he's waylaid by a colleague who slaps him on the back. Rex doesn't introduce me. I return to the table, grab my bag and head to the powder room. I feel as if I've been stared at all evening, judged and weighed to see if I make the grade as the movie star's wife. I need to a moment to catch my breath.

Of course, the powder room is full of chattering women. Repressing a sigh, I reapply my lipstick and then head back towards the party. A hand shoots out to halt me. It's Jack. I stare at him. His gaze is fixed on my feet. My heart pounds high in my chest. Can he not even bring himself to look at me?

'I guess congratulations are in order,' he says in a tight voice.

'It's not what you think,' I blurt out. 'There were reasons.'

There's a ghastly silence between us. People push past us, the band plays on but Jack and I are marooned in this smothered tension.

Then he grabs my hand and pulls me into the shadow of one of the Moorish arches. My body reacts with a zip of awareness at his touch.

'What possible reason can there be to marry a man who'll never love you?' he hisses at me.

'He was in trouble. A journalist found out his secret.' With

Jack, I don't have to lie. There's an immense relief in that. Keeping up the pretence for Ginny and Rita and in my letters to Esther is exhausting.

'Which made a hasty marriage essential.' Jack blows out a long breath and then raises his head to looks at me. The zing I feel is dampened by the distrust in his eyes. What must he think of me? 'Okay, but why'd you agree to it?'

Does he believe I'm a money-grubbing hussy who married Rex for a life of luxury? I can't bear him to think that badly of me and my words trip over themselves as I say, 'Because I had visa troubles and marrying Rex got me a Green Card.'

Deep frown lines appear between Jack's eyes. 'What kind of troubles?'

I look down, fiddle with the clasp of my evening bag. 'I had a friend, Freddie.' It feels strange saying his name in these surroundings, he would have *loved* The Cocoanut Grove. 'Back in England who was a rising star in the Communist Party. When the INS wanted to interview me before they renewed my visa, I thought they'd found out about him.'

Jack stares at me for a long moment. I hold his gaze because I have to. He must see I've nothing to hide. 'Is Rex treating you right?' he asks.

My head drops and I hesitate. I don't mean to. I'm just working out how to lie. But Jack spots it.

'If he isn't, you can leave.' He takes my hand, ducks his head to look at my face.

'It's not that bad,' I say hastily. His touch is as welcome as rain in a desert. I am starved of touch. 'It's just that he drinks.'

'We know!' Jack laughs wryly. 'Catering keep a vat of coffee on standby for Rex's hangovers.'

His frankness hits me in the gut, undoing all of my lies and pretences. Tears prickle behind my eyes. 'I can't get him to stop. I try but he just won't listen.'

'It's not your job, you hear?' Jack squeezes my hand. 'Only Rex is responsible for that.'

I blink to try to stop the tears from falling. It doesn't work. They cascade out of my eyes and down my cheeks. I fumble in my bag, looking for a handkerchief.

'Here.' Jack presses a perfectly laundered white square into my free hand. I'm dabbing at my eyes when an arch female voice says, 'So this is where you're hiding, Audrey. Rex has been looking all over for you.'

Jack drops my hand. My heart races as I step away from him. Who is this woman? What is she going to think finding me crying in a corner with a man who's not my husband?

'Mrs Seton.' Jack steps in front of me. 'The costumes in *The Three Musketeers* were incredible. You must be very proud.'

She must be the costume mistress then. I use the distraction to mop the remaining tears and stuff Jack's handkerchief in my evening bag.

Mrs Seton pats her tightly permed, grey hair. She's a matronly lady with a bust like a shelf, wearing an emerald-green cocktail dress. 'Well, thank you, Jack. That's always nice to hear.'

I lift my chin and step out from behind Jack. The longer I loiter, the more she'll think I've something to hide. Her sharp gaze switches to my face, assessing the smudges in my make-up. 'Thank you for coming to find me.' Though why I'm thanking the busybody I don't know. She's enjoying this far too much. 'Where did you say Rex was?'

'By the bar, dear. I'll take you over.'

She captures my arm and I have no choice but to walk with her. I feel as if I'm shrinking as I cross the dancefloor, becoming once again only the beautiful frock and perfectly coiffured hair.

'Jack Sorenson's a handsome lad,' Mrs Seton says. 'A girl could lose her head over those eyes of his.'

She's warning me off. How dare she? The rest of Crown know Rex's secret so she must too. I won't deny the attraction between us but Jack and I are only friends. 'A girl might,' I say firmly. 'However, I'm a married woman.'

She pats my hand. 'Very good, dear. I hope you don't mind me having a little word. I always find a stitch in time saves nine.'

Quite what that means, I don't have time to ponder. Rex sees me. His face is red, his eyes bloodshot. Mrs Seton hands me over to him as if I'm a mislaid parcel.

'Where've you been?' he slurs in my ear. 'I thought I'd lost you.'

'No.' I force a smile. 'Not lost.'

With Jack, I feel more found than I've done in years. He alone in this place sees the real me. To everyone else, I'm Mrs Rex Trent but Jack sees Audrey.

## 21

The cars arrive, windows down, music blaring from the radios. They follow the drive around to the back of the house. I've got the windows open as it's a warm July night and shouts of greeting and blasts of laughter float into me.

This is the fifth Saturday in a row that Rex has had a party in the bar on the top floor. I never see the faces of the men who come. I only hear the tramp of their footsteps up the back stairs, the muted rumble of their voices.

I'm watching *The Frank Sinatra Show* on our recently installed television set. Upstairs, the music gets going. Rex plays country music for his parties and above my head, Hank Snow is singing 'I'm Moving On'. I get up to turn the volume on the television up so I can hear Frank. Muffin jumps on the sofa and curls up next to me. Rex doesn't like her sitting on the furniture but on Saturday evenings, I forget about his rules. After all, I don't like him having thirty or forty blokes I don't know over for a party.

I watch the television until my eyes are gritty with exhaustion and finally call it a night after eleven. I know I won't sleep. I barely slept on the last four Saturday nights.

The music is louder as I climb the stairs but not loud enough to drown out the voices. Everyone sounds like they're having the most fantastic time. There's whooping and hollering as if they're all in on some tremendous joke. Reaching the landing, I smell cigarette smoke. It makes my stomach churn. Rex knows how I feel about people smoking in the house. I've begged him to stop people smoking up there but he doesn't listen.

I rush through the bathroom as 'Always Late (with Your Kisses)' booms above my head. In my bedroom, I close the windows against the din but that leaves the room hot and airless. Better that than lying awake listening to every laugh and grunt and thud.

I get into my queen-sized bed and Muffin takes up her usual spot, curled up next to my legs. The music has switched to 'The Rhumba Boogie'. The footsteps form a pattern as if there's people dancing immediately above my head.

I try not to imagine what's going on up there. The first week, when the noise levels didn't drop at midnight, I put my housecoat on and went upstairs. I intended to speak quietly to Rex and ask him to turn the music down so I could sleep. But what I saw through the window stopped me. He was dancing with a man, literally cheek to cheek, their bodies wrapped so closely together, you'd not get a reed between them. It wasn't Tony. I saw that much. And around them, others were playing pool, kissing, laughing, putting their hands in places hands do not normally go.

I was flustered and embarrassed and confused because what was going on was wholly outside anything I knew. Is this what Freddie wouldn't talk about? Are these the things men do together that he wouldn't explain?

As I tiptoed back downstairs, jealousy burned in my chest. Not because I wanted Rex to touch me like that. I accepted long ago that would never happen. But that someone touches him, dances with him, maybe even kisses him while I'm as chaste as a vestal virgin. The only living creature I touch most days is Muffin and it's not enough. I want to be held, caressed, kissed, experience *all* the things marriage is supposed to bring.

I lay in bed that night as the music thrummed above my head, feeling utterly out of my depth. Why had I not realised when he showed me the bar upstairs what went on there? Had I really thought he just had a few friends around to play pool? In truth, I had been hopelessly naïve. Just as Father and Freddie said.

I have since acquired a pair of earplugs. I put them in and the music drops to a muted hum but the beat seems to reverberate through the ceiling, down the walls and to my bed. I tell myself I'm imagining it as I turn over and put the spare pillow over my head.

Maybe I start to drift off but then I smell cigarette smoke and am instantly awake. I leap out of bed. My heart is pounding as if Father will walk through the door at any minute. The smoke from his pipe was the early warning that he was approaching. Everything inside of me would tense, wondering what mood he was in, whether he would yell and rage and hit.

I throw open the window to clear the air but that just makes the music louder. I have to stop the smoke getting in. My bedroom is my haven. I can't have it polluted. I open the cupboard, yank out a clean sheet and roll it up. I jam it into the space at the bottom of the door.

I cross to the window to close it. The party is spilling out onto the lawn. There's two men clutching each other, staggering drunkenly towards the fountain. I let the curtain fall. I do not need to see what happens next.

I curl up in my chair and rest my cheek against my bare knees. It's past midnight now but the party might go on for another couple of hours, maybe even three. I am unimportant in what should be my home and that makes me feel as worthless as Father always said I was.

I close my eyes and Jack's face appears. I hold the memories tight. His hand on mine. How he squeezed my fingers when I was upset. The sympathy in his grey eyes. His concern for me.

Then the woman I saw him with at the premiere pops into my mind. The gorgeous redhead in the cream sheath dress. For all I know, he's escorting her home after a night out. Yet I want to believe he's thinking of me as I'm thinking of him.

As I return to bed, I take his handkerchief from my bedside cabinet. I run my finger over his initials embroidered on it in blue and then press it against my cheek. If only it could summon him to me like in a fairytale. He'd ride up on his snow-white charger and rescue me from Rex's drunken clutches.

I sigh out a long breath which makes Muffin lift her head. 'Yes, I know I'm being ridiculous,' I tell her. I get back into bed, unfold Jack's handkerchief and lay it across my pillow. One day, I'll see him to give it back but until then, I cherish it.

* * *

In the cool light of morning, I'm ashamed of myself. I'm a grown woman. I do not need rescuing. Nor should I be weeping over a handkerchief like a Medieval maiden.

I made my bed by marrying Rex and if it's sometimes uncomfortable then I have to remember that the alternative was everyone finding out Rex was homosexual and me definitely being a laughing stock and, potentially, being deported. I try to imagine Father and Freddie's reactions to that. How I should have listened to their warnings that I was too flighty and silly to ever build a life for myself in America.

Yet somehow that thought doesn't have quite the same weight

as it used to. What's the point of proving people wrong if it leaves you miserable?

As Rex will not emerge from his bedroom for hours yet, I set about entertaining myself. I walk Muffin in Runyon Canyon, returning home as the heat starts to build. Then I head into Hollywood. I have lunch in my favourite diner and then head to the cinema.

Pride keeps me solitary on these Sundays. I could telephone Rita or Ginny but I cannot bear to admit Rex is still in bed after partying the night away with his friends. Explaining all of that would lead to too many questions.

The person I really want to talk to is Mum. She'd understand how hard it is. She'd also tell me appearances have to be maintained in the same way as, back home, the doorstep had to be clean and the lace curtains pristine.

I know that's what I'm doing. Just like Mum used to. I thought marrying Rex would make me feel confident, help me believe in myself but I feel even smaller than I did before. My own husband doesn't treat me well. What does that say about me?

My anger with Mum has evaporated. I now understand that loyalty to your husband comes before anything else. I wanted her to choose me over Father but she was bound by the invisible chains that tie wife to husband. She did her best even though I didn't realise at the time. She showed her love for Esther and me in the little ways, like making us clothes and saving her cheese ration. I wish I'd known those simple things carried so much love. I'd give a lot to have those sorts of kindnesses in my life now.

\* \* \*

When I get home, Rex is sitting on the terrace. He's in the shade but he's got his sunglasses on. His skin is pale, there's a sheen of sweat on his skin and he's unshaven.

'Where have you been?' he asks as I step out onto the terrace.

'To the movies.' I keep my voice as calm as possible. I know from bitter experience that he's on a very short fuse when he's hungover. 'But I'm back now. Can I get you anything?'

Sunday is Trudie's day off and Rex expects me to step into her shoes.

'You should be here when I wake up. I walked all the way round the house looking for you. I even went up to the darkroom.'

The darkroom was converted from an unused storeroom above the garage. I was excited about having a darkroom of my own but over the past couple of months, my passion for photography has somewhat waned. There just doesn't seem to be anything that inspires me any more.

'I'm sorry.' I apologise by default. Just as I used to much of the time with Father. 'I didn't know how long you'd sleep for.'

He harrumphs at that. 'Now you're *finally* back, you can make me bacon and eggs.'

I nod tightly. I hate it when he treats me like I'm staff.

In the kitchen, I tie on an apron and set to work. Rex likes his eggs sunny side up and I'm careful not to overcook them. When it's ready, I give him a call and get him a glass of water with ice to go with it. He's not asked for that but everyone knows you need to drink water when you've got a hangover.

He shambles through to the kitchen and sits down at the table. I busy myself washing up the frying pan. I'm drying it when he claps his hand over his mouth and dashes out of the room. The cloakroom door bangs shut after him. I hear retching and the toilet flushes.

My stomach roils. This will be my fault.

I hover uncertainly by the kitchen door. Should I go to him? Would that help or would it just make things worse?

Long moments later, he emerges. He looks even worse than he did before. His skin is pallid, his eyes bloodshot, his nose running.

He's tearing himself apart. I know he loves being a movie star but is it really worth destroying himself by living this half-life that makes him miserable?

He doesn't look at me as he walks past me. He's a big man; he towers over me. I shrink backwards, my back pressing against the worksurface as my shoulders hunch.

'Rex, I'm sorry—'

He grabs the plate and hurls it against the wall above my head. I shriek, covering my head with my hands as shards of pottery rain down. A rasher of bacon splats on the floor by my foot.

'Are you trying to poison me?' Rex stomps past me. 'What kind of wife are you?'

I start to shake. As if from far away, I hear Rex slam the kitchen door behind him. Seconds later, the front door bangs too. I sink down the kitchen cupboards until I'm curled in a ball on the floor. Something is damp and sticky under my bottom. Blood drips from a cut on the back of my hand. I press my other hand over it. It'll hurt like hell when the shock wears off but right now, I'm too stunned to feel it.

Muffin pads softly over and nudges me with her nose. I wrap my arms around her and the tears fall. How did I get it all so wrong? I've swapped living with one man who frightened me for another. How did I not see this side of Rex until it was too late?

## 22

On the first Saturday in September, I wake up in the very comfortable guest room at Ginny's parents'. For a second, I'm disoriented and then I remember. Ginny and Nate are getting married today and I'm her matron of honour.

Rex didn't come to the rehearsal dinner last night. He claimed he was too tired to drive to Pasadena after he finished at the studio. I doubt that but have learned to choose my battles.

There was an apology accompanied by a dozen pink roses after the plate-throwing incident. I accepted both even though resentment had seethed in my stomach. I briefly considered leaving but doing that after only five months would be an admission marrying Rex was a colossal mistake. I'm too proud for that.

The parties continue but the music has not been as loud since I checked into the Beverly Wilshire one Saturday night and charged it to Rex's account. There was an almighty row after that but I held my ground and told him I'd spend every Saturday at the hotel unless he toned down his parties.

We've established a fragile kind of truce since then. We live almost entirely separate lives apart from the occasions like this one when, for appearances' sake, we have to be together.

I go down to breakfast in my housecoat. Ginny is already there, fresh faced and beaming. She's excited to be embarking on the glorious adventure of marriage with Nate. They've bought a gorgeous little house in Glendale. It's white painted with a veranda and a neat little garden. When she showed me the three bedrooms, she said, 'We're planning on having two children and I'm hoping for a girl and a boy.' It felt like a knife in my gut. She's so lucky to have a future she can map out like that.

After breakfast, our hair is coiffured, our headdresses added and our faces made up. Ginny's nieces, who are eight and six, are flower girls and look absolutely adorable in their dresses which are cream with a lilac bow.

I dash back to my room to carefully put on my dress, which is floor-length, lilac silk with a sweetheart neckline and cap sleeves. When I return, Ginny scans me up and down and says, 'I half expected it not to fit as I thought you'd be pregnant by now.'

My face flushes as red as if I'd been scalded. 'We're trying,' I mumble as I take her gown from the hanger. I hate lying to her. My fingers are clumsy as I fasten the row of tiny, fabric-covered buttons but at least it gives me time for my face to return to its usual colour.

The ceremony is at noon and Rex has solemnly promised he'll be at the church by quarter to at the latest. He knows how important this is to me. I rarely ask him for anything but today, I need him to turn up and play the part of the doting husband.

All Saints Church in Pasadena looks like it's been transported from the Cotswolds, although the palm trees surrounding it definitely don't belong in rural England.

A wedding car drops me, the flower girls and Ginny's mum. I play pat-a-cake with the girls while we wait and adjust their circlets of flowers when they go askew. Ginny and her dad arrive as the bells in the tower begin to strike for the hour.

'Don't rush,' she says as I straighten her train. 'It's the bride's prerogative to be late.'

I twitch her veil into place and then give her a very careful hug. 'You look beautiful.' My throat clogs as I add, 'Nate's a very lucky man.'

They both are. They're in love and they're getting married and although I'm proud and delighted to stand by her side, it brings back all of the things I have given up by marrying Rex.

The opening chords of Mendelssohn's bridal march surge out of the church door. This is my cue. I pull my shoulders back, fold my hands around my bouquet and remember to glide. The congregation stands. I scan the heads for Rex, who is always easy to spot because he's so tall, but I don't see him. I keep my smile pinned in place as tension locks my jaw. I rang him this morning to remind him. So where is he?

Then my gaze snags on a pair of shoulders I do know. Jack turns his head as I reach him. I see the shock written there. I have to hope my face doesn't look the same because pretty much the entire church is watching me.

My ears feel like they're burning as I reach the front and take my place before the wide steps. Nate gives me a hasty thumbs up and I shoot a quick grin back at him. Does he know Jack? I'm sure Ginny doesn't, so what's the connection? And where is my errant husband?

There's a collective 'ahh' from the congregation as the flower girls scatter rose petals along the aisle. Everyone cranes their head to get the first look at Ginny but she's instructed me to keep my eyes on Nate. She wants me to report how he reacts.

He looks dazed and then a proud grin spreads across his face. It's adorable to see. Will anyone ever look at me with that amount of love? The thought makes my eyes turn to Jack, who's looking at me, not Ginny. He smiles and flutters go off in my belly.

At that exact moment, the church door is thrown open and Rex stands there. *Oh, no!* My throat closes with anger and frustration. Is he really going to ruin Ginny's entrance? Is this going to be another occasion when he makes everything all about him?

Heads turn and a whisper starts at the rear of the church and moves forward, as neighbour nudges neighbour and says, 'Oh my, is that Rex Trent?' until every head is staring in Rex's direction and not looking at Ginny at all. My face is bright red with embarrassment. What must people think?

An usher directs Rex to a pew at the back. Rex gestures along the aisle as if to say, *I want to be up there* but the usher stands firm. Grudgingly, Rex takes a seat on the back row just as Ginny reaches the steps.

I bow my head as the vicar starts the address. I look meek and devout as you'd expect of a minister's daughter but inside, I'm plotting what I'm going to say to my husband when the ceremony's finished.

* * *

As Rex emerges from the church, I grab him by the elbow and tow him around the side of the building.

'You were late,' I hiss. 'This is the only thing I've asked you to do in months and you couldn't even turn up on time.'

'Five minutes.' He shrugs. 'So what?'

His nonchalance does nothing for my temper. 'You arrived after Ginny.' I shake my bouquet of lilac and white roses at him. 'It's her moment and you spoiled it.'

'For two seconds.' He brushes his hair back with his hand as if he hasn't a care in the world. 'That uppity usher wouldn't even let me down the aisle.'

'He was doing his job,' I say in exasperation. Then anger makes me bold and I take a step closer to him and sniff his breath. There's already the sour smell of alcohol. 'Have you been drinking already? For heaven's sake, is it too much to hope you'll be sober until the reception starts?'

Rex's eyes narrow as the muscles in his neck tense. His head juts as he looks down on me. This is the moment when I normally apologise but I'm too incensed today. He's not going to intimidate me. 'Stop nagging. It's supposed to be a celebration.'

'Of Ginny and Nate's love,' I snap, before turning on my heel with a swish of my long skirt. 'So try not to end up so sauced, you can't stand up.'

The reception is at The Athenaeum on the California Institute of Technology campus. It's a beautiful cream building in the Spanish style. Ginny's father is one of the trustees and the staff at The Athenaeum have done everything possible to make her day perfect.

After more photographs on the lawns and beneath the beautiful arched colonnade, there's a short break before the wedding breakfast. I take a glass of champagne from one of the waiters and head towards a large tree. It's hot in the sun and encased in yards of silk and tulle, I'm a little overheated. I lost track of Rex some time ago. I suspect he's found the bar and is not moving.

I lean against the trunk and blow out a breath. From behind my shoulder, Jack says, 'Can anyone hide here or is it just for the matron of honour?'

I turn and smile at him. His hair is slicked back and he looks very dapper indeed in a grey, pinstripe suit with a navy tie. There's a single white rose in his buttonhole. 'What are you doing here?' I ask.

'You ask me that a lot.' He grins. 'Anyone would think you weren't pleased to see me.'

'Oh, I'm pleased.' My goodness, I'd forgotten how easy it is to talk to him and how light it makes me feel. 'But surprised. How do you know Nate?'

'I play pick-up basketball with him on a Monday night in Glendale.' He mimes dribbling the ball. 'He's the best player we've got.'

I remember Ginny mentioning Nate's basketball games and that he wouldn't miss them even for her.

'Small world,' I murmur. 'Ginny's my best friend. We used to work together.'

'You look beautiful, by the way,' Jack says with a gentle smile. 'In case no one has told you that.'

Heat rushes up my cheeks because his words say so much about my marriage. The days of Rex taking an interest in my clothes are long gone.

'Thank you.' I touch the white and lilac roses in my hair. 'Though personally, I think the headdress is perhaps a bit much!'

He grins. 'Maybe for a weekday.'

I meet his gaze and those grey eyes draw me inexorably in. The moment holds as everything else fades away. There's only Jack and me looking at each other. His eyes darken and I feel the pull deep in my belly.

I blink and look away. I can't do this. Not until I know if the redhaired woman (or any other woman for that matter) is part of his life.

'Are you here on your own?' I try to make the words sound

casual but it's obvious from the wry twist of his mouth that I've not fooled him.

'I came with the guys from basketball but, if you mean did I bring a date, then no.' He rests his hand on the trunk and then slides a glance sideways. 'I've still got a crush on a girl I bumped into outside the Chinese Theatre.'

'Oh!' My hand flies to my mouth. He feels it too! I'm not imagining this bond between us that only seems to strengthen each time we meet. But what can I say? I'm married. I should tell Jack to forget me but thinking of him is what gets me through the bad days with Rex. Some days, I still sleep with his handkerchief on my pillow.

'I think if you asked her,' I say slowly, 'she'd say she likes you too.'

Jack's face lights up. He takes my hand and my mouth goes dry as that zing runs up my arm and straight to my heart.

Then a gong sounds and a voice shouts, 'Ladies and gentlemen, please take your places for the wedding breakfast.'

Jack leans in and whispers, 'Will you dance with me later?'

I can't think of anything better! To be held in his arms, even if it's only for a single dance.

'Yes.'

* * *

After the speeches have been made and the cake cut, I go upstairs with Ginny to help her change into her going-away outfit. As soon as the door is shut behind us, Ginny turns to me and says, 'What's going on with Rex? He barely spoke to you during the meal and he's sure been knocking back the liquor.'

'I'm so sorry.' I'm mortified that on her wedding day, she's worrying about my husband. I bite my lip and then decide partial honesty is the only option. 'Rex drinks too much. I didn't know until after we were married. He gets sauced every weekend but he knocks it back on weekdays too.'

Ginny grips my arm. 'Why didn't you tell me?'

I shrug a little helplessly. 'Because it's the wife's job to smooth it all over and carry on.'

I didn't know when the wedding ring was slipped onto my finger that it bound me to silence about all of my husband's flaws. As husband and wife, there's a dividing line between you and the rest of the world. On the outside of that dividing line, I pretend everything between us is perfect. That's what's expected of me. In a good, solid marriage, I imagine there's space inside that line to discuss problems and work them out. Rex and I don't have that. We're two separate people locked together in lonely matrimony.

She must hear the catch in my voice as she dips her head to look at my face. 'Is he a mean drunk? Because if he is then, honey, you don't have to stay with him.'

I look at the ceiling as tears threaten. 'Only once,' I say, my hand covering the scar on the back of my hand. 'But he apologised and it's not happened since.'

'And I thought you had the perfect life,' Ginny says ruefully and then shakes her head. 'I feel bad about all the times I was jealous of you living in your beautiful house with your movie-star husband.'

I have a ridiculous urge to laugh that anyone, especially Ginny, would be jealous of me. I want to tell her I'm jealous of her adoring husband and her pretty house. I don't though because that would lead to questions I can't answer without betraying the enormous lie at the centre of my marriage.

I've just finished unbuttoning Ginny's dress when there's a knock on the door. Nate's voice says, 'Audrey, can you come down? There's a situation at the bar. We need you to talk to Rex.'

I blow out a long breath. *Now what?* 'I'm so sorry,' I tell Ginny.

'Go,' she says as she steps out of her wedding dress. 'I can manage.'

I run downstairs with Nate beside me. 'The bartender refused to serve Rex. Told him he'd had enough. Rex got antsy with him.'

'All right,' I say at the bottom of the stairs. 'Go back to your guests, I'll handle this.'

'On your own?' Nate looks appalled. 'I don't think—'

I don't want Nate's memories of this day to be hauling my drunken husband out of the bar. He's a good man. He deserves better than that.

'It'll be fine,' I say reassuringly. 'I know what to do.'

I hold my dress up and run down the stairs before he's got chance to argue. The room is decorated in the art deco style with elegant square lights and lots of mirrors. My husband is leaning heavily on the bar's marble top. There are half a dozen other men in there, all in shirtsleeves now. One of them is Jack.

My heart sinks. I can handle Rex's selfishness and unkindness when it happens behind closed doors but I don't want other people to witness it. Especially not Jack.

Rex is slumped forwards and hasn't noticed me yet. I take a deep breath and head over to Jack.

'Can you get everyone out of here?' I fumble for a reason that's more persuasive than me being horribly embarrassed. 'I... I have to make sure it doesn't end up in tomorrow's newspaper.'

'I know these guys. They wouldn't do that.' But Jack turns to them and says, 'Let's give the lady some space.'

I square my shoulders as I approach Rex. His face is pallid and sweaty, his eyes bloodshot. 'I think it's time you went home,' I say to him.

He pushes himself upright and points unsteadily at the barman. 'This guy won't serve me.'

'Because you've had enough, Rex.' I put my hand on his arm but he shakes me off. 'You need to go home.'

Rex wobbles as he turns to me. 'You're my wife. You're supposed to be on my side.'

'Don't take it out on Audrey,' Jack says. 'She's only telling you what's obvious to everyone.'

I glance at Jack. His arms are crossed, his gaze is intent on Rex's face. I didn't want him to witness this but I can't deny the reassurance of him standing beside me.

'Butt out, Sorenson!' Rex juts his head forward. 'This is nothing to do with you.'

'It is when you're disrespecting Audrey.' Jack takes a step towards Rex. 'It's time you went home to sober up.'

'You can't tell me what to do,' Rex yells in Jack's face. 'You're a nobody and I'm a fucking movie star.'

I want to drop through the floor. How dare he speak to Jack like that?

'Please—' I say, putting my hand on Rex's arm. He shakes me off and as I stagger backwards, I catch my heel in the hem of my long skirt. I'm falling when strong hands catch me.

As he pulls me upright, my body presses against Jack's. Every nerve ending is suddenly on fire. *Oh, my!*

'Steady,' Jack whispers in my ear. His breath against my skin makes my stomach flutter.

'Get your hands off her!' Rex grabs my arm and yanks me away. 'People might see!'

He lets go before I've got my balance and I totter until my back smashes into the marble counter of the bar. I gasp. Pain flowers, running out from the place of impact. My headdress tumbles to the floor.

'How dare you treat her like that?' Jack steps up to Rex. 'You clumsy oaf. Can't you see you've hurt her?'

Panic floods through me. This is heading in only one direction. I've got to stop it. I straighten but stop, wincing at the pain in my back.

Suddenly, it's too late to intervene. I watch in horror as Rex swings for Jack's head but Jack steps nimbly out of the way. Rex comes at him again, trampling on my headdress and landing a punch on Jack's shoulder. Jack socks him in the stomach and Rex lurches backwards. The contact seems to only enrage him further.

'You fucking bozo. I'll have you fired for this,' Rex yells as he staggers towards Jack, fists flailing. Jack lands an uppercut on Rex's jaw. Rex looks inordinately surprised as his head jerks backwards. Then he slowly slides down the bar until he's slumped on the floor, one foot resting on my broken headdress.

Rex points a shaking finger at Jack. 'Fired.' As his hand drops, his eyes flicker shut.

'I'm sorry, Audrey.' Jack flexes his hand as he turns to me. 'You should never have had to witness that.'

'No, I'm the one who should apologise,' I say. 'You shouldn't have been dragged into this.'

The barman startles me by saying, 'I'll call a taxi.'

As he leaves, Rex starts gently snoring. I bite back the urge to laugh. 'No permanent damage done then.'

Jack's staring at me with an intensity that worries me. 'Is he like this at home?'

I shake my head as my hand once again covers the scar on the back of my hand. Jack spots the movement. He gently removes my hand and looks at the scar. 'He did this to you?'

I run my hand over my face. 'He didn't mean to. He threw a plate at the wall. It shattered and this hit me.'

'That asshole!' Jack turns away from me, rubbing his hand over the back of his neck. 'I wish I'd hit him harder now.'

* * *

With the help of the barman, we get Rex to where the cab waits. Once he's in it, Jack catches my arm. 'Why do you stay with him?'

'Because I made my bed, I suppose.' I gesture hopelessly. 'And I worry what will happen to my Green Card if I leave.'

'There's got to be another way,' Jack says urgently. 'Even the INS wouldn't expect you to stay with him.'

I'm too wrung out to have this argument now. The ache in my back is making me feel a little dizzy. I'm exhausted. Today has shown me exactly how little Rex cares about me but I need time to work out what that means.

I kiss Jack gently on the cheek. 'Goodnight.' Then I climb into the backseat of the taxi. As it pulls away, I turn to look back. Jack stands, his white shirt bright in the floodlights, with his hand raised in farewell. He stood up for me today. No one has *ever* done that.

I wave until the taxi takes a bend and Jack is lost from sight.

## PART III

———

# MARCH 1953

INTERVIEWER: You had a well-publicised drink problem in the fifties and early sixties. What contributed to that?

REX TRENT: I drank because I couldn't be open about who I really am. These days, you'd say I was in the closet and, let me tell you, that is a real dark and lonely place. I drank to take away the shame of living a lie.

— INTERVIEW WITH REX TRENT –
BROADCAST ON HIS SIXTY-FIFTH BIRTHDAY, 27
FEBRUARY 1989

## 23

Rex Trent is in the Canadian Rockies to film RAIL CAR THREE. With his old playmate Tony Young part of the cast, the two have been frolicking in the snow together. Staff at the plush hotel the cast and crew are staying in say Trent is rarely seen without Young at his side. 'Tony has been staying in Rex's suite,' a source told us. We don't know what's going on after lights out but we're pretty darned sure they're not playing checkers.

— *EYEWITNESS*, MARCH 1953

'If it's a girl, we're thinking of Elizabeth.' Ginny runs her hand over her bump. She's five months gone and has never looked prettier. 'After your queen.'

We're sitting on the terrace. It's late morning, the sun warms my skin but there's a cool breeze off the hills. Muffin is asleep in the shade of the table. I sip my coffee, hoping my sunglasses hide my reaction as I blink back tears. I am wrung out with longing for a baby. I'm horribly and painfully jealous every time I see Ginny, which makes me feel like a terrible friend. I want her to be happy, of course, I do but I yearn for a life like hers, with a husband who adores me and babies to cuddle.

The telephone rings inside the house. Muffin lifts her head. I don't move. Trudie will be offended if I answer it.

'Did you decide on lemon yellow for the nursery?' I'm already planning her baby shower and want to make sure the colour scheme is spot on.

'Yes, it looks real pretty on the walls and—' Ginny breaks off as Trudie crosses the terrace towards us.

'Mrs Trent,' she says. 'Mr Stone's on the telephone for you.'

'Bother!' I say as I stand up. As Rex is away, a telephone call from Dirk will be a request for an interview or to attend some gala or other. In my husband's absence, I'm expected to remain in the public eye as if to remind everyone he does indeed have a wife at home.

I leave my sunglasses on the table and walk inside. Muffin follows at my heels. My footsteps echo as I cross the marble floor, punctuated by the rapid tap of Muffin's feet.

I pick the telephone up. 'Audrey Trent speaking.'

'I'll just put you through.' The voice at the other end is Jean, who replaced me at the agency.

There's a click and then Dirk says, 'Audrey, the studio need you to go to Canada.'

'Why on earth—?' I start to say but Dirk cuts me off.

'They need you to get Rex to see sense. Tony Young's up there with him.'

His words are like a punch in the stomach. Tony's in Canada? No wonder Rex left with a smile on his face! That lousy, lying snake. How dare he? He promised me he'd give Tony up, that he'd be as faithful as if our marriage was a real one. Was that all just guff to get me to agree to marry him? Because as it's barely a month since our first anniversary, it's starting to feel that way.

There's a rustle of paper and then Dirk adds, '*Eyewitness* have got photos. Damning ones.'

My stomach swoops because we're back where we were a year ago, only this time with photographs. My grip tightens on the receiver. I just know this is going to get worse. Muffin looks up at me with her deep, brown eyes as if she senses something is wrong.

'You still there, kid?' Dirk asks.

'Yes.' A pulse is throbbing in my temple. I press my fingers against it. 'There's more, isn't there?'

'*Eyewitness* has got someone at the hotel feeding them information. They know Tony's been staying in Rex's suite.'

'What?' There's a sudden tightening in my chest. 'How could he be so stupid?'

Anger screeches up my spine. I've been loyal; despite Rex's selfishness and the drinking and loneliness that has eaten away at my soul, I've done everything that's been asked of me. What was the point of all this if Rex was going to parade his feelings for Tony in front of the world only a few months later?

'That's what I need you to find out,' Dirk says. 'And you can tell him from me that if he keeps this up, he's going to have to find a new agent.'

'You don't mean that.' I know Dirk. His bark is worse than his bite.

Dirk laughs a little ruefully. 'Probably not. But that's our little secret, okay, kid?'

'Fine.' I fold my free arm across my chest. 'What do I need to do?'

'We've booked you on a PanAm flight to Calgary at eight thirty tomorrow morning.'

Automatically, I write down the details.

'Jean will courier the tickets to you this afternoon. A driver will pick you up at Calgary airport and take you to Lake Louise.'

I finish the call by promising to telephone Dirk when I arrive. Then I tilt my head back and stare sightlessly up at the ceiling. Of all of the utterly idiotic things to do! How could he be so reckless? Did he think no one knew him in Canada? He's a movie star! He'd probably be recognised in Outer Mongolia!

Muffin whines. I reach down to pat her. Force myself to take a breath.

I walk across the hall to the gilt-framed mirror. My face looks pale. There are lines between my eyebrows. On the table beneath the mirror is a photograph from our wedding. Rex and me outside the courthouse. Rex looks like the groom at a shotgun wedding. I'm smiling but there's a tiny crease between my eyebrows that gives my doubts away.

He promised to be true. Not only before the judge but on that fateful Saturday when I was summoned here. I've been true to Rex. I've not spoken to Jack since Ginny's wedding because I knew if I did, I couldn't trust myself to hold back this time. In those last five months, as loneliness grew rampant as weeds in my heart and Rex's secrets threatened to choke me, I've stood by him. And he's gone and blown all of that by jumping back into bed with Tony!

He really is the most selfish man that ever lived. When I get to Lake Louise, I am going to give him a piece of my mind. I've played nicely, I've bitten my lip and kept quiet at his bad behaviour time and again. I've begged and pleaded with him to give up drinking. Well, this time, I'm not pulling my punches. If he's not careful, he'll blow the charade of our marriage sky-high and what happens to me then? Nothing good, you can be sure of that.

I blow out a long breath. Ginny's outside. I've got to think up a reason why I'm needed in Canada. I run possibilities through my head as I head through the kitchen. Stepping outside, the sunshine makes me blink and I wish I'd not left my sunglasses on the table.

'Everything all right?' she asks.

'I have to go to Canada.' I slip my sunglasses back on, hoping she's not caught the strain written across my face. 'Rex needs me.'

'Is he all right?' Ginny turns to me, eyes wide. 'Has something terrible happened?'

'He's drinking too much again.' I clear my throat. 'It's making him late for his calls. The producers think I'll be able to help.'

'Has this been going on since the wedding?' Ginny grips my arm.

'Pretty much,' I say slowly. 'Look, I'm sorry to cut this short but I've got to pack. It's an early flight in the morning.'

'Of course.' Ginny levers herself carefully out of the chair, her hand instinctively cradling her bump.

As we walk inside, I say, 'Just how cold is it in the Rockies in March?'

'Pretty darned cold. You'll need plenty of sweaters and your fur topper.'

The fur topcoat was my Christmas present from Rex. I'm rather tired of the expensive gifts, which mean nothing, but if I don't take it, he'll be offended.

Ginny turns on the steps and looks back at me. 'You can ring me. From Canada. I barely sleep at the moment because of this one.' As she pats the bump fondly, I swallow around the enormous lump clogging my throat. 'So don't worry about the time.'

'Thank you.' I won't ring. I can't trust myself not to tell her all of the secrets if I do.

Once she's gone, I stand in the huge hall. Muffin comes towards me, her head tilted as if she's trying to work out what's going on.

I could pick her up and leave. Just walk away and let Rex sort out his own problems. I could start again somewhere new. Australia, maybe. I've done it before.

I don't want to run away. But I'm afraid of what Rex will say to me in Canada. Afraid of the decisions I'll have to make because of that. Afraid of feeling even smaller than I do already.

*Rex has done that to you*, that little voice says. *It's his fault you feel small. You owe him nothing.*

I rub my hands over my face again. That might be true but I've agreed to go to Canada. After that, who knows?

I look down at my dog. 'Come on,' I say to Muffin. 'We've packing to do.'

\* \* \*

My aeroplane tickets arrive mid-afternoon. I hear the bell ring as I'm deciding if I need the brown saddle shoes as well as the black loafers. I run downstairs. Trudie hands me the envelope. Inside, with the tickets, is the front page of *Eyewitness*.

In the largest photograph, Rex and Tony are talking by a lake. Their bodies are too close together, their gazes locked. My body goes entirely cold because you only stand like that with someone if even those few inches feels too much and you long for there to be no distance between you at all.

Over the page, there's another snap. In this one, they're emerging from a veranda that's cast in shadow. Banks of snow are piled up on each side of the path. Rex has his arm around Tony's shoulders, their heads are close together as if they're deep in conversation.

I take candid shots. I recognise moments that capture truth. It's written all over these. Rex and Tony care deeply about each other.

## 24

It's twilight when I arrive at Lake Louise. The sky is orange and pink, streaked with skeins of grey clouds. The lake looks like a huge skating ring. Snow-covered mountains encircle it. The air smells of pine forests and woodsmoke. I long to get out my camera. Perhaps if I check in quickly, I can come back out and take some photographs.

Chateau Lake Louise towers above me. It's very grand. A modern version of a French château with squat turrets at each end and in the centre and a lower wing running off to one side. The stonework is turned dusky pink by the sunset.

I shiver and tug at the edges of the fur topper. It doesn't have buttons, having been bought for Los Angeles rather than the Rockies. Despite Ginny's advice, I don't think I've got nearly enough clothes to keep me warm.

The driver takes my cases from the boot of the car and I walk up the steps to the entrance. I feel a little sick now I'm here. What on earth am I going to say to Rex that will make any difference? The studio and Dirk have overestimated my influence. He stopped caring what I thought a long time ago.

The receptionist gives me a key to our suite. I telephoned Rex last night and told him I was coming. I have to hope he's at least had the decency to get Tony to clear out. As the porter opens the door, I realise I'm holding my breath. I blow it out gently when I see the suite is empty.

As soon as the porter has left, I turn to the window to see the light has gone and it's dusk outside.

In the sitting room, chintz curtains cover French windows that open onto a balcony. There are two green, velvet sofas facing each other. The furniture is teak trimmed with brass. The drinks tray doubles as a table. On it are bottles of whisky, bourbon and brandy together with siphons of tonic and soda. I get myself a soda water and sit down. *The Long Goodbye* by Raymond Chandler is on the coffee table. My jaw clenches as I pick it up. Rex doesn't read fiction. There's a bookmark neatly tucked into it. It's an empty matchbook advertising The Windup Bar in Hollywood, which is a known hotspot for homosexuals.

I have a sudden urge to cry. I can see the two of them sitting together in an evening. Tony reading the book, Rex skimming through his script ready for the following day's filming. It's companionable, comfortable, maybe even loving.

I slam the book shut and drop it back on the table. They were here together while I was sitting alone at home with only Muffin for company. I believed him when he promised me he'd be true. How long has this been going on? Has he been with Tony for the entirety of our marriage?

I feel like a such an idiot for believing him. I married him to help and now he's gone and dug himself into an even bigger hole that even Dirk may struggle to get him out of.

Not knowing what else to do, I unpack. I've got the smaller of the two bedrooms. It's a pretty room with the same curtains as the sitting room and a queen-sized bed. The bed is piled high with blankets with a thick eiderdown on top. Just how cold does it get here at night?

After I've changed into a shirtwaist dress and freshened up my make-up, I decide there's no point hiding up here. Goodness knows when my husband will return. Sitting here worrying about what I'm going to say to him isn't going to help. Plus I'm hungry.

The dining room is filling up quickly. There are make-up girls, cameramen, the women from the wardrobe department, drivers, set makers, all sitting at the circular tables chatting about the day. I hesitate for a moment, scanning the crowd for Rex. There's no sign of him, which is almost a relief.

To my right, a woman says, 'What's Rex going to do now Audrey's here?'

My ears turn red. I swallow hard against the horrible mixture of embarrassment, rage and resentment that's swirling around in my stomach.

Then I remember Jack saying, 'Oh, Audrey,' at The Biltmore and my vision blurs with tears. Of course they all know! They knew before we married. They're his colleagues and it's pretty clear from the photographs in *Eyewitness* that he's done nothing to hide his relationship with Tony.

Should I go back upstairs? I'm sure the room service is very good in a place like this. Then a dapper man in his mid-forties stands and comes towards me. It's Paul Williams, one of the associate producers.

'Audrey.' He kisses my cheek. 'Thank you for coming.'

He guides me to a table near one of the wide picture windows. The lights from the dining room are reflected in the glass. I nod to the other people sitting there. Mrs Seton, who I met at The Cocoanut Grove and have disliked ever since; Ralph Doyle, cinematographer; Eric Schaltz, the unit man.

'Rex is still on set. They're shooting a night scene,' Paul

explains after a martini has been delivered to me and I've ordered a chicken salad to eat.

'How is shooting going?' I ask, fiddling with the twist of lemon that decorates my cocktail glass. This is what the producer cares about. It's his job to keep the production on schedule and on budget.

'Not as well as we hoped. Your husband has been...' He pauses, looks away. '...distracted.'

My hands knot beneath the white linen tablecloth. Paul's looking at me with concern. Am I supposed to play the broken-hearted spouse or does everyone know that our marriage is fake? After the comment as I came in, I'm betting on the latter.

My chin comes up. I've played my part. I can't be responsible for Rex's failure to do the same. 'What *exactly* are you expecting me to do, Paul?'

'Speak to him. Make him realise how serious the situation is.'

My breath hitches. Is that a threat? I wish Dirk was here. He'd know how to deal with this. I close my eyes for a second and try to think what my former boss would do.

'Which is?' I prompt.

Paul leans in and lowers his voice. 'Obviously, if Rex's true nature came out, the studio would have no choice but to let him go. It'd hit the schedule hard if we had to reshoot his scenes but this picture is too important to be derailed.' He coughs at the unintended pun. 'Discreet enquiries are being made in case we need to replace him. Gregory Peck may be available.'

My eyebrows shoot up. 'You'd replace him?' My voice comes out louder than I intended. A dozen heads turn towards us.

Paul gently shushes me. 'Only if we absolutely had to.'

\* \* \*

I'm sitting on one of the velvet sofas in our suite flipping through *Vogue* when Rex returns an hour later.

'How was your flight?' he asks as he reaches for the bottle of bourbon. He's wearing a cream cable-knit jumper that I'd swear he didn't own when he left home.

'Fine.' I put the magazine down. 'We need to talk.'

'Now?' Rex frowns. 'I'm famished.'

'Yes, now.' I take the page from *Eyewitness* from my handbag and lay it on the table next to *The Long Goodbye*. Rex takes a slug of bourbon and then picks up the torn page. I wait as his eyes scan the paper.

'What's the big deal?' he says with a shrug, sounding like a kid who's been caught with his hand in the sweet jar. 'Tony and I were only having a bit of fun.'

'It's a big deal because it makes it clear our marriage is a lie. That I'm your fake wife. Have you thought what that will mean for me?' My voice rises at the prospect of the humiliation if it becomes public knowledge. Louella Parsons will rip my reputation to sheds. Ginny, Rita and Esther will know I've lied to them. Father will believe I've made another colossal error because I'm such a terrible judge of character.

Rex shrugs as if none of that means anything to him. I know him well enough now to know that's very likely the case. I take a slow steady breath to tamp down the rush of fury that's sweeping through me. When I'm sure I can trust my voice, I add, 'And the studio think it's a big deal. Paul Williams had a chat with me. They're thinking of replacing you. Gregory Peck's available.'

Rex sits down on the sofa opposite me as if the wind's gone out of him. 'Peck? Hell! They can't do that.'

At least, I'm finally getting through to him. I lean towards him over the table.

'Whether they do is down to you, Rex. You have to give up Tony.' I put my hand on the book. 'I presume this is his.'

'Yes. He's—' He looks away, staring at the chintz curtains. 'That is, we've—'

The evasion twists in my gut. Enough with his lies. If I don't push for the truth, I'll feel like I'm shrinking away to nothing.

'Rex, I deserve the truth. What's going on between you and Tony?'

He knocks back half of the glass of bourbon, before glancing at me and then away. 'I love him.'

I grip the arms of my chair as suddenly, I'm tumbling back through time to that house in Camden with the smell of sour milk. Freddie loved Michael. He didn't say it out loud but that doesn't mean I didn't hear it. I'd been useful to Freddie and then he abandoned me when Michael came along and now Rex is doing exactly the same.

I trusted Rex because he promised he'd be faithful. I thought I'd never again feel as small and rejected as I did in that house in Camden.

I was wrong.

Inside my head, there's an insidious voice telling me I'm not worth anything. Father knew it, Freddie saw it. Rex believes it too. The men in my life I've cared most about all agree that I'm hopeless and useless and not worth anything.

I shake my head, trying to chase the voice away. I can't give into it now. *Come on, Audrey. You have to fight. You can't let Rex win.*

I smooth my shaking hands over my skirts. This is such a humiliating question to have to ask. How can he put me in this position?

That brings my chin up as I say, 'Have you and Tony been together all the way through our marriage?'

'No! I broke it off like I told you!' Rex gestures with his

glass and slops bourbon onto the carpet. 'But we bumped into each other when we came up here. I've been miserable without him. You've no idea what it's like. I just couldn't help myself when I found out he was on this shoot. It felt like it was meant to be.'

It's a relief of sorts to know he's not been lying for the entirety of our marriage. I do know he's been miserable. I've lived with that misery for the past thirteen months.

'He makes me happy,' Rex adds, his thick brows lowered. 'He's the only person I can be myself with.'

'We got married to protect you from stories like this and you've just gone and given *Eyewitness* an even better one. You've got to be more careful.'

Rex turns away from me and grabs the decanter again. 'Fine. I'll speak to Tony.'

There's silence between us for a moment. My brain is wondering how the conversation went when they were reunited. Clearly, they've not wasted any time which is surprising seeing as Rex pretty much threw Tony under the bus before we got married.

'I'm surprised Tony took you back,' I say slowly. 'Considering you let Dirk drop him *and* ruin his sister's career.'

'I didn't!' Rex splutters. 'That was all Dirk. I had—'

'You let him do it. You forget, I was there.' Then a thought hits me and I sit up straighter. 'Or does Tony not know what Dirk did to Ida?'

'He never needs to know.' Rex's eyes meet mine and there's pleading in them. 'Please, Audrey. Don't tell him.'

The last thread that was holding me to Rex unravels. All at once, I see the excuses I've made for him to Ginny and Jack are utterly hollow. Because if he'll lie to the man he loves then he'll have no compunction in lying to me again. If I can't trust him at all then how can we go on pretending? How can I continue to share a house with him?

I look at his face and it's still as handsome but I can see the weakness in his jaw now, the way his eyes narrow when he's lying to me, the cruelty in his mouth.

I have to get away from him and the bedroom opposite his is not far enough. I snatch up my handbag. 'You are contemptible,' I hiss at him. 'You claim to love Tony but you're lying to him too. That's not love, Rex. That's using people.'

The words crackle with truth. I can't call them back now. I won't. I march towards the door.

'Audrey, you can't walk out,' he calls after me. 'People will know we've—'

The door bangs shut, cutting off the rest of his words. My heart is pounding, my hands shaking. But I'm not sorry. I stood up for myself and if that makes him uncomfortable then so be it.

Voices are approaching down the hotel corridor. I plaster on a smile and start to walk along the corridor towards the lift. All of the doors are closed but there may still be people in those rooms, people who just heard every word I yelled at my husband.

I shrug. What did Rex think was going to happen? Did he expect me to be happy he's let the world see our marriage is a sham? My stomach clenches as I face the truth. Rex didn't think about me at all. He only ever thinks about himself.

A gaggle of girls pass me. They're all about my age, dressed in circle skirts with tight sweaters. Over the top, they all wear thick plaid shirts. I envy them their freedom, their independence. I gave all of that up when I married Rex and right now, it's feeling like a very poor deal indeed.

I really need a drink. As I wait for the lift, I shiver again. I rub my arms. Even in my cashmere cardigan, it's cold. I'll have to put more layers on tomorrow.

The lift deposits me on the ground floor. The lounge is at the front of the hotel. The burgundy damask curtains are drawn; a fire burns in the grate. I ask the waiter for a brandy, then take a seat in one of the wing-backed chairs by the window. I tilt my head back and blow out a long breath.

I feel eyes on me and turn my head. Jack sits near the fire. Suddenly, my heart is in my mouth. I've not seen him since Ginny and Nate's wedding but, boy, have I thought of him! I've imagined again and again what would have happened if we'd had the dance I promised him. If, when our bodies had been pressed together, I'd not been yanked off him by Rex.

His gaze meets mine. Behind his glasses, his grey eyes are beautiful. It's as if the distance between us contracts, that I'm being inexorably drawn towards him. I stand and walk towards him.

'Audrey, what are you doing here?' he says and then laughs. 'That's usually your line.'

'The studio asked me to come.' I take a seat on the leather Chesterfield next to Jack's seat. 'They wanted me to speak to Rex.'

Jack nods as if it's no surprise to him.

'Rex didn't manage to get you fired then?' I ask abruptly. 'After the wedding?'

Jack laughs a little ruefully. 'He tried but Harry King told him I'm too valuable to lose. He knows if he lets me go, MGM or Paramount will snap me up. I've been promoted since then. I'm Assistant Props Master now.'

It's said entirely as a matter of fact. I like that he knows his own worth. I wish I had that confidence. I thought marrying Rex would give it to me but it didn't. The words of Father and Freddie still rang in my ears. If I'd known my own worth, as Jack does, would their poor opinions have slid off me like water from a mackintosh?

'Congratulations.' I smile at him. 'I'm really glad you didn't get into trouble because of me.'

He smiles back at me and that warms me more than the fire is doing. I rub my arms. 'Why is it so cold in here?'

'The hotel is usually closed in the winter. They've opened early for the shoot but they're not really set up for it.'

I nod as understanding sinks in. 'Hence the heaps of blankets on my bed.'

'You'll need them.' Jack's beautiful eyes meet my gaze. I don't look away. I've waited a long time to see him again. 'Did no one warn you? We were all told to pack for the Arctic.'

I shake my head. 'Dirk failed to mention that.' A jolt of irritation runs through me. It's bad enough he sent me up here to confront Rex about Tony; he could have made sure I didn't freeze as well.

The waiter brings my glass of brandy and I swirl it around the bowl-like glass. It smells sweet and nutty. I knock back half of it, the rich liquid warming my throat.

'That bad, eh?' Jack asks.

'Worse.' I hesitate. I'm so wretchedly used to secrets. They're bread and butter to me now but why am I keeping them when everyone from the make-up girl in the dining room to Paul, the producer, knows the truth? '*Eyewitness* has got photographs of Rex and Tony. It makes it pretty obvious our marriage is a sham. I confronted Rex about it and he told me he loves Tony.'

'Christ, Audrey!' Jack reaches across the space between us and takes my hand. That zip of awareness is still there but what I feel more than anything is reassurance. And it's nice. Really nice.

I look down into my glass. 'The studio are threatening to fire Rex if he's not more careful.' I drink again. The alcohol warms my throat, thawing the tightness in my chest. 'I don't know what to do.' There's a relief in saying the words out loud. 'I honestly don't know why I'm doing this any more. I mean, I married him to keep his secret but if he's going to let the entire world know and damn the consequences then...'

'What happens to you?' Jack says softly.

'Yes.' I stare into the glass. 'I feel like such an idiot. He promised me there'd not be anyone else and I trusted that.'

'He said that?' Jack asks quickly.

'Yes.' I raise my eyes to look at him and hope he can read the raw longing in them. 'And because of that, I didn't contact you after Ginny's wedding, even though I wanted to. You have no idea how much I wanted to.'

'I wanted to as well.' He squeezes my hand. 'But I figured it had to come from you. You're the one with ties.'

I rub my free hand over my face. 'I've made such a terrible mess of it all.' I hear a log shift in the grate. 'I thought friendship and respect would be enough but it was clear pretty soon after we married that the real Rex was very different to the man I'd been dating. He's weak and selfish and sometimes mean.'

Jack tilts his head and studies my face. 'You seem different. You're not as wide-eyed any more.'

I laugh a little hollowly. 'Living with Rex can do that to a girl. He's got a talent for trampling on dreams.'

'Then why stay?'

He's asked me that before. I don't have any better answer than I did last time.

'I don't know.' I twist my watch around my wrist as I always do when I'm agitated. 'I haven't had time to—'

I break off as I hear someone enter the room behind us. A male voice is talking about his son who's newly back from Korea. Jack looks behind me. 'Paul and Mrs Seton,' he whispers.

I raise my eyes towards the ceiling. 'Not that old busybody!'

Jack gives me a quick grin of understanding. Then he points

to the door in the corner. 'Through there is the Sun Room. Then you're back in the lobby.'

I whisper a thank you.

He nods and then stands. I duck my head behind the back of the sofa and wait. 'I've glad I've seen you both,' Jack says loudly. 'I've got a couple of questions about the scene we're filming tomorrow.'

I peek around the edge of the sofa. Their backs are turned. I stand and dash as quietly as I can for the door. As I slip through it, I catch Jack looking at me over Mrs Seton's shoulder. He winks and I stifle a laugh as I close the door.

## 25

Surprisingly (and probably due to the brandy) I sleep well under my enormous pile of blankets but wake early, feeling cold. My lacy silk nightdress is no help at all. Winceyette like I wore back in Sheffield would be more the ticket in this climate. As soon as I wake up, my brain starts racing, trying to work out what on earth I'm going to do.

Rex wasn't here when I got back last night. By the fact he'd taken his toothbrush and washbag, I assumed he'd gone to spend the night with Tony. I can only hope my words got through to him and he's being more circumspect now.

I shiver and throw the covers back to grab my housecoat. When I pull the curtains back, there's a film of ice on the outside windows. I rub a patch of condensation away and peer out. It's still dark. I can stay here worrying about Rex until breakfast or if I hurry, I can catch the golden hour when the light is at its best. As photography always makes me happier, I decide the latter is the better plan.

I'm downstairs by quarter past seven. Through the wide windows facing the lake, the darkness is fading. As soon as I open the front door, it's clear I'm inadequately dressed even in my fur topcoat. Icy fingers of air brush every uncovered inch of skin. I wish desperately for a woolly hat and mittens instead of my fashionable shell cap and suede gloves. It's not snowed overnight but it's frozen hard. There's ice on all of the paths. I walk carefully down towards the lake, aware of the treacherous slipperiness beneath the soles of my saddle shoes.

It's worth it though as over the mountains to the east the sky turns pink, followed by apricot. When the sun strikes the icy lake, it glitters like diamonds. I take photo after photo, fascinated by the changing light, wishing all the time that I had Rita's skills with landscapes.

My fingers are numb by the time I finish. I blow on my hands to try to warm them before I put my gloves back on. As I turn to go back inside, I spot a movement off to the left at the end of the smaller block of the hotel. Two men are coming around the corner. One is Rex: I spot him by his height and the breadth of his shoulders. The other is Tony Young. They're holding hands.

My breath huffs out in a cloud. After everything I said last night! He promised me he'd be more careful and now he's doing this?

I glance around. There are a few people about. A groundsman, bundled up in a thick plaid coat and fur hat, is spreading grit on the paths; a couple who are about my age, who have come out to see the sunrise, are walking back towards the hotel entrance. Any of them could be the spy Dirk warned me about.

As Tony and Rex come towards me, a rage builds inside of me. I raise my camera to my eye and focus on the two of them. Maybe if I take these then Rex will realise the risk he's running. Something needs to make him come to his senses. I snap one of them holding hands, another as they smile at each other as they share a joke. I wind the film on and as I get them in the viewfinder this time, Rex is raising his hand to cup Tony's face. It's a gesture of infinite tenderness.

It's as if I've swallowed hot coals. Why has no one *ever* touched me like that? I want Jack to but it's not happened because I've been a good wife and kept away from him. Why did I bother if Rex was going to reveal the lies at the heart of our marriage to the whole world? As I press the shutter button, my hands are shaking. With longing, with loss, with yearning and with anger for what I've given up.

I sag back against the wall behind me. Cold seeps through my tweed skirt but I don't move. Rex really does love Tony. It's clear as day now I've seen them together.

\* \* \*

In the dining room, I get cornered by Mrs Seton. She keeps up a constant stream of fairly inane chatter as we eat our toast. When I comment on the cold, she looks at my pretty mauve sweater and says, 'Someone should have warned you, dear. I told all of my girls to bring union suits.'

Needless to say, my own undies are nowhere near as warm or practical as a union suit which can swaddle you in wool from ankle to breastbone. I gave up such practical garments when I arrived in Los Angeles and hoped I'd never need them again but it seems I have no choice if I don't want to freeze for the next week.

'Then I need to do some shopping,' I reply briskly, as this will be an excellent reason to make my excuses and escape. 'Where should I go?'

'Banff's the only option. The hotel reception can sort out a car for you.'

I didn't know what to do today and this seems like as good a plan as any other. At least it gives me a bit of breathing space and time to think away from the hotel. It's clear that the situation with Rex is impossible. The question now, as Jack asked last night, is what I'm going to do about it.

I order the car and return to our suite. Rex has been back long enough to create havoc in the bathroom. As I tidy up after him, memories of that last conversation with Freddie flit through my brain. I was so angry with him. He'd been so dismissive of me and our friendship, as if none of that mattered.

Absently, I clutch a folded towel to my chest and stare out at the lake. Six years have passed since then but Rex's betrayal hurts just as much. I thought life as a movie star's wife was worth giving up on the hope of being loved. I was utterly and totally wrong. Ginny and Nate have shown me that.

In truth, I have only one option: the D-word. Lee Miller got divorced. As did Elizabeth Taylor and Judy Garland. So why does the thought of it make me feel like a hussy who's no better than she ought to be? That's what Father would say.

I return the towel to the bathroom and snatch up my handbag. Father will be unhappy whatever I do. He always has been. I've never been anything but a disappointment to him. But I'm a married woman of twenty-four. Isn't it time to stop worrying what Father thinks?

The trip down to Banff is spectacular and distracting. There's less snow as we descend but the mountain scenery is still breathtaking. I make Bruce, the driver, stop the black Oldsmobile several times to let me take photographs. Each time I climb out, there's a stiff breeze that plucks at my clothes. It's more pronounced by the time we arrive in the town. Bruce drops me at Banff Avenue and asks if I mind being picked up at 3.30 p.m. as he's already arranged to bring another guest back at that time. I assure him that's absolutely fine.

Banff is like a frontier town out of a Western. There's a line of shops with cars parked outside but it honestly feels like the sheriff could ride in at any moment. Snow has been cleared from the pavements but still dusts the rooftops.

I locate a ladies' outfitters which stocks practical and warm clothes. I buy a union suit, woollen stockings, a woolly hat with flowers embroidered on it, scarf, sheepskin gloves and a coat that actually fastens. The lady who serves me is very understanding when I request to wear the outer layers immediately. She wraps my fur topper and flimsy shell cap with my new purchases, making them into two neat brown paper parcels tied up with string. I agree to collect them later and head off to find some lunch.

Outside, the wind has got up. It flattens my skirt against my legs and tugs at my new coat. I'm grateful for the warmth of the woolly hat as I walk up the street, looking for a café.

I've barely eaten since I arrived at Lake Louise but I make up for that over lunch, wolfing down a turkey sandwich and following it with cherry pie.

Being in Banff feels like playing hooky. I'm sure Dirk and the studio expect me to be at the Chateau waiting for Rex to come back from filming. But I have a life too. One that I've put on hold for my husband for too long, allowing my interests, including my photography, to take a backseat to Rex's needs.

I push my empty plates aside and peer out of the café window. I've got a few hours until the car takes me back to Chateau Lake Louise and all the problems that are waiting for me there. Until then, I'm going to do what suits me.

* * *

Despite the wind, which has got even stronger while I've been eating, I go for a walk along the river and take even more photographs, feeling more inspired than I've done in months.

When I change the film, I stash the one I took earlier in the zipped compartment of my handbag. I'll develop it when I'm in my darkroom where I can ensure only my eyes see the prints.

If I tell Rex I took them, will that be enough to make him more cautious with Tony? Or will he think I'm simply being difficult? I sigh – probably the latter. Especially as I didn't exactly mince my words last night.

I return to the café for a hot chocolate to warm up. As I drink it, snow starts to fall. The flakes are huge and fluffy. I watch them idly, reminded of the terrible winter of 1947 when we had six weeks of snow. It was as high as the windowsills. I helped Mum dig the path down to the gate every morning. When the fuel shortages kicked in, we spent our evenings by candlelight as if we were back in Victorian times.

It's hard walking against the wind and snow as I return to the ladies' outfitters to pick up my parcels. I'm buffeted by gusts that slow me to a halt and then have to battle on again. Clutching the parcels to my chest, I head to Banff Avenue. Snow swirls in my face, sticking to my eyelashes. I'm five minutes early and take shelter in the lee of the drug store.

A man in an overcoat and tweed cap walks towards me. He's ten feet away when I realise it's Jack. My heart leaps. What's he doing here? Then I remember Bruce saying he'd arranged to pick someone else up at 3.30 p.m. The thought of sitting next to him in the car for the journey back is both thrilling and frustrating. Because we won't be able to talk. Not like we need to with Bruce able to hear every word.

I grin as he approaches. I see the exact moment he spots me and does a double-take. His face lightens and he smiles.

'Audrey! What are you doing here?' Then he laughs rather ruefully. 'Will we ever stop asking each other that question?'

'Shopping.' I gesture with one of my parcels. 'And taking photographs.'

'It's pretty damned stunning, isn't it?' He raises a gloved hand and gestures at the mountain behind the town. 'Reminds me of home.'

'Oregon's like this?' I brush snowflakes from my nose. 'How did you ever leave?'

He laughs, low and gravelly. 'Not much call for prop makers where I come from.' Then he tilts his head and a slow grin appears. 'Like the hat!'

I self-consciously put a hand on it. 'I know it looks like a tea cosy but it's warm.'

'A very pretty tea cosy.'

I try to shoot him a look but snowflakes are sticking to my eyelashes.

He points along the street. 'Here's our ride.'

The black Oldsmobile pulls up at the rear of the line of parked cars. Jack opens the rear door for me. I walk carefully over the slush that's accumulated at the edge of the road, shifting my parcels into one hand. A gust of wind slams into me, wrenching the parcels from my hand. Jack's arm goes round me. One parcel tumbles into the footwell, the other falls from my hand into the slush.

'Let me.' Jack's arm cradles me as he helps me into the car. His sudden proximity is startling. I glance at his face. See the way the skin crinkles around his eyes, the smooth line of his jaw, the quirk of one eyebrow. My breath catches. Heat floods through me despite the cold.

He hands me the other parcel.

'Thank you,' I murmur.

What was that? But I already know the answer. It's the longing I've felt since Ginny's wedding. I want Jack to hold me, kiss me and make love to me. I want him to touch me in places I've never been touched...

I blush. Heat streaks up my cheeks. I press my gloved hands against them. Oh, my goodness! I shouldn't be thinking like this. I'm a married woman. But perhaps not for all that much longer. If I leave Rex, I'll be free. Free to explore whatever this is between Jack and me.

Jack gets in at the opposite side and slides across the seat towards me. His overcoat fans out around him and underneath its fabric, his hand reaches for mine. We exchange one secret smile and then stare out of opposite windows.

There's a tingle from where our hands touch that runs right up my arm. It's as if I've woken up. Not from sleep but from stupor. I've spent all this time worrying about what Rex needs and not thought about me and what I need. And suddenly, I know with absolute clarity what that is. I need a man who wants me as I want him. I want to be touched and held and loved.

I glance across at Jack and his head turns to meet my gaze. Those eyes! What they do to me!

The wind buffets the car. With my free hand, I grip the inside door handle. Another buffet comes and I hold on tighter. I clear a space in the steamed-up window and peer out.

Snow has covered the ground, forming knee-high drifts. Rows of pine trees line the road. Apart from the fact all of the conifers are bent by the wind, it looks like a Christmas card. Its sharp, clear beauty calls to something deep inside of me. A suppressed homesickness, a yearning for crisp, wintery mornings when everything seemed made new. For going out in the snow and coming back, chilled and ravenous to a roaring fire. For home.

I sit back against the seat as memories rush through me. Going sledging with Freddie. Wellington boots and wet gloves. Feeling free as a bird as the sledge carried me down the slope. Falling off, laughing, at the bottom.

The thought of Freddie doesn't bring the usual morass of emotions. I'm trying to work out why that is when Jack shifts to lean forward and asks Bruce, 'Do you think we'll get back okay?'

'Should do so long as you folks are in no rush.'

Jack glances at me and smiles. 'Take all the time you need,' he says.

The snow gets denser as we start to climb. Our pace slows to not much more than a crawl. The windscreen wipers creak under the accumulated weight of snow and ice. The light's fading now, darkness hastened by the weather.

When we stop ten minutes later, Jack shuffles to the centre of the seats to look through the windscreen. I peer around the passenger seat. All I can see is a lorry carrying a load of timber and half a dozen cars ahead of us. There's no traffic coming the other way. Snow has already carpeted that side of the road. A burly man, his cap pulled down low, trudges towards us through the snow and taps on Bruce's window.

'Tree down up ahead,' he says. 'Road's blocked. You'll not get up to Lake Louise tonight.'

'Damn, it's late in the year for that,' Bruce says before thanking the man. He winds the window back up and turns to us. 'I'm sorry, folks, but I'm going to have to take you back to Banff.'

'But that's twenty miles in snow that's getting deeper by the minute. Isn't there anywhere else?' The worry in Jack's voice reminds me that he's from the mountains of Oregon. I trust his instincts. If he thinks it's a bad idea then I'm not going to argue.

'There's a lodge at Castle Junction,' the driver says. 'It's pretty basic but they might be able to find you a couple of rooms for the night.'

I look at Jack, who shrugs as he meets my gaze. 'I don't mind roughing it. What about you, Audrey?'

A snow-bound cabin? With Jack? For a whole night? After a year of snatched conversations in very public locations, it feels like a gift from the gods and I'm not going to turn it down.

'Fine with me. I lived through the winter of '47. I'm sure I can manage a night in a cabin.'

Jack's hand tightens around mine. He doesn't look at me. He doesn't have to. I already know he's as thrilled at the prospect as I am.

## 26

The lodge is a little way off the highway. It's not much more than a wood cabin. The owners, Anya and Eric, are willing to take us in though even though they don't usually have guests at this time of the year. Bruce helps me and my parcels into the living room and then disappears into the kitchen with Eric.

I stand in the tiny, pineclad hall – hooks full of bulky coats, wellingtons lined up beneath – and feel suddenly self-conscious. Jack's beside me, peeling off muffler and cap. What if we've nothing to talk about when there's only the two of us? Our entire acquaintance has been condensed into these few intense meetings. There's been stolen moments at The Cocoanut Grove and beneath the tree at the wedding but we've never been alone together.

Anya emerges from the kitchen, wiping her hands on her apron. She's in her mid-fifties with the kind of weathered face that indicates she spends a lot of time outdoors and grey hair pulled into a bun. She shows me through the sitting room to the stairs and then up to my room. It's got pineclad walls, a square window with tartan curtains and a rag rug on the floor. An oil lamp burns on the bedside cabinet. There's a definite chill in the air.

'The bed's not aired but I'll bring up a hot water bottle for you later on. The bathroom's down the hall.' She hands me a towel and pats the sprigged garment folded on top. 'There's a night-gown here if you need it.'

I thank her for her kindness. Taking off my new coat, I spread it over the eiderdown. It'll help keep me warm tonight.

As it's too chilly to loiter, I return to the sitting room. It's also pineclad with two tweed-covered sofas, a small dining table under the window and a bookcase packed with novels and wildlife guides. It's lit by oil lamps which cast a gentle glow within the circle of light and deep shadows outside of it. The wind moans down the chimney. I shiver.

Eric, who's got a full head of grey hair and must be as tall as Rex, is adding logs to the fire.

'Do you have a telephone?' I ask. 'I should let my husband know where I am.'

'Sorry, ma'am,' he says. 'We don't. Too expensive for the tele-phone company to bring the line all the way out here.'

'I see. Yes, of course.' There's a stab of guilt that I won't be able to contact Rex. Yet I doubt he'll be anxious about me. He'll prob-ably be happy I'm not around and he can spend more time with Tony. 'I'm sorry to put you to all this trouble.'

'It's no trouble. We like having visitors.' Eric gives me a gentle smile as he rests his hand on the mantlepiece. 'It's just the old house isn't set up to keep folk warm at this time of the year. It's fine for Anya and me. We're used to it but most folks like a bit more in the way of comfort.'

'We'll be fine,' I say firmly although I've no right to speak for Jack. He just doesn't strike me as a man who needs a lot in the way of material comforts. Rex, in this situation, would be fussing that the beds are too hard, the room too cold, the food not to his taste.

Eric leaves the door slightly ajar as he leaves the room. Feeling the draught on my back, I give in to the urge to kneel by the fire. My knees sink into the rag rug beside the hearth. I hold my hands out to the flames and watch the fire crackle and spit. I used to do this at home when I got back from work. When my face is blazing, I sit back on my heels. There's a creak behind me. I look over my shoulder to see Jack descend the stairs. He's shed his coat and is wearing a Fair Isle jumper in blues and greys that brings out the beautiful colour of his eyes. As he comes towards me, I stand up.

'Are you sure don't mind spending the night here?' As Jack frowns, lines are scored between his eyebrows. 'It's not what you're used to.'

I laugh as I sit on one of the sofas. 'You're forgetting I grew up in wartime Britain. I survived ten years of rationing and the Sheffield Blitz. I'll be fine. And Eric and Anya couldn't be kinder.'

'They remind me of my grandparents.' Jack takes a seat beside me. 'They're just the same. Welcome anyone and never mind the trouble.'

'Are they in Oregon too?' I ask.

'My dad's folks moved into Bellingham, that's our nearest town, when Dad took over the farm. Mom's family were shop-keepers. Hardware store. My uncle runs it now. My grandparents moved into an Arts and Crafts home on the bay.'

There's an affection in his voice which makes it sound wonderful, as if they all get on together splendidly and there's never any arguments.

'Are you close?'

'I guess.' Jack shrugs as if he's never really thought about it which is more of an answer to the question than his words. 'I'm the only one who's moved away. Astrid, my sister, married a farmer and lives ten miles from home.'

There's a squirm of what feels uncomfortably like envy at the easy way he speaks about them. Like me, he's the only one who's roamed but it doesn't sound like he was running away.

'Astrid's an unusual name,' I say.

'Swedish grandparents. My middle name's Anders after my grandfather.'

My hands knot in my lap. I should reciprocate, talk about my family. I've avoided it since I came to America and yet if I want to know Jack, I have to let him know me.

I take a deep breath and say, 'I have one sister, Esther. She's two years older than me. I'm dotty about my nephew and niece. David and Ruth. They're the sweetest. I just wish I didn't live so far away.'

We're comparing notes about being an aunt and uncle (Jack's got two nieces who he clearly adores) when Anya returns with a bottle of amber liquid and two glass tumblers.

'A nip of this will warm you up,' she says, unscrewing the bottle of Canadian Club.

'My granddaddy drank this during Prohibition.' Jack stands to accept a tumbler.

'There was plenty smuggled over the border.' Anya pours him a very generous measure.

I blanch slightly at the huge slug Anya's poured into the glass. I'll be very tipsy indeed if I drink that on an empty stomach.

Anya waves the thanks away. 'Make yourselves comfortable. I'll be back with the rest.' A moment later, Anya carries a heavily stacked tray into the room. She rests it on a chair before tossing a gingham cloth over the table.

'Let me give you a hand.' I stand and go over to her. Between us, we unload plates, cutlery, a loaf of bread and a butter dish onto the table. I set places for Jack and me as Anya returns to the kitchen. Moments later, she returns with two steaming bowls, a wedge of cheese and jar of homemade chutney.

'The soup's chicken. I made it yesterday.' Anya moves one of the oil lamps to the table. 'I'm sorry it's not more but it's all I can rustle up on short notice.'

'You've done us proud,' I tell her.

Then we take our seats for the first meal Jack and I have shared. It's not Romanoff's or Villa Nova. There's no plush carpet or crisp linen napkins. No maître d' or à la carte menu. Just a gingham cloth and homecooked food.

And I don't want to be anywhere else.

## 27

While we eat, Jack tells me about growing up on a farm in Oregon. His dad was a big reader and as a family, they read plays together in an evening. Everything from Shakespeare to Chekhov. Whenever he got the chance, which wasn't often in rural Oregon, he went to the theatre. He talks about the Federal Theatre Project coming to town and how seeing plays performed brought the words alive.

He shrugs as he talks about making things and how he didn't realise it was a talent. It was only when he was at college on the GI Bill and got involved with student theatre that he realised it could be useful. Soon he was making props and sets for all of the college productions. He talks about his first job at the Pasadena Playhouse and it's obvious theatre is his first love.

I tell him about Muffin and the funny things she does. I mention Rita, Ginny and the camera club. I don't talk about Rex. If Jack notices the omission, he's too polite to mention it.

Anya brings tinned peaches and fruit cake for pudding. She's left the cheese so I add a thin slice and lay it on the cake.

'This is how we eat it in Yorkshire,' I say as I take a bite. The sharpness of the cheese is delicious against the richness of the dried fruit.

'You don't talk about it much.' Jack raises an eyebrow as his steady gaze meets mine.

Usually, I'd make a joke, say, *There's not much to tell*, and turn the conversation in a different direction. Instinctively, I clamp my arms together to make a barrier. He must see the movement as he pulls back slightly, my barrier making his own go up. I make myself stop, take a breath. I want Jack to know me. That means I have to tell him about the past.

'Home wasn't very happy.' I return the cake to my plate. I can't eat and talk about this. 'Father's a Methodist minister. He preaches Christian charity and forgiveness but there was none of that at home. He has a ghastly temper. We'd tiptoe around him, not knowing when he'd flare up next.' This is what I've done with Rex too but I don't want to think about him now. This evening is a gift and I don't want to spoil it by worrying.

'Father has very strict views on how girls should behave,' I continue. 'He wanted me docile and dutiful, ready for my future of marriage and motherhood.' I can't meet Jack's gaze. Instead, I trace the pattern of the gingham cloth with my index finger. 'He hated my interest in photography. Wholly unladylike in his view. I told you he sent me to secretarial college as soon as I'd got my school certificate.' I laugh briefly. 'If he'd had any idea that would lead me to marry a movie star, he might have acted differently.'

'I'm guessing he doesn't approve of movies either?'

'He thinks Hollywood is a den of iniquity and hopes God will smite it like Sodom and Gomorrah.'

Jack nods slowly as if he's considering and then, when his gaze meets mine, there's a twinkle of amusement in it. 'Sounds like he's met Dirk Stone and Harry King.'

The words are so unexpected that I laugh. 'Dirk's not that bad!'

'He is.' There's an emphasis to the words that I don't understand. I'm about to ask when he adds, 'You're not defending Harry?'

'Oh, Harry King's as black as they come! You need to count your fingers after shaking hands with him.'

'I'll remember that next time I'm summoned to see Mr King.' Jack grins fleetingly. 'What happened with your dad?'

'Esther joined the Land Girls when she turned seventeen. Once she left, Father and I rowed all the time. I had a friend, Freddie, I told you about him. Father didn't want me to see Freddie. The worst rows were always about that.' My hands curl into fists as the memories return. The smell of pipe smoke, the cold grip of fear, the sting of Father's hand as he hit me. My heart rate kicks up and I press my hand against my chest.

'Are you all right?' Jack asks softly. 'You don't have to talk about it if it upsets you.'

'It takes me back, that's all.' I attempt a smile but it's pretty weak.

'What about your mom? You've not mentioned her.'

'Mum was always in the background. For a long time, I was angry with her for never standing up for me but,' tears prickle behind my eyes as a lump forms in my throat, 'I understand that better now. Marriage can put a woman in a terrible position. Mum did her best.

'When I was seventeen, I left home.' I pick at the cake that's still on my plate. 'I didn't plan to. It was all down to Freddie.'

I tell him about the house in Camden, about what Freddie said to me. 'I felt such an idiot. I'd run after Freddie believing we'd be together and then he didn't want anything to do with me.'

'It sounds to me as if he'd already made his decision,' Jack says. 'He should have told you how he felt about Michael.'

'But he couldn't tell me the truth.' My hands jerk outwards. 'Homosexuality isn't talked about to girls. I knew next to nothing about it growing up.'

'Which is wrong in itself but we can't put the whole world to rights.' Jack looks me straight in the eye. 'But Freddie didn't have to let you believe you'd get married. He certainly could have been kinder when you landed on his doorstep. You'd stood up to your dad and walked out of home because you cared about him and then Freddie kicked you out because he didn't need you any more. What kind of friend is that?'

I stare at him. Because I wouldn't break Freddie's secret, I've not even told Esther the truth of what happened between us. My silence has weighed on me and then I added the weight of Rex's secrets too. There's no wonder I've felt choked by all I cannot say. But with Jack, that burden is lifted.

'He said some terrible things to me that day.' My voice comes out as barely a whisper. 'Things that have haunted me.'

Jack leans an elbow on the table and rests his hand on it. 'No friend does that,' he says firmly. 'Freddie was older than you. He led you on and that's not fair. Maybe he got his comeuppance by being left with a bunch of old Commies. Either way, you deserve better than that, Audrey.'

There's sincerity in his words and in his beautiful, grey eyes. He keeps saying that about me: I deserve better.

Do I? I've believed Father and Freddie's words for so long. Of course, I did everything I could to prove them wrong, right down to marrying Rex. Yet nothing stopped those words from echoing within me.

My gaze rises to meet Jack's. 'Why do you keep saying that?'

He stares at me for a painfully long moment, his head tilted to one side. It takes everything I've got not to look away, to allow myself to be seen by that searching case. 'You asked me something like that at the Biltmore.'

The overheated room comes back to me, the buzz of conversation, the too-sweet fruit punch. 'You told me you liked me and asked me why that was hard to understand,' I say slowly.

'That stands.' Jack smiles briefly and then raises his eyebrows. 'So why *is* it hard to understand?'

I close my eyes for a second. I have to find the strength to tell him the truth. Anything else ends this connection between us as if a blade has cut through it.

I have never put any of this into words. I don't know if I can now but I have to try. I take a deep breath, lay my hands flat on the table and say without looking at Jack, 'Father used to hit me when I didn't do as he said. There were other punishments too. Bible study, being sent to my room without tea, not being allowed a fire.' There's a sharp intake of breath from Jack but he doesn't interrupt. 'Somewhere along the line, I absorbed all the things he said about me. Including that I'm a hopeless dreamer who'd never make anything of her life. That's why I stayed in London in '47. Because I couldn't go home and admit I'd failed.' I look up and see Jack's eyes are shining with understanding. 'Freddie told me I was too naïve to survive in London and my dreams of Hollywood were childish. Those dreams were the only thing that kept me going living at home. Freddie knew that and I was so angry with him that I told him I would come to Hollywood and be a success and,' my voice goes very quiet as I say the final words, 'marry a movie star.'

Hot tears of shame prickle behind my eyes as it suddenly sounds really stupid. Proving your father and lost best friend wrong is a terrible reason for getting married. But there's more to it than that. The worries about the INS and my visa. The urge to help Rex to make up for failing Freddie.

But deep down, I had to show Father and Freddie that they were wrong. And I did but it all turned to dust. My marriage was always a sham but now it's utterly hollow. Even the reason why we got married doesn't exist any more if Rex is going to be open about his relationship with Tony.

I wrap my arms across my chest. Talking about the past makes me feel wretchedly vulnerable. Instinctively, I know I can trust Jack with what I've just told him but it doesn't make me feel any less like I've just turned myself inside out and all of my secrets are now written across my skin.

'Do you know what I see?' Jack says softly. 'I see a woman who was strong enough to get herself out of a lousy situation at home, brave enough to follow her dreams and once she'd got here, had enough determination to make a new life for herself.'

I look down at my hands. 'I didn't do anything special.'

'Yes, you did,' Jack says, taking my hand. 'There's nothing wrong with dreaming of a better life. Millions of people in this country are here because they did just that.'

'The American Dream,' I say softly.

'Exactly. That's what brought my grandparents here too. But you did it entirely on your own, Audrey. You came over here, you've made a new life for yourself and that takes guts.'

His skin is a little cold, the callouses rough against my palm. Jack wouldn't lie to me. He's not a silver-tongued charmer as so many in the movie business are.

'Is that really what you think?' I ask.

He shrugs as if to say 'of course' and that makes me smile because with Jack, it is that straightforward. He wouldn't say it unless he believed it.

'It seems to me,' he says, looking at our linked hands, 'that some folks, like me, are lucky enough to be born into a family that is there for them, who love 'em as they need to be loved. But other folks, like you, for whatever reason don't get that and you have to find the place and the people where you fit. That can be quite a journey and sometimes, there are mistakes along the way because no one gets a roadmap of how to find the place and the people that are home to them.' He raises his head and when his gaze meets mine, there's an intensity to it that I've never seen before. 'I guess what I'm saying is I'm never going to be thrilled you married a movie star but I understand why you did it.'

The vulnerability is still swooshing about, making my insides feel queasy, but there's something else now. A thrill of recognition, of being seen and accepted that is making my heart lift in a way that's completely new to me.

'I love Los Angeles,' I say, squeezing his hand. 'I have friends who are as close as family. But I don't have a home. Rex's house isn't that. It never has been.'

Sadness passes over Jack's face. 'It sounds to me that you've never really had a place to call home. Not if home is the place where you can truly be yourself.'

My eyes feel hot with tears. He's right. He's absolutely right and how unutterably sad is that? Only when I lived alone in my little flat in Fairfax Avenue could I truly be myself when I shut the front door behind me. Back home in Sheffield and living with Rex, I've had to pretend to be someone else, making myself smaller to try to please them.

No wonder I struggle to value myself when I spend far too much time shrinking to fit the role I've been given. If only I'd known that movie star's wife isn't all that different to minister's daughter. I am still expected to be seen and not heard, to quash my own thoughts and feelings for those of the man in my life.

I can't go back to living like that. I won't go on sweeping all of these messy, unsettling emotions back under the proverbial carpet. That's what my parents brought me up to do. To maintain appearances, to never let anyone see my emotions. I ran all the way to Hollywood and I've ended up doing exactly what I was brought up to do. I've stood by my husband as he's been reckless, thoughtless and selfish, exactly as Mum always stood by Father regardless of what he did. I always promised myself I wouldn't end up like Mum, yet I have.

There has to be a better way. There has to be a life where women can speak up when they're unhappy. Where maintaining appearances doesn't result in men's bad behaviour going unpunished. Where marriages can end if they're hurting the people in them.

If I want a home that's really a home then I have to divorce Rex.

I feel a roil of emotions as I make the decision. Fear, trepidation, anxiety are all swirling around but above that is glowing sense that I'm doing the right thing. Father views divorce as sinful but I believe it's a worse sin for two people who no longer get on to be locked together in lonely matrimony.

'What are you thinking?' Jack raises an eyebrow.

'I've made a decision.' There's a lifting in my chest as if the worries are releasing. 'I'm leaving Rex.'

'Well, hallelujah for that!' He grins widely before chinking his almost empty glass against mine. 'I'll drink to that.'

## 28

Jack's reaction makes me smile. There's something wonderfully straightforward about him and, after tiptoeing around Rex's moods for over a year, it's very refreshing.

Once we've emptied our whisky glasses, Jack adds wood to the fire which makes it snap and crackle again. I move the oil lamp over to the coffee table. As he sits beside me, the lamp's gentle light casts a halo of illumination between us.

There's a long pause with only the crackle of the fire and the wind moaning down the chimney. The silence that settles between us has an easiness to it which I've only felt with Freddie before.

'Okay, I understand why you married Rex,' Jack says, breaking into my thoughts. 'But I'd just told you how much I liked you. Did that not figure in this at all?'

'Be fair, Jack. I'd only met you three times.' I stare down at my gold wedding band and diamond engagement ring that have no meaning when your husband loves someone else. 'The truth is, I was mortified that you knew about Rex. I felt like such a blinking idiot. For a long time, I didn't want to see you. I couldn't bear the pity, you see.'

Jack colours. It's the first time his emotions are written on his skin. It strips him back a layer as if I'm seeing more of the man he really is.

'That's on me. If I'd not been as blunt.' He looks down and winces. 'Astrid says I came back from the war determined to speak the truth and damn the consequences. I'm sorry if that's what I did that night.'

I could accept the apology and move on but there's more here. I want to know this man. More than I've ever wanted to know anyone else.

'What happened to make the truth so important?'

'I lost a buddy.' He gestures. 'Actually, I lost dozens. That's the trouble with bombers. If a plane goes down, the whole crew are gone. Eight young lives snuffed out in an instant.' He grimaces and then gets up and walks to the fire. He adds another log and then turns back to me. 'It was Syd's death that hit me hardest. We met in training. He was from Seattle. He was a winger for his local ice hockey team and loved Glenn Miller and the Seattle Rainiers. We were deployed together. It was Syd I went to Matlock with. You remember me telling you about that?'

'Of course.' It's over a year but the conversation is crystal bright in my memory.

'In March '44, his plane was shot down over Germany. It hit me like a truck. I couldn't believe he'd gone. I went AWOL for two nights. I just couldn't bear to go back to base and Syd not be there. I should have been in big trouble but my Colonel took pity on me. He knew I'd not go off the rails if there wasn't good reason. Later, Betty, one of the WAAFs we used to meet up with, came to see me. She was as broken down as I was.' Jack runs his hand through his hair. 'You see, she'd been in love with Syd and I knew Syd had been in love with her. Neither of them had said anything.' He takes a gulp of air and I can feel how close the memories are. I reach out and take his hand. He smiles at me, gratefully but a little shamefaced at showing emotion.

'It was such a waste. They'd missed out on happiness. I hated that Syd died never knowing how she felt. I told myself I'd never make that mistake. That if I liked someone, I'd speak up.'

I nod slowly; too many people I knew lost loved ones during the war. I saw how grief burned them up, how heartbreak altered them. 'War changes you. I saw my home city pretty much destroyed. I was eleven during the Sheffield Blitz. I still have nightmares about it. It's one of the reasons I was so close to Freddie. He was in the shelter with us. He read *The Wizard of Oz* to me by torchlight the whole time.'

'Were you scared?' Jack puts his other hand on the top of mine.

'Terrified. Father was an ARP warden. He was out in it. I thought I'd never see him again.' I smile a little weakly and blink back tears. 'I loved him, you see. Even when I was fighting with him, I always wanted him to love me back.'

Jack smiles at me sadly. Then he shifts to stare into the fire. For a moment, the flames are reflected in his glasses.

When he turns back to me, his eyes are soft. 'As I recall, you owe me a dance.'

A flutter starts in my chest. 'I do.' I take his hand. 'I'm not sure what we're going to do for music.'

Jack's arm comes round me, holding me as people do for the last dance of the evening.

'I'm sure we'll manage,' he says. He starts to whistle 'Moonlight Serenade' and we gently sway, our bodies pressed together, only moving from foot to foot.

'Syd would approve,' he breaks off to whisper against my hair. 'He loved Glenn Miller.'

Jack starts whistling again and I rest my head on his chest, letting the familiar tune wash over me. Finally, I'm in his arms and it feels wonderful. I think of Syd and Betty and my heart aches for them. To love like that and never know the other felt the same. To never feel the joy of holding, touching, kissing.

The wind moans down the chimney; a log cracks on the fire. Jack holds me closer; his cheek rests on my hair. I glance up at him and he smiles down at me. 'Seeing as you're going to divorce that low-down rat you're married to...'

'Don't talk about him,' I murmur.

He strokes a stray hair away from my forehead. 'May I kiss you?'

I have waited so long for this. 'Yes!'

He smiles at how eager I sound. Our eyes lock for a long moment before his lips meet mine. He's achingly gentle. Yet it's as if a thousand volts of electricity have gone through me. My lips open. The kiss deepens. Something inside me cracks and I'm flooded with sensation. My whole body feels alive, rooted and yet fluid, tethered to this man but dissolving into sheer pleasure.

'Audrey?' Jack pulls away and looks at me.

I rest my hand against his face, cradling it as Rex cradled Tony's this morning. Finally, I'm experiencing a moment of such aching tenderness. 'Don't stop,' I say.

He trails kisses up my neck. I tip my head back and gasp as the feeling goes straight to my belly. There's a pulse of fire inside of me. He kisses me again and it sinks lower. I've never felt like this before. I want him. The desire is overwhelming, blurring my senses. All I know is Jack. All I ever want to know is Jack. Nothing else matters. I'm falling into him and it feels like flying. I cling to him, holding on as he takes me higher and higher.

\* \* \*

Later, we're in my bed and my head rests on his chest. His dark chest hair tickles my cheek but I don't care. I'm dazed and languid. Why didn't anyone tell me that's what *It* was like? Esther could have spilled the beans. Isn't that what older sisters are for? Now I understand why people do crazy things for love. I may never be sane again after this night with Jack.

He folds his hand around mine. 'Why didn't you tell me it was your first time?'

I blush, which is ridiculous after all we've done together. I duck my head against his chest to hide my hot cheeks. Then a horrible thought hits me. It seemed wonderful to me but perhaps I didn't do something I should have. I lift my head to look at him. 'Did I do something wrong?'

'No.' He chuckles deep in his chest. 'You were perfect.'

'Oh, that's a relief. I didn't want to...' I trail off because I don't have the words to talk about it. 'It's embarrassing to have been married over a year and never have done,' I gesture at the bed and him in it, 'this.'

He brushes a kiss over my hair. 'You'll have to make up for lost time then.'

I giggle. Those are difficult thoughts I'll have to deal with when the morning comes and we're forced to get out of this bed. But this unexpected and wonderful night has taught me one thing. I'm never living without this pleasure and delight again. Not for anyone and certainly not for Rex. 'If I'd known what I was missing out on, I'd *never* have agreed to marry Rex.'

Jack's arm tightens around me. 'I'm very pleased to hear that.' A long moment later, he adds, his breath soft against my ear, 'The wind's dying down.'

Now he's pointed it out, I can hear he's right. The restless moaning has gone, the wind has stopped buffeting the walls.

'I wish we could stay here forever.'

'In this bed?' Jack chuckles softly. 'Anya and Eric might have something to say about that.'

'Maybe if we explain that I've got a lot of lost time to make up for?'

He chuckles again. It's a delightful sound that comes from deep in his chest. 'Then we'd better get started,' he says.

**29**

We're woken by a particularly persistent cockerel.

Jack grins at me. 'Like being back on the farm,' he says as he gets out of bed.

It's not yet light and I have ten more luxurious minutes in the warm bed, enjoying the new and delightful sensations in my body. I get up as the light changes. It's the peculiarly intense glow which signals there is snow on the ground. I draw the tartan curtains to see a winter wonderland outside. Snow blankets the ground, creating mysterious mounds and gullies. Pine trees, draped in white, cluster around the cabin. In the distance are the mountains, imperious in their stark beauty.

I go downstairs to the sitting room which, without a fire, is very chilly indeed. Jack is outside helping Eric and Bruce clear the snow. For a moment, I stand at the window and watch him. Even under his bulky coat, I can see the power in his muscles and the strength in his arms. Arms that held me all night.

A blush streaks up my cheeks. I press my cold hands against them. I'm going to have to do a lot better than this or the entire world will guess what happened! However much I want to shout it from the rooftops, I need to keep it quiet until I've spoken to Rex.

There's a smell of frying bacon creeping into the room that's impossible to ignore. I locate the kitchen, where the range gives off a steady heat. Anya has a frying pan on the hotplate and is beating a batter mix for pancakes. When I offer to help, she hands me an apron and sets me to frying eggs. 'They'll be ravenous when they come in,' she says. 'Shovelling snow is heavy work.'

There's an unexpected joy in preparing food for Jack to eat. As the bacon crackles and spits, I imagine myself in a bright-yellow kitchen with Formica worktops cooking dinner for Jack. I'll be wearing a pretty, yellow apron and he'll kiss me as soon as he comes through the door and—

Then I shake my head. It's *far* too soon to be imagining things like that. No matter what happened last night, I'm not going to make the same mistake again. With Jack, I'm going to take things slow. Get to know him properly. Find out who he really is. Not who I imagine he is. This time, I'm going to be sensible. Dreams and fancies have only ever got me into trouble anyway.

Trouble I've got to face when we get back to Lake Louise. My stomach lurches at the thought.

I've made my decision. Now I've got to tell my husband.

\* \* \*

It's nearly one o'clock by the time we get back to Lake Louise. We had to wait for the snow plough to clear the road to Castle Junction and confirmation the highway was open.

The lake is coated in freshly fallen snow which glitters in the sunlight. The mountains feel closer, as if you could reach out and touch them.

Jack carries my parcels into the hotel for me.

'I've got to get to set,' he says as we wait by the lifts. By unspoken consent, we're keeping our distance. 'They're filming a fight scene and gubbins always get broken.'

'That's okay.' The urge to touch him is so strong, it makes my fingertips itch. 'I'm going to have a bath and then wait for Rex to get back.'

Jack frowns, creating deep score marks between his eyebrows. 'I hate you doing this.'

'I know.' We talked about it earlier. Jack volunteered to be with me when I told Rex, and although I'd love to have his steady, comforting presence, I got myself into this and I have to get myself out. 'I'll be all right.'

'Will you ring me? After you've—'

He doesn't need to finish the sentence.

'Of course.' The thought of what I'll say fills my stomach with lead.

Jack nods. 'Okay.' He glances around the wide reception area. There are only the girls behind the desk and they're busy discussing something in one of the ledgers. He drops a swift kiss on my cheek, his lips warm against my chilled skin. Then he's gone, heading towards the revolving doors that lead outside.

The lift dings as it arrives. I suck in a deep breath, hoist my parcels into my arms and step inside.

\* \* \*

'You're back then,' Rex says as he enters the suite that evening. He's peeling off layers of clothing as he speaks. 'Paul said there was a tree down on the road to Banff. Caused no end of trouble with the caterers as they come up every day. They had to bed down in the ballroom and then the food's been terrible all day as they'd only got leftovers to serve up. Christ, I'm starving!'

As I listen to this, my eyebrows rise. I shouldn't be surprised. After a year of marriage, I know Rex can bring any situation back to himself.

'We need to talk.' I say the words firmly but calmly which is good going as inside, I'm a mass of trepidation.

'Not again!' Rex rolls his eyes. 'I need my dinner.'

'It won't take long.' At least I hope it won't. I push a packet of crisps across the coffee table towards him. 'These should keep you going.'

He rips them open and grabs a handful which he shoves into his mouth. As he eats, I pour him a glass of bourbon. The siphon hisses as I get a glass of tonic water for me. I have to keep a clear head.

'What is it this time then?' Rex knocks back half of his bourbon.

I take a breath. There's no point hedging around it. I've got to come straight out with it. 'I want a divorce.'

The words land with an almost audible thud. I tense as I watch Rex's face change. The frown deepens to a scowl. My hands tighten on the arms of my chair. I'm poised for flight if it's needed.

'You can't,' he says flatly.

Does he mean I can't want one or I can't have one? I decide on the former. 'Rex, I can't do this any longer.' I sound enormously weary. 'And you don't want me around. You'll be much happier when I'm gone. Who knows, maybe you'll even drink less.'

'I only drink because I'm miserable.' He folds his arms and glowers at me. 'You don't know what it's like. Having to hide who I am all the time.'

'Then stop.' I thought long and hard about this as I walked

around the lake this afternoon. There is another option for Rex. He won't like it. He almost undoubtedly won't take it. It feels almost outrageous to suggest it but I'm the only person who can. Dirk and all the yes men who surround him certainly won't.

He jerks upright and stares at me. 'I can't. The studio. The press. Fucking *Eyewitness*. They're all out to get me.'

'Then get out.' I lean forward, my eyes fixed on his. 'Leave Hollywood. You told me at Romanoff's that you want to live in Italy. You and Tony could do that. In Italy, you could have a life together that's not about hiding and lying all the time.'

I see Rex close down as I'm speaking. He shakes his head as if he's trying to dislodge the words. 'I can't move to fucking Italy. That's just a pipedream.'

I slump back in my seat. 'Or you can stay in Hollywood and be forced to hide for the rest of your life.'

Rex's brows draw together as his chin comes up. 'That's just the way it is for people like me. You're just saying that so you can get a divorce—'

'I'm not!' I stare at him as if that will make him hear the truth in my words. 'It's obvious to me that Tony makes you happy. It's equally obvious that living without him makes you drink to forget how unhappy you are. Isn't it worth thinking about a life where you two could be together?'

He folds his arms and turns away from me. 'I'm not leaving Hollywood.'

'Fine.' I fold mine too. My stomach feels like rocks have settled in it. 'But I'm leaving you.'

'You can't.' He darts a gaze at me. 'I need you.'

'You need a doll you can wheel out to go to parties and premieres with you.' I raise my hand to stop him interrupting. 'Someone who looks the part and keeps the rumours at bay.'

He suddenly sprawls out in his chair. Due to his height, his legs almost reach mine. I hurriedly tuck my feet to the side. 'You've done that all right.' His lip curls in a sneer. 'Shame you're such a bitch to live with!'

The word is a slap in the face. I stiffen. It feels like all of the blood rushes from my head. I grip the seat arm and will myself not to shrink. Father made me feel small. At the end, Freddie did too. Rex has played the same game and always before it's made me fall into line. But I'm not going to let it happen again. I deserve better. Jack's made me see that. I deserve happiness and I'm never going to get it if I stay with Rex.

'Then you won't miss me when I'm gone.' My voice shakes on the last word. 'I don't want anything but my freedom. I'm not asking for money. I'll take nothing but Muffin, my clothes and the jewellery you gave me.'

'You say that,' Rex pushes himself up to standing and stomps across the room to the drinks tray, 'but what wife leaves without alimony? You must think I'm a fucking fool!'

'Money isn't everything.' My voice snaps with anger. 'All I want is my freedom. If you won't give it to me, I'll...' I cast around for something I can bargain with. I don't want to destroy him. He's weak and selfish but I won't see him hounded out of Hollywood for loving other men. What else can I use to persuade him?

Then I remember what he said forty-eight hours ago when we last talked in this room.

'I'll tell Tony what you and Dirk did to ruin Ida's career.' I lean forward, my chin jutting. 'How's Tony going to feel when he finds out you helped destroy his beloved sister's life?'

'You fucking bitch!' Rex spits the word across the table at me.

For a second, I quake. It's like fighting with Father all over again. I grip the edge of the sofa and summon up Jack's face: his quiet smile, his beautiful, grey eyes.

I swallow hard before I say, 'It's up to you, Rex. Let me go or the man you love finds out how low you'll sink to protect your career.'

'Get the hell out of here then!' He knocks back the rest of his bourbon and stands. 'I don't want to see you when I get back.'

'That's fine.' I stand too as I hate him looming over me. 'I'm already packed.'

'I'll tell the world it's your fault!' he yells as he heads for the door. 'That you're impossible to live with. That you're a nag who bosses me and I can't take it any more.'

I sigh out a long breath. If that's the price of freedom then I'll take it. The people who matter to me won't believe it. 'Tell them what you like.'

'You'll never get another job in Hollywood. No one who's anyone will want to know you.'

'Rex.' I sink back into my seat. 'I don't care.'

He turns to me with his hand on the door handle and then he stills. 'Promise you won't tell anyone.'

I sigh because it shouldn't even be necessary to ask. 'I've kept your secrets this long. I'm not going to start blabbing now.'

He nods as if that settles it and I guess it does for him. 'We won't meet again.' There's a heavy pause as if he thinks that will make me change my mind. 'My lawyers will deal with everything.'

I feel absolutely wrung out. 'Very well. Cheerio, Rex.'

He doesn't reply. The door slams shut behind him. I shudder and then I burst into noisy, painful tears. I curl up on myself, hugging my middle. I wish Muffin were here, nudging me with her wet nose. I can't wish for Jack. Not yet. First, I have to cry for the life I thought I'd lead when I married Rex. Cry for the hopeless dreamer I was when I married him.

It takes a long time. Tears are blotted by my collar, soak into my jumper. My heart aches for the mistakes I've made, for the broken trust, for the months of painfully empty married life.

My eyes are red raw when I finally sit up. I haul in a deep breath. It's over. I did it. There's a lot to sort out but at the end of it, I'll be free to start again.

I have to ring Jack. As I pick up the receiver, I catch sight of my left hand. I tug at the wedding and engagement rings, yanking them painfully past my knuckles. My hand feels lighter as I take them off. A tiny crack of hope is let into my heart.

## 30

'Did you sleep?' Jack asks the following morning, taking my hand. His glasses are smudged, his hair looks just as it does when he tumbles out of bed and he needs a shave but he looks absolutely glorious to me.

We're in a storeroom behind the hotel which he's using part of to store props. On one side are stacks of tables and chairs, and on the other are wooden crates containing champagne bottles, a lethal-looking pickaxe and a selection of strangely glossy fruit. The place smells strongly of detergent and wood chippings.

'Not really.' I yawn behind my hand, my breath creating a white plume. I still feel jagged from the confrontation with Rex. And I've got to get back to Los Angeles, the list of things that needs doing stretches terrifyingly ahead of me.

Tempting though it was to spend another night with Jack, we couldn't risk it in this hothouse of a hotel where gossip runs rife. The receptionist didn't ask any questions when I requested a single room for the night. She also booked me onto the ten thirty flight to Los Angeles. Bruce will pick me up in half an hour to take me to Calgary airport. I left my cases in reception and crept out in the half-light before dawn to meet Jack. 'Did you?'

He shakes his head. 'I couldn't stop thinking about you.' He reaches into the pocket of his plaid jacket and takes out an envelope which he hands to me. 'I wrote this in the end.' It's got my name on the front in tiny, crabbed writing.

'Thank you.' I turn it over. Should I open it now? Or would that be—

'Open it later. On the plane or when you get home.' He runs his hand through his hair as I'm learning he does when he's struggling to find the right words. 'I wanted you to have something to remind you that this wasn't all just a crazy dream.'

I laugh at that, take a step closer to him. 'I know quite a lot about crazy dreams. I chased one all the way across the Atlantic.' I rest my forehead on his chest. 'You're not a dream, Jack Sorenson. You're 100 per cent real and 100 per cent wonderful.' My arms come round him. Instantly, he's hugging me back, holding me tight against his body.

I sigh out a long breath. This is what I needed last night. This is what I yearned for in my narrow single bed as I tossed and turned, worrying about all of the things that need doing to unravel my life from Rex's.

He chuckles gently. 'You won't say that when you know me better. I've got all sorts of annoying habits, you know.'

It's a reminder that we barely know each other. Circumstances have propelled us past the normal stages of a relationship. That was the other thing I worried about when I couldn't sleep. Will I discover he's just as flawed as Rex when I really get to know him?

I pull back as a thought hits me and I can't stop myself from blurting out the question. 'You don't drink, do you?'

He blinks behind his glasses, his eyes soft with understanding. 'I like a beer sometimes, and you know, I don't say no to a whisky on a cold night.' He pulls me back to him and cradles the back of my head. 'But you don't need to worry about that.'

'I seem to be worried about everything,' I murmur against his jacket. 'Leaving Rex is going to be a lot more complicated than marrying him was.'

Jack raises his head and looks down at me. 'You need a good lawyer. Someone out of the Hollywood set who doesn't drink with Dirk or Harry at the Beverly Hills Country Club.'

He's reminding me that Hollywood is a small town with too many allegiances that run beneath the surface. 'I'll ask Ginny. Her father's a partner in a law firm in Pasadena. I need someone who understands immigration too.' Because that's the other thing that kept me awake. 'I need to find out what happens to my Green Card after I divorce Rex. I'm still worried that if the INS find out about Freddie, they'll think I'm a subversive.'

Jack frowns. 'I'd love to be able say you were worrying about nothing but these are crazy times.'

Unexpectedly, it's reassuring that he doesn't dismiss my fears. It makes me feel that he treats me as a grown woman capable of dealing with anxieties. Not a child to be coddled and controlled.

I look him straight in the eye as I say, 'I *really* don't want to be sent home.'

Jack tugs my tea cosy hat off and runs his hand over my hair. 'If I can speak on behalf of the United States of America, I think that would be a terrible waste. Why should Great Britain get to keep the delightful...' he kisses me, soft as a butterfly's wing '... delicious...' another kiss with a little more edge this time '... Audrey Wade...' a deeper kiss '...when she's needed here?'

'Needed?' I manage to whisper. My head is spinning, my legs starting to feel a little weak. I want to pull him even closer, kiss him even deeper and do all of the things we did in the snow-covered cabin.

'Don't doubt that,' Jack says against my hair.

After that, we don't speak for quite some time. Only the fact that I've a plane to catch forces to me to pull away. I rest my forehead against Jack's as he rebuttons my jacket.

'Write to me,' he says. 'Let me know you get back to LA okay.'

His concern warms me. It's been such a long time since anyone cared in that way.

'I have a roommate, Rick. I think you'll like him,' Jack adds before dropping a kiss on my cold nose. 'Come over when I'm back. I'll introduce you.'

I smile up at him. 'That sounds wonderful.'

It's not just an invitation but a promise. We *will* be part of each other's lives. I imagine me meeting Rick, laughing with him and Jack in their yard. Introducing him to Ginny and Rita. And Muffin, of course.

As I step away from the warmth of his body, I add, 'Do you like dogs?'

It's going to be a major problem if he doesn't because Muffin and I are a team.

But Jack grins. 'Love them.'

## 31

I don't like the noise of aeroplanes. The constant thrum makes me anxious. I wish Jack was with me. I'd give a lot for a hand to hold. But I'll settle for reading the words he wrote when he couldn't sleep last night.

There's no one in the seat next to me. Two businessmen chat across the aisle. The stewardess in her natty blue uniform offers them coffee. I've already got mine. As I wait for it to cool, I take the letter from my handbag and rip the envelope open.

*Dearest (because that's how I think of you) Audrey,*

*You'll never know how much I regretted not asking you on a date when I bumped into you in the commissary at Crown. Maybe we could have spared ourselves a whole load of heartache because I knew even in those few short moments outside the Chinese Theatre, you were pretty damned special. I wish I'd taken you dancing, to the movies, introduced you to my friends and my folks. In short, done it properly because that's what you deserve.*

*I should have said this in the cabin but I guess there were*

*other things on my mind. (Don't blame me for that, I'm only
human and I have longed to kiss you for months!) Audrey, I'm in
love with you. If you need time to get over your marriage that's
fine, I'll wait as long as it takes. Just know there'll be a welcome
for you when you're ready at 310 Brockmont Drive, Glendale.*

    *Love Jack x.*

Oh, my goodness! I press my hands against my heart which is
beating very erratically. He's in love with me? I want to cry and
laugh and wave the letter for everyone on the plane to see and
then quickstep down the aisle.

I read the letter again, slower this time, savouring each word.
My heart is glowing that much, I wonder the other passengers
aren't pointing at the great pulsing orb in my chest. The second
time, I spot that at the bottom it says *P.T.O.*

I turn the page and there's a list headed:

*Things you don't know about me yet*

I grin. I imagine him sitting in bed writing this as last night
dragged its heels towards sunrise. They're the questions you
might ask on a first or second date when you're getting to know
each other. The questions we've skipped past entirely in our
topsy-turvy love affair.

I take a sip of coffee and start to read.

1. *Favourite Book – To anyone else I'd say* Dubliners *by
   James Joyce but the truth is it's* The Hardy Boys Mystery
   of Cabin Island
2. *Favourite Movie –* Citizen Kane *(a work of genius and if you
   don't agree with me be prepared to argue your case)*

3. *Favourite Meal – Isterband (It's Swedish. Pork sausages and creamed potatoes. Grandma Ingrid makes the best I've ever tasted)*

4. *Earliest memory – riding in the green tractor with Dad. I was four. This was the first time I was allowed to ride in one. Blew my mind!*

5. *Music (can't get this down to only one favourite) – Blues – Howlin' Wolf and Muddy Waters. Folk – Woody Guthrie and The Weavers. Country – Hank Williams and The Carter Family*

6. *Politics – Democrat*

7. *Biggest Fear – Ever having to get in a Liberator bomber again*

8. *Dream job – Props Master*

9. *Hobbies – listening to music, reading, playing the guitar (badly), skiing, basketball*

10. *Best way to spend a weekend – (with you? Or is it too soon to say that?) Okay, then drinking coffee, playing records, reading, up at Big Pines for the snow in the winter, on the beach in the summer*

I grin at the 'with you' comment. I don't think it's too soon. Not after our night together. His way of spending a weekend sounds wonderful.

I run my finger down the list again. It's endearing that he's confessed the Hardy Boys is his favourite book. Mine is *The Wizard of Oz* and I feel just fine about admitting it now. I've seen *Citizen Kane* and it is good. It'll be fun to debate with him what makes a truly great movie. For me, it's got to leave you feeling happier than you were when you went into the cinema, which is why *Citizen Kane* will never be my favourite. His musical tastes are very different to mine. I've heard of Hank Williams but not the others.

Is this what the start of a relationship should feel like? The thrill of finding out where we're alike and where we're different? An effervescent bubble of excitement as if I've been drinking champagne whenever I think of him? I've never felt like this before. Is that a sign it *is* love?

I shake my head. I promised myself I wouldn't rush in. Jack's told me to take my time. I mustn't let my past unhappiness propel me too quickly into being with Jack. He's always telling me I deserve better than life has thrown at me so far. Well, what he deserves is a woman who's free and ready to be with him. Not one who's all tangled up in the end of her marriage.

Until then, there's letters. As he's just proved, you can say a lot in a letter. With over two hours to go until we land in Los Angeles, I've plenty of time to write a list to send back.

I rummage in my handbag for some paper and pull out the letter on Dirk Stone Talent Agency headed notepaper which had my outward flight details on it. I rip Dirk's name and the address off, turn the paper over and start writing.

\* \* \*

It's after six when I pull onto Ginny's drive. I've already been to Rita's to pick up Muffin. I told her straight out that I'm leaving Rex and once she'd recovered from the shock, she knocked my socks off by saying I'm welcome to stay with her for as long as I need. Her kindness has left me feeling a little choked. I'm lucky to have such wonderful friends.

Ginny ushers Muffin and me into the sitting room. The lamps are lit, the colours are warm and welcoming. There's a richly patterned rug on the floor and a vase of yellow and white carnations on a side table. It smells of furniture polish and citrus from the huge bowl of fruit on the coffee table.

I take a seat on the sofa and blurt out the news, my hands knotting in my lap as I go through my carefully prepared speech again. She looks absolutely blindsided for about five seconds and then says, 'Is it because of his drinking?'

'No,' I say, not meeting her gaze. 'He's in love with someone else.'

'Jeez, who?'

'No one you know,' I say quickly. 'Someone he met on set.'

'Is this really why you went to Canada?' She crosses her arms on top of her bump. 'Don't kid me, Audrey. I saw *Eyewitness*. It doesn't take much to read between the lines.'

I put my head in my hands as I blow out a long breath. 'I promised him I wouldn't tell.'

'If he's done the dirty on you with Tony Young, you've got every right to shout it from the rafters!' Ginny smooths her maternity smock over her stomach.

I sigh. I know my loyalty is misplaced. 'I don't want to destroy Rex,' I say quietly.

'Then you're a better woman than me. I'd want to scratch his eyes out.'

'I have thought about it,' I admit with a small smile.

'How long have you known Rex was... you know?'

I scrub my hands over my face. She's going to think me an absolute idiot when I confess. 'Since before we married,' I say slowly. Muffin comes over and sniffs my feet. Instinctively, I reach down to stroke her, needing the comfort in her soft, white fur.

'Then why the Sam Hill did you marry him?'

I wince. Ginny knew me back then. She was always telling me to go out with a nice, normal guy, not waste my time dreaming about movie stars.

'Because he was in trouble and I could help and that was pretty heady for a girl like me.' I spread my hands. 'Plus marrying him sorted out my visa worries and got me my Green Card.' I draw breath and shrug a little hopelessly, knowing that what I say next will definitely rile her up. 'Because my father told me not to and I had to prove him wrong.'

'Of all of the darned stupid reasons for getting married!' Ginny gestures in frustration. 'You have to know with every fibre of your being that you can't live without him. That's what marriage takes. That's what gets you through the rocky times, the days he's making you flip your lid, the days you make him flip his lid.'

'I know that now!' My voice rises as tears clog my throat and my eyes start to prickle.

She must see that because her face softens. She nudges me with her elbow as she says, 'Why didn't you tell me you were unhappy?'

'I wanted to!' I blink to clear the tears away. 'I hated keeping secrets from you. But how could I tell you without betraying Rex's secret?'

Ginny's arm comes over my shoulders and she gives me an awkward side by side hug. 'Did no one ever tell you that it's okay to spill the beans to your best friend? Known exception to all secrets.'

I pick up my handbag to search for a handkerchief. 'You're making that up.'

'I'm not.' She grins. 'How else would women take care of each other? Did your mom not tell you?'

I shake my head, saddened by all the secrets Mum kept. 'I don't think anyone told my mum.'

Ginny squeezes my shoulder and then releases me. 'We got to

get you out of this. You need a darned good lawyer. I'll ring Dad. He'll know who can do it.'

'They need to understand the immigration rules too.'

'Shucks, I'd forgotten about that.' Ginny scoots to the edge of the sofa. Then she stops, the expression on her face halfway between a grimace and the happiest of smiles.

'What is it?' I'm instantly behind her, a hand on her arm.

'He kicked.' She presses her hand against the side of her belly.

I smile with her, caught up in her delight. 'That's amazing!' The jealousy is muted now. Leaving Rex changes everything. Now children could be in my future. Hopefully, with Jack, although (as I keep telling myself) it's too soon to be having thoughts like that.

But because it crossed my mind, it prompts me to ask, 'Ginny, how did you know Nate was the one?'

She's gripping the arm of the sofa, ready to lever herself out. She lets go, blinks a couple of times and then folds her hands across her belly as she says, 'It was easy with him from the start. I never had to try to be something for him. I guess you can say being with him was as effortless as being on my own. Not always, mind. We get tired and cranky and fall out like any other couple. But when it's good, that's how it feels.'

I nod slowly. Her words soothe some of the knots in my stomach. Maybe I can trust the way I feel with Jack. Right from the beginning, it felt easy, just as Ginny described.

'Why?' Ginny asks suddenly, her gaze fixed intently on my face. 'Have you met someone?'

'You can't tell anyone but yes. Jack Sorenson.' It's a joy to just say his name. 'Nate knows him. They play basketball together.'

'Wait?' Ginny grips my arm. 'Is he the one you were chatting to under the tree at the wedding?'

I press my hands against my heated cheeks. 'Yes.'

'I saw the two of you together and you looked different. Happier than you've ever done with Rex, that's for sure.'

I glance shyly at her as I add, 'Well, Jack was at Lake Louise too and—'

Ginny looks at me in astonishment. 'Audrey, did you—?'

I nod, biting my lip.

'Start from the beginning.' Her eyes are wide. 'And tell me *everything!*'

## 32

'Mrs Trent.' Trudie hovers by my bedroom door, surveying the organised chaos of boxes and cases that surround me.

I told her on Saturday morning that I'm leaving. There was a long and painful pause, then she nodded once and said, 'Very good, ma'am.' Since then, she's pretty much left me to it, which avoids any more awkwardness between us.

'Yes?'

'Dirk Stone is here to see you.'

Dread settles like a rock in my stomach. 'Did he say why?'

It's Tuesday afternoon. I spent the weekend packing. Yesterday morning, I telephoned the lawyer Ginny's dad recommended and I have an appointment with him tomorrow afternoon in Pasadena.

'Only that it's urgent,' Trudie says.

I sigh heavily and then shake my head. Dirk has been behind everything else in our marriage. I should have guessed Rex would wheel him in now. But if it's a last-ditch attempt to keep us together then he's had a wasted trip.

'Very well.' I look down at my white blouse which is streaked in dust. 'Put him in the dining room. Make him some coffee and tell him I'll be down in two minutes.'

As the door closes behind her, I hastily undo the buttons of my blouse and throw on one of the three which remain hanging in the wardrobe. It's butter-yellow silk with a Peter Pan collar. I smooth the creases from my navy circle skirt, change into matching ballerina pumps and apply lipstick. I nod at my reflection. Ready for battle.

There's a tingling sensation in my chest as I walk down the spiral staircase. I suck in a deep breath, square my shoulders and cross the hall.

'Audrey. Always a pleasure,' Dirk says as I enter the room.

'Don't give me that, Dirk. Why are you here?' I take the seat diagonally opposite him. He's got his briefcase in front of him, lying flat on the table. A cup of coffee by his elbow. He takes his cigarette case from his pocket. 'Mind if I?'

'Yes, I do. Go outside if you want to smoke.'

'Aren't we uppity today?' Dirk shoots me a look which is hard to read and then pops a mint ball in his mouth. 'Rex told me about your little tantrum.'

Cold swirls in my belly. My hands form fists, my nails pressing into my skin. Then I force myself to take a breath. This is what Father used to do. Insult me. Call me names. Until my head spun and I couldn't think straight. 'Call it what you like. I'm still leaving.'

Dirk pushes his briefcase to one side and leans across the table, his hand stretched towards me. 'What would it take to make you stay?'

'Nothing is going to make me—'

'What if we increased your allowance? Say, another hundred bucks a month?'

That's a lot of money. If that was all I cared about, it might be enough. But as I told Rex, money isn't everything. I cross my arms. 'No.'

'How about a vacation? All expenses paid. The Caribbean is nice this time of year. Or Europe. You could visit your family.'

*They really do think I can be bought!* My chin comes up. 'No.'

'You're playing hardball, Audrey.' Dirk grins as if this is all a game. 'Last offer. A house by the beach. Your own place. Rex wouldn't come near. You'd still attend public events with him but other than that, you'd live your own life.' Dirk smiles confidentially at me. 'Within limits, of course.'

Boy, they really must be desperate! But with Dirk, the conditions are just as important as the offer. I can guess what those limits would be. The same old rules which allow men to do what they like, while women remain pure and chaste. I scowl. 'No.'

Dirk sits back in his seat. 'That was the carrot.' He takes two buff-coloured files from his briefcase and tosses them across the table to me. 'These are the stick.'

The cold spirals out from my belly and lands in my chest, making my breath catch. Why didn't I expect them to fight dirty? I worked for Dirk. I know the depths he'll plummet to to get his own way.

'I've done everything that was asked of me,' I say hotly. 'I've been the perfect fake wife. It's Rex who's blown everything by getting together with Tony and not caring who sees them. You cannot honestly expect me to sit quietly here while everyone finds out my husband is in love with another man? Louella and Hedda Hopper will tear me to shreds!'

Dirk picks up his cup. 'Leave me to worry about *Eyewitness* and the gossip queens. Your job is to stand by the man you married.'

There's a clear emphasis on the word job and it makes my jaw tense. 'I'm not your secretary any more. You don't get to order me about.'

'Read the damn files and then tell me that.' Dirk smooths his moustache. 'I'll wait.'

My stomach is a mass of nerves. What has he got up his sleeve? He's calm but intent, like a predator stalking its prey. He thinks he's got the trump card.

Well, whatever it is he can take a running jump! I take a deep breath and open the first file.

There's a photo of Freddie. I gasp at the shock of seeing him again. Then I look at Dirk, my eyes wide. 'Where did you get this?'

'I got you checked out. Last year, before you married Rex. There had to be a reason why you were spooked by that appointment with the INS.'

I'm momentarily lost for words. I stare at him in dumb horror. Then the emotions start to pile up: betrayal, anger, fear.

'How *dare* you?' I spit the words at him.

'I had to be sure you were a good investment.' He shrugs. 'I was only protecting our boy.'

'Investment?' My voice is high. 'Is that all I am to you?'

There's a painful tightness in my chest. I thought he liked me. Respected me even. He told me I was the best secretary he'd ever had. He gave me the watch on my wrist. Did none of that mean anything? I bite down on my bottom lip and blink furiously so he doesn't see I'm close to tears.

'It's nothing personal, kid.' Dirk's sounds entirely reasonable, as if people treat each other like this every day. 'I needed to be sure you weren't a Red. It wasn't going to help Rex any if you turned out to be a subversive now, was it?'

'I trusted you,' I say through the pain in my throat. The words fall like stones. Dirk looks momentarily confused as if it's an emotion he's not familiar with. I swallow hard before adding, 'When I agreed to marry Rex, I thought we were all in on this together. That we were a *team* of sorts.' My voice cracks on the word 'team' and I grip the edge of the table to steady myself. 'How can you turn on me like this just because I want out?'

Dirk doesn't have to spell out what he intends to do with this file. I already know he's going to use it to blackmail me into staying. The man who sold Ida Young down the river to protect Rex's career (and the hefty income he gets from it) will have no scruples about threatening me. My vulnerability is my immigration status.

I have to get over the shock that he's prepared to do this and work out what my next move is because I absolutely cannot let him win! I wish Jack was here. I need his steadying presence.

I look again at the photograph of Freddie. My vision blurs with unshed tears. I blink them away. My lost friend is speaking to a crowd of men in donkey jackets and overalls outside what look like factory gates. He's a little older, he's filled out from when I last saw him, his shoulders are broader, he's grown into that square jaw. He's gesturing as he speaks; a lock of hair has fallen across his forehead just as it always did. My heart squeezes with affection, regret and grief. If only things hadn't ended as they did. I've missed him so much.

'He left the Communist Party in 1950. He's a Labour Party councillor now in a place called Finchley. Got a reputation as a rabble-rouser.'

I turn over and Freddie's standing on a stage, addressing a crowd of people. It looks like a town hall. Freddie's impassioned, gesturing wildly. I wish I could hear his words. I can tell from the hands waving programmes, the faces turned towards the camera, that he's making an impression.

'Greenwood teaches art at Archbishop Hutton's School for Boys.'

He didn't get his dream job designing sets then. I guess that was too much to hope after he had to leave university but I can imagine him teaching. He'd be passionate about it, committed to bringing the best out of his pupils.

'He shares a flat with a Michael Grey. They're flatmates to the outside world but you and I know they're both queers.'

He sneers as he says the word and the prejudice is suddenly blindingly clear. He doesn't like men like Rex and Freddie. He thinks he's better than them. Can I use that? Can that get me out of this terrible situation?

'You have no right to judge him. He's twice the man you are,' I manage to grind out through gritted teeth.

'I doubt that.' Dirk pops a mint ball in his mouth. 'Clearly, you're a fan of faggots but I doubt the headmaster at Archbishop Hutton's will see it the same way. Unless you drop this ridiculous talk of divorce, this file lands on the headmaster's desk and you can bet Fredrick will be out on his ear.'

I'm vibrating with anger now, my hands shaking, my heart pounding. 'I've not seen Freddie in five years! You cannot drag him into this.'

Dirk shrugs. 'I use what I've got, kid. You know that.'

I knot my shaking hands together in my lap. 'How did you know about Freddie?' I demand.

'I've a man in London. Investigates when I need it. Runs errands for me. He dug it up and I asked him to look again after Rex rang me from Canada.' Dirk leans back and folds his hands behind his head. 'Now I'll admit that it's a bit thin at the moment. You've not seen Greenwood since '47. It's hard to make you out to be a subversive—'

It's what I've always feared. And Dirk, being the shark that he is, has smelt out my weakness. Because that's what he does. He finds weaknesses and exploits them to get what he wants. Why didn't I see it before? I worked with him, for heaven's sake. Why did I think he'd treat me any differently?

*Because you're naïve*, a little voice says. *Too trusting. Silly. Weak.* But the words don't hurt like they used to. Jack thinks I'm pretty special just as I am. And I'd rather be naïve and trusting than a snake like Dirk!

'Which was reassuring when I looked last year,' Dirk continues. 'But my man's very creative. All it needs is a few letters, a report of telephone calls, some donations to the British Communist Party and we've got a file that the INS will be very interested to see.'

Fury and fear make me leap to my feet. I plant my hands on the table and lean towards him. 'That's fraudulent! You can't just make things up!'

'Oh, pipe down, kid. What'd you think the FBI's been doing for the HUAC? Did you really believe they'd got evidence on all of those people who've been hauled before the Committee?'

I stare at him, cold seeping into every party of my body then I sit down heavily. 'But that's *wrong!*'

'I put a lot of work into you and Rex. You think I'm going to let it go to waste?'

'You've not lived with him.' I hate how my voice wobbles. 'You have no idea how impossible he is. He's drunk all the time. He's selfish and mean and sometimes even cruel.' I point at the scar on the back of my hand. 'He did *this* when he threw a plate at the wall above my head and I had bruises for weeks after Ginny's wedding—'

'Yes, the wedding. Where your *boyfriend,*' Dirk sneers, 'gave my client a black eye. I knew something was going on when you didn't tell me. Can you imagine what'd have happened if the papers had got hold of that story?'

My stomach plunges painfully. He knows about Jack? I look down as I blink away the shock. I take a breath and remember the way it felt when Jack stood up for me. I won't have Dirk think badly of him. My chin comes up. 'Jack was defending me against my drunken husband.' I put both hands on the table and stare across it at Dirk. 'Who you were entirely happy for me to marry even though you knew he drinks far too much.' I throw my hands up. 'For goodness' sake, Dirk, you didn't even warn me!'

'You got your Green Card, didn't you?' He makes an impatient turning gesture with his index finger. My eyes narrow but I close the file on Freddie and open the second one.

It's a list of dates with actions Jack allegedly took next to them. I feel queasy now, my head spinning. I force myself to focus and run my finger down the list.

*Signed petition in support of Hollywood Ten.*
*Donated to Committee for the First Amendment.*

'Half of Hollywood did that!' I protest. 'The half with any decency.'

'And look where it got them!' Dirk snaps back. 'Forced to recant like Bogart. Or blacklisted like Marsha Hunt.'

'Jack wasn't even in Hollywood in '47!'

Dirk crosses his arms and raises a single eyebrow.

The list continues with conversations Jack is supposed to have had with unfriendly witnesses of the HUAC, occasions where he spoke out against the Committee, a fundraiser he allegedly attended to support striking workers, links to organisations accused of being fronts for Communism and that he attended a concert by The Weavers.

I recognise The Weavers from Jack's list but I have no idea why they're in this file. Is that the only nugget of truth in a bundle of lies or is Jack actually a Red? He's told me he's a Democrat and the HUAC have looked on some Democrats as pretty suspect. I think back to what Jack said when I told him about Freddie; something about Freddie being punished by having to stay with a bunch of Commies.

That doesn't sound like a man who's actually a Red. I have to trust that. What I definitely can't do is let Dirk see my doubts. He'll be onto that in no time and before I know it, he'll be trying to convince me Jack is a drinking buddy of Khrushchev's.

'This is quick work.' I twist my watch around my wrist. 'Who told you?'

'About Sorenson? I've had my eye on him since The Cocoanut Grove.' Dirk pops another mint ball in his mouth. 'I did a bit of digging. Always best to be prepared.'

My stomach plunges. That's nearly a year ago. This isn't something Dirk's thrown together in a couple of days. He's had his spies on Jack for months; that's why this file goes back so far. That makes me even angrier. My teeth clench as I bite back the urge to scream at him. I want to tear the blooming thing to shreds but I'm absolutely certain he's got a copy. I ran his filing system for too long to not expect that.

Dirk smooths his moustache again. 'Did you think I wouldn't put two and two together when you disappear in a snowstorm together?'

There's someone at Chateau Lake Louise who's feeding information to Dirk. No matter how careful we were, someone was monitoring our movements and that incenses me.

'Who told you?' I say through gritted teeth.

'Mrs Seton.'

I shudder. That interfering busybody. I knew I didn't like her!

Dirk sees my reaction and grins. 'She's a spy for the HUAC too. And if you don't give up Sorenson, this file goes to the Committee and your young man can expect a visit from the FBI with a pink slip.'

I shiver; I know what comes after the pink slip. Jack will be required to appear before the HUAC and they'll ask him one question: *Are you or have you ever been a member of the Communist Party?* Even if he says 'No', they'll want him to name the names of those who have. And, if the information in the file is not a total fabrication, then he'll know people who believe in trade unions and the right to strike, who want workers to be properly paid and not exploited. If he refuses to answer (and I already know him well enough to know he won't incriminate others), he'll be black-listed. He'll lose his career. He'll never work in Hollywood again.

I cannot put him through that. The FBI investigation, the subpoena, being required to testify before the Committee and then losing the job he loves. Jack cannot be subjected to all of that because of me.

'You are a weasel. A lying, conniving weasel.' I lean across the table and hiss the words at Dirk. 'I wish I'd never met you.'

'Just doing my job.' Dirk closes his briefcase with a snap. 'You can keep the files. I've got copies. You've twenty-four hours to make your decision. If you don't agree to give up this talk of divorce, the files go to the relevant authorities. You can wave goodbye to your Green Card and Sorenson can expect a visit from the Feds.'

He stands and, automatically, I mirror him, our chairs scraping against the marble floor. He grabs the handle of his briefcase and swings it off the table.

There has to be a way to prevent this. I know Rex's secret. If I threatened to go to *Eyewitness* and the newspapers, would that make Dirk stop? Or—

It comes back to me in a rush. The threat I threw at Rex when I asked him for a divorce.

'I'll tell Tony Young what you did to Ida.' The words tumble out of me. 'That you and Rex were the ones who ruined her career.'

Dirk laughs hollowly as he turns to look at me. 'Go ahead, kid. You'd be doing me a favour.'

I stare at him, confusion swirling in my gut.

'Young's got to go. Rex will kick up a stink about it but it's for his own good.' Dirk shifts his briefcase into one hand and then crosses his arms. 'That might have worked on Rex but you're talking to the organ grinder now. Not the monkey.'

The image is spot on – Dirk turning the handle on the organ while Rex dances to the tune – then the sheer disrespect of it hits me.

'Do you not care about him at all?'

Dirk moves to the door. 'I care about the money he makes me. I invested a fortune in Rex. Because of him, I'll be able to retire to Palm Springs. But only if I keep him earning.' He nods. 'Before close of business tomorrow. If you decide to leave anyway – and I don't recommend it – the locks will be changed on this place and you'll be escorted off the premises.'

My mouth drops open. 'I agreed with Rex I could stay until he comes home.'

Dirk tilts his head and looks at me as if I'm a particularly slow pupil. Then he points at his chest. 'Organ grinder. Whatever you decide, everything goes through me from now on.'

He opens the door and Muffin trots in. She takes one look at him, then goes down on her front paws and barks at him.

Dirk pointedly steps round her. 'And if you go, you take the fucking dog.'

## 33

As the front door closes behind Dirk, I sit down heavily in the nearest chair. My head drops into my shaking hands. My heart is racing, there's sweat under my arms even though my body feels entirely cold.

I didn't think Dirk would sink that low. Making up lies about me to tell the INS. Ruining Freddie. Taking Jack's past and turning it into something wholly different. Using fear and intimidation to make me stay in my marriage.

I leap up and pace to the window. Well, he can shove it! And Rex too! I am not going to be blackmailed into staying! If I have to go back to England then, blast it, I will! At least the British government isn't having a witch hunt to weed out suspected Communists.

But then I'd never see Jack again. My heart plummets at the thought. I've only just found him; I can't give him up.

What Dirk's threatened is worse for him. Jack will lose his job. He'll have to leave Hollywood. I have no idea how hard it would be for him to find work elsewhere. Would theatres hire him if he'd been blacklisted by the studios? I can't put him that position. It's simply not fair.

I turn and pace back to the chair. I'll have to play ball. Stay for now and then make plans to leave and go to Mexico or somewhere Dirk and Rex will never find me.

I know Jack said he'd wait but that could take months, years even. I don't want to wait that long. I don't want to wait at all. I want to be with Jack, if he'll still have me after all of the trouble I've brought on us both.

This is all my fault! I've been stupid and trusting and hopelessly naïve. Father was right. I am a terrible judge of character. I've gone and dragged Jack into this because he cares about me. And he shouldn't because I'm not worth it. I'm just as hopeless as Father always said I was. One night of love and a few kind words don't change that. I am what I've always been. A useless dreamer and I've sleepwalked myself into this catastrophic mess.

I'll have to telephone Jack and tell him it's over and I cannot see him again. That's the only thing to do. I'll say I've changed my mind and I'm staying with Rex.

Even the thought of it leaves me breathless with loss. I grip the chair back to steady myself. To continue living with Rex in this soulless mausoleum? I'd rather die!

There has to be another way. I just have to think! I know all of Rex's secrets. If I threaten to go to Hedda Hopper and Louella Parsons, would that be enough? Maybe. I don't know.

There's a tap on the door and Trudie enters. 'Are you all right, ma'am?' she asks as she picks up the coffee tray. 'You look kinda pale.'

'It's nothing,' I lie. Hastily I gather up the files from the table, press them against my churning stomach and fold my arms over them. 'If you'll just make me a pot of tea though, that would help.'

Trudie nods and leaves. I sit down again. Not knowing what else to do, I open the file on Freddie. I stare at each of the photographs. Now the initial shock has worn off, there's a quiet joy in seeing his picture. He's doing all right. He's left the Communists but he's still fighting for workers' rights. He and Michael are together.

Suddenly, tears are pouring down my face. I'm crying for Freddie and all of the times I've missed him. For the friendship we had and lost. For the idiots we were when we last saw each other. We made it too black and white. Because he couldn't be with me as I wanted him to be, I let him go. He walked away because I was an embarrassment in his new life. If only we'd been old enough to know there are very few friendships as deep and true as ours. That however hard it felt at that time, our lives would be better if the other one was in it.

I raise my head and wipe the teardrops from the photographs. I wish I could talk to him. I stare at the photographs as if that will magic him up and I'll hear his voice again.

I close my eyes and try to take myself back to Sheffield. I never do this voluntarily; it only ever ambushes me when I'm upset. I grip the top of the table to steady myself and imagine our hall with the smell of pipe smoke and stewed tea. My heart-beat speeds up, the fight or flight instinct kicking in. I step out of the front door and imagine myself walking down the garden path, past the vegetable beds that filled each side during the war. My shoulders drop as I get further from the house. At the end of the path, waiting by the post box, is Freddie. He turns and grins at me. It's the older Freddie, the one from the photographs.

'You can't let the bullies win,' he says, his eyes soft with understanding. 'You're stronger than you know, Audrey.'

I sob and the sound shatters the image. My eyes pop open.

How I've missed him! But I'm not alone now. I've got Jack in my life and Ginny knows the truth. What would they tell me to do?

I suck in a deep breath. I should tell Jack what's happened. Then a ghastly thought hits me like a punch. What if this scares him off? I couldn't blame him if he decides the risks are too high. We've barely had a chance to get to know each other. Why would he choose me when that brings with it the risk he'll end up blacklisted?

I sit down heavily again. Is this what Dirk intends? Does he believe the threat of the HUAC will be enough? That Jack will act to protect his career and tell me, regretfully no doubt, that he cannot see me again?

I've not had time to think since our night together in the cabin but I know he's important. Losing him would be like a hole opening up in my life. A hole that might just swallow me up.

If I lose Jack then I might as well go home. I'd miss Ginny and Rita dreadfully but I couldn't stay in Hollywood. It's not the place I thought it was. Behind the glitz and the glamour, it's a dirty business. I've closed my eyes to that for a long time. But Dirk's forced me to look at it straight.

I take a deep breath. I have to trust Jack. If he's the man I think he is, then he'll stand by me. If he's not then I'm going to find out really fast. But in the long run, it's better to know now. If I'd known how weak and selfish Rex really was then I wouldn't have married him. Not even for a Green Card.

I check my watch. It's twenty to five. Jack should be on his way back from the set soon. I wouldn't normally make an international call but needs must when the devil (or in this case, Dirk) drives. I just need to make sure Mrs Seton isn't anywhere around when he speaks to me.

Who'd have thought she was such a sneak? I shouldn't be shocked. I've known these things were happening in Hollywood and yet it's different when you're the one who's been betrayed. Did she take the photographs of Rex and Tony that were in *Eyewitness*? Did they give her more money than she was getting from Dirk?

I go completely still as the realisation hits me. She's not the only one with photographs! I took ones of Rex and Tony together and they're even more incriminating. The film is still in my handbag. I've not had time to process it.

Trudie comes in with the tea tray. I take it out of her hands before she has a chance to set it down. 'I'll take this with me,' I tell her. Then I add, 'And take the rest of the day off.'

She rarely comes into the darkroom and never when I'm working in there but I'm not taking any chances. I need to develop these photographs and see if they're as unequivocal as I think they are. They might just save my bacon.

* * *

I ring Jack later that evening, pouring out to him down the crackling line all that Dirk said. He's silent for a long moment when I finish. My heart starts to thump hard and painfully. What if he doesn't want to risk my plan not paying off? I can hardly blame him. It's a huge gamble.

'You're choosing me?' he says softly. 'Dirk threw all of that at you and you're still choosing me?'

'Yes.' I swallow hard against the dread that's clogging my throat. 'I want to find out where this goes.'

'Me too.' His words are firm and fervent. 'I didn't expect you to be blackmailed though.'

'And you,' I remind him. 'That's worse. You could lose your job.'

'Not sure I want it in a town that'd do this.' There's a pause. I imagine him running his fingers through his hair as he does when he's thinking. 'I wouldn't have let you go, you know. No matter what Dirk Stone threatened me with.'

All of the tension goes out of me in a whoosh. Abruptly, my legs feel like cotton wool. I press my hand against the table to steady myself.

'I wouldn't have blamed you.' My voice is barely a whisper. 'You can't have expected all of this when you kissed me.'

He chuckles softly and my stomach flips. 'No, but I've waited over a year for you. I'm not going to be scared off. And if your plan fails, then they make movies in England.'

My hand flies to my chest as my eyes widen. 'You'd do that?'

'I'm not going back to Norfolk, though. Too damned flat.'

I laugh, although tears are prickling behind my eyes. I never expected that. Logically, it's far too soon to be making plans like this but Dirk has forced us into it. If I have to leave, I won't go alone, and that's far, far more than I ever hoped for.

'Let's hear what Dirk cooked up about me?' he adds.

I read the list to him.

'I've never hidden my anger at what the HUAC are doing,' he says when I read the next allegation to him. 'If that's enough to get me a pink slip then all the decent folk in Hollywood are damned.'

He makes a few more choice remarks as the list goes on. I can hear his anger crackle down the line.

'Well, he got that right,' he says at the end when I mention The Weavers.

'What's wrong with a folk band?'

'They're blacklisted. Can't perform on radio or television. They were dropped by their record company earlier this year.'

'Blooming McCarthy has his fat fingers in everything.'

Jack chuckles. 'Going to say that to Dirk?'

The chuckle makes fire flame in my belly. I miss him. I wish he could hug me. And do other things...

'Maybe. He's made me mad enough.'

'I wish I could do this instead of you,' Jack says softly. 'It eats me up that I can't be there.'

That makes my heart swell. That wish to make things easier for me. I could get used to that. But before I can have any hope of it, I have to fight this battle.

'I can handle it. I've dealt with bullies before.' My fingers knot in the telephone cord, pulling it tight. 'He thought I was the Minister's perfect daughter but actually, I was always the Minister's rebellious daughter.'

Jack laughs. 'Thank the Lord for that!'

## 34

'You didn't have to come in,' Dirk says as Jean shows me into his office. 'A telephone call would have been fine.'

I glance around the room. It's not changed much. There are still untidy piles of paper covering Dirk's desk. His cigarette case sits next to the telephone. Does Jean buy him Pall Malls as I used to and keep the jar of mint balls topped up? On the wall behind the desk are the photographs of Dirk's clients, with Rex top and centre. Seeing his picture makes my stomach harden.

'I came to show you these.' I take the prints out of the envelope I brought them in and slap them down on his desk.

The first is of Rex and Tony holding hands. I spent ages working with the enlarger to make the images fill the paper and be clear and crisp. In the second, they share a joke, their hands still entwined. It's their faces that speak in this one. They both look to be on cloud nine, buoyed up by love and happiness. The last one is when Rex cupped Tony's face.

Dirk sucks in a breath through his teeth when he sees that.

'I've got copies and the negatives are with my lawyer.' The poor guy's secretary was baffled when I arrived at nine this morning with an envelope I insisted she give to him as soon as he stepped through the door. 'The copies are with a friend who will mail them to *Eyewitness*, Louella Parsons and Hedda Hopper if I don't call her by midday.'

That bit was Jack's idea. He said I shouldn't give Dirk time to regroup and find another way to threaten us.

Dirk reaches for a cigarette and then roots around under the papers to find his lighter. I make a show of folding my arms, popping my hip and tapping my toe. I see myself reflected in the glass of the photographs. I'm wearing a suit that Ginny lent me. The navy sheath dress fits me like a glove. Over it is a matching jacket piped in cream. I'm wearing cream gloves, shoes and shell cap to complete the outfit. I look older. A woman, not a girl.

Dirk blows smoke at the ceiling and then pulls the photographs towards him. 'In exchange for these, you want what exactly?'

'The files on Jack and Freddie destroyed. A formal undertaking that you'll not do anything to jeopardise Jack's career, Freddie's job or my right to stay in the USA. The wording for that will come from my lawyer.' That bit was Ginny's idea. Seems she imbibed some legal jargon over the family dinner table. 'Rex makes no objection to our divorce and you keep Jack's name out of the newspapers.'

Dirk looks at me as if he's never seen me before. Then he claps slowly, the sound sharp in the quiet room. 'Looks like you got me. I didn't think you'd got it in you, kid.'

I narrow my eyes, not sure if it's a compliment or not. 'My name's Audrey. Not kid. And I worked for you for ten months. Guess I picked up a thing or two.'

He points to the photographs. 'Just out of interest, where did you get the snaps?'

There he goes again, underestimating me. 'I took them.'

Seeing his eyes widen brings a rush of satisfaction. 'With the top-notch camera Rex gave me for Christmas last year.'

'Christ! He's the agent of his own downfall.' Dirk laughs ruefully. 'Except he's got me to catch him. I tell you it's a thankless job.' Then he stands and leans on the desk, looking me straight in the eye. 'You win, *Audrey*.' He puts heavy emphasis on my name. 'You know I can't risk these seeing the light of day. You'll get your divorce.'

I'm about to say thank you like the well-brought-up girl I am. Then I bite my tongue. 'My lawyer will be in touch,' I tell him instead. It's the kind of thing Dirk would say at a time like this.

I move to the desk to gather up the photographs. I pick up the first two but Dirk's got his finger on the one of Rex cupping Tony's face. 'How do I know I can trust you? You could leave here and still sell these to *Eyewitness*.'

'Except I won't, Dirk. Because I'm not a low-down snake like you.' I lean on the opposite site of the desk and face him. It feels good, powerful. It feels like I'm finally his equal, rather than just the secretary. 'You brought me into this. You picked me to be Rex's girlfriend and wife. You trusted me with all of that. I guess you're going to have to trust me a bit longer.'

He sits down heavily in his desk chair. 'As soon as the divorce is through, I want the negatives.'

I snatch up the last photograph and put it back in the envelope. 'Fine.'

I stride to the door and then take a moment to look back. He's stubbing out his cigarette with short, angry movements.

'Cheerio, Dirk.'

He doesn't raise his head.

I close the door, take a breath and smooth my skirt with trembling hands. Now it's over, I'm shaking. My chest feels tight and I want to cry. But there's one thing I have to do before I leave.

I stop by Jean's desk. 'Do not trust him,' I murmur, my voice low to make sure the girl occupying Ginny's desk doesn't hear. 'He's a scoundrel of the first degree.'

Her eyes widen.

'And if he offers to introduce you to any movie stars, say no.'

'But he wouldn't...'

'Oh, believe me,' I say. 'He would.'

## PART IV

# JUNE 1953

INTERVIEWER: Your marriage to Audrey ended in 1953. You said to me before we came on air that you owe Audrey an apology. Why is that?

REX TRENT: Well, firstly I should have been more gracious when she wanted a divorce. I let some things happen back then that I'm not proud of. Secondly, because she told me to get out of the movie business and go live in Italy. Audrey, if you're watching. I finally took your advice. Tony and I bought a little place on Capri last year and we've never been happier.

— INTERVIEW WITH REX TRENT –
BROADCAST ON HIS SIXTY-FIFTH BIRTHDAY, 27
FEBRUARY 1989

## 35

Well, here's a turn up! Audrey Trent has divorced Rex. I've put the word out to Rex's people to find out what happened but they're completely schtum. All I know is that Audrey got a quicky divorce in Reno and returned to LA this week as a single woman.

— LOUELLA PARSONS, *LOS ANGELES EXAMINER*, 4 JUNE 1953

As the train passes through the outer reaches of Los Angeles, I'm alight with excitement and anxiety. I put a hand on my stomach to calm the flutter of nerves. It's three weeks since I saw Jack. He came to Reno and we had four wonderful days together at the ranch I was staying at just outside the city. It was the highlight of my time in Nevada which otherwise was simply spent waiting for the required six-week residency period to expire, at the end of which I could get a divorce. I'd saved quite a bit while I was with Rex and that paid for the ranch. As other women gossiped and flirted with the cowboys, I kept myself to myself, hoping not to be recognised as Rex's erstwhile wife.

It's two days since I left Reno's courthouse and kissed one of its enormous white pillars in gratitude for my divorce. Tradition has it that you then throw your wedding ring in the Truckee River but, as I left mine in Canada, I skipped that part and rushed straight back to the ranch to finish packing.

Jack has promised to meet my train. I rest my hand on my travelling case which sits on the sofa next to me. I'm in one of the parlour cars, sitting in a comfy sofa facing into the carriage, able to watch the spectacular views of the Pacific coast through the huge windows that curve up to the roof. By my feet is Muffin who, after entertaining the other passengers in the early part of the journey, is finally asleep.

In my travelling case is a bundle of letters from Jack, all of which are precious, but also a letter I never expected to receive which is like gold to me. It arrived with a letter from Esther, who I wrote to as soon as I arrived at the ranch to tell her I'd left Rex. When the letter arrived, I noticed it was thicker than usual. I thought she'd perhaps sent a photograph of David and Ruth to cheer me up but when I opened the envelope, her letter was wrapped around another one. It said simply *Audrey* in Mum's handwriting.

I flip open the case and take it out. I know it almost by heart but it that doesn't change the impact it has every time I read it.

*Hello love,*

*I'm ashamed of myself that this is the first letter I've written you in all the time you've been away. I'm sorry. I've let you down. From what Esther tells me, you maybe needed a word from your old mum now and then. I should have done that. I shouldn't have let your father stop me.*

*Esther tells me you've left your movie star because he wasn't kind to you. I'm that sorry you had to go through it, love. I want you to know I'm proud of you for standing up for yourself if he wasn't treating you right. That's brave. You've always been brave. Braver than me, anyhow.*

*I hope this new chap is good to you. You deserve it; you always have. I should've told you that a bit more too.*

*I wish I'd been as brave as you. There were times when I thought of taking you and Esther and walking out. I never found the courage to do it though. Too worried about what other folk would think.*

*Your father is busy raising money for a new church organ and that takes him out and about a great deal, which I'm not complaining about. We rub along all right these days. But he doesn't need to know everything that goes on in this house. Esther says she'll send my letters with hers to save on the postage. I hope you'll forgive me, love, and write back but I'll try to understand if there's been too much water under the bridge.*

*All my love,*

*Mum x*

I sobbed like a baby when it came. I cried because I missed her and for all of the times when I'd needed a hug or a kind word and couldn't have it. I cried for the years when she was lost to me and my heart ached for her. I cried because she still loves me and because unbelievably, she was proud of me even though I'd done the unthinkable and left my husband.

There's a lump in my throat as I read it again. I wrote back immediately and told her that of course I forgive her and that I was absolutely thrilled to get her letter. I gave her Rita's address as I'll be living there for the foreseeable future.

I turn to the window and crane my neck to try to see the tower of Central Station. I slip on my jacket. Straighten my hat. Apply a fresh coat of lipstick. Muffin wakes up, stretches and yawns. 'Not long now,' I tell her as I clip her lead on.

I'm standing by the door as we pull up to the platform with my cases by my feet. I scan the waiting people looking for Jack's face. What if he can't make it and he couldn't let me know? Or worse, if he's changed his mind?

I try to remember his steady smile, the warmth in his beautiful eyes. The way he says my name as if he's waited a lifetime for me.

*He'll be here. You can trust him*, I tell myself. There's still an unpleasant swirl of anxiety in my stomach, though.

The moment the train stops, I've got the door open. I climb down onto the platform and Muffin jumps down behind me. I summon a porter and hand over my two large cases but keep hold of my travelling case. As I walk down the platform, I'm frantically scanning the crowds looking for Jack. Where is he? Did he get the day wrong? Or forgot? Now I know him better, I've discovered he gets very engrossed in whatever he's doing and can easily forget the time.

Tears tingle behind my eyes. I've been really looking forward to this. I've imagined our meeting multiple times. What he'll say. What I'll say. His arms going round me. That first kiss.

Disappointment sours my stomach. Do I wait? Or do I get a taxi to Rita's? But what if he's only caught in traffic and is on his way?

The attendant takes my ticket and we're out into the lobby with a wooden vaulted roof and tiled floor. There are people everywhere: dashing to catch trains, sat waiting, reading the paper or chatting.

We approach the square central desk. There are running feet

behind me. Muffin pulls on her lead and barks, the kind of bark when she's pleased to see someone. I stop, just as a hand falls on my shoulder.

'Audrey! I went to the wrong platform.'

I drink him in. He's tousled and untidy as usual. His glasses are smudged and his hair's a mess but his grey eyes smile at me as if I'm the most precious thing in the world.

'I thought you weren't coming,' I blurt out.

'Never.' His arms come round me and he pulls me towards him. 'God, am I pleased to see you!'

The kiss is everything I dreamed of and more. His lips are gentle but questioning and the answer is there. *Yes, I've missed you too. Yes, I want you too.*

He lets me go but his hands remain on my waist. 'I've got something to ask you,' he says. His grey eyes are studying my face, checking for my reaction.

Is he going to propose? A white beacon of hope lights in my heart but I quell it ruthlessly. The ink is barely dry on my divorce. It's far too soon to be thinking of marriage. I'm determined not to rush into things. I'll wait until Ginny's words are true and every fibre in my being knows I cannot live without this man.

'Something I should have asked in the commissary at Crown.'

'Okay, I'm listening.' I raise my hand to check my hat, which has slipped slightly during the kiss. I push the kirby grip in more firmly.

'Audrey Wade, and I can't tell you how pleased I am that that's your name again,' Jack grins, 'would you like to go dancing on Saturday night?'

My grin answers his. 'Too right I would.'

He drops a quick kiss on my lips. 'What about the following Saturday?'

'Yes, then too.'

Kiss, deeper this time.

'And the one after that?'

'Definitely.'

Kiss, long and languid and turning my belly to fire.

A throat is cleared behind us. We hastily take a step apart. Heat rushes to my cheeks. If Father could see me snogging in a public place, he'd be appalled. That thought doesn't sting like it used to. Mum still loves me and is proud of me and that's enough.

'Let me take those,' Jack says to the porter. He swings my cases from the trolley and slips something into the man's hands. The porter tips his cap to him.

'My car's just outside.'

I think back to the girl I was when I arrived in Central Station three years ago with a head full of dreams. Hiding my insecurities behind a new wardrobe and a determination to make a life for myself. If I'd known then I'd marry a movie star, I'd have been on cloud nine. I wish I could warn her to take care, to not trust people unless they definitely deserve it and that movie stars are human beings with faults and failings just like everyone else.

I'm not that girl any more. I've grown up. Yet as I follow Jack, a picture forms in my mind. I see us in a few years' time, returning home from vacation. Jack carrying the luggage. Me holding a curly-haired little girl by the hand and pushing a pram with a bouncing baby boy in it with Muffin trotting along behind.

That's what I want. A life built together. And, if we're lucky and the stars align, a family too.

There's no harm in dreaming about that. Because as Jack said, dreams can have power. Mine brought me across the Atlantic and eventually landed me here, with Jack. And there is nowhere I want to be more than that.

## EPILOGUE
### NOVEMBER 1955

INTERVIEWER: You came out as gay five years ago. What made you take that decision?

REX TRENT: The world changed. The old prejudices disappeared. And I'm getting old. I didn't want to die having never been open about who I am. I did a lot of things I'm not proud of pretending to be straight. I should never have married.

INTERVIEWER: Which time?

REX TRENT: All of 'em! I was a lousy husband. There's no wonder they kept on divorcing me.

— INTERVIEW WITH REX TRENT –
BROADCAST ON HIS SIXTY-FIFTH BIRTHDAY, 27
FEBRUARY 1989

'There's a bottle in the bag in case she wakes up and she's

hungry.' I gingerly hand Ginny the carrycot where Ingrid is *finally* asleep. 'There's also a clean nappy, muslins, the rattle she likes—'

'We'll be fine,' Ginny says firmly. 'I have taken care of a baby before.'

As if to prove her point, Eddie, who's now eighteen months old, toddles on chubby legs through the door. 'Auntie Aud!' he lisps.

I put the bag stuffed with Ingrid's many essentials on the floor, grab him under the arms and swing him up in the air. 'How's my favourite boy?'

He squeals with happiness until I set him down on his feet again. Then he grabs my hand with a decidedly sticky one of his own and tugs. 'Trains.'

'Not right now.' I unpeel my hand from his. 'When I get back.'

Ginny leans against the worktop in her neat as a pin kitchen (I honestly do not know how she does it. Since Ingrid was born, our kitchen resembles a bombsite) and looks at me with concern. 'You feeling okay about this?'

'Not really.' There's a flutter of anxiety in my belly and a tightness in my chest. 'What if she doesn't believe me?'

Ginny spreads her hands. 'Then you'll know you tried. That's all you can do, honey.'

I nod and then straighten my shoulders. 'Righto. I'd better go.' I kiss my fingers and press them against my daughter's cheek. It's downy soft, and as always, ignites an ache deep in my heart.

\* \* \*

Jack and I married in March of '54 and bought a house in Glendale not far from Ginny and Nate's. He works at MGM now. He was ready to leave Crown and Harry King behind and MGM made him an offer he couldn't refuse.

Before we married, we went to Oregon to meet his family, who are the nicest people imaginable. Seeing him with his nieces brought a huge lump to my throat and I knew then he'd be a good dad if we were lucky enough to have children. Before Christmas '53, I sold the jewellery Rex had given me for a surprising amount of money and bought two liner tickets to Southampton.

I wasn't going to make the same mistake twice. I needed to know Jack got on with the family who still talk to me. Esther pronounced him 'a really nice bloke' (high praise indeed!), Bill and he talked intently about carpentry and David and Ruth called him 'Uncle Jack' from day one.

Mum and I had an emotional reunion at the very chilly botanical gardens in Sheffield. It was beyond wonderful to see her again. We hugged and cried and tried to pour all of the past seven years into the hour we had together. She was a bit shy around Jack, seeming not to know what to say to this slightly shaggy American, but later whispered to me, 'He gets my vote, love. He treats you right. I can tell.'

Father refused to see me. I wasn't surprised but it still hurt. Since Ingrid was born, I've found it even harder to understand how he can turn his back on his own child or why he doesn't want to know his granddaughter. I send Mum photographs with my letters and she sends tiny booties, cardigans and hats she's knitted.

After I got back from Reno, I got a job in the personnel department at Cal-Tech in Pasadena. I was still typing contracts but these were for the scientists who came to teach and research. I liked the quiet campus with its Mediterranean buildings. It felt like a million miles from the movie business.

Rex's career flourishes. He was nominated for an Oscar for *Operation Exodus* this year but he didn't win. Rumours still flurry around him. I don't know what happened between him and Tony but Jack heard Tony moved to New York and is making a name for himself on Broadway. I'm sad for Rex that they've parted but I tried in our last conversation to offer him a different life and he chose not to take it.

What can I tell you about Jack? He's my rock and my friend. He makes me laugh every day. He takes care of me, believes in me and can still spark desire with a single look. I waited and married him when I knew with every fibre of my being that I couldn't live without him.

Our daughter was born in April and we named her Ingrid, after Jack's wonderful grandmother (and my favourite female movie star) and Joan for my mum. It's been a rollercoaster ride ever since. She's yet to sleep through the night. Jack and I are permanently exhausted. I can't remember the last time we had a night out. Yet I've never been happier.

Rita's a surrogate grandmother to Ingrid and Ginny is the most stalwart friend imaginable. She thinks what I'm doing today is a mistake but I'd sleep even less if I let another girl walk blindly into marriage with Rex.

I've arranged to meet her at the Formosa Café, legendary hangout of movie stars. They say John Wayne once made himself scrambled eggs in the kitchen after drinking that much, he passed out in one of the booths. It's exactly the kind of place which thrilled me when I first arrived in Hollywood. I've chosen it because it's close to the Warner Brothers lot which is where she works.

The jukebox is playing 'Only You' by The Platters. Above the green, leather booths are rows of photos of Hollywood luminaries. I'm shown to a seat and scan the pictures above it: Bette Davis, Dinah Doyle and Humphrey Bogart.

A girl comes in and I recognise her from the photographs I've seen in the newspapers. Tall, pretty, heart-shaped face, blonde hair in a ponytail, wearing a tight sweater and a poodle skirt. I wave a little awkwardly.

As she walks over, the jukebox clicks over and 'Rock Around the Clock' by Bill Hayley and the Comets blares out. It's a reminder that the world's changing. Rock and roll has exploded onto the music scene. I'm twenty-seven but it makes me feel about a hundred and ten. It's aimed at teenagers, like the girl who's walking towards me. Emma Finch. Rex's new fiancée.

'Hello,' I say as she sits down. 'Thank you for coming to meet me.'

There's a huge sapphire on her ring finger that winks in the light. At least he had the decency to buy her a new rock and not reuse the one I left behind.

She frowns, the lines marring her perfectly smooth forehead. 'I still don't know why you wanted to see me, Mrs Sorenson.'

'Audrey, please. I want to talk to you about Rex.'

The waitress comes to the table. I ask for coffee; Emma orders dim sum and an orange juice.

Emma's gaze focuses on my collar. I look down and spot the splodge of pureed banana. Blast! We're moving onto solids and it's rather hit and miss.

I pick up my napkin and dab at it but it's not going to come off. 'My daughter,' I say by way of apology. 'She's six months old.'

Emma nods politely but I can tell she's not interested. Babies are far removed from her life as yet.

'How old are you?' I ask suddenly.

'Nineteen.' She crosses her arms as her chin lifts.

Goodness, she's even younger than I was. Rex is now thirty-one and he really has snatched her from the cradle!

I remember being nineteen as if it was yesterday. Proud of being finally out in the adult world, bashful around people older than me, embarrassed by my mistakes, bewildered by all the things I didn't know. Hating being reminded how young I was.

Because of that, I make no comment and ask another question, 'And you work at Warner Brothers?'

'In the make-up department.' She beams. 'It's my dream job.'

I remember that feeling. I said the same about working for Dirk and look how that turned out!

'Is that where you met Rex?' I ask.

The waitress brings our drinks. Emma nods before sipping her orange juice through a straw. 'He was loaned to Warners and was working on a spy film. I didn't do his make-up, but he used to ask me to bring him coffee.' She flips her ponytail behind her shoulder. 'And it kind of started like that.'

I bite the inside of my cheek as memories spool. Chatting to Rex at the Cock'n Bull, the rush of elation when he asked me out, that first date at Romanoff's, dinner at Villa—

I push them away. This isn't about me. This is about what I can do for Emma.

'When was this?' I ask, fiddling with my teaspoon.

'We started dating in September.'

My heart squeezes painfully. Two months! I bet it's been just as much of a whirlwind for her as it was for me.

'And when did you get engaged?'

She twists the ring around her finger. 'Ten days ago. He asked me at L'Escoffier Room where we went for our first date.' She blushes prettily. 'The ring was on top of my lemon cheesecake and everyone cheered when I said yes.'

I bite back a sigh. Did Dirk have a hand in that? It's exactly the kind of thing he'd stage-manage and then have a photographer on hand to snap the happy couple afterwards.

The gleam of pride in her eye confirms what I feared. This time, Rex hasn't told his prospective bride the truth. She's going into this believing not only that he loves her but that he'll *make love* to her. She probably hopes for children with his beautiful, brown eyes and square jaw.

This is what's been keeping me awake at night, wrestling with whether I should tell her what I know or if the promise I made to Rex back in Chateau Lake Louise should be kept. Jack, with his ability to cut through things, said, 'If you'll feel bad if you don't then you've got to try.' Which is what's brought me here about to detonate a bomb under this girl's happiness.

I take a deep breath. 'Emma, I have to tell you something. It's going to be hard to hear but I want you to at least listen.'

She presses her lips together and then nods sharply.

'Rex will have swept you off your feet. I have no doubt you believe you're in love with him but, you see, that's not the real Rex.'

She gestures sharply as if to push my words away.

'Just hear me out, okay?'

She licks her lips but doesn't speak.

I continue, 'There's two things you need to know about Rex before you marry him. Firstly, he's homosexual.'

She pulls back as if I've slapped her. 'He is not! How can you spread such dirty lies about him? He's told me it's all trash made up by the papers.'

I look up at the ceiling and bite back a curse. If only I'd kept the photographs of Rex and Tony but I did as I promised and sent prints and negatives to Dirk when I got back from Reno.

'I'm not lying, Emma.' With an effort, I keep my voice calm and soft. 'When I was married to him, he was in love with another man.'

She leans back against the booth and crosses her arms. 'I don't believe you.'

'I can see that.' I take another deep breath. 'He also drinks when he's unhappy which is a lot because he's having to hide—'

'He told me he drank when he was with *you*,' she interrupts. 'But that was because you were hell to live with. He won't be like that with me. *I'll* make him happy!'

I close my eyes for a second. I should have guessed he'd blame me. Isn't that the classic man's story? *She didn't understand me but I'll be different with you.* And women fall for it all the time.

I close my shaking hands around my coffee cup. 'You won't, Emma. Rex will never love you as you deserve to be loved. It's not his fault. It's just the way he's made—'

'You're making all of this up because you're bitter. He told me he couldn't take it any more, that you nagged him and bossed him and made his life a misery. It won't be like that with us.' She blinks rapidly, which makes her look like a startled fawn. 'He's taking me to Italy on honeymoon. On the *Queen Mary*. Where did you go? A weekend in Palm Springs, was it?'

I sag back in my chair. She thinks I'm the enemy. She'll never believe I came here as a friend. That makes me feel enormously sad.

'Okay, so don't believe me but just hold on a minute while I give you some advice. First, do not trust Dirk Stone. He's a manipulative, lying scumbag who'd smile at you as he stabs you in the back.' She opens her mouth to protest and I hold my hand up to stop her. 'Trust me. I worked for him and I still didn't realise until it was too late. Secondly, talk to your friends. There's no secret you can't share with them. I got that one wrong and it made things a whole lot harder.' My throat clogs as I think of the weight of Rex's secrets. I reach into my handbag and I put a business card on the table between us. 'And if you find yourself in need a lawyer, ring this guy in Pasadena. He'll see you right.'

It's all I can do for her. I gather up my handbag and stand. Then I offer her my hand. She frowns but in the end, she takes it. 'Good luck, Emma. You're going to need it.'

She visibly scoffs at that.

The waiter arrives with her dim sum. I nod at the plate. 'Enjoy your lunch. I'll pick up the cheque on the way out.'

I settle up with shaking hands and step out into the sunshine. I get into the car and then rest my head against the steering wheel. I'm trembling. It feels like my girdle is the only thing holding me up. I suck in a deep breath, feel the elastic press uncomfortably on my post-baby tummy.

I tried. That's worth something. When the gossip columns are full of rumours about the state of their marriage and their inevitable divorce, I'll know I did my best. But she's protected by the self-belief that's the joy and the curse of youth. I slam my hand against the dashboard. Blast Rex for getting his lies in first! He's spun an entirely different story of our time together and one that paints me as the wicked witch he couldn't wait to get away from.

I sit up and let my shoulders drop. Then I put the car into reverse, exit the parking space and turn into the traffic on Santa Monica Boulevard.

Instead of heading for Glendale, I turn into Lake Hollywood Park and follow the road until I see it. I pull over on the scrubby edge of the road and climb out. High on the hill is the Hollywood sign.

I stare at it. What power it has! It called to me across the Atlantic Ocean with the promise of glamour and sophistication and I answered that call, upping sticks, leaving Blighty behind and rocking up in Hollywood.

This is the dream that still holds Emma. It's the other reason I couldn't reach her. You have to grow out of it yourself. No one can pull you out. In truth, that's what Esther and Father tried to do and I fought them tooth and nail. I can't blame Emma for doing the same.

Rex and Dirk forced me to see it for the tawdry façade it is. They tore the curtain away and revealed the grubby shenanigans that make Tinseltown tick. There's a grief in that. It's why I don't come this way very often any more. But today, I want to face it. Because it's time to let it go.

I close my eyes and I'm back in Sheffield as Freddie and I grasp palm to palm as we say, 'Hollywood!' I see me at twenty-one staring up at the sign with wide eyes on my first day in Los Angeles. I remember the thrill of getting the job with Dirk and believing I was finally part of the movie business. The moment on the terrace at Rex's house when we looked at the Hollywood sign together. The premieres I attended, the incredible frocks and beautiful jewellery I wore.

I did it. I lived the dream. And it wasn't worth a hill of beans compared to what I've got now as wife to Jack and mother to Ingrid.

I blow a kiss up to the sign and then I shout, 'Cheerio!' at the top of my voice. It stirs the hawks and they swoop in circles in the cobalt-blue sky.

I get back in my car and head for Glendale where my daughter is waiting.

\* \* \*

## MORE FROM ALEXANDRA WESTON

Another book from Alexandra Weston, *The Hollywood Governess*, is available to order now here:

https://mybook.to/HollywoodGovBackAd

# HISTORICAL NOTE

The idea for *The Lavender Bride* came when I read an article in *The Guardian* about Rock Hudson which mentioned that he married his agent's secretary to hide his sexuality. I knew about Lavender Marriages from my research for *The Hollywood Governess* but they were usually between two people who both had secrets they wanted to hide. This seemed a very different proposition and I thought (as novelists tend to do) 'there's a story there'.

## Rock Hudson and Phyllis Gates

Rock Hudson was a huge star in the fifties and sixties with a clean-cut, 'boy next door' image. I knew him from the rom-coms he made with Doris Day in the sixties of which *Pillow Talk* is the most famous. He also starred in serious dramatic roles including *Giant* (for which he was nominated for an Oscar) and *All That Heaven Allows*. Homophobia was widespread in the fifties and if Rock's sexuality had become public knowledge, it would have destroyed his career.

Phyllis Gates was born in Minnesota in 1925 and worked as an air hostess and as secretary to a New York talent agent before moving to Hollywood. She started dating Rock in 1954 when she was secretary for his agent, Henry Wilson. Rock and Phyllis married a year later. They were physically intimate during their marriage (although it was often unsatisfactory for Phyllis). Phyllis claimed she had no idea about Rock's sexuality until after the marriage ended in 1957. Others have disputed that, believing she must have known and stayed with Rock because she liked the money and the lifestyle. After reading Phyllis's memoir *My Husband, Rock Hudson* (1987) written with Bob Thomas, I believe she didn't know. It's clear she loved Rock. Phyllis never remarried and twenty years after their divorce, bought the house in West Hollywood that they'd lived in together.

Although the idea for *The Lavender Bride* came from Rock and Phyllis's relationship, Audrey is not based on Phyllis and Rex only shares some physical characteristics with Rock. Rex has a very different personality to Rock. I gave Rex issues with alcohol as that is not uncommon in men who are forced to keep their sexuality hidden.

Audrey and Rex do however frequent some of the same places as Rock and Phyllis (including The Cock'n Bull, Villa Nova, L'Escoffier and Scandia, all of which are mentioned in Phyllis's memoir). Phyllis, like Audrey, had a flat on Fairfax Avenue and Rex's house is on the Bird Streets like Rock and Phyllis's.

What I did use was Henry Wilson, Phyllis's boss, setting her up with Rock as a way to clean up his image after the scandal rag, *Confidential* printed stories hinting at Rock's sexuality. Just before Phyllis and Rock's marriage, Henry Wilson gave *Confidential* a story about another client's criminal record in exchange for them agreeing not to publish a story about Rock's former lover. It's from this that I got the idea of Dirk swapping the story about Ida Young to protect Rex's secret.

If you think Dirk's a pretty dastardly character then Henry Wilson was a lot worse! He reputedly slept with all of his male clients (if they were unwilling, he blackmailed them into bed with him) and defrauded Rock for many years.

## McCarthyism and the Second Red Scare

In the early fifties, Senator Joe McCarthy alleged there were Communists in government and other positions of power. The House Un-American Activities Committee (HUAC) started investigating Communism in Hollywood in 1947 which led to the imprisonment of The Hollywood Ten and the beginning of the Hollywood blacklist. McCarthy wasn't part of the HUAC but his allegations added fuel to their activities.

Everything I included in the book is reported to have happened. The FBI did tap phones and carried out surveillance on suspected subversives. There is no *proof* that the FBI fabricated the evidence which was sent to the HUAC but it is strongly suspected. The blacklist destroyed careers, affecting not only the individual in question but their family too. People were not permitted to travel to or reside in the USA because of suspected links to Communism. Charlie Chaplin was refused permission to return to the US in 1952 after Senator McCarthy labelled him a Communist. It was 1972 before Chaplin was permitted to re-enter America to accept an honorary Oscar.

I have simplified Audrey's immigration situation for the sake of fiction but the fear of being sent home because of her connection to Freddie would have been very real.

## Confidential

I based *Eyewitness* on *Confidential* magazine which started in 1952. *Confidential* was an early example of tabloid journalism. It aimed to find the scandals and gossip the studios didn't want to be known.

Prior to *Confidential,* the Hollywood studios had a symbiotic relationship with the print media. The studio's publicity department fed magazines, like *Photoplay,* stories about the stars which the magazines were happy to print in exchange for exclusive interviews and invitations to premieres and parties. This allowed the studios to strictly control the public image of their stars.

*Confidential* was the first publication to disrupt all of that. It was feared and loathed by movie stars. However, there were those in the industry who, like Mrs Seton, sold stories to *Confidential.*

*Confidential* was published quarterly and then bi-monthly but I needed things to happen faster than that so *Eyewitness* is a monthly magazine in the book.

## Homophobia in the 1950s

Senator McCarthy didn't only target Communists; he also aimed to remove homosexuals from government roles, asserting they were more susceptible to blackmail and therefore posed a secu-rity risk. This purge of homosexuals from government roles was later labelled the Lavender Scare.

Social attitudes to homosexuals were extremely negative. Homosexuality was illegal in both the UK and the US. The views of Audrey's father would have been commonplace. There was a general belief that gay men were predatory and could not be trusted around children.

Dirk's threat to reveal Freddie's sexuality to his employer would have resulted in instant dismissal. There was also a lot of ignorance about homosexuality particularly among girls because (as Audrey complains) no one told them about it.

*Sexual Behaviour in the Human Male* (colloquially known as *The Kinsey Report*) was published in 1948 and provided the American public with information on various aspects of sexuality (including sexual orientation) which had previously been taboo. Audrey reads the book after her fateful last meeting with Freddie and it shapes her attitudes when she's discussing sexuality with Rex.

The Hollywood studios were often aware of their star's sexu-ality but did everything they could to hide it. Universal Pictures loaned Rock Hudson the money to buy a house in a very private setting to help keep his sexuality secret. There were, however, places LGBTQ+ people could go. In the book, Rex is followed by a journalist from Will Rogers State Beach. An area of the beach, often referred to as Ginger Rogers Beach, has been a popular spot with the LGBTQ+ community since the 1940s.

**Music**

We associate the fifties with rock and roll but that only became mainstream in 1955. Prior to that, the charts were full of what we'd now call crooners and easy listening. In the early fifties, some radio stations were playing the music that would inspire rock and roll (for example, Howlin' Wolf ) and I've included some of those artists in Jack's list.

I've created a Spotify playlist of the songs that feature in the book which is perfect to listen to while reading *The Lavender Bride*. You'll find the playlist at: https://open.spotify.com/playlist/26cHWxEQJ8EStyDeuOvWg1?si=a96c338faf60422f

# ACKNOWLEDGEMENTS

Huge thanks to my amazing editor, Emily Ruston for her invaluable advice and support while I was writing this book. She helped me to shape the story, talked about my characters as if they were living, breathing people from day one and came up with the idea for the epilogue. Thank you to Cecily for her fabulous copy-editing skills and for picking up my mistakes. I'm also grateful to Niamh Wallace for her wonderful marketing expertise and everyone at Boldwood Books who have done so much to promote my books. I'm very proud to be part of #TeamBoldwood.

I've dedicated this book to my Dad because he's been such a huge part of it. He shared his recollections of Sheffield in the late forties which helped shape the chapters about Audrey's life in Yorkshire. I know there's been a lot of questions, Dad. Thanks for answering them so cheerfully even when you weren't feeling on top form. I'm only sorry I didn't manage to get Davy's tomato sausages in!

I also want to thank Margaret Bell for finding the first-hand account of the Sheffield Blitz for me.

Judith and Bruce Rich very generously answered my questions about growing up in America in the fifties and provided me with incredibly useful information that allowed me to flesh out the reading I'd done. I'm very grateful to them both for taking the time to answer my questions so thoughtfully.

Jenny and Richard Pearson talked to me about their recollections of growing up in the fifties and about the prejudices towards homosexuals at that time. The information they shared helped me to understand the realities of life for Freddie and Rex. I really appreciate Jenny and Richard's support for me and my writing.

Thank you to Amy Thompson for her bid in the Auction of Promises to raise money for the East Yorkshire Food Bank. Thanks for supporting such a worthy cause and I hope you enjoyed *The Hollywood Governess*.

Finally, the biggest thank you goes to Tim. Firstly, for using his photographic talents to make me and my books look good. Secondly, for everything he's done to support me while I've been writing this book. From cups of tea brought to my writing shed to tracking down research books and endless amounts of moral support, I am incredibly grateful for everything. I wouldn't have got this book written (and hit my deadline) without him.

# ABOUT THE AUTHOR

**Alexandra Weston** is a historical fiction writer whose novels are inspired by forbidden love in Golden Age Hollywood. She fits her writing around her two day jobs as a solicitor and a creative writing tutor, and lives in East Yorkshire.

Sign up to Alexandra Weston's mailing list for news, competitions and updates on future books.

Visit Alexandra's website: www.greenmanwords.co.uk

Follow Alexandra on social media here:

facebook.com/61556666098594

x.com/alexweston46

instagram.com/alex_l_weston

## ALSO BY ALEXANDRA WESTON

The Hollywood Governess

The Lavender Bride

# Letters from
## *the past*

Discover page-turning
historical novels from
your favourite authors
and be transported
back in time

*Join our book club*
*Facebook group*

https://bit.ly/SixpenceGroup

*Sign up to our*
*newsletter*

https://bit.ly/LettersFrom
PastNews

# Boldwood

Boldwood Books is an award-winning fiction publishing company seeking out the best stories from around the world.

**Find out more at www.boldwoodbooks.com**

Join our reader community for brilliant books, competitions and offers!

Follow us
@BoldwoodBooks
@TheBoldBookClub

Sign up to our weekly
deals newsletter

https://bit.ly/BoldwoodBNewsletter

Made in United States
Cleveland, OH
28 March 2025

15613679R00207